Presented To:

From:

Date:

THE CHILDREN OF ETERNITY

THE CHILDREN OF
ETERNITY

A Novel

KENNETH
ZEIGLER

DESTINY IMAGE® PUBLISHERS, INC.
PO Box 310, Shippensburg, PA 17257-0310
"Promoting Inspired Lives."

This book and all other Destiny Image, Revival Press, MercyPlace, Fresh Bread, Destiny Image Fiction, and Treasure House books are available at Christian bookstores and distributors worldwide.

For a U.S. bookstore nearest you, call 1-800-722-6774.
For more information on foreign distributors, call 717-532-3040.
Reach us on the Internet: www.destinyimage.com.

ISBN 13 TP: 978-0-7684-4146-8
ISBN 13 Ebook: 978-0-7684-8814-2

For Worldwide Distribution, Printed in the U.S.A.

1 2 3 4 5 6 7 / 16 15 14 13 12

PART I

CHILDHOOD'S END—THE WAR IN HEAVEN

CHAPTER 1

"THERE IT IS AGAIN," SAID 10-year-old Christopher Pace, looking up at the green forest canopy and into the bright blue sky beyond. "It was like the sound of wings, only very big ones I think."

"An eagle maybe," replied his friend, 19-year-old Jerry Anderson, glancing up from the place where his fishing line met the clear stream water. "You see them around here from time to time."

"No, not an eagle," insisted Christopher, adjusting his straw hat to block out the glare of the sun, which glistened through a gap between the trees. "It sounded way bigger than an eagle. I think there are more than one of them too."

"If you're going to become a successful fisherman, you'll need to learn to keep your voice down," replied Jerry. "The fish can hear you, you know."

"Maybe," said Christopher, "but I bet you they don't understand a word we say. They don't know that we're fishing for them."

Jerry just shook his head. "At least keep your eye on the lure."

"I don't need to," said Christopher. "My looking at that shiny thing isn't going to help. It only helps if the fish sees it and decides that it looks good enough to take a bite out of. When he does, I'll know."

"Unbelievable," muttered Jerry.

"You don't think I'd make much of a fisherman, do you?" asked Christopher, who had finally focused on the business of fishing again.

Jerry seemed surprised. "Now why would you say that?"

"Because you were thinking it," replied Christopher. "Fishing isn't everything, you know. Our Lord and Savior Jesus spent a lot of time around fishermen, but He only did a little bit of it Himself. He was able to convince fish to swim right into the fishermen's nets. I guess He was able to talk them into surrendering. The only time that the Bible even suggested that Jesus might have gone fishing was in the twenty-first chapter of John, verse nine, when the disciples found Him cooking fish over a fire by the Sea of Galilee. Who knows, He might have talked those fish into surrendering too."

"Sounds like you know the Bible quite well," said Jerry.

Christopher nodded. "Pretty much word for word."

At this point Jerry was looking at Christopher incredulously. "You've memorized the entire Bible, chapter and verse?"

"Yes," replied Christopher. "Actually, I read it in the original Hebrew and Aramaic."

"You're pulling my leg."

Christopher stared at Jerry. He looked a bit offended. "Why would I do that?"

Jerry didn't answer. He turned to the west to see what looked like a flock of something moving through the skies above the trees.

"There, you see, there are even more of them this time," said Christopher. He hesitated, "Do you feel it?"

Jerry hesitated. Whatever had been there had moved on. "I think so. I felt a sudden chill. It wasn't the air that was cold. It was, well, sort of a chill within my spirit."

"Yes," confirmed Christopher, "I felt it too. It was the chill of an evil thing passing by." He slipped down off the boulder he had been sitting on and gazed into the sky for a long time. "I think we need to leave. Something is wrong. It's gone away for now, but I think it may come back."

"What has gotten into you today?" asked Jerry. "We've been out here fishing plenty of times, but today you seem really distracted. Your mind isn't on fishing."

"It isn't," confirmed Christopher. "I've felt like something was wrong since I got up this morning."

"Like what?" asked Jerry. "I mean, what could possibly be wrong here? It ain't like this is Earth."

"Yes, I know, Jerry," said Christopher, whose eyes continued scanning the sky. "There's nothing out there now."

"Maybe it was just a group of angels flying past," suggested Jerry. "They fly through these parts now and again."

"Angels don't make you feel like that," said Christopher. "Believe me, I know."

Jerry nodded understandingly. "I reckon you would. You know, I've lived in Heaven for all of my life, really. You'd think that I'd know all about angels, but I don't. Oh, I've seen them in the forest from time to time, and I've seen them in the City of Zion too. They always give you a friendly hello and all. They're very nice, but I've never had one as a friend, not really. My dad says that they travel in different circles from us. They are our trusted friends, but they go their way and we go ours."

"I've grown up around them most of my life," said Christopher. "I've been raised by angels since I was three. I loved them right from the start. Their being around makes me feel good, safe. They've held me, taught me, comforted me…angels are love, and they know a whole lot."

Christopher paused. For a moment he seemed sad. "Still, sometimes I miss my life on Earth. I was only there for three years, but I still remember those years. I had parents—real parents. They loved me. I loved them. I know that I'm going to see them again…someday. I've been promised that. Still, I miss them."

Jerry nodded, placing an arm over his friend's shoulder. "I think I can understand you missing your parents; really, I do. I know how I'd feel if I were separated from my mom and dad. What I can't understand is you missing Earth. Look around you—could any forest on Earth be more beautiful than this one? Is there any ocean on Earth more beautiful than the Crystal Sea of Heaven? My friend, everything you could ever want is right here."

Christopher just nodded.

"Like I said, I can't see why you miss such a place as Earth," continued Jerry, giving his line a tug. "I'll tell you this for sure; my brief experience with that place didn't endear me to it, not one bit. From what I've read, everything there keeps changing. Nothing is permanent, nothing assured. There is disease and death, floods and earthquakes.

"A doctor on Earth killed me while I was still in my mother's womb. She let him do it—wanted him to do it. Doctors are supposed to try and cure people, not brutally murder them. What kind of doctor does that sort of thing…and what kind of mother allows it? Isn't a mother supposed to love her child? Isn't that the way it's supposed to be?"

Christopher nodded, looking over at his friend. "That's the way it's supposed to be. Still, you don't know what was going through her mind right then. Earth isn't Heaven, you know. All kinds of things happen to people there that just don't happen here. It sounds to me like there's still a spiritual wound deep down inside of you that hasn't healed."

"Yeah, I guess there is," said Jerry, whose eyes were affixed upon the waters.

"That can't be healthy," continued Christopher.

"Maybe not," continued Jerry, "but it doesn't matter. I'm never going to see her again anyway. That's what my heavenly parents told me. That's why I was given to them and not to the angels, like you were. If a child from Earth is going to be reunited with their parents again some day, they're either raised by the angels or by their nearest kin here in Heaven. She ain't coming here. I reckon I don't even have any earthly next of kin here in Heaven."

Christopher was troubled by Jerry's words. He'd never heard him speak like that. He decided that it might be best to let the subject drop for the moment.

Still, Jerry didn't seem to want to let it drop just yet. "If that is what Earth is all about, I don't want to have any part of it. Here in Heaven I was given real parents, parents who really and truly love me, and I love them. On Earth, people steal from each other, hurt each other, and even kill each other. I don't see why the Father even bothered to create it. I don't see why He continues to put up with it."

"Because the Father loves us," continued Christopher. "He loves us even though we do bad things. I guess it's just the way He is. But we were talking about angels."

Jerry paused. "Yes, about angels. What is it like where you live? You know, we've been coming out here for months now, and I've never gotten around to asking you that. I reckon I figured it might be too personal a question."

"Oh, not at all," assured Christopher, thankful that the direction of the conversation had turned once more. "I'd love to tell you about it. You see, there are eleven of us living in our home. It is a great big home in the meadow. The others, they're all like me. They lived on Earth for a time, but we all died very young. I'm the oldest one right now. We all know we'll see our parents again. Their names are in the Book of Life too. Until then, the angels look after us. They teach us and show us love, real love. They even play with us. Sometimes older people come to our home, people the angels had taken care of a long time ago. They still stay in touch with the angels that raised them. They still love them very much.

"The angels teach us all we need to know to live in Heaven, but I especially like the stories that the angels tell us. There is one story I like the best. It's a true story. It's a story about a man and his wife. The man's name is Chris, just like me. His wife's name is Serena. Chris lived here in Heaven not far away from here, but his wife had been sentenced to Hell, to a place called the Great Sea of Fire. Satan treated her really bad; he treats all humans that way…but for some reason he hated her more."

"I met Chris!" exclaimed Jerry. "I met him a few different times. The first time was here by the stream. He seemed real nice. He lived with his mother over in the meadow. Sometimes we'd all go fishing together. Then, one day, he went away. I never saw him again."

"That's because he was special," said Christopher. "Once you come to Heaven, you don't remember a lot of the people you knew on Earth because they're not coming here. That's what the angels taught us. The Father makes it that way because He doesn't want us to be sad because people we may have loved on Earth are now being punished in Hell. It is better that we don't remember them.

"But Chris eventually remembered his wife. He knew that he had to try and save her. He loved her so much. But, in Hell, someone had already rescued her from the Sea of Fire. His name was Abaddon the Destroyer, a powerful dark angel. He was a dark angel, not a demon… there's a difference."

"Yeah, I know," said Jerry. "The dark angels didn't go to war against the Father and the other angels during the War in Heaven. They were sentenced to Hell for another reason."

"Yes," confirmed Christopher. "After Adam and Eve fell, those angels were told to watch out for Adam and Eve's children and grand-children, to help them along if they could. But something went wrong. They ended up telling the people whom they were supposed to protect that they were gods. They even began mating with them and producing angel-human hybrids. Some of those children were not so good.

"Anyway, those angels were sentenced to Hell for what they did. It was one of them that helped Serena. He hid her away from Satan, protected her from the demons. When Chris found out about this, he sent an angel called Aaron to carry letters from him and his mother to Serena. They even sent her seeds to plant from his mother's garden. It made Serena feel much better. You see, she knew that she was still loved, even though she was in Hell.

"But soon, Satan came looking for her. Abaddon knew that he couldn't hide Serena from him forever. So Chris and several of his friends here in Heaven went to rescue her. Several hundred angels went along to help. And in the end, the Father showed mercy to both Chris and Serena and sent them back to Earth to give them a second chance at life. There they go around preaching the Gospel to this very day, trying to save other people from Hell."

"That's a wonderful story," noted Jerry. "I've heard it too. Still, I wonder why the Father showed such mercy to Serena."

"Only the Father knows," replied Chris. "But I know the Father had a very good reason…He always does."

Jerry nodded. He reeled in his line only to cast it out again.

"You said the angels teach you," observed Jerry. "My parents taught me to read, write, and do math. My mom was a schoolteacher back on Earth. She even taught me algebra. Don't know that I'll ever use it."

"I learned algebra a few years ago," noted Christopher. "I really like math. Now I'm studying analytic geometry. I'll be moving on to calculus soon."

"Calculus," repeated Jerry. "That's pretty complicated stuff for a ten-year-old."

"I'm almost eleven," noted Christopher.

"Yeah, but still, I thought kids your age played and had fun."

"I guess, but I don't play so much anymore," continued Christopher, gazing out at the fishing lure glistening in the filtered sunlight.

"Kids your age should play," replied Jerry. "My mom says that it's healthy for them to play."

"Maybe," said Christopher, "but I have something to do, and I need to get about doing it. Our Lord Jesus knew there were important things He needed to do when He wasn't much older than me. On a trip to Jerusalem with His mother and father, He disappeared for a time. They finally found Him in the temple talking with the priests and scribes. When they asked Him why He had gone off without telling them, He said that He had to be about His Father's business.

"Even when we are young, the Father can speak to our hearts and tell us what He wants us to be doing. Well, I want to know about the universe that the Father created. Knowing about it will be important someday. I want to know all that I can know. I've spoken to the Father about it, and He liked that I was interested. He told me just last week that I should go and seek out Professor Faraday. He said that he would teach me. I've met with Professor Faraday and it's all arranged. He and his wife will be taking me into their home. I'll be leaving in just a few days to begin my studies."

"I'm happy for you, but I'll be sorry to see you leave," said Jerry. "I've sort of gotten to like you, even if you are a lousy fisherman."

At that very moment a fish, a large trout, bit Christopher's hook. The fishing pole slid out of his hand. He tried to get a grip with his other hand, but it was too late. A few seconds later, the pole was caught among some rocks at the water's edge.

"Get it! Quick!" hollered Jerry.

Christopher made a mad lunge for the pole, sliding on the loose rocks along the way. He landed flat on his belly. He reached out with his right hand to grab the fishing pole as it started to slide into the water.

He got a firm grip with his right hand, then the left. He got up on his knees and pulled back on the pole, but it was too late. With all of the slack, the trout had managed to turn around and bite into the line, even as the hook slid from his mouth. He quickly swam away, and the lure dropped to the bottom, four feet down. Christopher reeled in the line with the bob intact, but no lure or hook. He shook his head as he rose to his feet. "Woops."

Jerry stepped up to his side. "Like I was saying, watch the lure." He scanned the water, then pointed to the place where the lure had settled to the bottom. "There it is. All you'll need to do is take off your shirt and shoes and jump on in and grab it. I'll be here for you."

Christopher focused on the lure shimmering in the sunlight. For a moment he shivered. "Couldn't you get it for me, Jerry?"

"You lost it," Jerry replied. "I figure it's only fair that you go in and get it. Nothing is going to happen to you. The current is slow and the water isn't that deep. Anyways, I'll be right here for you. The water probably isn't even over your head. No, I'm sure it's not."

Christopher set his fishing pole down and took two steps toward the water, then stopped once more. Why was he hesitating? *I can do this.* Abruptly he reached out toward the lure with his right hand. He focused his full consciousness upon it, but he didn't move.

All the while Jerry stood there looking at his young friend. Then he looked toward the lure. Was it moving?

A moment later, the lure was in motion. It burst forth from the surface and flew into Christopher's hand as if magnetized. Christopher's fingers entwined about it. Then he looked toward Jerry.

"Wow!" exclaimed Jerry. "Christopher, how did you do that?"

"I'm not sure," admitted Christopher, stepping back from the water. "I just thought about it being in my hand, and a moment later it was there. I think the Holy Spirit gave me the power to do it. I mean, we can both gate from one place to another, right? We think about being there, a swirling tunnel of mists and stars appears in front of us, and we walk in. A few seconds later we walk out of the mists and we're wherever in Heaven we want to be. If we can do that, what is wrong with doing this?"

Jerry looked at Christopher doubtfully. "Yeah, but that's different."

"How is that different?" objected Christopher. "We are using God's Holy Spirit. Nothing should be impossible. We should be able to move mountains—Jesus said we could. If we can move mountains from here to there, then I can move that fishing lure." He handed the lure to Jerry. "Here, it's yours. I don't think I'll have much time for fishing from now on."

Jerry accepted the lure and the hook. "Have you ever done something like that before? I mean, made things move by just thinking about it?"

"Sure," confirmed Christopher, "this was the third time. It was easier this time. I think I'm starting to get it."

Their discussion was interrupted by a distant explosion coming from somewhere toward the northeast. They both turned in that direction and were suddenly silent. They could hear other noises—the crackling of electricity and the sound of distant thunder, but it wasn't a storm.

"I think we need to get home," said Jerry.

Christopher nodded. They both picked up their fishing poles, and they were off. At first they were walking, but they quickly picked up the pace, following the trail that led to Jerry's home about a mile away. They came to a sudden stop as a bolt of lightning, and then another, cracked across the sky, passing nearly overhead. This was quickly followed by several balls of orange fire traveling swiftly in the other direction.

"What's going on?" asked Christopher, noticeably shaken.

"I don't know," said Jerry, gazing into the sky. "I ain't never seen anything like this."

Another round of lightning and fireballs followed about ten seconds later. The lightning seemed to be coming from a single source somewhere to the west and above the trees, while the fireballs seemed to be converging from three different places toward the source of the lightning. It seemed as if a battle was going on overhead.

Again the boys were on the move toward Jerry's home. It was quite a bit closer than Christopher's. Perhaps Jerry's parents would know what was going on. As they ran, a thought crossed Christopher's mind. It wasn't a pleasant one, and it didn't make any sense either. Maybe he had just heard one too many stories. It was then that the sound of wings returned, only this time much closer. Christopher turned to the left to see two huge, bat-winged creatures descending through a hole in the forest canopy. They were coming straight for them. They passed only a dozen feet over the boys' heads, then swung around, landing on the trail about 50 or so feet ahead of them. Both boys came to a stop.

The bat-winged creatures had two arms and two legs and wore black leather armor held together with what looked like golden studs. They had the pale faces of incredibly old men, and both were brandishing long, sharp swords. Both boys knew only too well what sort of beings these were.

"Demons," gasped Jerry. "But what would demons be doing here in Heaven? They were cast out thousands of years ago."

The demons approached the boys slowly. Both Christopher and Jerry resisted the urge to take off running. As fast as these creatures could move, it wouldn't have done much good. Gating out would have been a better option, but they didn't do that either. They just stood there in amazement.

"Peace be with you," said the demon on the left in a deep, gruff voice. "I assure you, we mean you no harm. We have been given strict orders by our master to in no way harm the saints of Heaven."

For a moment, neither of the boys said anything. Jerry finally broke the silence. "What do you want from us?"

The demon smiled a sort of evil-looking smile. "What do I want from you? I want nothing, nothing at all. But know this, there is war in Heaven. My lord and master has returned to claim that thing that was his in the beginning. He has returned to assume his rightful place as the leader of all of the angels. This bickering among the angels has been going on for far too long.

"The time for peace and reconciliation has come, but that peace can only be won through war. My master must utterly crush the angelic forces of Michael and Gabriel. There can be only one angelic master and that is Lucifer."

The two human youths looked at this dark being dubiously but did not immediately respond. Christopher felt a mixture of fear and confusion. Yet, in the end, it was his curiosity that ruled the moment. "And the Father is OK with all of this?"

"He is," confirmed the demon. "He agrees that this undeclared war among the angels has gone on for too long. There was a meeting among all of the parties involved. At that meeting my master expressed an interest in returning to Heaven and unifying all of the angels under his rule. He wanted to do it through negotiations if possible and through force if need be. Regrettably, Michael and Gabriel resisted my master's gestures of peace, and thus we are forced to bring my master to power through force of arms.

"But the Father set forth one provision, a provision we will gladly comply with. We are to do no harm to the saints, the human inhabitants of Heaven. They are the sons and daughters of God. We shall abide by that provision. Our grievance is with the angels, not with you. Stay out of our way, take no part in this conflict, and you will come to no harm. For the moment, for your own safety, return to your homes and stay there. We cannot guarantee your safety if you stray into the battlefield."

"I think we need to do as he says," said Jerry, turning toward Christopher. "You can stay with us until this is all over."

Yes, that was probably the smart thing to do, and Christopher knew it, but he wasn't about to bow to the wishes of an unholy enemy of God. "But I live with the angels, in a house not far from here, over in the next meadow," Christopher objected. "I was raised by the angels. They've been very good to me."

"You keep poor company," noted the other demon, stepping forward, "very poor company indeed."

"You *did* live with the angels," corrected the first demon. "The house you speak of has been burned to the ground, and the angels who have poisoned your minds with their lies have been vanquished or have fled. Don't worry; none of the human children living there have been harmed, at least not seriously. Accept your friend's offer and remain with him until this war comes to an end. It will make your life far less complicated. In time, you will learn to accept us."

"I reckon that the quality of life here in Heaven has just dropped a whole lot," said Jerry, almost under his breath.

"I'd be careful of my attitude if I were you," said the second demon, glaring at the youth.

Christopher's confusion, and yes, his fear, was beginning to subside. It was being replaced by a new emotion—anger. It was not the kind of anger that simply lashed out at people who might have displeased him. This was a different type of anger, a righteous anger against evil and injustice, and the ultimate sort of evil was standing there right in front of him. "Those angels at the mansion didn't do anything to harm you. You had no right to hurt them or threaten my friend."

"I had every right," snarled the first demon, "and I'll go on hurting them. The angels who follow Michael and Gabriel are our sworn enemies. In time, they will either accept our master, Lucifer, or they will be all the sorrier for their stupidity. Perhaps we will lock them away in Hell for a thousand years, separated from the love of the Father; or even better, throw them into the Great Sea of Fire to suffer for as long as the sea roars.

"Such will be the fate of those who oppose us. As for your friend, he needs to be careful how he addresses us. His attitude could be taken the wrong way. Those who choose to side with the angels will meet the same fate. So stay out of this war, boy."

In that moment, Christopher's anger overflowed, yet it was a controlled overflow, deliberate and planned. "You're going to lose this war, and do you know why? Because you have no heart. You're a dried up husk of what was once an angel. I'm not going to stand by while you hurt others."

"And what are you going to do, boy?" snarled the first demon. "We are a great and powerful race. I've personally tortured ten thousand of your kind in Hell—watched them whimper like frightened little children—and I enjoyed it. I would have no problem with doing the same thing to you. You humans are pathetic little creatures."

"And hurting helpless people makes you great?" asked Christopher.

Those words made the demon's anger boil to the surface. He stepped forward and backhanded Christopher, sending him flying at least eight feet. He landed flat on his back. Much to the demon's amazement, Christopher didn't cry. In fact, his eyes had taken on an icy cold stare. "And this makes you great?" he asked again, sitting up. "I had a different term in mind to describe you."

The demon approached him, fire in his eyes. He seemed an unstoppable force.

"Leave him alone!" demanded Jerry, stepping into the demon's path.

The demon pushed the youth out of the way as if he were no more than a rag doll. A second later he stood towering above Christopher.

"No, Grenlak," warned the other demon. "You're exceeding our mandate. We are not to harm the humans."

"I haven't harmed this little one yet," laughed Grenlak, "I've hardly even started."

"You should listen to him, Grenlak," said Christopher. "You'll live longer that way."

Grenlak laughed again. "Oh, is the little one threatening *me* now?"

"Believe what you want to," replied Christopher. "But don't put a hand on me again. You have no right to touch a child of God."

Grenlak reached down and grabbed Christopher again, this time by the wrist. That is when it happened—the burning glow. It radiated out of Christopher's hand and into the greyish flesh of the demon's arm. Grenlak immediately stumbled backward as his entire arm was engulfed within a burning red glow. He drew his arm to his chest, trying to extinguish the flames, but this was no ordinary fire. It spread quickly from his arm to his torso. Grenlak shrieked in agony as he tumbled to the ground. The fire spread to his other arm and then to his legs, yet it didn't ignite the dry leaves on the ground.

Within 20 seconds Grenlak was fully engulfed within the fiery glow. His flesh and armor disintegrated in the intense heat.

The other demon rushed toward Christopher, his sword drawn, but he didn't get very far. A second later, he too was engulfed within the fiery aura that had leaped from Christopher's open palm. He too tumbled to the ground. He writhed in total agony, shrieking in a shrill, inhuman voice. Within a minute, piles of dark gray ash were all that remained of the two demons.

By this time, Jerry had made his way to Christopher's side. There was a nasty, deep gash in Christopher's cheek where the demon had struck him, but already it was healing. Christopher seemed totally exhausted, only about half conscious. Jerry held him in his arms, not sure what to do.

"That really took the life out of me," murmured Christopher. "He really shouldn't have hit me like that."

"How did you do that?" asked Jerry, glancing back toward the two piles of ash that had been demons but a minute ago.

"I didn't do anything," said Christopher. "It had to have been the hand of the Father that saved me. I was simply a willing vessel."

It was several minutes before Jerry was able to help Christopher to his feet. By then the gash on his cheek was almost completely healed. "Come on," said Jerry, "it won't take us long to reach my house."

"No," insisted Christopher, "we've got to get to my place. We've got to help the other children."

"I don't think you're in any shape to help anyone," insisted Jerry. Jerry concentrated for a moment. A blue mist formed before them, alive with what looked like twinkling stars. "Come on, we'll take the shortcut." Jerry helped Christopher into the misty cloud, where they vanished.

They walked through a short corridor of cool mists, emerging only a few seconds later a dozen feet in front of Jerry's front porch where his parents were standing. They were relieved to see the two boys safe and sound.

Jerry's father, Bill Anderson, had the appearance of a man in his late 40s, although his real age was well over 130 years. His mother, Sarah, was nearly as old, though she looked no older than her husband. They could easily have taken on a younger appearance if they had wished, but it just wasn't their style. No, this was the proper appearance for the parents of a son in his late teens.

"What happened?" asked Sarah, running to the two boys. She noticed the almost-healed scar on Christopher's cheek.

"We ran into a pair of demons in the woods," said Jerry. "One of them hit Christopher. I reckon he didn't much care for the way Christopher spoke to him. But you should have seen what happened to the demon after he hit Chris."

Jerry was interrupted as yet another cloud of blue mist formed nearby. A man dressed in farmer's overalls stepped from the glowing, sparkling phantasm. It was Cy Davis, a neighbor from over in the next meadow.

"Bill, we've got problems," said Cy. "I swear to you, my daughter and I were visited by demons, the kind straight out of Hell."

"We've seen them too," confirmed Bill, "and I guess the boys ran into some in the woods."

Cy turned to Christopher and Jerry, a look of concern on his face. "You boys OK?"

"Yeah, we're OK," replied Jerry. "One of them hit Christopher…but not hard. He'll be fine."

Cy noticed the nearly healed gash on the youth's cheek. "This is crazy. I just don't understand how those demons could possibly be here. I thought that the Father would have prevented them from coming."

"I've got to get over to my house," said Christopher.

Cy shook his head sadly. "I'm afraid it's not there any more, son. The demons burned it. Don't worry, all of the children got out. A few got burned a little, but they healed pretty fast. They were just scared, that's all. My daughter and I took three of them in. Other neighbors took in the rest. Still, that place is crawling with demons right now. I really wouldn't go over there now. Maybe tomorrow."

"I reckon we're at war," said Bill, walking over to Cy.

Christopher leaned over to Jerry. "Please, Jerry, don't tell anyone what happened to the demon after he hit me. Let's just say they flew away. Don't tell them what I did, not yet."

Jerry looked at Christopher, surprised at his request. "Why?"

"Please…just trust me," whispered Christopher.

"I think they're going from house to house," said Bill. "They told us to stay in our homes, not to interfere. They said that they would tell us when it was safe to come out. It looks like we're right in the middle of a war zone. They've been commanded by the Father not to harm us so long as we don't interfere in this war of theirs."

"Look, Bill…me and some of the other men are going to make our way to Zion to see the Father. He'll know what to do," said Cy.

Bill glanced over at his wife. She nodded.

"We're going to meet over at Lester's place in about an hour," continued Cy. "There'll be about six or seven of us going. We'll gate out to Zion from there."

"OK," confirmed Bill. "I'll meet you there."

Cy nodded. The mists formed once more. He stepped into them and vanished.

Bill turned to his wife. "I'll need to get ready."

"OK," she said, as Bill headed for the house. She quickly turned to Christopher. There was still a trace of blood on his cheek, but the scar itself was gone. She reached down to have a look. "No permanent damage," she said. "But the demons who came here to our home said that they wouldn't hurt any of us. This war was between them and the angels."

"I guess you just can't trust demons," said Christopher, smiling slightly.

"So, what happened after he hit you?" asked Mrs. Anderson—Sarah.

"The other one stopped him," said Christopher. "He said something about hitting me was beyond their mandate or something like that. A minute or so later they were both gone."

"I'm just thankful that you two boys didn't get seriously hurt," she said.

"Well, if we would have, it would have healed in a few minutes anyway," continued Jerry. "Remember when I broke my leg jumping off that rock down by the creek?"

"How could I forget?" replied Sarah. "You were scared for a minute or two until the bones came together and healed. You were afraid that your leg would stay broken and twisted. But that doesn't happen, not here. The Father takes care of us."

Sarah hesitated. "But why not now? I wonder if there is something that we may have done to bring this thing on ourselves."

"I don't reckon I know what it might be," said Jerry.

"I don't either," said Christopher. "I just talked to the Father a couple of days ago and He didn't say anything about being upset with us."

"Well, we should know more when your father gets back from the Holy Place," said Sarah. "Then we'll know what to do."

A few minutes later, Bill returned from the house. He was wearing a long, white robe, the sort that most people wore when they made a journey to the Holy Place at the very heart of the City of Zion. The Father never said this was a requirement. Still, it had become a tradition among most of the saints. People wanted to look their best when they came before the Creator of the universe.

"I don't know how long this is going to take," Bill said. "I don't know what the conditions are in Zion. I guess I'll know soon enough."

"Be careful," cautioned Sarah, taking Bill's hand in hers.

Bill chuckled. "I always am." A blue mist filled with twinkling stars appeared before him. He stepped into it and faded from view.

"Well," said Sarah, turning to the boys, "no point in waiting out here. Why don't we head into the house? It's getting kind of warm."

Christopher was sure that he saw the trace of a tear in Sarah's eye, but he didn't say anything. He could sense how she felt right now.

The boys walked into the log cabin that was the heavenly mansion of the Andersons. The inside of the house was quite rustic. It wasn't a particularly large home, yet it was pleasantly furnished with fine wood furniture, a stone fireplace, and shiny hardwood floors with a variety of mismatched throw rugs. Christopher had been here several times before, yet the ambiance of this place always impressed him. It was very unlike the modern home of his parents on Earth, and equally dissimilar to his home here in Heaven, which struck him as being a bit austere. Angels weren't the universe's best interior decorators.

No, this place had the feel of a well-kept, backwoods home of the 1920s or '30s. It had old-style electric lamps and fixtures, though they operated on a wholly different principle from those of early twentieth-century Earth. The water faucets utilized hand pumps to bring the water into the basins. He figured that Jerry's parents went with the appliances and furnishings that were the most familiar to them.

The boys headed into Jerry's bedroom where they could discuss what had transpired in the forest, away from Jerry's mother. Christopher figured that Jerry would have some questions for him. He wasn't disappointed.

"OK, why did we just lie to my mother about what happened in the woods?" asked Jerry, closing the bedroom door behind him. "I always tell her the truth. Relationships in this family are based on trust."

"You didn't say anything," corrected Christopher, "and I didn't lie to her. What did I tell her that wasn't the truth?"

Jerry had to think a few seconds on that one. Christopher had a point. "Yes, but it was misleading."

"Maybe," admitted Christopher. "I've been reading books on American history in one of the libraries in Zion. I spend a lot of time there. One interesting book was about American politics during the Cold War."

"I've heard of the Cold War," replied Jerry.

"Well, during the Cold War there were certain American military secrets that were even withheld from the president himself—deep, dark secrets. Some were violations of international law. If the president knew about them, they would have counted him as part of the illegal activity. They couldn't risk that. His not knowing gave the president what they called plausible deniability. It kept him out of trouble.

"If we told your parents about what happened out there in the woods today, we would put them in danger too if the other demons found out. I don't want to put your parents in danger, do you?"

"No," confirmed Jerry. He hesitated before continuing. "You know, what I find real…well…troubling about you is that you don't act or talk like most ten-, I mean almost eleven-year-olds. You don't really play, and you don't read the sorts of books that most kids read. I mean, do you ever read books like *Tom Sawyer* or *Twenty Thousand Leagues Under the Sea*?"

"I've read them both," replied Christopher.

"OK, but sometimes the things you say are sort of creepy."

"I was mostly raised by angels, not ordinary parents, and not wolves," retorted Christopher.

"I get that," replied Jerry. "But you do problems in analytic geometry, whatever that is. You know your Bible like no one I know, and you study American political history in fantastic detail. And after all of that, you still can't tie a decent fly to go fly fishing with."

Both Christopher and Jerry were laughing now. It broke the growing tenseness in the room.

Then Jerry continued. "What you did out there in the woods…do you think you could teach me how to do that?"

"I think so," said Christopher, with not a second of hesitation in his voice. "You can gate from one place to another in Heaven with pinpoint accuracy. That takes thousands of times more energy and control than what I just did. I think it's important that you do learn it."

For the next hour and a half, Christopher explained to Jerry what was involved in what he had just done. Then Jerry tried it for himself. More than three hours later, Jerry rolled a small ink pen several inches across a table with nothing more than the power of thought. It wasn't so much mustering up the power to do it as it was mustering up the faith to do it. The power wasn't resident within the individual but within God's own Holy Spirit who permeated all of Heaven. It became a matter of convincing himself that all things were possible, even when common sense urged that they were not.

In the coming days and weeks, mastering such an ability might become a matter of survival. Yes, they could escape a demon by simply gating away 1,000 miles or to another level of Heaven entirely, but did they truly wish to spend their eternities constantly on the run? No, it would be better to stand and fight and vanquish their foe if possible—and apparently it was.

CHAPTER 2

IT HAD BEEN DARK FOR several hours when Bill Anderson emerged from a glowing cloud of blue and onto his front porch. His wife and the boys were there waiting for him.

"I was starting to get worried," said Sarah, stepping forward. "Well… how did it go?"

Bill's expression was not encouraging. "Not too well. We arrived just outside of the great walls of Zion, at the gate where we normally enter." Bill paused. "There were people running everywhere. In all of my years in Heaven I have never seen panic like I did today. I mean, there was never any reason for it. People were gating out all around me, tens of thousands of them. It was impossible to enter into the city with a flood of people trying to get out. Not many people were in the mood to talk to us either, but those who did talk painted a real grim picture.

"The angels and demons had been battling in and above the streets all day. They were still battling. There was smoke drifting everywhere. Parts of the city were in flames. Many people had tried to reach the Holy Place to seek sanctuary, but at least some were turned back by roving bands of demons. Both angels and demons alike were urging the human population of Zion to leave. I swear, I never thought I'd see a day such as this."

"Did you try to gate right into the city itself?" asked Jerry.

Bill shook his head. "Son, you know that doing that is forbidden. You have to walk beyond the walls of the city before you can gate in or out."

"Dad, I had the feeling that it was more an issue of etiquette than a hard and fast rule," said Jerry. "In an emergency, I think it would be allowed."

"I don't know about that, son," replied Bill. "We weren't about to put it to the test."

"Mr. Anderson, could you tell who is winning this war?" asked Christopher.

The hesitation in Bill's answer was not encouraging. "From what we were able to learn, this was a sneak attack by an enemy who had been preparing for years. The angels were caught completely off guard and were falling back. Many had been captured. As you all know, angels can't gate like we can. They can't travel instantly from one place to another simply by thinking about it. That ability is reserved for the Father and His children. Wherever they go, angels have to either walk or fly.

"But there are physical gates that they can use, rings of stone and metal like the one in the meadow not far from here. The angels use those to move great distances. Now, our ring is what they call a local gate. It allows angels to move mainly from one place to another on this plane of Heaven. But there are also the main gates, one or two on each level of Heaven. They allow angels to travel anywhere, even back to Earth or to the depths of Hell.

"Apparently, the demons entered through those gates and managed to gain control of them. That is how they got here in the first place. Then they spread out to the local gates, controlling them as well. They've managed to cut the angels off from each other. They've got them in full retreat on all sides. They're keeping the pressure on them, not allowing them to get organized."

"But still, don't the angels have something like a two-to-one numerical advantage over the demons?" asked Jerry.

"Something like that," replied Bill, sitting down on the porch swing. "The thing is, nearly half of the angels are on Earth right now, and they have no way of getting back with all of the gates controlled by the demons." Bill paused. "No, that's not quite true. I heard that the angels managed to hang onto control of a few of the gates. In fact, I heard that they have managed to keep the demons completely out of the second level of Heaven. It's become a sort of fortress, and humans have been helping angels get there so they can regroup.

"We heard that a legion of the angels had finally managed to make a stand at a place called Ceranda, not far from Zion, but that they were quickly being overwhelmed by huge numbers of demons. A group of humans helped wounded angels by the tens of thousands to gate from there over to the second level of Heaven and safety. They created their own gate, then led the angels hand in hand through it, hundreds at a time. While they did that, others held the demons off for a time with some kind of new weapon that they had fashioned. Word of their resistance is spreading. All over Heaven humans are joining the angels in their fight against the demons."

"That's why the demons are threatening us," reasoned Sarah. "They don't want us to get into the fight."

"That's about right," confirmed Bill. "But we can't just stand by and let this happen. The angels are going to lose this war unless we get involved. A meeting has been called at the church this evening. We're going to try and get the whole community together and see what we can do. We're sending out runners to let everyone know. The meeting starts in less than two hours. We need to get ready."

Sarah nodded as Bill headed off into the mists to spread the word to their neighbors. "Well, let's get ready. It sounds to me like we're going to have a long night ahead of us," she said.

As Sarah entered the house to prepare, Jerry turned toward Christopher. "That meeting at the church may be a good place to let the people know that we have authority over these demons. You could tell them what you've done. Some of the others have to have that same power. Maybe we all do—we just have to realize it, that's all."

Christopher hesitated. "Are you ready to bet everything on that?" he asked. "Are you willing to bet the eternities of this entire community on one isolated event in the woods? That's what we would be doing. Jerry, I don't even know exactly how I managed to do it. I was angry and frustrated, and I just acted. Maybe when the people of God are backed into a corner, they will find the power to do just what I did. But your father didn't return with stories of that kind of thing. No, he mentioned that some people were able to come up with some kind of weapon—a gun I guess, by the sound of it."

"People need to know," insisted Jerry.

"We've been all over this before," objected Christopher. "Plausible deniability, remember?"

"I haven't forgotten," said Jerry. "I just figure that we need to do something, that's all."

"We will," confirmed Christopher, "just not now. Right now we need to listen and plan. Before we jump in, we need to have all of the facts. We really don't know anything yet. Maybe we'll know more after the meeting tonight."

A bit over an hour later, the three entered the glowing mists and emerged in front of their community church. Their church looked very much like the picture book example of a small town, community church with its white exterior, large stained glass windows, and high steeple. It was the main gathering place for their far-flung, yet close-knit community. The building sat in the middle of a small, grassy meadow about three miles from the Andersons' home. Tonight it was bustling. Groups of people were gating in all over, and everywhere people were gathered in small groups discussing the terrible curse that had befallen the community.

Sarah and the boys quickly made their way toward the large, wooden front door. Beyond, in the well-lit church, still more people were gathered. Some sat in the wooden pews, while others stood around in groups.

This church was large and could easily accommodate 500 people. They would have a standing-room-only crowd tonight.

"We'll try and sit near the front," said Sarah, moving through the crowd of familiar parishioners. Everyone knew everyone else here. It was part of the very nature of Heaven. You instantly knew anyone and everyone you encountered, whether it be in church, in Zion, or in the forest beyond. It was a gift from God: there were no strangers in Heaven.

Sarah had found space in the third pew back when Jerry pointed out a pretty, dark-haired woman talking with a group of people near the front of the church. "Remember this morning when I was telling you about my meeting with Chris Davis years ago? Well, that's Jennifer Davis, Chris Davis's mother. We're likely to hear quite a bit from her before this night is over. When Serena was in Hell, Jennifer sent her things like clothes, food, and seeds. I suspect that she will be put on the demons' black list real quick. They're already on hers."

Over the next 20 minutes, the rest of the congregation filed into the church until it was completely filled. Bill, Cy, Jennifer, and several others sat up on the platform and would be addressing the congregation. Cy opened the meeting in prayer, then presented to the assembled multitude what they had discovered at the City of Zion. It was not an encouraging story.

One of their group had even managed to brave the raging flow of people fleeing through the great archway and got beyond the wall and into the city. He spoke of collapsed buildings, rubble filling the streets, and angelic battles still raging above the southern regions of the city. However, the city itself was firmly under demon control. All of the saints who remained within the walls of the city did so at their own peril.

There were reports that some of the citizens had managed to reach the Holy Place with its promise of sanctuary, but these were unverified reports. Even the member of their group who had managed to enter the city hadn't stayed very long. It was just too chaotic and dangerous there.

They also heard more about the battle at the place called Ceranda. Both the demonic and angelic forces had taken serious losses there. Yet the demonic forces had virtually unlimited reinforcements available. Had it not been for the humans who had evacuated the wounded angels to the safety of the second level of Heaven, hundreds of thousands of angels might have been captured. This was the place where a few brave humans had fired the first shots of the war, officially drawing humanity into the conflict. They had used a weapon that, interestingly enough, had first been fired in Hell to cover the escape of Serena Davis. They called it a particle rifle, and it had been developed by the great scientist Nikola Tesla. Along with Johannes Kepler and Niels Bohr, Nikola was leading the growing human resistance. It was curious that the human resistance was being led by scientists rather than by military or religious leaders. This brought a slight smile to Christopher's lips. "Scientists rule," he murmured.

Christopher listened intently to the reports; he did the math. Apparently his conflict in the forest had not resulted in the first demonic casualties. Actually, he was a bit disappointed.

When Jennifer Davis took the podium, the sparks really began to fly. She wasn't mincing words. "This has been coming for a long time," she began. Her voice was that of a fire-and-brimstone preacher, stirring the congregation to action. "We don't have a choice here, and if you think we do, you're sadly mistaken. We must get involved. Do you really want to live your eternity in a Heaven where the angels are ruled by Satan?

"We have children here left homeless by the demon attack, children who suffered burns in the fire that consumed their home. They were pushed callously and thoughtlessly to the side amid the demons' lust for revenge against the angels. The children's only fault was being in the way. These are the same demons that have tortured your forgotten loved ones in Hell. Do you want these same torturers to be teaching the children of Heaven? Their hands are covered in blood, and make no mistake, it is human blood."

She stretched out her hands before the people gathered. The symbolism was effective.

"She is quite a talker," whispered Jerry to Christopher.

Christopher only nodded. Here was another soul touched by Serena Davis. It was curious the number of times the Serena Davis incident came up. It was interwoven into the present conflict at so many levels. It had pushed forward the development of a weapon that was apparently very effective against the demonic invaders. It had brought the members of the human resistance together. It had even touched lives locally—namely, Jennifer Davis. Perhaps he was drawing lines and connecting dots that didn't really exist, but he didn't think so.

"It was the Father's wish that we remain unaware of the plight of our lost loved ones," she continued. "Indeed, we were left unaware of even their existence. Imagine suffering throughout all of eternity, knowing full well that not so much as one person is aware of your plight or even your existence. Imagine being forgotten even by your loved ones. But that is their fate, brothers and sisters.

"The Father desired that we should not grieve over those whom we are powerless to help. But I tell you this: there are times when I wish we could all remember those lost to us in Hell, remember them so that the crimes of these invaders should sink deep into our consciousness."

There was a long pause. Jennifer's piercing eyes scanned a room full of people who had her full attention.

"Several years ago, after a most traumatic incident that raised my awareness to the plight of those lost in the fires of Hell, I made the conscious decision to remember all of my lost loved ones. I went to the Father, and the Father honored my request.

"Yes, I grieve for them now, but I live in this world of ours with my eyes fully open. I understand the precious gift that the Father has given us. I look upon the lost and say, 'There but for the grace of God am I.' There but for the sacrifice of Jesus go all of us. The anguish of Hell is separation from God, but the torments of Hell are the deeds of its foulest inhabitants. Do you really think that Satan is going to keep his word to us?"

"He will," came a voice from the back of the church.

All eyes turned to see a demon in a long, black robe at the door, his bat-like wings folded tightly behind him. Yet this being did not take on the appearance of a pale old man, but rather that of a dark-haired, clean-shaven man who appeared to be no more than 35 years of age. He stepped in, flanked by two others whose appearance was not unlike his. All in all, they were quite handsome beings in every respect, from their well-groomed hair to their flawless skin. Were it not for his wings, he could easily have passed as human.

"I am sorry to interrupt your service," continued the demon, "and I am sorry that we have disrupted your lives; however, it was necessary." His eyes scanned the congregation thoroughly before he continued. "I am Lieutenant Kragow, commander of this cohort. I have come to tell you that you are no longer limited to your homes. You are free to come and go as you please.

"Our concern was for your safety. We couldn't have a child of God wandering unknowingly into the line of fire in a battle. However, this is no longer a war zone. The angels of Michael and Gabriel have fled. Most of us will be rejoining our legion; only a few will remain. They will remain to assure your safety. I do caution you, however, to make no attempt to visit the City of Zion during the next few days. There are still pockets of resistance there as well as unstable and crumbling buildings. Do this for your own safety. I assure you, all will be rebuilt, all set right."

The unexpected visitation had caught all by surprise, to say nothing of the eloquence of this demon commander's speech. It was, in the end, Jennifer who responded.

"For thousands of years, your master has been the sworn enemy of all humanity. Now, suddenly he wants to be the ruler of the very race whose job it is to safeguard us. Back where I come from we have a saying about that. We call it 'the fox guarding the chicken coop.'"

That brought a few chuckles from members of the congregation, here and there. Mostly it brought a hushed silence.

For a moment it seemed as if the demon lieutenant did not seem to understand the reference. Then he responded. "We are not foxes, and you are not chickens. During those thousands of years you speak of, it was us and our testing of humanity that separated the goats from the sheep. I hope that you will forgive me, but I overheard your previous comments about our activities in Hell. I wish to respond.

"You find what we did to the humans sent there to be reprehensible. That is your right. But allow me to ask you this: Would you prefer to have the likes of Genghis Khan or Adolph Hitler here in your midst? What would their presence and that of those like them do to the environment of Heaven? Like it or not, we serve a useful purpose in the history of humanity. If you prefer an analogy, so be it. The Father separates the wheat from the chaff, and we in turn burn that chaff. When this war is won, the only thing that will change is that the angels of Michael and Gabriel will be compelled to share the burden that we have shouldered alone for so long. Those that refuse to do this task are not worthy of the name 'servant of God.' Their fate shall be to become chaff."

"A very noble speech," retorted Jennifer, "but I know better. If you were listening to what I said, then you must know that I am aware of exactly what goes on in Hell. I have loved ones there even today, my brother for one. Yes, I remember my loved ones sentenced to that realm, and I have watched what you do to them. To confine them is one thing, but you haven't stopped there. You hurt them and go on hurting them. What you do is zealous and excessive. You drive them to madness with your torments, and you enjoy it; indeed, your master revels in it, creating ever more elaborate methods of eternal punishment.

"You started with pits of boiling filth and oceans of flames, but you didn't stop there. Your methods evolved into cities of altars where helpless humans are eaten alive by birds of prey—eaten to the bones—only to regenerate and have the whole ordeal repeated again and again. You created great steam-driven engines of torment where the shackled victims were randomly impaled on spikes, burned with acid, and broiled in molten metal. According to you, this was all done in the name of justice?"

"Yes, it was done in the name of justice," confirmed the demon. "Know this, the Father sent these people to us for a reason. He knew what we would do to them, but He sent them nonetheless. He knew that we would do our job. Out of love for you, His true children, He wiped these people from your memory. He did it for a reason, so that you would not grieve for them. It was all part of His divine plan. I tell you, they are unworthy of your grief. But you chose to ignore His plan; you chose to remember them. Now you reap the harvest of your foolish decision, of your disobedience. To you this has become a personal vendetta when it should not be."

Jennifer replied, "I watched my own daughter-in-law suffer in your Sea of Fire. I watched my own brother burn in the eternal flames of a fire pit; so yes, to me this is personal. I know your kind only too well. You speak of doing your job. And what job is that? There is a difference between the executioner and the torturer, sir, and you and your kind are the latter. You do not belong here any more than Genghis Khan or Adolph Hitler. Hell is your home, and I will not rest until you are once more cast out of Heaven and back to that place where you belong."

A growing applause arose from the congregation. Further debate would have been futile. The demon lieutenant and his two escorts departed. For several minutes the congregation continued in their cheers of defiance. Jennifer finally quieted the masses.

"There you have it, my brothers and sisters," she began. "That is what we are dealing with. They will mix some truth with their lies, but they are still lies. I've opened the books in the Hall of Records that no one else wishes to see, the black books. I've witnessed firsthand their contents, and I tell you this—Satan's minions are master torturers. For the sake of the children, I will not subject this assembly to any further description of what I have seen in those pages. I have already said more than I should have, and I ask your forgiveness for that. But the leopard cannot change his spots and neither can the minions of Satan. Hell is their home, not Heaven. We must stand with the angels, for they have stood with us more times than we can possibly know."

The congregation was in agreement: they needed to stand with the angels in their struggle—but how? What could they do against the fiery swords of the demon armies? It seemed a futile struggle. In the end, committees were established to study the situation and make recommendations. They all agreed to meet again in three days.

As Christopher left the church with the Andersons, he had become even more determined to get into this fight. But what could he do? Taking down two demons was one thing, but he was dealing with an entire demon army of over 100 million. Even dealing with the two this afternoon had left him feeling weak. Yes, it had to be the power of God acting through him, but why him? Why not someone older and wiser?

"It's not by might, not by power, but by My Spirit, sayeth the Lord," he murmured. Surely there had to be others who could do what he had done. As he faded off to sleep that night he prayed for guidance. He had discovered an incredible gift, yet he still was unsure how to use it.

❖

Jerry stared intently at the metal lure glistening in the filtered sunlight of the forest. He had been doing so for nearly five minutes.

"Picture it rising," insisted Christopher. "Know that it can be moved. Be sure that you can do it…don't doubt."

Jerry's face took on an even more determined scowl, yet nothing happened. A moment later he turned away. "I can't."

"You can't because you believe you can't," replied Christopher. "As long as you believe you can't, you never will."

Jerry's face took on a puzzled aspect. "Say what?"

"What," replied Christopher.

"No, I didn't mean for you to say what," said Jerry, frustration in his voice. He sat down on a nearby boulder and stared out at the waters of the stream. "Why do you have to take everything so literally?"

"My upbringing, I suppose," said Christopher.

"Sometimes I just don't understand you," said Jerry, whose gaze hadn't moved from the water. "Just a couple of days ago things seemed so simple. I had my eternity all planned out. I'd go fishing with my dad, walk in the woods, go talk to God in the Holy Place…those kinds of things. My life was perfect. Then yesterday had to come. This is Heaven, not Earth. It isn't supposed to be like this."

"But it is," said Christopher.

"Now it is," confirmed Jerry.

Christopher sat on the boulder beside Jerry and looked out at the stream for the better part of a minute before responding. "Do you think that is all that God had for you? I mean, the things that you just mentioned."

Jerry seemed puzzled. He looked toward Christopher. "What else could there be? I mean, this is Heaven, we're supposed to be happy."

"Yes, it is, and yes, we are," confirmed Christopher, "but that's not what Heaven is all about. I'm starting to think that a lot of grownups here think just that way. On Earth there are places called rest homes, where older people go to sit and relax and eventually die. You don't die in Heaven, not in body, but I think some people here are starting to die in spirit. I learned a new word for it awhile back; that word is *apathy*.

"You don't stop growing and learning just because you die and go to Heaven. This isn't a rest home in the sky. This is a place where the Father trains you, if you let Him. It is the second phase of our existence. I've seen people in the City of Zion do incredible things. I've seen them create sweet sounding musical instruments and other wonderful things through the power of thought alone. They push the human imagination beyond its limits.

"On the first level of Heaven, Professor Faraday is creating scientific marvels beyond anything that humans back on Earth could even dream of. He's made spaceships that travel faster than a beam of light, taking you anywhere you want to go. Here you can live your dreams. Here you can become all you can possibly be, and that is the very image of His firstborn Son, Jesus. Along the way you can gain a lot of knowledge and wisdom. That's what I want to do. What do you want to do, Jerry?"

Jerry suddenly smiled. He jumped from the boulder and turned back toward the lure. "What I want to do is to try and levitate that lure."

"Don't *try*," replied Christopher. "Do or do not...there is no try."

"Who said that?" asked Jerry.

"Yoda," replied Christopher.

"Who is Yoda?" asked Jerry. "Was he one of the angels who taught you?"

Christopher smiled and stepped down from his perch. "Are you going to do it or not?"

Jerry didn't answer. His expression had taken on an uncharacteristic calmness. He was still focusing on the lure, but he wasn't struggling. A moment later it floated gently into the air. Yet Jerry's expression hadn't changed. For nearly a minute it hung motionless about four feet above the ground.

"Nice," said Christopher, his arms crossed.

Suddenly, the lure shot off to the left as if propelled from a gun. It ended up imbedded half an inch into the bark of an oak tree 20 feet away.

Jerry looked to Christopher in amazement. "I didn't do that."

Christopher laughed. "No, I did. Imagine that lure flying right into the forehead of a demon, just like David's sling fired a stone into Goliath's head. It would ruin the demon's entire day."

Both boys shared a good round of laughter. Jerry went to the tree to retrieve his coin-shaped lure, but it wasn't easy. It was wedged into the wood tightly. By the end of the afternoon, Jerry could move the fishing lure effortlessly about. He could even move stones that were easily ten times heavier than the lure. Christopher was also practicing the trade, though on a grander scale, moving large rocks that were easily 30 pounds in weight. They agreed not to speak of this to Jerry's parents, at least not yet. If they were going to teach these skills to the people of the community, they first had to master them. Until then, they would keep a low profile.

During the days that followed, the boys made many treks down to the stream, not to fish, but to continue exercising their newly learned skill. They invented games to make the learning more fun, as well as to test what could and couldn't be done with this newfound ability.

On one day, Jerry pondered if it was possible to pull oneself up into the air by their bootstraps. It was part of an old joke his father had told him, but could it really be done? Christopher vowed to try. He attempted to levitate himself.

What had started off as a joke became a surprising reality when Christopher managed to levitate himself about four feet off of the ground for a good ten seconds. His ability to levitate heavier objects was improving.

But they did more than just practice their gifts of levitation. They traveled to other places as well. Christopher insisted that they take some time each day to visit the children who had been raised by the angels along with him and now lived with other families. Most of them looked up to Christopher as one would admire an older brother. Christopher would play with them, though play wasn't really part of his life anymore.

The boys also discovered that several adults who had been raised by these very angels in their youth had returned to the meadow to help. They planned to rebuild the home of their youth, and teach these children themselves if need be.

From them, Christopher learned bits and pieces of information about the War in Heaven. It was not going well for the angels. Many of them had been captured and were being held prisoner in a variety of undisclosed locations. Others had fled to the second level of Heaven where they were trying to regroup. Still others fought an ongoing battle with the demonic forces, yet they were always outnumbered, always on the run. Apparently, a huge number of angels remained stranded on Earth with no way to return to Heaven.

There were other stories of a growing and very organized human resistance, yet Christopher could get no specifics about this movement. Perhaps these people hid their identities for a reason.

Still, these were secondhand stories. Christopher longed for the truth, and there was only one place that would be found—in the Holy Place, in the very heart of the City of Zion. Yet the word was that Zion was deep within demon-occupied territory.

A week passed, and the boys saw neither demons nor angels in the sky. Apparently this backwoods location on the third level of Heaven was not of any real strategic interest to either side. To some it seemed like a refuge. Other people of the area spoke of revolt against the demon hoards; yet, here at least, there were no demon hoards to be found. Despite the community's insistence on becoming involved in the conflict, complacency was beginning to set in.

Jerry's parents had a middle-of-the-road attitude. They spoke of the need to act, but couldn't decide what course of action to take. In the end, they did nothing.

On this day, the seventh day, Jerry and Christopher were in the forest again by the stream. But this time they weren't honing their skills of levitation; they were fishing. A sort of strange melancholia had descended upon them both. They knew that they had to do something, but like so many of the others, what it was eluded them. To make it still worse, the fish weren't biting.

"I've been thinking about that night at the church," said Jerry. "I've been thinking about what Jennifer Davis said."

"She said a lot of things," said Christopher, whose gaze remained fixed on the bob floating 30 or so feet out.

"Yeah," confirmed Jerry, "but I was thinking about what she said about remembering her loved ones in Hell. She willingly chose to remember when no one else would. I wonder why she'd do that."

"Because of Serena," replied Christopher.

"Maybe," replied Jerry. "But later, after Serena was rescued, she chose to regain all of her memories of Earth, and the Father granted her request." Jerry paused. "I mean, my dad realizes that he must have known his father. He speaks of gaps in his memory of Earth. Surely his father was there, but he can't remember him. Neither can my grandmother. She can't remember her own husband. To them he has become a phantom.

"They both admit that he must be in Hell. There is no other explanation. But knowing that he exists and is in Hell is not like knowing him. The way it is now, they're sort of detached. It doesn't have the emotional impact it might otherwise have. I don't know. Does that make any sense?"

"Sure," replied Christopher.

"I don't have any experiences like that," continued Jerry. "Everyone I ever knew and loved is right here in Heaven. I'm totally disconnected from Earth. But you aren't. Are there gaps in your memory of Earth? I mean, I know you were real young when…well…you know…"

"When I died," said Christopher. "It's OK, you can say it. I remember that day very well, though sometimes I wish I didn't. For that matter, I remember all of my life on Earth perfectly. There are no gaps. I remember my parents. I even remember my three older brothers, Jamie, Brandon, and Tyler. They are much older than me. They're all in their twenties now and still right there on Earth. Sometimes I look in on them using their books in the Great Hall of Records. Their future is not yet written. I'd like to think that they'll end up here eventually, but I just don't know."

Christopher paused, anticipating Jerry's next question. "I know… why do I remember when almost no one else does? I'm not sure. There are just so many unanswered questions."

"Maybe it's time we got some answers," suggested Jerry, "now that we know the right questions to ask."

Christopher knew where this conversation was going too. "We need to go to the Holy Place, but it may be pretty dangerous; it is right in the middle of demon-held territory. I'm not sure that the demons would allow us anywhere near the Holy Place."

"As I see it, they don't have the right to deny us access to the Father," said Jerry. "After all, according to the demons we have met, this war is between them and the angels. It doesn't concern us. We should be allowed to come and go as we please."

"So they say," replied Christopher. "Still, they are demons."

Jerry nodded. "Are you up for it?"

"Yeah, I think so. We can't just sit here."

"Shall we go tomorrow?" asked Jerry.

"We go tomorrow," confirmed Christopher.

And so the plans were made. They discussed their options and alternatives all afternoon and well into the night. They really didn't know quite what to expect. They prayed for guidance. Tomorrow they would meet with the Father.

CHAPTER 3

O**N THE MORNING OF THE** eighth day following the incident in the woods, Jerry and Christopher rose early. They donned the traditional white vestments of persons who intended to make a pilgrimage to the Holy Place. Fortunately, Christopher was able to wear the old white robe that Jerry had long since outgrown. They set off through the sparkling mists toward the entrance to the City of Zion.

It seemed but a short walk through the cool, blue mists before they arrived at the gates of the city. Before them rose the mighty wall that surrounded this great metropolis. On any ordinary day, this place would have been abuzz with people going into and out from the city. That was not the case today. The quiet was positively eerie.

In places, clouds of smoke still arose from the city beyond the wall. Still, the boys couldn't evaluate the extent of the damage from where they stood. A great white marble wall, 100 feet high, surrounded the city, blocking their view of the streets and buildings. To evaluate the condition of the city beyond, they would have to pass through the great archway 50 yards before them.

The archway, one of 12 entrances into the city, stood fully 50 feet high and 100 feet wide. It was undamaged, but was guarded by at least 50 winged demons dressed in armor. They were spaced out across the width of the entrance in two rows. Each held what looked like some sort of long, metallic spear. They didn't appear to be very friendly.

Christopher turned toward Jerry and took a deep breath. "Demons are creatures of habit and duty. They will expect the older of us to do the talking. That would be you. They would be suspicious, even offended, if I spoke on our behalf."

"All right," replied Jerry. "What should I say?"

"Don't worry what you shall say, for in this very hour the Lord shall tell you what to say," said Christopher.

"Matthew 10:19," replied Jerry.

Christopher smiled broadly. "Very nice, Jerry. OK, here we go. Are you ready?"

Jerry definitely looked nervous. "Into the valley of death rode the two."

Christopher smiled slightly. "Rudyard Kipling would have been proud."

They boldly advanced toward the archway. All the while the demons watched them carefully. These demons had taken on a visage not unlike the one that had appeared at the church a week ago. Except for their black bat-like wings, they appeared in all manner human. One toward the center advanced in their direction. He had the appearance of a man in his mid-30s, a handsome man at that; stranger still, he wore a pleasant smile.

"Greetings, children of the most high God," he said. "I am Lieutenant Vigaran of the Seventeenth Cohort, Fifth Legion. I regret that my orders are to allow none to pass on this day. The city beyond these walls is not safe. Even now the streets are being cleared, and routes to the Holy Place are being given priority for those who seek communion with the Father. I assume that is where you are going."

"You assume right, sir," said Jerry, in as pleasant and respectful a tone as he could.

"I ask you to be patient with us," said the lieutenant. "We have over ten thousand of our forces securing the city, making it safe for you. We do not wish to bar you from communing with the Father, but our concern is for your safety."

"I can understand that," said Jerry. "Tell me, has the City of God been damaged badly?"

"The damage is extensive," confirmed the lieutenant. "Should a wall collapse at the wrong time and injure a child of God, I fear that we may be held accountable. We made a promise to the Father that no child of His would come to harm due to our actions. We intend to keep that promise. It is dangerous enough for the inhabitants still within the city. We do not wish to compound that danger by allowing additional people to enter."

Jerry nodded. "Do you know when we will be able to enter?"

"I do not think it will be much longer," assured the demon, "a week, perhaps less."

"I understand," said Jerry. "We shall return in a week."

"I do appreciate your understanding," said the demon, his smile growing. "It is my sincere hope that the children of God will one day come to trust and depend on us. I know that trust will not come easily; but we hope that, in time, we will be able to earn it."

Jerry smiled as best he could. "I hope so too, really I do." With those words, Jerry turned and walked away. Christopher followed. "I'm gating out, follow my lead."

The starry mists materialized before them and they vanished into them. Jerry glanced behind him.

"Are we going home?" asked Christopher, looking over at his friend.

"No," said Jerry, "not quite."

A moment later, Christopher felt the cold wind as they materialized on the snowy ridge of a mountain. The cold wind seemed as if it were blowing right through him. He saw a great alpine valley before him. Through its center ran a mighty glacier. He turned around to see the magnificent City of Zion far below and about 20 miles away. The city dominated a high plateau just beyond a forested river valley. The city itself stretched out for nearly 30 miles. From here they could see that all was not well. Smoke still rose above portions of the great metropolis. The heaviest damage was around the Great Hall of the Angels near the center of the city and those parts of the city farthest south, along the route of the angels' retreat. It hurt Christopher to see the most beautiful city in the universe in such a state.

"I wanted to reconnoiter our situation," said Jerry. "I probably should have brought us here before. We're nearly three miles above the city."

"You've been here before?" asked Christopher.

"Yes," confirmed Jerry. "Actually, the last time I hiked up here from the valley with my dad. It took us a couple of days, but it was worth it. I enjoy high places. I wish we had wings like the angels—flying could be fun."

Christopher smiled. "So you *do* have goals and dreams beyond fishing throughout eternity."

Jerry smiled. "Yeah, I guess I do."

Using their heavenly, God-given vision, the boys could see the city in perfect detail. Their sight was eight or ten times that of the clearest vision one may have possessed on Earth. It was not a binocular vision. Objects didn't look any larger; they were just far clearer.

"Remember the demon telling us that he didn't wish to allow any additional people into the city?" said Jerry.

"Of course," confirmed Christopher. "That means that there are people within the city, the residents who decided to stay. I guess the demons didn't have the authority to make them leave."

"Bingo," replied Jerry. "If we were to step out from a building within the city, a library maybe, they may just assume that we had been there all along. They wouldn't have the authority to make us leave. Now all we need to do is to gate unseen into a building, preferably one close to the Holy Place. Then we could make a beeline to the Holy Place from there."

"The Hall of Records?" suggested Christopher. "I can see it from here. It doesn't look like it was damaged. It's a really big building, one could almost get lost in it. We could gate onto the fifth floor, section J. That place isn't near any windows. I don't think anyone would see us. It would be less than a mile to the Holy Place. It's a great plan. That is, if it's possible to gate into the city. I've never tried."

"I reckon it's time to find out," said Jerry. "Sounds like you know the way…you lead."

Christopher concentrated and the misty stars appeared before him. He entered, followed closely by Jerry. A few seconds later they stepped into an aisle with books stacked high on crystal shelves on either side. Christopher had been right. Due to the way the tall bookshelves ran in this part of the hall, no one could have seen them enter from any other location.

"Looks like it worked," said Christopher, looking about to confirm what he already suspected—they were alone. "You'd think that lots of people would come here. After all, this is the place where the events of every human life in the history of Earth are recorded. But they don't. In fact, I rarely see people here."

"I can tell you I don't come here," confirmed Jerry. "Matter of fact, I've only been here once. My mother brought me here to see this many years ago. I don't think my father has ever been here. He says that the stuff here is best not known."

"I come here a lot," said Christopher, raising his hands and turning about to see all of the books. "Each book represents the life of someone who lives or had lived on Earth, even if he or she only lived there a few months. The books are color-coded. If they're gray, that tells you that person is still alive and on Earth. The white ones are the books of the saints, those of us who are right here in Heaven. And the black books... well...they're the books of the poor people who didn't make it here...if you know what I mean."

"Perfectly," said Jerry, who was still gazing around to confirm that they were indeed alone.

"All you have to do is open one of these books and turn to a page. The cover tells you whose book it is. You look at the words inside, but you only see them for a few seconds. Then the whole world of this library vanishes, and you are right there watching that person's life. They can't see you or hear you, but you can see, hear, and even smell what is going on. It's sort of like the story *A Christmas Carol*, where Ebenezer Scrooge is traveling with the Ghost of Christmas Past. None of the people Scrooge saw could see him either. The ghost told him that it was because all of the people he saw were merely shadows of things that were."

"That's all very nice," said Jerry, "but how did you know that this one aisle was so secluded?"

"Because I come here often," said Christopher. He walked over to one particular gray book. He picked it out almost instinctively from the other books around it, many of which were also gray. He caressed its binding. "This is my mother's book. I come here to get closer to her. I open her book, and I'm with her. She spreads the Gospel wherever she goes, and sometimes I'm there with her." Christopher hesitated. "You know, sometimes I feel like she actually knows that I'm there."

Jerry walked toward Christopher. He saw the trace of a tear in his eye.

Christopher gently returned the book to its place. "I've been doing this for an awfully long time. One of the angels showed me how. Since then I've come here. I visit my father's book too. It is only a few rows over."

Jerry placed his hand on Christopher's shoulder. "Well, now that we know it can be done, what next?"

"I guess we make our way to the Holy Place," said Christopher. Suddenly the youth went quiet. He placed his finger to his lips. "There's someone here."

The two boys made their way across the translucent floor to a corner where they felt they might have more cover. Yes, there was no doubt about it—the sound of footsteps could be heard, and they were drawing closer. The two boys remained totally silent, totally motionless. What now? Should they gate out? No, they held their ground.

A shadow slowly crossed the floor in front of them. They held their breath.

Then a young man dressed in white turned the corner before them. He appeared to be somewhat younger than Jerry, perhaps 17 or so. When they saw him, they both knew his name—Jonathon.

"I thought I was alone here," said the light-haired youth in a soft voice as he approached the two friends. "It's OK. I'm a friend, just another child of God. I was just two aisles over doing some research when I saw the glow. I guess you gated in, right?"

"Right," confirmed Jerry.

"Research?" asked Christopher. "What kind of research?"

Jonathon seemed to have to think about that one. "Well, how can I describe it? I guess you could call it detective work of a sort. I'm trying to learn all that I can about this conflict. There are so many wild rumors flying around that I had to come here and find out what the truth was for myself. And I'm here to tell you that the truth is way stranger than fiction."

"Are you from the city?" asked Jerry.

"Actually, no," replied Jonathon. "I live on the third level of Heaven, along with my great-grandmother Gladys and my great-grandfather

Bud. We have a mansion that overlooks the sea on one side and beautiful meadows on the other. We even have a tennis court in our backyard where I play tennis with my great-grandfather—that is, when we're not all going fishing." There was a pause. Jonathon was looking at Jerry in such an odd way. Then he smiled. "You like to go fishing too, don't you?"

"Why...yes," replied Jerry, "but how did you know that?"

Jonathon's smile widened. "I wasn't trying to pry. I guess it just takes one fisherman to know another one."

Jerry smiled slightly. "I guess so."

Christopher thought about Jonathon's unusual observation. He knew that there were people in Heaven who had an uncanny ability to read other people—it was almost like telepathy. But most of those people had been here in Heaven for centuries. It wasn't the sort of gift that you picked up overnight. They were sort of like Yoda, only taller and less wrinkled. "How old are you, Jonathon?"

"Seventeen," replied Jonathon, "and I lived all of those years, short three minutes, in Heaven. You see, I died at birth. When I first came here, I was taken by the angels to my great-grandmother Gladys. She raised me in the knowledge of the Lord. Later, my great-grandfather Bud arrived to help her. They've been wonderful. I love them very much, and they love me. One day, so I've been promised, my parents and others of my family will be here with me too."

"It sounds to me like we're all very much in the same boat," said Jerry.

"Boat?" asked Christopher. "What boat is that?"

That comment brought a round of laughter from both Jonathon and Jerry.

"Is he always like that?" asked Jonathon.

"Yeah, pretty much," confirmed Jerry. "He was raised by angels."

"Oh well, I suppose it's better than being raised by wolves," said Jonathon.

It was about that time that Christopher got it. "Oh, yes…the same boat, as in the same circumstance."

"Yeah," said Jerry, looking toward Jonathon, who just nodded in agreement. "But how long have you been here, Jonathon, and how did you get here?"

"The same way you did, I suspect. The demons were guarding all of the gates. I tried several of them. So, when all else failed, I infiltrated the compound in a way only we humans can."

"You gated in," deduced Christopher.

"I think I just said that," confirmed Jonathon. "Actually, I was here in Zion when this whole thing started. I was right across the street, over there at the library, studying ancient Egyptian when it began."

"Ancient Egyptian?" asked Jerry.

"Yeah," confirmed Jonathon. "I enjoy studying other languages, ancient languages especially. I've learned twenty-three so far."

"Twenty-three different languages?" exclaimed Jerry.

"Is there an echo in here?" asked Jonathon. "Yes, twenty-three languages. Those include both the angelic and demonic tongues. Under the present situation, that may become useful.

"Anyway, there was a terrible explosion that rocked the entire building. I went running out into the street just in time to see a volley of demon fireballs blow out one entire wall of the Great Hall of Angels. The rubble came crashing to the street hundreds of feet below in a great rumble, then a huge cloud of dust came billowing down the street at high speed…and I ducked into the Great Hall of Records. I mean, it's one of the best built buildings in all of Zion. I thought I'd be safe there until the battle ended. Anyway, it offered a tremendous view of it all with its huge thick windows. So I just waited.

"At first the angels fought very well. They were converging from all sides on the demons that were attacking the Great Hall. For a time, I thought that they would surely crush this demon raid on the Holy City. But the demons just kept coming. It wasn't a raid; it was a full-scale invasion. You should have seen it: angels and demons battling in the sky over Zion—hundreds, then thousands, then millions of them. The sky was darkened by their black wings. There were lightning bolts and fireballs flying everywhere. And in the end, the angels were forced to withdraw."

Jonathon continued, "Hours went by, and the demons just kept streaming out of the Hall of Angels. I figured that they were coming in through their main ring in the Hall of Angels, and here I was only a mile and a half away from ground zero. So I waited and watched.

"The streets were filled with people by now, and some had been injured by falling and flying debris. Well, so much for the demons' promises that humans wouldn't be hurt during this conflict. They're demons, what do you expect?"

"Yeah, we've seen firsthand how they keep their word," said Jerry. "We don't want their kind around here."

"I'll say amen to that one," said Jonathon. "I'll tell you, Jerry, they've caused real chaos here. I never thought I'd see panic in Heaven, but I don't know what else to call it. The streets were full of it on that first day. Some people were trying to head for the Holy Place, but some of the fiercest fighting between the angels and the demons was in that direction. Most were turned away and so headed for the gates of the city. Some even decided to violate the rules and gated out right from the city street. That's when I realized that it could be done.

"I figured that was what I'd do when it was time to leave, but I decided to stay for a while. I decided I'd use the books to get a clearer picture of what was going on. I selected books of friends of mine who lived right here in Zion. I figured that they wouldn't mind, and it would allow me to see the conflict through their eyes. I saw plenty and learned even more. I stayed in here for hours, going from book to book, seeing this war from all angles, even through the eyes of an angel.

"Then I went to the book of a friend of mine who lives only about a mile away from here. He studied science and math with Johannes Kepler. I mean, this guy is a real brain. While the fighting was going on, he assembled several high tech weapons by just thinking about them. Now, that's real talent. I can materialize matter too, but I'm here to tell you, I'm not *that* good. Through his book, I found out that the angels had managed to keep the demons off the second level of Heaven and were preparing to launch a counterattack near a place called Ceranda. It's a hilly region about twenty or so miles south of the city."

"We heard about that battle," noted Christopher. "It doesn't sound like it went too well."

"That depends on who you ask," replied Jonathon. "The demons had the angels outnumbered five to one, and the angels had to eventually retreat, but it was a psychological victory nonetheless. It was the first time that the angels and humans stood side by side and took up the fight, and I'm here to tell you they did serious damage to the demon forces. I should know, I was there.

"I jetted out of here in a hurry to help gate the wounded angels to safety on the second level. I personally guided about six hundred angels to safety. They'd have been demon fodder if I hadn't. After the battle, I caught up to my friend David. He'd actually used that weapon I told you about in the battle. I tell you no lie...it literally disintegrated the demons. He called it a particle rifle.

"Normally an injured demon, like an injured angel, would regenerate. But I'd bet that the demons hit by those particle beams won't regenerate anytime soon. They were blown into way too many pieces. The inventers of the particle rifle also created a smaller version of it: a particle pistol."

Jonathon pulled his robe aside to reveal a pistol strapped to his belt. It looked like something straight out of a science fiction story.

"I managed to talk my friend David into making one for me," said Jonathon. "I'll tell you this: it sure beats a sword. A demon doesn't stand a chance against one of these. It more than evens up the odds. I never leave home without it."

"How does it work?" asked Christopher, examining it more carefully.

"I really don't know," admitted Jonathon, "at least not exactly. It somehow harnesses the power of God's Holy Spirit and creates a beam of high energy particles moving at incredible speeds. That is how David explained it to me. I'm not nearly the science geek he is. But I do know how to use it."

"So, you came back to the Hall of Records to do more detective work," deduced Christopher.

"Yeah, I couldn't see staying home," replied Jonathon. "I couldn't just hang around doing nothing. I decided to come here and see what I could find out. I've been here for two days. I know exactly what Satan has up his sleeve, and I know what plans the resistance has to oppose him. Would you believe that there is even a resistance movement in Hell? It's led by this big dark angel called Abaddon."

"The same Abaddon that rescued Serena," deduced Christopher.

"Right on," confirmed Jonathon. "He rescued her mother too, as well as about a thousand other humans in Hell. They've built themselves quite a fortress. There is so much here to learn. I just find a thread and follow it wherever it leads. Maybe you could help me. The three of us working together could accomplish so much more than I could alone."

"But we're not staying here," said Jerry. "We're on our way to the Holy Place to talk to God." He paused. "Would you like to come with us? It seems to me that you may learn more from the Father than you could following these threads of yours, even with our help. Then, afterward, you could come back here if you felt you needed to."

Jonathon nodded. "Yes, you have a point there. It's not that far, and I don't think it's nearly so dangerous as it was a few days ago. I haven't spoken to the Father since this all began. Yes, thank you…I think I will go along."

The boys made their way to the northeast staircase, a grand marble spiral, one of six, that ran from the ground floor all the way to the highest floor of the magnificent building. They cautiously descended to the ground floor, keeping an eye on the street beyond the huge windows. The streets were empty. To Christopher, that in itself seemed strange. In the eternal daylight world of the City of Zion, the streets were perpetually busy. No vehicular traffic was allowed on these broad streets; they were reserved exclusively for pedestrians. Yes, it took time to get around the city on foot, but who was in a hurry? In a world of true eternities, time was almost meaningless. Anyway, one didn't become tired. Walking ten miles was as easy as walking one.

Reaching the ground floor, the boys scanned the avenue beyond to confirm that no one was around and headed out the glass door. The wide marble steps that led down to street level were dusty and cluttered with small debris.

Jonathon looked across the avenue to see his favorite library largely in ruin. "The library took several direct fireball hits just minutes after I ran into the street. The destruction of all of those books is a terrible loss."

"At least you weren't in there when it happened," said Christopher.

"True," replied Jonathon. "I think most everyone got out when the shooting started."

"Maybe, when this is all over, the Father will replace the books that were lost," suggested Jerry, scanning the devastation all around them. "It looks like this part of the city got hit pretty hard." He turned to gaze at the Great Hall of Records. It was a monolithic building that stretched for several city blocks and rose over 120 feet above the street. It was an incongruous mixture of tall Greek columns and marble floors, combined with walls that were largely made of thick glass and shimmering metal. He'd been told that this particular metal was called titanium and that it was very light yet strong. All in all, the building had survived the attack very well. A few of the columns had sustained significant damage, and some of the metal framework was dented and the glass cracked, but otherwise it was intact.

They stepped out into the broad, gold-paved avenue to discover that it was littered with debris, and yes, even traces of blood could be seen here and there. They began the short trek to the Holy Place, ever mindful of their surroundings. The streets were almost deserted. Here and there they spied a shopkeeper cleaning up the mess in and around his or her place of business, or a resident of the city watching them from a window. He took note of one woman restoring a shattered window of her shop with little more than a touch of her hand. Yet it was far from business as usual in Zion.

Business within this city was conducted in a very different manner from that on Earth. For one thing, few of the wares here were built in the conventional sense with physical tools and manual labor. Most of it was the product of imagination and force of will. Works of art were created through thought, and they materialized right before the customers' eyes. These items were neither sold nor bartered but given freely as between loving brothers and sisters, and to the artisans, the making of these things was a labor of love.

But today there was no commerce in the shops or open-air markets. Indeed, little remained of many of the once-busy establishments. It was a truly sad state of affairs. Would things return to normal? Christopher wanted to believe that they would, but first they would have to rid Heaven of its invaders.

Farther along the avenue they encountered a winged demon standing motionless in the shadows of a partially collapsed building. A wave of apprehension swept through the group. Yet, as they passed, the demon seemed to take no notice of them whatsoever.

"That was creepy," said Christopher, glancing back toward the demon, who still hadn't moved. "Didn't that demon lieutenant we met at the entrance to Zion mention something about thousands of his kind at work clearing the streets between there and the Holy Place?"

Jerry scanned their surroundings. "Yeah, he did. But where are they?"

"That was what I was wondering," said Christopher. "There is a lot of work to be done, but I don't see any of them doing it."

"I was told the same thing when I arrived," replied Jonathon. "I think they're stalling, buying time. They'll probably come up with one excuse after another in the coming days and weeks. They feel threatened by us—that one we just passed did, though he said nothing. They don't want us meeting with the Father. They can't have us organizing a rebellion while their forces are spread thin fighting the angels. But I'll tell you this, my friends: I'm game for a rebellion the first chance I get."

Christopher pondered Jonathon's words for a moment. There were a few statements that struck him as odd, though he focused on only one of them. "Why didn't you join this friend of yours, the one who gave you that gun? I mean, you were involved in the battle at Ceranda. Why not just stick with them?"

"I still may," replied Jonathon. "I just wanted to get all of the facts before I throw in lots with anyone. I want to be certain that I'm supporting the right people. There are several different resistance organizations out there. They are all well-meaning. Each has a slightly different game plan. Still, the way I see it, some of those plans just aren't workable. No, I want to throw in lots with the group that has the best chance of success. I want my efforts to count for something."

"That makes sense to me," said Jerry, whose eyes constantly scanned his surroundings.

They continued walking, sometimes having to make a detour around large piles of rubble in the streets. It made Christopher sad. He loved this city, much like one may love a close friend. To see it so hurt him deeply.

Then, just a few hundred yards from their destination, they encountered a virtual mountain of rubble where once had stood the Great Arch of the Via de Gloria. It commemorated the victory of the angels over the minions of Satan during the first war in Heaven, almost 100 centuries ago. It became clear that it hadn't been destroyed by a few random fireballs. No, it had been the target of intentional demolition, a symbolic act of vengeance by Satan against those who had vanquished him and his dreams of glory all of those years ago. The rubble towered at least 25 feet above the street from curb to curb. The boys could hear the songs of praise from the Holy Place beyond. They were so close, but there was no way around or over this barrier.

"What now?" asked Jerry, looking up at the remnants of the stone arch that had once stood proudly, nearly 100 feet above the street.

"We'll need to backtrack," said Jonathon. "There's a side street about an eighth of a mile back. We can loop around and come in on Ascension Way. With a little luck, that route will be clear."

The others agreed. Jonathon led the way. They made their way back to a narrow side street on the right. The narrow street was littered with rubble fallen from the tall buildings on either side. It took over five minutes just to navigate their way 100 yards through this obstacle course. At last they reached Ascension Way, only to be confronted by three demonic guards.

"You boys shouldn't be back here. It isn't safe," said the most formidable of the three.

"Sorry," said Jonathon.

"I don't believe I've seen the three of you around here before," said the guard, who appeared to be in charge. "Who are you, and where are you from?"

Christopher was amazed at Jonathon's quick response. "My name is Jonathon, and these are my friends Christopher and Jerry. We are from beyond the river. We've come here to be closer to the Father."

It wasn't just the fact that Jonathon had thought so quickly on his feet that surprised Christopher, but that he was speaking to the demons in the common tongue of the demons. It was a complex variation of the angelic language. In turn, it had brought a smile to their potential adversaries.

"You have learned our language," noted the second.

"Why, yes," replied Jonathon, still speaking in the demonic dialect, "I learned it several years ago. Now I'm coming to realize that it may well be the dominant angelic dialect here in Heaven within the next few years. I think it's a good idea to practice it. I hope I'm speaking it correctly; I don't wish to offend."

A smile appeared upon the demon leader's face. "No, my friend, you are not offending us at all. In fact, you speak it with hardly an accent. We are flattered that you have taken the time and trouble to learn it. I am Zurel, and these are my associates Klat and Sataring."

"Yes…very good indeed," said Sataring. Klat nodded in agreement.

"I was hoping to have the opportunity to practice with those who could be a true judge of my ability or lack thereof," continued Jonathon.

"So many of your kind dislike us intensely," said the second demon, "though we do our best to win your approval."

"I don't dislike you," said Jonathon. "As for the others, give them a chance to get to know you better. I think they'll come around in the end. I realize that your kind have served a useful function through the years. We humans have a saying, 'It's a dirty job, but someone has to do it.'"

Jonathon's comments elicited a round of good-natured laughter from the three demons. It was clear that they had taken an immediate liking to this young human.

He engaged them in conversation for several more minutes. They spoke of what Heaven would be like once Lucifer assumed control of the angels. The demons assured the group that nothing would really change for them. All of the damage would be undone, and Zion would arise an even more beautiful city than before. Indeed, Lucifer would do almost anything to enrich life for the human inhabitants of Heaven.

Jonathon seemed to anticipate every aspect of the conversation, and his words seemed to actually endear the demons to him. Christopher had never seen anything quite like it. What was this power Jonathon possessed that even soothed the hearts of savage demons? Then came the most probing question.

"Tell me, my friend," said the second demon, "would you like to see Lucifer rule over the angelic hosts once more?"

There was the question. Short of lying, how would Jonathon wiggle his way out of this one?

Jonathon gave not the slightest hesitation in his response. "Allow me to put it this way, my friend," said Jonathon, looking the demon straight in the eye. "Your master spoke directly and frankly to the Father. The Father knew well his intentions, for He saw into your master's heart, as He sees into all hearts. He granted him permission to negotiate with Michael and Gabriel, to come here and wage war with them if it came to that. So, clearly, all that has happened is within the will of the Father. If it is in the will of the Father, who am I to debate it? Who am I to presume to counsel the Father? So, as I step back and watch these events unfold, I see the will of the Father, do I not?"

"Well spoken," said the demon leader. "Would that more humans felt as you do. Thousands of years ago during the first war in Heaven, we made a terrible mistake. Yes, I openly admit it. We sought to oppose the Father's decision to create humankind, and in doing so we opposed the Father's will. We sought to do it by force. It was a war that we couldn't possibly win. Even our master has confessed this very thing to the Father. Now we simply wish to reinstate Lucifer to his rightful place in Heaven as leader of the angels. We are willing to serve the children of the Father; we will do it gladly. I only wish there were more such as you."

This day was full of surprises. Christopher could hardly imagine a demon, a minion of Satan, making such an admission.

"I hope that we shall have the opportunity to meet again," said Jonathon, extending his hand in friendship.

The demon gladly accepted it. "As do we. It will be our pleasure and honor to serve you, son of God."

The demon's compatriots nodded in agreement. The three boys continued on. They were relieved to see that the road was clear all the way to the Holy Place. It was over a minute before anyone spoke.

"Jonathon, how did you do that?" asked Jerry.

"That was pretty neat, wasn't it?" replied Jonathon.

"Jedi mind trick," said Christopher.

"What's a Jedi?" asked Jonathon.

"It's a long story," said Christopher. "I'll tell you about it later."

"I'll be looking forward to it," said Jonathon.

"What I think he means is: How did you get those demons to become so agreeable with you?" asked Jerry. "I thought for sure that they were about to seriously question us...maybe send us away."

"Simple," assured Jonathon. "I told them exactly what they wanted to hear. In doing so, I left them open to a suggestion of my own. They will feel kindly disposed to me the next time we meet. They will trust me, and I will be able to use that trust to our advantage."

"You read their minds," deduced Jerry.

"Yes," confirmed Jonathon. "Believe me, they are very pliable. That is unusual. Demons were once angels, and angels are usually hard to read, not to mention influence. My great-grandparents are easy to read but nearly impossible to influence, especially my great-grandfather. Once he has made up his mind, good luck trying to get him to change it."

"The weak-willed are easily influenced," said Christopher.

"Exactly," replied Jonathon. "Let me tell you your next question: How do I read minds? The answer is that I don't know. Everyone in Heaven can discern the name of everyone else. I can simply discern most everything else that is there. I've been able to do it for a long time. However, the influencing part…well, that has only come in the past year or so…and I'm getting better at it all the time."

"Like I was saying, Jedi mind trick," repeated Christopher. "You gotta love it."

Jonathon hesitated. "Obi-Wan Kenobi…yes, *Star Wars Episode Four.*"

"How did you know that?" asked Christopher.

"I didn't, you did," said Jonathon, smiling slightly.

Jerry didn't respond, although he did smile.

All the while the sound of praise grew. Before them were a series of great marble columns, spaced out about every 20 yards around the perimeter of the Holy Place, a marble floored, open-air plaza many miles across. At the center was the very presence of the Creator of the universe. They were almost there. Christopher hoped that the answers to their questions were only a few minutes away.

Chapter 4

T HE BOYS STEPPED ACROSS THE threshold and into the Holy Place—they had made it. Before them was a vast open-air temple surrounded by marble columns that did little more than designate its perimeter. One could not gain an appreciation of its true size from here.

Christopher had once seen it displayed on a map in a library within the city. According to the map, the Holy Place was about eight and a half miles across and perfectly circular. Never had he seen this place so filled with the children of God.

It contained no seats of any kind; it was simply an open area in the middle of the city. The floor of the Holy Place had always intrigued Christopher. It had the color of gold—more or less—and was seamless throughout; yet this gold had a strange translucent quality that made it seem almost glass-like. At times it seemed to almost glow.

At the very center of it all, upon a sort of platform, was the physical presence of God. He sat upon a great throne surrounded by beasts of the sort described in Revelation. Here too were the 24 elders who worshiped God continually. Christopher had never actually seen God's presence up close. There were so many people here, all wanting to get as close as possible to the physical presence of the Father. The area within a few hundred yards of the Father was always the most densely packed.

As people came and went, new people took the places of those leaving, and thus got closer to the Father. To get within 100 yards of His presence could take several days of patient maneuvering. To get within 100 feet could take weeks, and those at the very front basking in the brightness of His glory could well have been there for years. Even from here, more than four miles away, Christopher could see the great radiance coming from that place.

But it didn't really matter how close someone got. Anywhere within the almost 27 square miles of the Holy Place was as good a place as any to speak to the Father one on one. A person had simply to sit down and open his or her heart. Saints could hear God's voice and feel His presence as if He were sitting right in front of them. They could hold a clear, two-way conversation with Him. Afterward, they would feel renewed and refreshed, filled with His Spirit and His love.

Not having been here during the past week had left Christopher feeling drained and troubled. Now at last he was in God's presence once more. Normally, he would head into the Holy Place at least a mile before sitting down and communing with the Father. Doing that today would be difficult indeed. There were so many people here. They would be doing well to go several hundred yards.

As always, the people were involved in a number of different activities. Some stood with their hands raised to the Lord. Others sang or played musical instruments, some in groups, some solo. Still others sat there talking with their heavenly Father. As always, the place had a wonderful atmosphere about it. It was the presence of the sweetest Spirit in the entire universe. For a moment, Christopher just stood there in silence, basking in the presence of the Lord.

"Christopher, over here," said Jerry, pointing toward an open area not far away. "We can sit there."

On his way there, Christopher couldn't help but notice the pretty, young girl sitting on the ground with her hands partially raised in praise. She was clearly of Asian descent, perhaps three or four years older than he was. She sat very still, like a beautiful statue, her eyes closed. Christopher wasn't sure why his attention had been drawn to her more than any of the other people around him. He could discern her name, Lilly. At least that was the name she went by. He wondered if Jonathon could tell him more about her. No, that wouldn't be proper. He joined his friends who had already taken their places sitting upon the golden floor.

"Ready?" asked Jerry, looking at the others. They nodded in agreement, closed their eyes, and opened their hearts.

Christopher felt the warmth of the sun shining down upon him as he felt the glory of the Father surround him. Then something unexpected happened. His surroundings faded to black and the songs and voices of all of the other worshipers seemed to vanish into the distance. This wasn't normal, yet Christopher remained motionless. Several minutes passed, yet still he didn't move. Even as he heard footsteps around him, he remained motionless.

"Would you look at this!" exclaimed Jerry.

Christopher opened his eyes. They were no longer in the Holy Place. He was sitting on a Persian carpet covering the floors of a very long, dimly lit hallway. The walls were mostly made of dark-colored wood, with off-white columns imbedded into them every dozen feet or so. Also mounted along the walls were what appeared to be some sort of lamps that glowed with a dim, amber light. About halfway down the long hallway on the right, a double wooden door stood partially open.

From beyond that door streamed an undeniably strange radiance. It wasn't particularly bright, shifting from an almost pink hue to orange. Christopher turned to see that he was sitting only about 15 feet from the end of the hallway where a tall window took up most of the wall. It was apparently night, for he saw that only darkness lay beyond the clear glass. Jerry and Jonathon stood by that window, gazing out into the darkness in wide-eyed wonder.

"Christopher, you've just gotta see this," said Jerry, who only glanced back at his friend for an instant.

Christopher rose to his feet and looked out into the darkness. Now he could see stars out there. It was night. He approached the window. "Where are we? How did it get to be night all of a sudden?"

"Is it night?" asked Jerry. "I think you need to take a closer look."

Christopher looked up into the sky to see a firmament filled with the brightest stars he had ever seen. Yet the pattern of these stars was unfamiliar. His vision panned down to where he perceived the horizon could be; but there was no horizon. His gaze drifted ever lower to behold nothing but stars—above, below, and everywhere. "Oh, my."

"We're in space," deduced Jerry, smiling from ear to ear. "This is a home in space."

Christopher had to think about that one. "But wait a minute, if we're in space, shouldn't we be weightless or something?"

"Yeah, we should be," confirmed Jonathon, "at least according to anything I've ever read."

"But we're not," replied Jerry. He reached out to the glass of the window cautiously. "The window seems to be warm and vibrating."

Christopher reached out to touch the glass to confirm Jerry's comment. He was right. It was then that Christopher heard a sound. "Wait, I thought I heard a voice." He turned toward the partially opened door about 50 or 60 feet away. "It came from down there."

Cautiously, the three boys made their way toward the door. Christopher got there first, stopping just short of the door and staring at the warm glow that emanated from the room. He took a deep breath and then one more step. He turned to behold the source of the light. He was looking into a large room, well-furnished with finely cushioned chairs and couches. It was like a grand study that may have been part of a great mansion from a century past.

A huge globe of the Earth sat not far beyond the door, cradled in a dark, wooden frame. To the left was a stone fireplace in which a small fire popped and crackled. The plastered walls had a number of paintings depicting finely rendered scenes of galaxies, stars, and planets, and the floors were glossy, made of the finest hardwood with a few throw rugs here and there. The wood glistened in the primary source of light, which in reality didn't come from within the room at all. Beyond a great set of tall windows that took up the entire far wall was a thing of wonder: a luminous nebula painted in glowing clouds of pink and orange. The clouds stretched from one side of the window to the other and from top to bottom. Imbedded within the distant mists were stars far brighter than those seen within the night sky, enshrouded in swirling blankets of blue mists.

"Amazing," gasped Jonathon, stepping up to Christopher's side. "Did you ever see the likes of this? It's an emission nebula, and a big one too. I've seen things like this through my great-grandma Gladys's telescope, but I've never seen one this close. It's in places like this that stars and planets are born. Amazing."

Then Christopher's attention was drawn to a high-backed armchair with fine red leather upholstery. In that chair was a girl who looked like the one he had seen in the Holy Place. She was staring straight at him with an absolutely contagious grin on her face.

<hr />

"Father, they're here," she announced, a giggle in her voice.

"Yes, I know," said a strong voice that emanated from another high-backed armchair that was facing the windows and the nebula beyond. "Come in, My children."

Christopher recognized that strong deep voice. He had heard it many times. It was the voice of the Father. He slowly walked toward the chairs that had been placed around a coffee table near the middle of the room. All the while the girl gazed at him with that wonderful beaming smile. Yes, there was no doubt about it: this was the same girl he had noticed in the Holy Place.

He was only a few steps away from her when he turned to view the source of the voice. For the very first time, Christopher came face to face with the physical manifestation of the Creator of the universe.

Somehow, the Father's physical appearance was not quite what he had expected. He was not some great glowing being or an old man with a long, white beard. He looked very much like any human being. There was nothing in His physical appearance that made Him particularly stand out. Christopher figured that He was about 6 feet tall and of average build. He had the appearance of a man in His mid-40s. He was clean shaven, with brown, curly hair. His eyes were blue, and His skin was the very essence of smooth perfection. He wore a sort of purple robe and slippers on His feet.

Still, there was something about His eyes. There was a deepness about them, and a kindness. His presence made Christopher feel very much at ease, even though he realized that he was gazing upon the very Creator of everything. The slightest of smiles came across the Father's face.

"Does My appearance live up to your expectations?" He asked.

Christopher didn't know what to say. And before he was able to formulate an answer, the Father answered.

"Not quite what you expected," He chuckled. "Actually, I get that a lot." He motioned to the chair at His right. "Please, Christopher, My son, sit here at My side. We have much to discuss."

Christopher made his way around the chairs and sat at the Father's side. The Father took Christopher's hand in His. There was nothing unusual about the feel of that hand—no electricity, no sense of power, just a warm, soft, human hand. Yet Christopher knew beyond a doubt that he was touching greatness.

"I've been looking forward to this meeting," continued the Father. The Father turned to see that Jonathon had fallen to his knees before his Creator, as had Jerry. He smiled. "Come, My sons, to your feet. We have much to discuss. Please, be seated, be comfortable. Know that I love each of you very much, and I am very pleased with you. You have all done very well. You have made Me both happy and proud, and you shall do greater things still."

Jerry and Jonathon rose to their feet and made their way to the remaining two chairs. All the while their eyes were upon the magnificent being before them. It was Jonathon who spoke next.

"Incredible," he said.

Again God laughed. "Thank you. I am glad to have you here with Me."

"You have a really nice place," said Jerry. "It has such a wonderful view."

God nodded, His smile broadening. "Thank you, Jerry, it serves Me well."

"I don't understand," Jonathon finally admitted. "I've come to talk to You many times before, but this is so different."

"Yes it is," confirmed the Father. "What we have to discuss today is very important, so I have brought you all here."

Jerry and Jonathon sat down, though they seemed a bit nervous. It was only then that Christopher noticed the four cups on the round table before them. Had they been there before? He didn't think so.

"I've prepared something nice for all of you," announced the Father. "Cinnamon tea for you, Christopher; coffee with cream for you, Jonathon; spring water for you, Lilly; and for you, Jerry, mint tea."

"Thank You, Father," said the four, almost in unison.

Christopher took a sip of the tea. It was exactly the way he liked it. Then again, what else could he have expected?

"All of you came to talk with Me," began the Father. "Lilly has been here for several days. We have had a wonderful time together, haven't we?"

"Yes, we have," confirmed Lilly, smiling with a truly angelic smile. "I've really enjoyed being here again." Lilly turned to the others. "And

I've learned so much. But we've been waiting for you. Father said you would come, and now here you are."

"You've been waiting for us?" asked Christopher. "I mean, the three of us?"

"Yes," confirmed the Father. "Invaders have entered into the most beautiful land in all of creation. And I need to call my greatest warriors to arms to vanquish them."

For a moment, silence ruled the room. Only the crackling of the burning wood in the fireplace broke the silence. Clearly, the Father was waiting for a response. It was Jonathon who provided it.

"Father, I'm confused," he began. "Satan and his demons were trapped in the depths of Hell. Wasn't it You who released them?"

"Yes, it was," confirmed the Father. "Every so often I gather together the leaders of the angels—all of them. Even those angels that have fallen are called. I bring them together so that they may talk. You could say that they are given an opportunity to air out their differences. In addition, I give them counsel and instructions. It is generally a good time of fellowship."

"Generally?" asked Jerry.

"Yes, generally," replied the Father. "The conversation between the leaders of the angels is usually very constructive. They discuss how to best help each other and how to make the most effective use of their time and talents." There was a pause. "That is with the exception of the angel of the morning. He was created the most beautiful of all of the angels. He went by several names. To some he was Phosphorus, the Bright and Morning Star, but I had named him Lucifer. He was My chief minister, the spokesperson for all of the angels.

"In the beginning, he served Me very well. Yet, as time passed, he became enamored with his own importance. When I decided to create man after My own image, he objected strongly. He couldn't understand why I would want to create a race of beings who would become My children, a race of beings that he and his fellow angels would serve. In the end, he and those loyal to his cause revolted against Me and the other angels. There was a war in Heaven, yet he and his minions did not prevail.

"I could not bring Myself to destroy them, so I cast them out into outer darkness, cut off from the rest of My creation. There they were, free to set up their own kingdom if that was their wish. Even still, I called Lucifer forth to join the other angels at the time of the meetings. It gave him an opportunity to settle his differences with Michael and Gabriel, to make peace with them. The angels have been at war with each other for far too long. But all he would ever speak about was My children and their weaknesses. He accused them of all manner of crimes, so great was his hate for them.

"Then, but nine days ago, he challenged Michael and Gabriel. He desired to ascend to his former position here in Heaven. He spoke of a peaceful transition if possible, but he was willing to engage them in war if that was not possible."

"And You allowed it," deduced Christopher.

"Yes, I did," confirmed the Father. "Even My Firstborn had reservations about My decision. You see, the time had come for the bickering to end between My servants. If they could settle their differences through negotiations, that was good, but if a final war was necessary, so be it."

Christopher could hardly believe what he was hearing. He could not, for the life of him, understand why the Father had done what He had done.

"You doubt the wisdom of My decision?" asked the Father. There was the slightest of smiles on His face. Christopher knew that He was not offended.

"I would never do that, Father," replied Christopher, "I guess I just don't understand."

"This war, terrible as it is, was necessary," continued the Father. "The angels had to be given the opportunity to reconcile their differences. But there is another reason that this war had to happen. You know that reason already."

The others looked at Christopher in surprise. A few seconds later Jerry nodded, yet he said nothing.

It was another few seconds before Christopher finally responded. "Some of the saints are treating Heaven like a rest home in the sky."

"Yes," confirmed the Father. "Very good, Christopher. As you already know, many of My children have lost their vision of the future." The Father scanned the eyes of the children, which were all upon Him. "They see Heaven as a destination, a place of final rest. This is not the case. Heaven itself is a journey. You do not stop growing simply because you have left the troubles of Earth. Two of you had but a brief experience upon the Earth, the other two none at all. With the exception of Lilly, you have been largely spared the trials and tribulations of living on Earth, so you do not fully realize the relief that comes with an arrival in Heaven. Many who were very concerned with their spiritual growth on Earth are not so concerned here, and so they have grown little in Heaven or not at all…"

For a moment the boys looked toward Lilly, though she did not return their gaze. Lilly was different, of that much Christopher was certain. What had happened to her on Earth?

There was a pause, as if the Father was awaiting a response. It was Jerry who finally replied.

"Father, I think I was guilty of that, even though I didn't spend any time on Earth," said Jerry. "I thought that my eternity would be one filled with fishing and mountain climbing. Now I'm starting to realize that there is more to Heaven than relaxation." Jerry hesitated. "There is even more to it than praise and worship, though that's important too. We've got to grow. We've got to become more like Your Firstborn, Jesus."

The Father smiled broadly. "Very good, Jerry, you've learned the lesson already." He turned to the others. "You all have. The day is coming when humanity will play a vital role in My plan for the universe. To accomplish that role, you must grow."

"What is that role, Father?" asked Lilly, her almond eyes growing wide. "I still don't know."

The Father laughed good-heartedly. "You will, My dear, and soon, but now is not the time. I promise that the four of you will be among the first to know. But before that happens, there is a task you need to complete. Some might call it a quest, even an adventure."

That word brought a smile to Jonathon's lips. "Adventure?"

"Yes, Jonathon," laughed the Father, His tone bordering on the dramatic, "an adventure, a real adventure. It won't be easy—adventures rarely are; but it will be exciting and worthwhile, and it involves all of you. The four of you are a team. You must learn to work as a team."

The Father turned to Christopher. "You and Jerry are particularly fond of the writings of Rudyard Kipling. I too enjoy his words. Though not always spiritually enlightening, they describe very well the struggles and the realities of life on Earth. Here are some words from Kipling to you: 'For the strength of the pack is the wolf, and the strength of the wolf is the pack.' Each of you is a wolf in My service. Your strength is in Me and in each other. Singly each of you has a portion of that strength, a special gift, but it is only as a group that you are an effective fighting force capable of warding off even the most powerful aggressor, whether he plays by the rules or not.

"You see, wars are not without their rules. My children, this one is no exception. Satan made many promises to Me before this war started. He agreed to abide by certain rules, and already he has broken many of them."

"What else can you expect? He's Satan," interjected Jonathon.

The Father nodded. "Sadly, that is very true. He had so much potential, yet he has wasted it, wallowing in his own bitterness and envy. However, the age of Satan shall soon come to an end, and the four of you shall be instrumental in bringing about that end."

"Us?" asked Jerry. "But we're just kids."

"Don't underestimate yourself," cautioned the Father. "You are My son; you have limitless potential. You simply need to have faith in yourself and in Me. I tell you this—your work is only beginning; in time you will come to do things that you can hardly imagine now...incredible things."

"But I don't know what they are," objected Jerry. "I watched Christopher reduce two demons to ashes in the woods last week. He can lift heavy objects by just thinking about it. Jonathon can read minds and make people do what he wants them to do. I want to be part of this thing, Father...more than anything. I just don't know what to do."

The Father smiled. "Jerry, take My hand."

Jerry reached out. The Father took his hand in His. Their eyes met.

"Jerry, you have a most precious gift," said the Father. "I Myself have imparted it to you. But you will need to discover it for yourself, and you will. The four of you must learn to work as a team. I shall send you to a place where that will be possible. You will know when it is time for you to begin your ministry. But until then, get to know each other. You have so much in common."

The Father paused. "I would like to introduce to you your sister Lihua Hue, although she prefers the name Lilly. She is from the nation of North Korea, and she spent over seven years on Earth. The day is coming when her mother will be joining her here, so I have assigned the angels to look after her. But those angels have been taken prisoner by Satan. It is up to the three of you to comfort and protect her now. Likewise, she shall safeguard you."

The boys gave Lilly a friendly greeting. None could quite get over that smile of hers. It was practically angelic and made her look all the more beautiful.

"Before you leave, I want to give you two pieces of advice," said the Father, scanning the group. "Mind them well, and they may win the victory for you. Never give into fear, even when your situation looks bleak. If you do you show weakness, you hand the enemy the victory that is rightfully yours. Second, trust and love one another, for the strength of the wolf is the pack."

The children agreed, promising the Father that they would do as He asked. Then they simply faded from the room—that is, all except Jerry. He looked around to see that he was now alone with the Father.

"I wished to have a word with you in private, away from the ears of the others," said the Father, leaning forward toward Jerry. "Something is troubling you. It is standing in the way of your ministry."

Jerry seemed very nervous. "I don't know if I understand."

"You do," insisted the Father. "It is a thing that troubles you more than anything in your life, though you have rarely admitted it."

Jerry hesitated. "It's about my birth mother, that is, the woman who would have been my birth mother. I've thought about her a lot, especially lately."

"Why is that?" asked the Father. His voice was not angry, far from it, but it was insistent.

"Lord, You know," replied Jerry.

"Yes, but do you?" asked the Father.

"I can't understand why she gave me up," said Jerry, wetness coming to his eyes. "Why didn't she love me? Aren't mothers supposed to love their children?"

"Are you sure that she didn't love you?" asked the Father.

"How could she?" asked Jerry, the tears now streaming down his cheeks. "I mean, she had a doctor murder me. How can you love someone yet decide to have them killed?"

"You may be surprised by the answer to that question," noted the Father, rising to His feet. He stretched out His arms to Jerry. Jerry rose to his feet and fell into the arms of his loving Father. "You have lived in darkness regarding this issue for far too long. What you don't know is poisoning your spirit. You know how to find out the truth, though you have resisted doing so. I leave the next step to you."

<hr />

Jerry materialized out of the mists into a field full of green grass and yellow flowers. Before him the others were waiting.

"We thought you may have gotten lost," said Jonathon, almost jokingly.

"The Father wanted to speak to me about something," replied Jerry. "Maybe I'll tell you about it later, but not now, OK?"

"Sure, no problem," said Jonathon, who really didn't seem interested in pursuing the issue.

Jerry gazed around him. Behind him, beyond the meadow, was a mighty forest of tall oak trees. Before him the meadowlands sloped slightly upward to meet a beautiful three-story mansion built to Victorian specifications. The white mansion was surrounded by a wide porch supported by ornate columns. "Where are we?"

"Oh, welcome to my home," said Jonathon with pride in his voice. "This is where I live with my great-grandparents. It's a really neat place, and we've got plenty of room...come on."

The foursome made their way up the hill toward the house, which appeared to sit on the very crest of a ridge in the meadow. As they reached the ridge, a truly incredible view greeted them. The meadow sloped gently downward, ending at a sheer drop-off that must have plummeted 20 or 30 feet at least. Beyond it, as far as the eye could see, stretched the waters of a mighty ocean.

"The northern shoreline of the Crystal Sea," said Jonathon. "It tends to be a bit cool even during the summer. Still, there is some seriously great surfing around here. You don't get super big waves, mind you, but they have just the perfect shape. If you'd like, I could teach you all how to surf."

Christopher looked over at Jerry, then at Jonathon. "I don't think surfing is quite what the Father had in mind when He brought us together."

"You never know," replied Jonathon. "It builds split-second timing and coordination."

"You may be right," said Lilly in a soft voice. "It may be helpful."

"Right on," said Jonathon, giving Lilly a thumbs-up sign. "I can show you how to make your own surfboards, or I could make them for you."

"That would be nice," said Lilly, smiling ever so faintly.

"I don't agree at all," objected Jerry. "God Himself has given us a mission, a quest if you will. I don't think we can treat it so lightly as to just go surfing. We have to prepare ourselves, come to understand how to best pool our talents."

"And how do you propose we do that?" asked Jonathon. "How exactly do we prepare for a mission when we don't even know what it is?"

"By making a surfboard," said Lilly.

Christopher and Jerry looked at the slight Asian girl incredulously. Her expression was not one that spoke of levity. She was really serious. Christopher's doubts about this team were growing. He and Jerry seemed to take their commission from the Father seriously. Apparently, the same couldn't be said about Jonathon and Lilly. He was very tempted to make a comment to that effect, yet he held his peace.

It was then that Christopher noticed a young, blond woman walking from the house in their direction. His God-given vision could distinguish her features in detail even from 50 yards away. She appeared to be in her late 20s, perhaps 30. She was of a medium build with hazel eyes and an expression that was practically angelic. Christopher had rarely seen a more beautiful woman.

Jonathon looked toward Christopher, then toward the woman. He smiled. "Oh, that's my great-grandmother, Gladys. She looks very good for ninety-five, don't you think? She prefers the young look. She often goes out surfing with me. She is really good."

"I'm more accustomed to somewhat older-looking parents," said Jerry. "My mom and dad prefer to take the appearance of people who are about fifty."

"I didn't know that you were back, dear," said Gladys, placing her arm around her great-grandson. "And you brought friends with you. Maybe they would like to stay for lunch."

Jonathon took a moment to introduce his friends to his great-grandmother. Then he proceeded to tell her about his adventure and his face-to-face encounter with the Father.

"Let's talk about it over lunch," she suggested, leading the group back toward the mansion. The group followed her up a well-worn trail that led past the tennis court and to the front door. They walked across the porch, in through the front door, and toward the dining room. Gladys had her guests sit around the very long dining room table while she headed into the kitchen and out of sight.

"Your great-grandmother seems very nice," said Lilly. "She has a very bright aura about her. It is very clear that she is a very loving person."

"I think so," said Jonathon. "Then again...I'm sort of biased. She raised me from the time I was a baby. She has always been there for me."

"And she'll be there for us," said Lilly. "The hand of the Father is upon her. She is destined to do great things for Him."

Lilly's comments struck Christopher as being rather strange. Did she know something that he didn't? She had a gift all right; but what it was, he wasn't quite sure.

Only a few minutes had passed when Gladys returned with five grilled cheese sandwiches and five lemonades on a tray. Then she sat with the children at the table. "OK, honey, why don't you tell me how you met your friends?"

And so he did. His great-grandmother listened quietly to Jonathon's story. When the telling was done, she was amazingly calm.

"I am so proud of you, Jonathon," she said. "I am happy for all of you. We have plenty of room. My mansion has twelve bedrooms, more than enough for all of you. I'm so thankful that the Father sent you all here. Bud and I will take care of all of you." Gladys paused. "Oh, Jonathon, that nice young man David was by yesterday. He brought you something. It's up in your room."

Jonathon immediately headed to his room, thundering up the steps two at a time.

"Wow!" hollered Jonathon. The excited shout was followed quickly by his thundering return. In his hands was something that looked like a weapon straight out of a science fiction movie. "A particle rifle," he announced, displaying the weapon to the group. "This thing has about three times the punch of my particle pistol. You can even adjust the power setting using this control here on the side. You don't want to use the maximum power setting if your target is only ten or fifteen feet away. David told me all about it last week. I know Grampa would just love to get a look at this thing."

Jonathon turned to his great-grandmother. "By the way, where is Grampa?"

"He's not here," said Gladys. "He headed off with a group of men to find out what they could about this war. He promised that he would be back tomorrow evening. He fought in Patton's army in Europe during World War Two. I think he intends to fight in this one too. He has been very upset about what has happened."

"That's my great-grampa Bud," said Jonathon.

"You're an awful lot like him," said his great-grandmother. "You're both warriors for Christ. I don't intend to sit on the sidelines either, not this time. I plan to get into this war. I asked your friend David if he could make me one of those rifles too. Actually, I was mighty good with a gun in my time. I do not intend to live in a Heaven where Satan rules over the angels. He had his chance. I intend to see that he doesn't get another. David said that he couldn't promise that he would have time to make another for us, but he did leave you something else."

Gladys walked into the living room and to a large wooden desk. She pulled a large, rolled-up paper from the top drawer and brought it into the dining room.

"I'm sorry I didn't leave this for you in your room, dear," she said, unrolling the paper on the large table. "David said that these were the plans, schematics, for the weapon. He thought you may want to make one for yourself."

Jonathon laid the weapon on the table and drew closer to the complex diagram. He studied the plans for about half a minute, then shook his head. "Oh boy, this is way beyond me. I couldn't even begin to materialize something that complicated. I don't know anyone other than David who could…" He paused. "Well, maybe someone. Maybe the person who taught me could do it." He looked at his great-grandmother.

Gladys laughed. "Don't look at me, honey. I couldn't do it. Believe me, I tried. I'm pretty good at materialization, but not this good. If I could, I'd make one for each of us. We could charge on out and teach these moth-eaten demons a thing or two, kick their little arseys back to Hell, where they belong!"

That comment elicited a round of laughter from the whole group. There was no doubt about it: Christopher liked Jonathon's great-grandmother. She seemed a lot more passionate than her great-grandson about this war.

"Ma'am, I take it that you're really pretty good at this materialization thing…I mean, causing things to appear out of thin air," said Jerry.

"You don't have to make it sound so dramatic," laughed Gladys, "and yes, that's what I do. I learned how to do it pretty soon after I arrived here, almost thirty years ago. That's how I made the sandwiches and the lemonade. I really don't do much cooking anymore, not in the traditional sense anyway. It is also how I make all of the clothes we wear. In a way, I suppose I've become a fashion designer."

Gladys got up from the table and headed over to a nearby closet. She reached in and pulled a rifle from it that looked identical to the one that her great-grandson had already set out on the table. "This is the one I made. It took me most of the morning to materialize it, following the diagram your friend left me. I made it part by part in my sewing room, then put it together. The parts all fit together just fine. It looks real enough, but it doesn't even power up. I probably made a bunch of mistakes in materializing it. It's not like materializing a dress or a surfboard."

The word *surfboard* made Jonathon's eyes practically light up. "Speaking of surfboards, we should be just about at high tide, shouldn't we?"

"Just about," replied Gladys.

"It should be good surfing today," continued Jonathon. "I could feel the sea breeze the minute I hit the ridge. I was thinking of taking my friends down to the workshop and making some surfboards for them."

"Sounds good to me," said Gladys, who seemed just as excited about the prospects of surfing as her great-grandson. "They may even appreciate some quiet time on the beach, but first things first. Don't you think you should show your friends to their rooms before we head out to the beach…let them get settled in a bit?"

"Oh yeah, that might be good," confirmed Jonathon.

"In the meantime, I can make swimsuits and beach sandals for all of them. I have a pretty good idea of their sizes," said Gladys. "You take them on down to the workshop later. It will just take a few seconds for me to clean up here."

"I'll help you, ma'am," offered Jerry.

Gladys laughed. "Oh, no need."

As the group looked on, the now empty plates vanished from the dining room table, even as Gladys rolled up the diagram.

"Dematerialization," she said. "I'll be up in a few minutes. Dear, take that weapon and the diagram up to your room."

"Yes, Grandma," said Jonathon, taking the diagram from his great-grandmother and picking up the rifle. "Come on, I'll show you to your rooms. They'll be just down the hallway from mine." The group filed up the steps.

"So nice to have so many children in this house," said Gladys, watching the last of the kids head up the stairs. She headed for her sewing room. "Thank You, Lord, for answering my prayers."

CHAPTER 5

"SOMEHOW THIS ISN'T COMING TOGETHER quite the way I thought it would," lamented Christopher, sitting on the very comfortable canopy bed in his new room.

"How do you figure?" asked Jerry from a chair a few feet away. "Jonathon's great-grandmother seems very nice, and you can't hardly beat the accommodations."

"Oh, that isn't what I mean," said Christopher. "What I mean is…well…I don't know, I expected this all to be a bit more intense. I wasn't expecting this to end up as a trip to the beach. I thought we'd be training."

"The day is still young," said Jerry. "I've got to believe that the Father knew what He was doing when He sent us here."

"I suppose you're right," said Christopher.

Their conversation was interrupted by a knock on the door. In stepped Jonathon's great-grandmother.

"I made you two pairs of swim trunks each," she announced, handing the clothes to the two boys. "There is a blue pair and a black pair. I also made each of you a pair of sandals for the beach and a couple of nice shirts for an expedition in search of the perfect wave or just relaxing. Oh, and I picked up a few towels for you too. Those white robes are fine for a trip to the Holy Place, but not quite so good for the beach."

"Thank you, ma'am," said the two boys almost simultaneously.

"Enough of this 'ma'am,'" said Gladys. "Why don't the two of you just call me Grandma? I think it's appropriate. I'm here for you, come what may."

"Thank you, Grandma," came the once again almost-simultaneous reply.

"I look forward to getting to know you better," said Gladys. "I think we're going to have plenty of time. Well, we're all going to meet down in the dining room in about fifteen minutes."

Gladys headed on to the next room, Lilly's room. It was about half a minute before Christopher spoke.

"Does this girl, Lilly, seem just a bit odd to you?"

"Maybe a little," replied Jerry. "Why do you ask?"

"I don't know," admitted Christopher. "I guess it's some of the things she says. It's like she knows a whole lot more than she lets on."

"Jedi mind trick?" joked Jerry.

Christopher smiled, though slightly. "Maybe. Well, let's get ready for a day of fun at the beach."

Jerry nodded and headed off to his room.

There's an awful lot of Jedi around here, thought Christopher, putting his robe in the closet and getting ready for a day at the beach.

About 15 minutes later, the group met in the dining room, all ready to go. Once again, Lilly caught Christopher's attention. Grandma had made her a modest, orange, one-piece bathing suit. "Very nice," said Christopher.

"Thank you," replied Lilly, in a soft voice.

The group made their way down the hallway to a large room, the work room. Here, mounted on the wall, were several different surfboards.

"Grandma and I make them ourselves," said Jonathon. "My grampa isn't so much into surfing. He prefers to swim, especially on calm days." Jonathon looked over at Christopher and Jerry. He pointed at two surfboards leaning up against the wall. "I think these would be about right for you guys. They're good boards for beginners."

Then he turned to Lilly. "You may need a somewhat lighter board." He headed over to a large table in the middle of the room and focused on it.

Christopher was quite impressed as he watched the front tip of a white surfboard begin to appear about an inch above the table. Slowly but steadily ever more of the board materialized. All the while, Jonathon's gaze was upon the place where the board seemed to be forming out of thin air. It took him the better part of five minutes to complete the task, as the group looked on. When the task was done, Jonathon handed the board to Lilly.

"Thank you, Jonathon," she said, in a quiet voice.

"Well, surf's up," said Jonathon, grabbing his own board and heading out a door that opened to the outside to a path that led toward the sea. The group followed.

The drop-off at the end of the meadow was not nearly so drastic as Christopher had imagined. The incline may have been 30 degrees at most, and a well-worn trail led down the slopes in a sort of switchback fashion, leading to the beach 40 feet below. To their right, the sloping terrain that separated the beach from the meadows above gently curved, giving them a panoramic view of the coastline. The beach itself was composed of a light tan-colored sand with a few rounded boulders here and there. The waves of the Crystal Sea were not particularly big—maybe three or four feet high—but they broke in a very regular pattern from left to right about 100 or so feet away from the shore.

"A perfect day," said Gladys, pointing to the waves.

"Nice," agreed Jonathon.

The group dropped their towels about 50 feet from the water's edge and moved on toward the foaming waves. After just a few minutes of instruction from both Gladys and Jonathon, the group made their way out into the surf.

The water was distinctly chilly to Christopher. It was, at best, 70 degrees. Still, he was up to giving the whole thing a try. They paddled out through the surf.

After about half an hour of falling off of the surfboard, Christopher came to the conclusion that this was clearly not a sport that he was a natural at. The same could not be said about Lilly. She seemed to get the hang of it after two trips in. Perhaps she had done this before. Jerry wasn't faring all that much better than Christopher, but he seemed to have a bit more determination.

To Christopher, this whole thing was a bit pointless. He couldn't see how this activity was helpful in achieving their goal. In the end, he retreated to the beach and watched the others from there. About 15 minutes later, Lilly joined him in his vigil.

"You seemed to be doing really well," said Christopher, turning to Lilly. "I guess you've surfed before, right?"

"No," replied Lilly, "this was my first time."

"Well, you seem to learn fast," said Christopher, who had become a bit nervous.

"You want to know about me," observed Lilly.

Christopher hesitated. "Yes, I guess I do. But I don't want to pry."

"You're not prying," assured Lilly. "Actually, it's important that you know."

"OK," replied Christopher.

"So, I'll tell you," said Lilly, smiling slightly. "We have some time. As the Father told you, I was born in North Korea. My mother was not very popular with the government of his holiness Kim Jong Il."

Christopher picked up on Lilly's sarcasm right away, though he decided to say nothing about it. It didn't seem appropriate. He'd read a bit about this ruthless dictator, enough to realize that living in his country must have been a living hell.

"My father died when I was just four years old," she continued. "He died of a disease that may have been curable almost anyplace else, but North Korean hospitals are very poorly equipped, and my family didn't have sufficient political connections, so he died. My mother and I lived with my grandparents for a time. But when my grandfather died a year later, we found ourselves on the street, left alone to fend for ourselves. Single women trying to take care of children in North Korea are not very popular with the government. They are a bother, really.

"The fact that my mother was a practicing Christian in an underground church didn't help our cause. Others in the church tried to help us, but it wasn't very long before her activities landed us in a concentration camp. So there we lived, under conditions that I doubt you could imagine. She did her best to feed me...but you see, prisoners in the camps are expected to grow their own food, and she wasn't a particularly strong woman. Yet, through her faith, and God's help, we survived. She said that God had chosen me for great things. At the time, I didn't understand it."

"I'm sorry," said Christopher. "I guess it was real rough."

"It was," confirmed Lilly. "What made it worse for us was that the Holy Spirit of God fell upon me in that camp when I was five. Somehow my mother knew it was going to happen. I was given a gift of prophecy, among other things, and I immediately started to use it. Words came out of my mouth that I didn't even understand. I only knew that they were from my heavenly Father. My mother was overjoyed, but the guards at the camp were not. I spoke out against them, against their superiors, and against the government. They backhanded me many times, placed my hands in boiling water, even branded me on the cheek, yet still I prophesied against them.

"But worst of all, my prophecies were coming true. The guards became very afraid of me. Yet, seeing what was happening, prisoners all over the camp—and several of the guards as well—were giving their lives over to Jesus Christ. Though Bibles were not allowed within the camp, my mother was a living Bible and led many people to our precious Savior."

Christopher shook his head sadly. He placed his arm around Lilly. "I'm so sorry, Lilly. I lived on Earth too, but my experience was a wonderful one. I had loving parents, a good home, and I lived in the greatest country on Earth. I guess I still look back at Earth and see only the good things. My friend Jerry has a very different view. He never saw the light of day there. Looking at Earth from a distance, he feels like it is a very evil place. Maybe it is."

"It doesn't have to be," replied Lilly. "There are good people there, really there are. I saw some of them in the camp, people who tried to help us. But Satan and his demons have ruined our home world. They tempt and destroy, entering the minds of the rich and powerful—people whose minds and moral fiber have already been weakened by their own greed and desire.

"I became a threat to people who were desperately holding onto power that could only be bought through the blood and toil of those weaker than they were. The words of the righteous were a threat to their very way of life. In the end, they found a way to get rid of me. I was shipped off to another camp called Holding Place Twenty-Two when I was seven...to a hospital where they did medical experiments on me. I died of typhoid fever, which the doctors themselves had infected me with. They silenced the messenger—but not the message.

"The day after I died, his majesty Kim Jong Il died also. It was a death that I had prophesied, and a prophecy that had led to my death.

Now I'm here, and I'm going to take the battle right to Satan and his legions of demons—we all are."

Christopher was overwhelmed by the story of this brave girl. Never in his entire life had he encountered someone quite like her.

"You think that I was being weak by giving in to Jonathon's impulse to go surfing," said Lilly.

Christopher felt practically naked before Lilly. Had she been reading his mind all along? "No...I mean, well...yes, I guess I did."

"It's OK," said Lilly, placing her arm around Christopher as well. "You are very intense, very driven by our crusade. That is good and that drive will serve us well. But you still lack vision. You are about to see why we are down here at the beach."

A few seconds later there was a flash to the northwest, beyond the bluffs to their right. The flash was followed by another, then another. Bolts of lightning and balls of fire flashed across the horizon. It was nearly a minute before low, distant rumbling filled the air, accompanying the visual display with sound.

"A battle," deduced Chris, rising to his feet.

"Yes, a battle," confirmed Lilly.

"That's why we're here," said Christopher. "This is why you went along with Jonathon's idea of going surfing. You wanted us to see this."

"Yes," said Lilly.

By now, even the surfers had taken notice of the terrible firestorm beyond the cliffs to the north. Gladys and Jonathon sat on their boards just beyond the breakers watching in wide-eyed amazement, while Jerry made his way back through the swells toward the shoreline. A minute later, Jerry had joined Christopher and Lilly on the beach.

"I reckon the war is coming to us," he said, gazing out at the firestorm in the sky.

"Not quite yet," replied Lilly, her eyes never turning from the pyrotechnical display.

"What do you figure we should do?" asked Jerry.

"Nothing," replied Lilly. "We're not ready yet."

It was another several minutes before Gladys and Jonathon joined the group on the beach. By then a cloud of smoke was rising up into the sky below the firestorm.

"That's the town of Phillipsburg over there," observed Gladys.

"It looks like the demons are attacking it," said Jonathon.

"They are," confirmed Lilly.

"My husband said that the people over there had been openly siding with the angels," continued Gladys. "I guess the demons have decided to make an example of them. Right now, I sure wish that I could materialize weapons that actually worked."

After another ten minutes the bombardment ended. The cloud of dark smoke drifted off to the west, away from them.

"We need to head back up to the house," announced Gladys. "I think we have some planning to do."

Twenty minutes found the group gathered around the dining room table talking strategy. Yet even after three hours, none of them, not even Lilly, had a workable plan. In the end they decided to take a chance and gate over to Phillipsburg.

Gladys retreated to her sewing room, and within ten minutes had materialized a nice dress and shoes for Lilly and shirts, socks, trousers, and good walking shoes for the boys.

"These aren't your typical clothes," she said. "They are fire and puncture resistant. They may even deflect a sword thrust or two."

Christopher looked at Gladys incredulously. "You can make clothing like that?"

"Sure, if I need to, honey," she replied. "These are likely to be very hard times, so I guess I need to think a bit out of the box, as they say."

Twenty minutes later the group materialized on the road just outside Phillipsburg. What they saw filled them with horror. The town had been virtually leveled, and there were burned and suffering people all around them, people who no longer had homes. Yes, their glorified bodies would heal within a few hours, but the pain that they felt now was all too real.

Lilly went right to work. She moved quickly from person to person. Her very touch removed their pain and even accelerated their healing.

Jonathon had brought his particle rifle with him. He scanned the skies for any sign of demonic invaders, yet they were long gone. "Too bad," he lamented, "I'd really have liked to disintegrate a few of those demons. Too bad."

It didn't take long to piece the story together. The demons had arrived in force—tens of thousands of them. They blasted the city from above and attacked the citizens in the street. They spoke of giving the humans of Heaven a taste of the anguish felt by their brethren in Hell. They spoke of the townspeople paying the price for siding with the angels. Amid the crying of the townspeople, the resolve of the children was strengthened. There would be no more time for play. The time had come for their training to begin. Some ideas were finally beginning to crystallize within their minds. For them, childhood was over.

Well past midnight Christopher and Jerry were awakened by a strange sound from somewhere outside. It was like the crackling of powerful electricity. They met in the dimly lit hallway and walked down the steps. Reaching the ground floor, they heard sounds coming from the workroom and headed in that direction. They were both tired. They'd only gotten a few hours of sleep. They had sat around the kitchen table the following evening for hours, yet they hadn't accomplished a whole lot.

The workshop door was open just a crack, and a shaft of light emanated from the brightly lit room beyond. They opened the door fully to find Jonathon standing there with the particle rifle in his hand. He looked up at Christopher and Jerry.

"Hi guys," he said. "You can't sleep either?"

"No," lamented Jerry. "I feel like I'm carrying the weight of all of Heaven on my shoulders. I'm praying for guidance, but I'm not getting anything."

"It was the same with me," said Jonathon, "so I came down here to the workshop. I was just test firing the rifle. Sorry if it woke you up."

"That's OK," said Christopher. "I'm sort of curious to see how it works anyway."

"Come on, then," said Jonathon, heading out the door and into the meadow. "You can squeeze off a few rounds for yourself. It doesn't run out of ammo; it draws power directly from the Father's Holy Spirit. It channels that power into a beam of pure, destructive energy. I'm here to tell you…it's a thing of beauty."

The boys walked about 100 feet from the house, nearly to the trail that led down the slopes to the beach. The night was dark and full of stars. Jonathon pointed to a boulder exposed by the low tide at the water's edge, just barely visible by starlight.

"Watch this," said Jonathon, flipping a switch along the side of the weapon. Immediately a growing hum came from the weapon. Two small red lights just in front of the stock lit up. "That sound was the capacitor charging up." Jonathon directed the weapon at the boulder. "This is just fifty percent power," he announced. He slowly squeezed the trigger.

A brilliant beam of light erupted from the weapon accompanied by an electric crack. The 15-foot-diameter boulder practically exploded, scattering glowing fragments of rock for 20 feet around. The boys watched in total amazement.

"Now you try it," said Jonathon, handing the weapon to Christopher. "You sight using this scope on top."

Christopher carefully lined up his shot, placing ever more pressure on the trigger. The weapon fired, blasting another several feet of rock off of the top of the boulder.

"This is some weapon your friend gave you!" exclaimed Christopher, handing it back to Jonathon.

"This isn't the one David made," corrected Jonathon. "This is the one my great-grandmother made."

"But I thought that one didn't work," said Jerry, gazing at the glowing boulder 150 feet away.

"It didn't," replied Jonathon. "Then I decided to open it up and take a look inside. It only took a minute to find the problem. One of the modules had a small piece of insulation on the plug that was preventing it from making good contact. I just cleaned the base and sealed it in again. It works fine now."

"So she could make more of these," deduced Jerry.

"Sure, I guess so," said Jonathon. "Let me tell you, I don't know anyone who can do materialization as well as she can, and that includes David. My grandma has way more experience than he does."

"She could make hundreds," continued Jerry.

"I don't see why not," said Jonathon. "She enjoys doing this sort of thing. I'm starting to think that maybe I could give it a try too."

"We might be able to equip a small army," concluded Jerry.

"Yes," said Jonathon. "Still, my grandma is only one person. I imagine she could make eight or ten of these a day. At that rate it would take a long time to make enough of these to equip an army. I don't know if we have that much time, and it usually takes years to master the skills of materialization. I've worked on it for seven years to get to where I am now. I might be able to make one of these, but I'm just not sure."

"Teach me," said Jerry. "I want to learn."

Jonathon nodded. "Sure, but it's tougher than you think."

"I still want to try," replied Jerry.

"Me too," chimed in Christopher.

"OK," said Jonathon. "Let's head back to the shop. It's going to be a long night."

It was a long night, but a fruitful one at that. Within an hour, Jerry had managed to materialize a block of gold on the table through nothing more than the power of thought. Then he moved on to more complex items. An hour later he had materialized a surfboard—a good one.

Jonathon was absolutely astonished. "People just don't get the hang of this like you have—not this fast. It took me over a year to get as far as you've come in a couple of hours."

"I'm not getting much of anywhere," complained Christopher, just a little bit frustrated. "I can move a two hundred-pound boulder with my mind, but I can't seem to do this."

"It's completely different," said Jonathon. "I've never been any good at telekinetics, and believe me, I've tried. Grandma is pretty good at it, but it wasn't a gift passed down to me, I'm sad to say." Jonathon paused. "I want to try something." He unfurled the schematic of the gun. He pointed to a component. "Take a look at this one, Jerry."

Jerry looked at it. Indeed, he focused his entire being on it. It was more than just pen and ink on paper; there was a feel to it that he couldn't explain. He felt it within him. He could picture every detail of the component in his head.

"Yeah, I think you're getting the picture," said Jonathon, looking over at Jerry and then back at the diagram. "It's sort of like the books in the libraries of Zion. There is more than just print in them—they have a life of their own. You don't just read the book; you feel the book. It imparts to you much more than just words; it imparts detailed concepts."

Jonathon unscrewed the access panel of the particle rifle and pulled from it the thumb-sized component. "OK Jerry, here is what the thing really looks like. Now, materialize it. Don't doubt that you can do it. Forget what I said about it being difficult. Don't think about that at all, just do it."

Jerry took a deep breath and started to concentrate. He imagined the thing that was already in his mind taking shape on the table before him, and it began to do so. It was happening very slowly, but it was happening. It was the better part of five minutes before he finished.

Jonathon picked up the component that looked like a crystal on one side and had tiny metal prongs on the other. "It looks real enough, but will it work?"

Jonathon slipped the new component into the rifle and closed it up. He headed back outside. The others followed. He stopped at the slope. "OK, what you just materialized is a power distributor. If it is not exactly correct, the weapon won't even power up. Let's see what happens."

Jonathon flipped the switch. To everyone's amazement the capacitor began to hum. Jonathon directed the weapon back at their target rock. He pulled back on the trigger. A beam of brilliant, high energy particles erupted from the gun, practically blowing the rock apart and reducing the sand around it to glowing, bubbling glass.

Jonathon seemed as amazed as everyone else. "Guys, that was one hundred percent power! If that component had been anything short of perfect, it would have fried. Congratulations, Jerry! You just accomplished in a few hours what it would have taken most people ten years to learn. Maybe it's time to see if you can build the entire thing piece by piece."

Jerry went back to the diagram, and Jonathon selected another part for him to materialize, then another. One by one they appeared on the table. Jerry wasn't even keeping track of how many components he had materialized; he just did it, and as each component was completed the table was cleared to make the next one. With each part his speed increased.

The light of dawn had come to the eastern horizon as Jerry finished the final part. He felt so tired. He looked up to discover that Jonathon had assembled the parts into another gun.

"Do you really think that thing is going to work?" asked Jerry.

"I really don't know," admitted Jonathon, "but if I had to make a wild guess...my answer would be yes."

Again they made their way to the edge of the meadow. Their target rock was nearly submerged by the rising tide, yet it was easier to see in the growing light of dawn.

"You do the honors," said Jonathon, handing the weapon to Jerry. "Let's not put too much power to the coil on this first shot, maybe twenty-five percent."

"OK," said Jerry. "Let's see if it even powers up."

Jerry practically jumped when he switched it on and the capacitor began to hum. He quickly regained his composure and dialed the power to its lowest setting: 25 percent. He took aim. He struggled to keep his hands from shaking. His aim was a bit wide. He missed the rock completely and hit the water beyond. A wave shot away in all directions from the impact point as a cloud of steam billowed into the air.

"Yeah!" shouted Jonathon.

Jerry lowered the weapon, looking at it in amazement. It had actually fired.

"Let's try fifty percent," suggested Christopher.

"OK," said Jerry, dialing up the power one more notch. Again he took aim. There was a loud report, as this time he hit the rock head-on, leaving none of it remaining above the waves.

"Crank it up to full power. Let's see what that thing's got."

"OK," said Jerry, turning the dial the whole way to the right.

The hum of the capacitor increased in both volume and pitch. Jerry selected another rock and took aim. The rock was practically disintegrated by the powerful beam of high energy particles.

"I don't know how you did it," admitted Jonathon, "but you just materialized a functioning particle rifle in about an hour and a half. Only the Father Himself could have possibly granted you such a gift as this."

"I think we've all earned a good night's sleep," said Christopher. "Way to go, Jerry. Between you and Grandma Gladys, we may just manage to make enough of these things to equip a small army."

"Don't forget me," objected Jonathon. "I'm not all that sure that I can't do it too. We'll find out after we all get some sleep."

Christopher and Jerry agreed. They made their way back up the stairs to their bedrooms amid the growing light of dawn. As they faded off to sleep, they still weren't quite sure what the path before them looked like, but they now had another weapon in their arsenal.

CHAPTER 6

IT WAS NEARLY NOON WHEN Christopher opened his eyes to the sound of voices coming from the first floor below. They seemed to him to be the voices of people who were rather excited. He jumped from his bed and got himself dressed. He headed quickly downstairs to discover his friends and several other men gathered in the dining room.

One man, a short, dark-haired man who appeared to be about 40 years of age, held in his hands a particle rifle. He examined it closely, his eyes full of wonder. He was talking to Jerry.

"What an incredible weapon," he remarked, "simply fantastic. And you say that you materialized it after only a few hours of practice?"

"Yes sir," confirmed Jerry.

"I finally managed to make one too, Grampa," said Jonathon stepping forward. "But it took me three tries to get all of the pieces to work. Jerry has a gift from God—there's no other explanation."

At that moment the dark-haired man caught sight of Christopher. A broad smile came to his face. "And this must be the fourth member of your group—Christopher."

"Yes, it is," confirmed Jonathon, as they walked over to Christopher. "Christopher, this is my great-grandfather Bud."

The man extended his hand to Christopher. "Welcome to our home, young man. Jonathon has spoken highly of you. Apparently, you have had quite an adventure."

"Yes sir, we have," confirmed Christopher.

"My wife has all of you kids calling her Grandma, so I guess I'll follow suit on that one. You kids can call me Grampa or Grampa Bud, whichever you prefer. All of my grandchildren and great-grandchildren on Earth called me that."

Bud glanced over his shoulder to see that the group was gathering around the table. "We're about to get started. A group of us have been traveling all over Heaven to find out as much as we could about this conflict. We all agreed to meet back here this morning to share what we've learned. You're welcome to share what you've learned as well. I think what you young people have learned is important."

Christopher followed Grampa Bud back to the table, where the others had already gathered. There were four men and three women around the table in addition to the children and Grandma Gladys, and Christopher was certain that all of them would have something to share. He hoped that he would learn a lot about what had happened in Heaven since the invasion.

Bud and his group had only recently learned of the fate of the town of Phillipsburg, a place that most of them called home. It made the meeting all the more emotional. Apparently, about two dozen people had been taken captive during the raid. One of them was the wife of one of the men present.

"How could such a thing as this happen in Heaven?" the man asked, tears coming to his eyes. "Jean and I lived a Christ-centered life on Earth, and we have been good citizens of Heaven for nearly a hundred years. How could the Father possibly have allowed this to happen here? How could He have allowed demons to take Jean prisoner?"

"Maybe it has happened to strengthen us," suggested another.

"Yeah, by throwing us to the wolves?" asked yet another.

It was a comment that held undeniably disturbing ramifications. Had God thrown them to the wolves, or at least allowed the wolves to attack them?

Bud calmed the growing rumblings. "Look, if we allow ourselves to get all emotional about this, we won't be any good to anyone. We need to think this out, but only after we have all of the facts. We don't need to be bouncing off of the walls. I want to hear everything that you folks know about what is happening here."

Apparently, Bud held considerable influence among the group, for they settled down almost immediately. Then, one by one, they spoke of what they had learned in many diverse places within the Kingdom of Heaven.

One of the men spoke of visiting the second level of Heaven, where the angels were trying to regroup. Apparently, they were being assisted by a team of humans who were both ferrying them to the safety of the only level of Heaven that Satan's forces couldn't reach and helping in the development of a battle plan. The human resistance was organized, and they had developed powerful weapons that were indeed effective in combating the demons.

Gladys brought to the group's attention that several of those sitting at the table not only had such weapons in their possession, but also had the ability to fabricate more. This very fact placed a degree of power in their corner. They just needed the time to make enough of the weapons and find as many people with the gift of materialization as they could. Yet this also could make them a target of Satan's forces. They would need to be on their guard.

Another spoke of terrible atrocities against saints and angels alike on the first level of Heaven, where a growing human resistance movement had already been brutally crushed by Satan's forces. The same could well happen to them if word got out that they were arming themselves before they had enough of these weapons and were ready for battle.

And the question as to why God was allowing this to happen came up repeatedly. Christopher, the youngest person at the table, delivered the answer to that question. He spoke of the "rest home in the sky" analogy and of God desiring greater things for His people. Heaven was not an end unto itself but a means to perfection. Christopher was surprised to find that his comments met with general agreement from those present, especially after he spoke of his very personal meeting with the Father.

Nearly two hours had passed before Lilly finally rose to her feet. The group grew strangely quiet as she addressed them. "These are dark times," she began, her dark eyes intense, "but can there truly be light without darkness? The Lord of Hosts would have you know that you have been chosen to bring the light of His justice back into Heaven. You are His sons and daughters. You have far more power than you know.

"You, all of you, will have a part in driving Satan from this place, and when it is done, it is you who shall judge the angels, every last one of them…even Satan himself. Be not quick to anger or quick to act. Rain does not wear down the mountain overnight, but a little bit at a time. The day is coming when you shall act, but that day is not now. The day is coming when you shall set the captives free, but it is not today. But when that day comes, there shall be no doubt in your minds."

Those gathered around the table had no doubt that they had heard from the Lord. The path was becoming clear. Most immediately, they would see to the needs of the people of Phillipsburg. Second, they would manufacture the weapon in great quantities; and third, they would begin to assemble an army. They would do it quietly, but they would do it.

As the people departed, they did so with new hope. Each had a sense of purpose and a mission to fulfill. They would drive Satan out of Heaven as they brought new direction to God's people. Today would be the first day of a new age in Heaven.

Even as the last of the guests departed, those living within this home went to work. Their main goal would be to build as many of the weapons as possible. Gladys was the most prolific at building the rifles. She could materialize eighteen of them on a good day. Jerry was nearly as good at 16, while Jonathon managed to produce 8.

The others did their best to learn Heaven's most difficult trade. Although a relative newcomer to the trade, Grampa Bud was able to make very good housings and mechanical parts for the weapons, and Christopher and Lilly took up the job of assembling the materialized parts.

As the days passed, they added new efficiencies to the process. Grampa Bud spoke of Henry Ford's production line, in which each person on the line became an expert at one or two particular things. By implementing these improvements, their production nearly doubled.

More people skilled in the art of materialization joined the effort, and within three days eight people were working on the assembly line. They worked long hours with little sleep, and within another week had produced nearly 1,200 functioning weapons. And as the number of weapons increased, so did the number of people skilled in their use.

The weapons were distributed to the people of the nearby towns of Phillipsburg and Newtown. The people formed an effective militia, well-trained in the use of the new weapons. Sentries were posted to scan the skies for approaching demons, even as a defense plan was devised. If the demons came again, the people would be ready.

Yet no matter how long the day had been, the four children of Heaven met each morning and evening to talk and pray. They learned how to be a team and how to most efficiently use their gifts.

Occasionally, demon patrols passed by the house, yet the four always assumed the role of quiet and peaceful children of God. Of course Jonathon never missed the opportunity to charm their demonic occupiers. The Jedi mind trick, as Christopher called it, was becoming ever more effective.

Another week passed uneventfully. God seemed to have hidden the children beneath His wings, yet that was all about to change. It was a warm afternoon as Lilly sat in a small clearing amid the forests not far from the mansion. She was meditating when she felt the dark presence. She turned to see three winged demons in black leather armor standing not far away. She rose to her feet to face them.

"Isn't this the pretty one?" said one of the demons to the others. "I wonder if she is one of those who have been plotting against us."

The others laughed in a low guttural tone. It was clear that part of their intention was to scare her. They seemed a bit surprised when it didn't work.

"Perhaps we should take her with us for questioning," suggested another.

"Perhaps we could do more than that to her," said the third, as a fourth and a fifth demon joined the group.

Lilly remained motionless as she spoke. "Tubor, is your soul not dark enough already without threatening a child of God?"

The first demon seemed surprised. "How is it that you know my name?"

"By the same means that I know the names of Cenaka and Verkon," said Lilly. "Leave me in peace."

"I asked you a question, girl!" objected Tubor, taking a step forward as he drew his sword.

"I think we should treat this little wench as we would one of her condemned sisters in Hell," said Cenaka.

"What would you do, Cenaka?" asked Lilly, taking one bold step forward. "Would you shackle me to a black altar and let the birds have their way with me, consuming me again and again throughout all eternity? That is the ordeal that you enjoy watching the most, isn't it? You particularly like to do women that way, don't you? There is a sickness within your soul, Cenaka. You think that being the cause of eternal pain to others somehow justifies you. It doesn't."

"How dare you speak to me in such a manner?" demanded Cenaka.

"I dare because I am your master, not the other way around," replied Lilly. "If you are truly to become the servants of God once more, you must also learn to serve the sons and daughters of God. If you cannot do this, then you have no place in Heaven."

"I think this one needs to learn some manners," said Verkon, who took a step forward.

The flapping of even more wings spoke the arrival of a sixth and seventh demon. Still, Lilly seemed unaffected. She turned about to find herself in the middle of a shrinking circle of what was now nine demons.

"I think we need to take her back for questioning," said one of the newly arrived demons. "We need to see what will make her squeal."

Lilly weighed her options. Could she really take on nine demons alone? "The strength of the wolf is the pack," she said.

"And what is that supposed to mean?" growled Cenaka. "You're supposed to be a sheep and we are the wolves."

"I disagree," said a voice to Cenaka's right.

The demon turned to see Christopher standing there. "Move along, boy," he warned. "This doesn't concern you."

"If it involves my sister, it involves me," said Christopher, taking several steps forward. "You need to issue an apology to her and leave," he continued, his voice totally without emotion. "As she told you, we are the masters here, not you."

"Who are you to make demands of us?" asked another demon, approaching the youth.

"A child of God," replied Christopher, giving the demon an icy cold stare. "This isn't Hell, and we are not damned souls. You have far exceeded your mandate."

"And how would you know about our mandate?" asked yet another demon.

"The Father told him—He told all of us," said Jerry, stepping from the forest about 30 feet from Christopher. In his hands he held a particle rifle. A second later, its capacitor powered up with a hum that all of the demons could hear. "The strength of the pack is the wolf."

"You are one of them," accused another demon. "You are members of the human resistance. We may do with you as we please."

Another five demons swept in, landing near the edge of the clearing. Then three more joined them. They were ready for battle.

"If you are familiar with that weapon, then you know what it can do," said Christopher, in a loud enough voice for all to hear. "If you leave right now, you may live to fight another day."

"I see only one with a weapon," said Verkon, turning to Christopher. "I advise you to surrender."

"I don't need a weapon like that," announced Christopher. "I am quite able to reduce you to dust where you stand, and it won't be the first time I did it to one of your kind—far from it. Now leave, but only after you have apologized to my sister."

"It is just the three of you against all of us," said Verkon. "You are in no position to make demands."

"I think you'd better make that four," said Jonathon, stepping into the field from a blue mist that had suddenly appeared. "Still, all of this is pointless." He walked up to a nearby demon who had already drawn his weapon. "My friend, you don't want to do this; your master gave strict orders not to harm any humans unless they were aiding the angels. These children were doing no such thing. They are innocent. Please believe me, we're your friends."

The demon hesitated and then nodded. "This boy is right," he said. "We are overstepping our authority and you know it, Cenaka. These children have done nothing wrong. Do we want to bring down the wrath of the master upon us? We need to apologize to this child and leave."

"You're mad, Hadron!" accused Cenaka. "I am the ranking minion here, and you shall do as I say."

"You do not outrank the master," argued Hadron, pointing his sword in the direction of Cenaka. "I will not allow you to hurt these children."

The tension was building, Christopher could feel it. This would be their first test—that was only too clear. But were they ready?

"Enough!" growled Verkon, looking about at the children. "I'll take this little wench in for questioning myself—and you will not interfere."

As Verkon advanced toward Lilly, Jerry took aim at him with his particle rifle. Two other demons also approached Lilly. A line had been crossed.

What happened next was totally unexpected. Lilly waved her arms at the demon, who was now only five feet in front of her, and he was thrown as if by a giant hand through the air. He was tossed forcefully into another demon some 30 feet away.

Then Cenaka advanced toward Lilly, only to be engulfed within an explosive fireball that erupted from the tip of another demon's sword. That demon in turn was run through by a third demon, even as a blast from Jerry's particle rifle fired into the crowd, hitting and practically disintegrating one of the two demons approaching Lilly from the rear.

Jonathon drew out a particle pistol hidden beneath his long, flowing cloak and took out two other demons in rapid succession. Their boiling blood and shattered flesh was scattered for a radius of 20 feet. Yet even as he took the second shot, a fireball launched from another demon's sword was on its way toward him. But it never got there. It seemed to be deflected by a transparent shield of force that had materialized a mere ten feet in front of him. Jonathon looked to see Lilly making some sort of gesture in his direction.

Out of the corner of his eye, Christopher saw a demon running toward Jerry, his sword drawn. With only a second to act, Christopher stretched out his hand. The demon flashed into a glowing ball of fire and then into dust, all before reaching Jerry.

To Christopher, the whole battle seemed to be moving in slow motion, but in reality it couldn't have lasted more than 20 or 30 seconds. In the end, only two of the demons managed to survive. They leapt into the sky to get away. Jerry took a shot at one, yet it was a clean miss. Jonathon got a bead on the other, but the shot was too long. He holstered his weapon.

The four friends walked toward each other amid the field of blood. They embraced.

"I was afraid that I was done for," admitted Lilly, a tear coming to her eye.

"Not possible," said Jonathon, in his typically confident voice. "The strength of the wolf is the pack."

"And the strength of the pack is the wolf," said Christopher.

"We really did it," said Jerry. "We were a team. I think we're ready."

"We had better be," observed Christopher. "Those demons will surely report what happened here…and they probably know where we live. Next time, we will face even more of them."

"Bring them on," said Jonathon. "We will be ready for them."

"Yes, we will," confirmed Lilly. "This was the test the Father told me about, and we passed it. Our time has come."

The four made their way back to the house, gating the distance rather than walking. They emerged from the starry mists in front of the mansion. Grampa Bud was standing right before them, a particle rifle in his hand.

"I heard the sound of weapon fire coming from the forest," he said. "I was heading out to investigate."

"Grampa, there's been trouble," announced Jonathon, and he quickly filled in his great-grandfather on the events that had just transpired.

By now, Grandma Gladys was also there. She too held a particle rifle in her hand.

"We knew that this day would come," said Grampa. "We'll need to contact the militia in Phillipsburg and Newtown."

"We'll fight at your side," said Grandma.

Within minutes, the community was on high alert. About 20 armed men and women joined the family at the mansion. They watched the skies for the rest of the day, yet no demons were sighted. The vigil ran through the night and into the next day, but still no demons made their appearance.

During their regular morning gathering around the dining room table, Lilly spoke of a strange revelation. "I had a dream last night," she began. "I was standing in a dimly lit room with walls of rock on three sides and a wall of thick, metal bars on the other. It was some sort of cell, I think. It was barren, totally without furniture. There was a girl about my age there and two young women—each had been shackled by their wrists and ankles to one of the walls. I think it was to prevent them from gating out. Their clothing was dirty and torn, and they themselves seemed in a terrible state. I think they may actually have been tortured.

"One of the women spoke to me and asked for my help. She said that her name was Christa Carter, and that she had vital information for General George Washington. She pleaded for me to free her and the others from their demon captors. She said hundreds of them are trapped in a horrible dungeon that the demons have fashioned right here in Heaven. The demons even threatened to transport her and those around her to Hell where they could be more properly interrogated and punished…out of the view of the Father."

"They couldn't do that," objected Jerry. "If these women you speak of are of Heaven, they are sanctified, washed by the blood of Jesus. The Father wouldn't possibly allow it."

"He hasn't moved against the demons up to this point," observed Jonathon.

"Except through us," observed Christopher. "Still, this dream doesn't make any sense. The General Washington I know about was a general in the American Revolution. He went on to become the first president of the United States. But that was two hundred and fifty years ago."

"True," confirmed Jonathon, "but remember where you are. People's purpose and their duties in Heaven often mirror those on Earth. His experiences on Earth may simply have been in preparation for the purpose he was destined to serve in Heaven. He is one of the most important leaders of the human resistance movement."

Christopher turned to Lilly. "Can you be sure this wasn't just a dream?"

"I can," confirmed Lilly. "I even know where they are being held: below the Hall of Angels within the City of Sarel. That city is right here on the fourth level."

"So what are we supposed to do?" asked Jerry.

"You're to set the captives free," said Grandma Gladys, stepping out from the kitchen and into their midst. "Don't you see? This is why the Father called you all together. This is what you've been training for. The battle in the forest happened to show you that you can do this—no, you *must* do this. It will be hard to do…I've been to Sarel. I know what sort of place this Hall of Angels is—it's a fortress, and the prisoners are probably being held in the deepest part of it. But the four of you must go there, and you must do it alone."

"So…we'd need to gate into this dungeon in the Hall of Angels and release the captives, even as we fight off the several thousand demons who try to stop us," deduced Jerry. "That should be easy enough." There was a definite tone of sarcasm in his voice.

"Not that easy," cautioned Jonathon. "If they are truly being held within the Hall of Angels, the building is surrounded by a field of energy that prevents us humans from gating in. All of the Halls of Angels have one. It insures their privacy. I read it in a book in one of the libraries in Zion. If it prevents us from gating in, it will probably keep us from gating out."

"OK," said Jerry, "so we'd not only need to know where within the building they are being held—but we'd also need to know how to get there."

"Right," confirmed Jonathon.

"You wouldn't happen to know where we could find a floor plan to the building, would you?" asked Jerry.

"Actually, I would," said Jonathon. "It is in the library straight across from the Great Hall of Records in Zion. "I looked through that book once. That's how I knew about the force field."

"You're talking about the library that was totally destroyed during the battle for Zion," noted Christopher.

"Yeah," said Jonathon, "that one."

A look of dismay swept across the faces of everyone at the table. Jonathon looked over to where his great-grandmother had been standing, but she was gone.

"The Holy Spirit of God might guide us," said Lilly. "I've been guided by His Spirit before."

Jonathon nodded in agreement but said nothing. Indeed, silence dominated the room for the better part of a minute.

"Look, we have to do this," said Christopher, "and I think we need to do it real soon."

"The Hall of Angels in Zion has no doorways or windows on the outside," noted Lilly. I think it can only be entered from the roof. I wonder if all of the Halls of Angels are that way."

"The Hall of Angels in Sarel has an entrance from the street level," said Grampa Bud, entering the dining room at his wife's side. "It is one of the few halls that does." He placed a large book upon the table. "Is this what you were looking for?"

The golden colored book's title, *The Angelic Culture*, was imprinted on the cover.

"That's the book!" said Jonathon excitedly. "Grampa, how'd you get it?"

His great-grandfather smiled broadly. "When you told me about this book about a year ago, I got curious. Your great-grandmother and I went into Zion to have a look at it. Your great-grandmother went ahead and materialized a copy of it for me. I never cared much for sitting around in a library reading books…so here it is. As I recall, there is a floor plan for the angelic hall in Sarel. The author used it as an example of a typical angelic hall. I assume that it's accurate. As I remember, it is quite detailed."

"Lilly, did you see where the demons were holding the human prisoners?" asked Grandma Gladys.

"No, I'm sorry, I didn't," replied Lilly.

"Did you get a look through the bars and into the corridor?" asked Grampa Bud.

"A quick look," said Lilly, who went on to describe what she had seen.

Grampa Bud opened the book on the table and went to the pages that described the layout of the building. The map went on for several pages. It was the better part of 20 minutes before he made a determination.

"From what you told me, I think what you saw was here." He pointed to a series of corridors in a subbasement of the structure. "If you're right about the dimensions of the cells and the layout of the corridors, this has to be the place. You see, the angelic halls are used mainly as a place for angels to rest and meditate. The individual rooms need to be larger than eight feet square to accommodate an angel's wings.

"These rooms here were used as storage rooms. Apparently, the shackles and bars were added later—by the demons. Problem is, these corridors will be tough to get to. It will be a long walk from the one and only entrance. Who knows how many demons you may run into along the way?"

"But we have to go," insisted Lilly.

"But you can't go it alone," insisted Grampa Bud. "I could go in with you. I've got over three hundred well-trained soldiers we could bring along. They're mostly World War Two and Korean War veterans, strong and fit as the day they left boot camp. A bunch of them are former U.S. Marines—pretty tough characters. Armed with particle rifles, they'd be a practically unbeatable force. A number of them lived right there in Sarel before this whole thing started. They already know the lay of the land. With less than a week to prepare, we could be ready. We could gate right into the center of the city. I suspect that we could get in and out of that prison in twenty minutes—rescuing the prisoners and taking a lot of demons down in the process."

"Grampa, I don't think we have that long," said Jonathon.

"We don't," confirmed Lilly. "If we don't get Christa out of there within the next two days, it won't matter."

For hours they made their plans. They plotted the shortest route to the place where they assumed the prisoners were being held. It was a truly torturous route through the maze of passageways, and fully 300 yards. In addition to that, they had to consider what the purpose of this facility was: a resting and meditation place for the angels. Along most of the corridors were resting and meditation cubicles. Suppose the demons now used it for the same purpose? There could easily be tens or even hundreds of thousands of demons in those cubicles. If the alarm were sounded, they would be hopelessly outnumbered.

This rescue mission was looking more difficult by the minute. But before they could consider their options further, they would have to get a look at the place, size up the demon troop strength, and look at their defenses.

That afternoon Grampa Bud and Grandma Gladys accompanied the children into the City of Sarel on a reconnaissance mission. They gated into a place that had once been a park near the center of the city. The trees here were mostly burned, leafless hulks, and the city that surrounded the park was beaten and battered. It seemed even more badly damaged than Zion.

There were still plenty of people here trying to clear the rubble and rebuild their lives. But plenty of demons were here as well—more than the group would have liked to see.

The group made their way to the Hall of Angels. They were dismayed to discover that it was surrounded by demonic guards, while great numbers of the bat-winged warriors patrolled the skies above it. The humans of the city seemed to stay clear of the area.

"Well, so much for blending into the crowd," noted Grampa Bud, as he gazed about at the demons. "We couldn't even risk gating in here. The demons would open fire on us before we could even draw our weapons. If we gated into the park in force and marched on the Hall of Angels, they'd see us coming a half mile away."

The group had nearly completed a circle of the building when Jonathon came to a stop. "Wait here," he said, making a beeline toward a demon guard some 100 feet away.

"What's he doing?" asked Lilly.

"Just hold up," said Christopher, "I think I know what he has in mind."

Jonathon boldly approached the demon, which abruptly turned in his direction. Three other demons saw the young human approaching and moved to intercept him. Everyone was surprised when a smile appeared upon the first demon's face.

"Jonathon," said the demon in a pleasant tone, "it is nice to see you again." The demon extended his hand and Jonathon accepted it.

"Hello, Zurel," said Jonathon, using the common language of demons to address him. "As my people say, it can be a small Heaven."

"Indeed," said Zurel. "What brings you to Sarel?"

"Exploration," said Jonathon. "I'm trying to keep up with the goings on in Heaven. These are historic times; I want to experience them."

"That could be dangerous," said Zurel. "The war still rages all around us."

"My friend," Jonathon continued, "exploration is usually hazardous to one degree or another...but the firsthand knowledge it yields is priceless."

Again the demon smiled. "I shall not debate you on that issue. What have you learned?"

"I've learned enough to realize that your kind are very methodical and organized. I've met many of your fellow beings, like you, that I can honestly say I like. Though sometimes I've found your kind to be a bit rash and impulsive."

Zurel nodded in agreement. "Nor shall I debate that. Be patient with us."

Jonathon smiled broadly. "Oh, I intend to be."

"Is there a problem?" asked the first demon guard to intercept Jonathon.

"Not at all," assured Zurel. "This is my good friend Jonathon. He is one of the few humans I have met that I can actually call a friend."

"I hope I'm not trespassing," said Jonathon. "I just saw Zurel over here, and I had to say hello."

"No," said the second demon. "We welcome humans who accept us. We will win this war, and when we do, we will serve the humans of Heaven."

"I believe that," said Jonathon.

The second demon waved off the third. "I will not interfere further with your reunion. I appreciate your attitude, young Jonathon. I wish unto you a pleasant day and look forward to serving you in the future."

With those words, Jonathon found himself alone with Zurel. "You folks seem a bit tense. Is something wrong?"

"No, not really," assured Zurel. "There are rumors that the angels under the command of Michael and Gabriel are planning an offensive. The human resistance is helping them."

"I'm not surprised," replied Jonathon, shaking his head. "I heard in my travels that you have some of the rebels right here in the Hall of Angels."

"We do," confirmed Zurel. "After all, we can't have them going around stirring up the population."

"No, I guess not," said Jonathon. "How many have you captured anyway?"

"The last number I heard was three hundred and twenty-six," replied Zurel.

"That is sure a lot," said Jonathon. "Where do you keep so many of them?"

"In the lowest level of the Hall of Angels for the moment," replied Zurel, "in a place that was used for storage. We have the most dangerous ones here. Some of them are little more than children, but they can be just as dangerous as the adults. We have to shackle them tightly to the wall to contain them. After all, these are not like the damned souls of Hell. These people are far more difficult to control. That is why we keep them here in a place where they cannot gate away."

"That's curious," said Jonathon. "What keeps them from being able to gate away?"

"Well, as long as they are tightly shackled, they can't gate," continued Zurel. "After all, they must walk through the tunnel they create, and if they can't walk they can't escape. But there is another thing. These angels of Michael and Gabriel liked their privacy, so they created a bubble of nerloft around this place."

"Nerloft?" asked Jonathon. "What is that?"

Zurel smiled. "Oh, nerloft is a sort of spell that can be placed around a building to prevent ethereal tunnels from penetrating it. I believe you call them wormholes or gates."

"Oh," said Jonathon. "So, it goes around the entire building?"

"Yes," confirmed Zurel.

"And it has a source, right?"

"Yes," replied Zurel, "The source is a circular room right in the middle of the building. I've been told that the device that does it all looks somewhat like a glowing tree of multicolored crystals."

"Sounds pretty cool, I'd love to see that," said Jonathon.

"So would I," laughed Zurel. "It is heavily guarded at all times. I've never even been near it. I may be a lieutenant in the master's service, but I'm not trusted that much. That thing is a key component of the defense of this place. It lies directly below the great ring, the one we use to transport ourselves from one level of Heaven to another, or even directly back to Hell, which is where our human prisoners are probably going to be transferred."

That revelation shocked Jonathon. "That doesn't seem quite right. I mean, these are sons and daughters of God, sanctified by the blood of Jesus. I'd think that there would be serious consequences if that was done. I think that the Father would be very displeased about the whole thing. Don't you agree?"

The demon hesitated. "Yes, that may be so…nevertheless, that is the master's command, and it must be followed. It may be that we will be ordered to return them to Heaven when this war is over, so we will take great efforts to keep track of them. I have been told that they will be kept in holding cells and spared any real torments."

Zurel paused. "But I doubt that that shall be their fate. I suspect there are those in the master's service that would insist on more severe treatment of the prisoners. Many of my species truly hate your kind, especially the true sons and daughters of God. They would like nothing better than to throw one of them into a fire pit or crucify one of them in much the same way that your Savior Jesus was crucified. I have heard talk of such things among the ranks."

"That's monstrous!" exclaimed Jonathon, as he realized too late that he probably shouldn't have said that.

"I agree," said Zurel, "and I am not at all happy with the prospects. It puts all of us in a very unfavorable light. Still, I would not be so bold as to question the orders of the master, and I'm sure that he would not object to such harsh treatment of your people."

This line of questioning wasn't getting Jonathon anywhere. He refocused his questions. "Do you think that it would be possible for a human inside of the Hall of Angels to gate from one place to another?"

Zurel seemed in deep thought. "I would assume so. That may be the reason that the human prisoners within this place are so tightly shackled to the wall, to prevent them from wandering around. Still, even if they did escape, they would eventually be caught. At any given time there is as many as 30,000 of my kind within that building. After all, we need to rest too, just like the angels you are more familiar with. We utilize the cubicles along the many passageways as places of rest and contemplation."

The question that Jonathon asked next served no real purpose. He was veering back off topic. After all, he had gathered all of the information that he really needed. Still, he felt compelled to ask. "Zurel, what do you contemplate about?"

Again Zurel seemed deep in thought. His expression seemed almost blank.

"I'm sorry, my friend," said Jonathon. "I realize that was a very personal question."

"No," replied Zurel, "it was a fair question. I contemplate my freedom."

"Your freedom?" asked Jonathon. "I don't understand."

"I doubt that you would, my friend," said Zurel. "Only an angel in Satan's service would. You may think that the humans damned to the torments of Hell are Satan's only captives, but I tell you that this is not the case. Those who serve him are as surely his captives as those who suffer within the pit. Our pain is different, of course, but it is pain nevertheless. For so long I missed the wonders, the blessings of Heaven. I missed the presence of the Father's divine Spirit."

Jonathon nodded. "I think I can understand that."

"I am a warrior," continued Zurel. "I would like to think that I am one of the best. It is the reason that I have risen from humble beginnings to the rank of lieutenant. I am not a torturer of humanity, Jonathon, please believe me. My job as a member of Satan's regular military is to keep order in Hell, to put down any human rebellions that may arise."

"There have been human rebellions in Hell?" asked Jonathon, his tone of voice speaking of his surprise.

"There have been many," replied Zurel. "Most were short-lived. However, even as our forces embarked upon this war of conquest, we were in the midst of the most serious rebellion that I have ever seen. An organized and well-equipped group of humans supported by a dissident sect of angelic beings known as the dark angels were at war with us. Indeed, they had won an important battle on the very day we launched our assault on Heaven. We should not have embarked on this campaign. We had serious problems at home.

"Still, the master's plans would not be changed, and so here we are. During our absence, the rebels have launched other attacks—bolder attacks, or so I have been told. The last one was upon the City of Sheol, the most important city built with demon hands. It has been completely destroyed by some terrible weapon. I had friends stationed there. I cannot help but wonder if it would have happened had we delayed this war and taken care of business at home before embarking upon this far-flung venture. I suppose I shall never know."

"I think that a lot of beings have suffered as a result of this war," noted Jonathon.

"Such is the nature of war," said Zurel. "I will tell you this, my friend: I had been looking forward to this conflict—I openly admit it. To walk through the meadows of Heaven once more was an experience I have longed for. But now that I am here, I question the wisdom of this conflict. This is not the Heaven of my youth. My compatriots are turning it into a wasteland in order to gain control of it.

"You cannot imagine how much I appreciate people who think as you do. Yet, I fear that in the end, even if we triumph over our enemies, this place will not be the same. We will serve a people who both dislike and distrust us. I cannot envision such a place being Heaven, can you?"

Jonathon was shocked. He placed his hand upon this mighty demon's shoulder, and it was not a well-planned deception on his part. He truly felt sympathy for this being. He had to leave. "I need to be off. I do hope that we get a chance to meet again. I hope you find the freedom and the peace you deserve."

"It was good to see you," replied Zurel.

Jonathon moved on. He discovered that the others had kept walking so as to avoid suspicion. It took several minutes before he at last caught up to them. "I've learned all that I need to know," he said. "I have a plan."

CHAPTER 7

THE CHILDREN GATHERED ONCE MORE around the dining room table. They had plans to make and little time to make them. Jonathon began by telling what he had learned from his conversation with the demon Zurel.

"You've got the Jedi mind trick down perfectly," said Christopher.

"You don't understand," said Jonathon, "I didn't use it at all. Zurel told me all of those things of his own free will, and I know that he was telling me the truth."

"Why would he do that?" asked Grampa Bud.

"I'm not sure," admitted Jonathon. "But I think I know how to get in."

Jonathon opened the book once more to the diagram of the Hall of Angels. He concentrated on the page for a few seconds. Abruptly, a three-dimensional schematic of the building appeared floating above the table before them. "Good job, Grandma," said Jonathon, glancing over at Grandma Gladys. "You materialized the book perfectly."

"I guess being a perfectionist pays off," said Gladys, smiling broadly.

Jonathon nodded. "Here is what I was thinking: the teleporter ring is located directly above the field generator..." He paused. "My friend David is the real expert on all of this. He has been teaching me, but I'm uncertain about my facts. However, I think that it may be possible to gate into the complex, right into the prison level, if someone was positioned directly above the Hall of Angels when the ring was active. The wormhole formed by the ring would interfere with the field protecting the facility, producing a gap in the field directly above the building, and making it possible for us to enter. We would be able to exit the same way—waiting for the ring to activate and then gating out."

The usually quiet Lilly looked at Jonathon incredulously. "So we'd have to find some way of hovering above the building unseen until, by chance, the ring was activated?" Lilly turned to Christopher. "You and I have the power of levitation. How much weight can you levitate and for how long?"

Christopher had to think about that one. "Well, I've levitated myself. I'm sure that I could levitate two people. I don't know for how long."

"I could probably do the same," noted Lilly. "We may be able to get in. But how would we get out with several hundred people?"

"You wouldn't have to levitate anyone," said Jonathon. "Distance is no object in gating. Creating a wormhole a billion miles long is no more difficult than forming one a mile long. What is directly above the Hall of Angels on the fourth level of Heaven?"

There was a momentary silence. Everyone in the room looked around at each other.

"Someplace on the fifth level of Heaven?" asked Jerry.

"Bingo," said Jonathon. "We would need to be at the exact same latitude and longitude as the Hall of Angels, only on the next level up. It would differ in location by only one dimension."

"Would something like that actually work?" asked Grandma Gladys.

"I think so," said Jonathon.

"But where would that place be?" asked Grampa Bud. "Jonathon, it could be in the middle of an ocean."

"It could, Grampa, but it isn't. I've checked. It happens to be in the middle of the Ion Desert. We go there, wait for our window of opportunity to open, and then gate in."

"Gate into a place we've only seen on a map?" asked Lilly.

"Yeah, that's about it," confirmed Jonathon.

"It wouldn't work," objected Lilly. "You can't even be sure that the floor plan on that diagram is accurate. Someone is going to have to go down there and find out. Then they could reach out to the group and guide them in."

"Who could do that?" asked Jerry.

"I could," said Lilly. She turned to Jonathon. "You could gate to exactly where I was, even if I was in that dungeon. You managed to sense my thoughts before and gate straight to me in the forest."

"But how would you get into the dungeon?" asked Jonathon. Then the realization of what she was suggesting hit him. "No, you can't be serious."

"I am serious," insisted Lilly. "If I were sneaking about their fortress, perhaps with a particle pistol on my person, I would probably end up in that dungeon."

"After they interrogated you, or worse," said Grampa Bud. "No, that's just too much of a risk."

"And if I don't, then hundreds of innocent people get sent to Hell to experience who knows what. Don't you see? I have to do this—*we* have to do this. This is what the Father brought us together for."

"Lilly is right," said Christopher. "I don't like this idea either, but the time has come for us to place all of our faith in the Father. He will not abandon us."

"But it shouldn't be Lilly who goes; it should be one of us guys," said Jerry. "I'll volunteer."

"You say that because I'm a girl," said Lilly, just a trace of anger and frustration in her voice. "I'm the best choice. I can reach out to Jonathon from anywhere in Heaven, I'm sure of it. I'm not so sure about you—it's just not your gift. You'll need to have Jonathon with you. He understands how this complicated gate is going to work. If something goes wrong, he is the one who will be able to figure it all out."

Lilly's logic was impossible to argue with. In the end, the group agreed. All afternoon was spent working out the details. At best, it was a thin and risky plan. So many things could go wrong.

Just two hours before sunset the group gathered in the meadow behind the mansion, all ready to go. They could hear the pounding waves in the distance and feel the gentle breeze. There was a perfect sense of the calm before the storm.

"The sun will set about an hour earlier in Sarel than it does here," said Grampa Bud. "Everything is all set."

"Grampa, please...no heroics," begged Jonathon.

Grampa smiled slightly but said nothing.

"It's time," said Grandma Gladys. She hugged each of the children. "Come back safe." She tried to keep her spirits and her smile intact.

Lilly walked over to Jonathon. She gave him a kiss on the cheek. "I have faith in you, Jonathon. Find me, rescue me, rescue all of us."

"No worries," said Jonathon, bowing slightly. "I'll be your knight in shining armor, fair maiden. We all will."

The others followed Jonathon's lead, bowing before Lilly. She giggled slightly. They all seemed so noble, so brave. How could she possibly have asked for three braver or nobler knights?

Jonathon was doing his best to exude an air of total confidence, yet he quivered slightly. Lilly's life—maybe even her eternity—was in his hands. Could he really do all that he claimed he could do? Right now he wasn't so sure.

Lilly stepped away from the group. "Father, into Your hands I place my life and my eternity."

"Amen," said Christopher. "You can do it. We'll see you in a few hours."

"Sure will," said Jerry.

Lilly only nodded. She raised her hand and a mist filled with sparkling stars materialized before her. A moment later she stepped into the mists and vanished.

For a few seconds, silence ruled the meadow. Jonathon was next to create a field of blue sparkling mists. "We're off to the Ion Desert," he proclaimed, "latitude thirty-four degrees, fifteen minutes, twelve seconds north; longitude one hundred seventeen degrees, fifty-two minutes, eleven seconds west."

The three boys picked up a large stack of weapons and stepped into the glowing mists and faded away.

Bud and Gladys grasped each other's hands and their weapons. It was time. Gladys raised her hand to form the third corridor that would lead her and her husband to the City of Sarel. The wheels of their plan had been set into motion.

Darkness was falling as the young girl in the blue dress and long cape was dragged into the main audience chamber deep within the Hall of Angels in the City of Sarel. With a demon holding her roughly by each arm, and another following closely behind, she was brought before the demon commander.

The audience chamber was composed wholly of white marble and was larger than most rooms within the Hall of Angels, measuring about 30 by 50 feet. The 12-foot-high ceiling was supported by very plain marble columns spaced about ten feet apart along the left and right walls of the chamber. Indirect illumination of the chamber came from behind a cove line that ran the entire way around the chamber about a foot from the ceiling. Along the back of the chamber a set of heavy, blue drapes ran from just below the cove line to nearly the floor.

The only piece of furniture within the room was a high-backed chair, the color of polished brass, which was placed about five feet in front of the drapes. Here the demon commander sat, his icy stare trained upon the pretty girl who had been dragged before him.

The bat-winged commander was an undeniably handsome being with dark eyes and even darker hair. He was clean shaven and wore a long, purple robe fringed with gold. Upon the second finger of his right hand was a ruby ring that glowed from its depths. "And who do we have here?" he asked.

"This human tried to gain entrance into the hall, my lord," said one of the demons walking behind the others. "She demanded that we release her sister or face the consequences."

"Did she now?" asked the commander, rising to his feet. "And who is this sister of yours, young human?"

"Her name is Christa Carter," said the girl.

"I know that name," said the commander, placing a finger to his forehead. "Yes, she was captured but four days ago. We determined that she was a spy for the human resistance."

"This one may well be one too," noted the demon guard. "She had on her person a dagger...and this." In one hand the demon held a very nasty looking dagger, while in the other hand he held a particle pistol.

"My, my," said the commander, "aren't you the bold one? Things do not look good for you, my dear. What did you propose to do with that weapon?"

"Nothing," said the girl, "so long as you released my sister."

The guards chuckled in a guttural tone.

The commander took several steps toward the girl. "You know what I think? I think you're a member of the resistance too...and not a very intelligent one. Where did you get that weapon?"

"A friend gave it to me," she said.

Her response was quickly followed by a hard twist of her arm from one of her demon escorts, which caused her to wince in pain.

"You'll have to do better than that," said the commander, a slight yet devious smile coming to his face. "What is your name, child?"

The girl looked into the demon's eyes. There was not so much as a trace of fear in her almond eyes. "My name is Lihua Hue, but most people just call me Lilly."

"A pretty name for a pretty girl," said the demon commander, stepping before her. He placed his hand under her chin. "If you'd like to remain pretty, you will answer my questions completely and honestly. Do you understand?"

"Yes," replied Lilly, her eyes locked with those of the commander.

"Where are you from?" asked the commander.

"I was born on Earth, in the nation of North Korea," she said. I died about seven years ago, and the Father brought me here."

"Very good beginnings," said the commander. "Now, let us continue. Who do you work for?"

"I work for the Father," said Lilly. "He sent me here."

The commander pulled back the hood of Lilly's cloak and grabbed her dark hair. He pulled her head back roughly. "You'll need to do better than that, little wench. We know that you work for the human resistance. I need to know who sent you. Was it Washington? Kepler? Who?"

"It was the Father," replied Lilly, struggling with the demons that still held her. "And I have a message for you, Kemrick. You have been weighed in the balance and found wanting. So here are the words of the

Father: 'Before the sun rises on another day you shall be brought down by the very people you have persecuted. In that instant you shall know that the words of the Lord are true.'"

The demon commander flew into a rage. He struck Lilly across the face with his hand. His ring cut deep into her lip, causing blood to flow. Yet Lilly neither cried nor whimpered. She quickly made eye contact with him once more.

"Time answers all questions, Kemrick, and it will reveal the truth of my words," she said, her voice intense and certain.

The commander reached back once more, yet stayed his hand this time. "I think it is time that you were reunited with your sister," he said, anger lingering in his voice. "You shall endure that thing that she endures; and come tomorrow's sunset, you shall join her in a journey to a place where you can be more adequately punished, a place where you will come to know the real meaning of agony." He looked toward the demon guards. "Take her away!"

Lilly was dragged from the audience chambers and down the hallway beyond. All the while Lilly observed every detail, every turn, and every side chamber. She was taken down a long, winding stairway, deeper and deeper into the great monolithic structure that was the Hall of Angels.

"What you experience tonight will be but a taste of your future, little wench," said the one demon. "In Hell you will discover the true meaning of hopelessness."

Lilly's mind reached out in search of Jonathon, yet she couldn't find him. Was it the field of force that surrounded this place, or was he simply too far away to contact? Right now she wasn't sure.

It was several minutes before she reached the lowest level of the Hall of Angels. Here she heard the sound of weeping, praying, and even praising of the Father as she was led past one small cell after another, each cut off from the corridor by black, metal bars. In each it was the same story. Human men, women, and even children had been shackled hand and foot to the walls, three per cell. She could feel the sense of helplessness, even hopelessness here. Could she really help these people?

"No, your fate shall not be as merciful as theirs," snarled one of the demons, who had suddenly taken on the pale, wrinkled facial features of an incredibly old man.

Lilly realized that the demon had done this to frighten her. She did her best to ignore the creature.

At last they came to a series of short corridors on either side of the main corridor. Stone steps led down to heavy, metal doors with what appeared to be a small window on each. Yet each window was shuttered by a metal slide that prevented Lilly from getting a glimpse of what lay beyond. These too were cells; that much was clear. Yet it wasn't sorrowful lamentations that arose from the chambers to her left, but cries and screams of pain.

The demon stopped and turned Lilly to the left. As Lilly turned, she saw another demon in the corridor. She recognized this one: it was Zurel, the demon that Jonathon had spoken to. Yes, she was certain of it. For a moment she caught his gaze, but just for a moment. He turned around and walked the other way.

"This is the one," said the demon on Lilly's left, leading her down the stairway to one of the metal doors. "We're going to reunite you with your sister. In fact, we'll allow you to share her fate...and have some quality time together."

The demon pushed the metal slide on the door aside and forced Lilly's face up to the opening. Within she saw a stone room that was maybe 12 feet on a side. It was a foul-smelling place illuminated by a single torch mounted to the back wall. Within this grim chamber were five humans, three men and two women. Their wrists were shackled firmly to the wall, forcing their arms wide apart. Their ankles too were shackled to the wall, forcing them to stand with their legs spread wide. A heavy black metal band held them at the waist, rendering them unable to move.

And on the floor were large rats—dozens of them—with unnaturally large, sharp teeth. They tore into their helpless victims in a feeding frenzy, reducing their bare feet to little more than ragged hunks of stringy red meat. Some of the rats had even climbed up onto their prey to feast upon their legs and flanks. All the while the victim's bodies regenerated, creating new meat for their eternally voracious tormentors.

Lilly turned away in disgust, but the demon pushed her back to the window. "Take a good look," he said in a loud, sneering voice. "There is your sister. Before the night is over she'll tell us all she knows. Perhaps watching the same thing happen to you will loosen up her tongue."

"This shouldn't be happening here," said Lilly. She tried not to cry, yet the tears began to flow.

"Why?" asked the demon, "because there are no rats such as these in Heaven? Of course there aren't. These are imports straight out of the master's kingdom. But we needed them. Our little pets will keep you company until we transport the lot of you to Hell tomorrow evening. Then we shall really get creative."

The other demon unbolted the door and roughly pushed Lilly into the room. As the demons entered, the rats immediately scattered in fear, fleeing into a series of holes and crevices on the far wall, leaving their victims gasping and crying in fear.

"Well, have any of you had enough?" asked the demon. "Would any of you care to give us the information we require? Who knows…if you cooperate, we may see fit to release you."

The bloodied and disheveled victims looked up at the demon with weary eyes. Yet no one seemed in the mood to cooperate.

"Our suffering is but for the moment," said one of the men near the back wall, the one who seemed to have gotten the worst of it. "But our reward for our sacrifice will be eternal."

"I wouldn't know about that," hissed the demon. "Who knows... once we transport you to Hell, God may even forget about you. You may end up stuck there with all of the other sinners."

"Not likely," said a woman. Lilly recognized her as Christa.

"We shall see," said the demon, leading Lilly toward an empty set of restraints beside Christa. "We thought that you might like to spend some time with your little sister. She came looking for you. We thought it was only fair that the two of you be reunited. Still...it doesn't have to be this way. If you tell us all about your mission, we may spare her the torments that you have endured."

At first Christa seemed confused. Then she responded, apparently willing to play along. "I can't tell you anything, even to spare my sister." She looked over at Lilly. "I'm so sorry, sis. I hope you can forgive me."

Lilly only nodded.

"Take your shoes off, little wench," demanded the demon. "We don't want to make too much work for the rats, do we?"

Lilly had little choice. She removed her shoes. Then the demon ripped away her cloak, leaving her dressed only in her short-sleeved, knee-length dress.

"I think your arms need to be exposed as well," said the demon. "It will expose a bit more good meat to the rats." Then the demon slammed her against the wall. Within two minutes she was locked into the manacles.

Lilly quickly discovered that these manacles were far more insidious than she had at first thought. Although their outsides were smooth enough, the insides were a different matter—rough and barbed, so as to encourage the wearer not to struggle within them quite so much.

"The rats are terrified of us," said the other demon. "We bred them that way. But they have no fear of humans. In fact, you're their natural prey. The minute we leave the room, they'll be all over you. This is your last chance to tell us what you know. Once we leave…it may be morning before someone looks in on you."

None of the prisoners said a word. There was nothing to be said.

"Have it your way," said the demon, heading for the door with its compatriot. "It is likely to be a long night for the lot of you—not being used to the pain of the damned. Still, I expect that you will have plenty of time to adjust to it."

The demons vanished beyond the heavy door, and it shut behind them with a dull thud. The sound of the bolts reengaging quickly followed.

For a moment, one of the demons gazed at the prisoners through the small window as if to confirm that all was as it should be. At first the rats seemed reluctant to emerge from their hiding places, but after about a minute the first of many returned. By now, many of the prisoners had to a large degree regenerated. It was a new feast for the rats. Within another minute they had renewed their feeding frenzy; only this time they had an additional course on the dining table.

Lilly winced in pain as a particularly fat, gray rat lit into her little toe. She tried to resist, yet it was futile; moving her feet only resulted in yet another form of pain as the barbs on the inside of the manacle dug into her tender flesh. Within seconds, the rat had gnawed and ripped the toe from her foot. As the blood flowed, two other rats took notice of their new guest, their red eyes gleaming in the light of the single torch. They began to move toward her.

The demon seemed pleased with what was happening, and the shutter on the window closed. Lilly heard the footfalls fade away beyond the door.

"Who are you?" gasped Christa, struggling with her pain. "I only know you from a dream."

"I'm here to rescue you," said Lilly.

"Some rescue," gasped one of the men on the far wall.

"It is," assured Lilly, gazing in disgust at the rat who had already consumed her toe, bone and all. "It starts right now."

A fraction of a second later the rat was hurtling through the air. It hit the far wall with such tremendous force that its blood and guts were scattered for several feet around. Then Lilly focused on one eating its way up Christa's leg. It too hit the wall with force. Within a few seconds rats were flying everywhere. Others seemed to be twisted apart or ripped in two. Within three minutes all of the rats had been killed or had taken shelter within their holes.

Lilly looked across at the man who had first spoke. "As I said, I'm here to rescue you."

"But who sent you?" asked the other woman, who was little more than a girl herself.

"The Father," Lilly replied. "You're all getting out of here. Just believe."

Lilly focused on her wrist manacle. She tried to imagine how its locking mechanism worked. She focused the full force of her mind upon it. It vibrated, and those vibrations really hurt. A trickle of blood was running down her arm before she relented.

"I can't," she gasped. "We'll have to wait for the others."

"What others?" asked the other man shackled to the far wall.

"I'm part of a team," said Lilly. "It may be best if I didn't explain it all now. You've just got to trust me...trust the Father who sent me."

"I do," said the man.

"Praise Him, praise Him, for He will set the captives free," sang the other young woman in a voice barely above a whisper.

The others joined in, even Lilly. Still, Lilly was really scared. She hadn't been so scared since the day doctors at the concentration camp in North Korea had begun surgery on her without anesthesia. That had been the beginning of the end of her life on Earth. She prayed for strength, not just for herself but for all of the rest as well.

"Please, Jonathon, find me. Please come and get me," she said, almost under her breath. "I'm so scared."

"Still nothing," lamented Jonathon, who was now sitting on a large boulder, staring up at the stars.

They had arrived in a hilly region of the Ion Desert. It offered a panoramic view of the more level desert plains to the west. It was still very hot—over 90 degrees. And the winds that had been considerable when they arrived had died away to a gentle breeze.

This was a largely uninhabited region of the Father's Kingdom. Only a few hardy desert dwellers called this region home. On the horizon they could make out the few campfires of the dwellers of a tent village some five or so miles away.

"I wonder who would want to live in a place like this?" said Jerry, fanning his face with his hand. "I prefer the deep, cool forest."

"But not everyone does," noted Christopher, staring out toward the distant campfires. "Heaven is a place for all humankind. The people who grew up in Egypt or the southwest deserts of the United States may find a place like this to be the sort of Heaven they prefer. Heaven is fashioned for everyone."

"We should have never let her go in there," said Jonathon, placing his face in his hands.

"I don't reckon that you were going to stop her," said Jerry. "Her mind was made up."

"This is all going to work out," said Christopher. "The Father sent us on this mission, and it's going to work out."

"But how do we know it was *this* mission?" objected Jonathon.

"I know," said Christopher. "I don't have any doubts."

"I don't either," confirmed Jerry. "You didn't seem to have any doubts when this all began, Jonathon. You were as sure of yourself as you ever were."

"It was easy when Lilly's life wasn't on the line," replied Jonathon. "Who knows what is happening to her in there? Suppose I'm wrong?"

"You're not," said Christopher. "This thing may take time. Just don't lose faith."

"I'm trying not to," said Jonathon.

"Do or do not...there is no try," said Christopher.

Jonathon turned to his young friend. The expression on Christopher's face told him that he was very serious. Jonathon stepped off of the rock and took several steps up the canyon; then he just kept on going.

"What's up with Jonathon?" asked Jerry, who started to follow him. Christopher stopped him.

"Let him go, Jerry. He needs some time."

"We don't have much time," said Jerry.

"We have enough," countered Christopher, "let him go."

Jonathon followed the dry canyon into the hills for about 20 minutes before he stopped. He was barely able to see his way in the starlight. He turned around to see the campfires in the distance. Then he looked up to see the bright blue star high in the western sky, a star as bright as all of the other stars in the sky combined. It was the main source of light illuminating his surroundings this night.

No, it wasn't a star. It was the planet that was the fourth level of Heaven. He stared at it for a moment. How very beautiful it was. Lilly was out there on that point of light. He shouldn't have let her go into that demon stronghold alone. He shouldn't have walked away from the guys for that matter. Was he running away from his responsibility? Suppose that fleeting moment of opportunity to gate into the Hall of Angels came and went while he was way out here?

"Oh Lord, what do I do now?" he asked.

"You wait for the right moment to rescue Lilly," said a Voice out of the darkness.

Jonathon was startled. He turned to see a white-robed figure step out of the shadows and into the soft, blue light. It was a Man with long, flowing hair and a short beard. His expression was kind and understanding. Jonathon knew Him immediately. "Jesus…Lord!"

"Hello, Jonathon," said Jesus.

"Lord, You're here," said Jonathon.

Jesus laughed kindheartedly, "Of course I am. It seems to Me that we need to have a talk."

"Oh yes, Lord," confirmed Jonathon. "I'm so confused…confused and scared." He walked toward Jesus and fell into His arms. Jonathon began to cry.

Jesus placed His arms around the distraught youth. "It's OK, Jonathon, I'm here now. I'll help you."

"I was so sure of this plan—that it would work," began Jonathon. "I let Lilly go into that awful place. I was so proud of myself; I thought I had it all figured out. I was going to be her knight in shining armor. I was going to gate in and save the day. I was so full of it."

"But now you doubt yourself," deduced Jesus. "Every leader has had his moments of doubt, those times when he asks himself if he is really the right person to be making the important decisions. There have been times when I had My doubts too."

"But we were a team, Lord," said Jonathon. "Who am I to appoint myself the leader? That's what I've done."

"You didn't just do it," corrected Jesus, "our Father did."

"What?" asked Jonathon. "I don't understand."

"Look back over the past few weeks," said Jesus. "If it had not been for you, Christopher and Jerry would never have reached our Father. They would never have met Lilly. Isn't this correct?"

Jonathon had to think about that for a moment. "I guess so."

"In the forest three days ago, who first sensed that Lilly was in danger?"

"I did," replied Jonathon.

"And who came up with the plan of gating in so as to surround the demons?"

"I did," said Jonathon.

Jesus grasped Jonathon gently by his shoulders. "And who figured out this plan?"

"I think we all did," replied Jonathon.

"But who was the guiding force?"

"I suppose I was," said Jonathon.

"You suppose right, My friend," said Jesus, smiling broadly. "You were not wrong the other times, so why do you suppose you're wrong now?"

Jonathon didn't answer. He truly didn't know what to say.

"You can't answer that question because there is no answer," continued Jesus. "You aren't wrong. Our Father has been guiding you all along, and He will continue to guide you. His Holy Spirit shall lead you into the Valley of the Shadow of Death this very night…but you should fear no evil, though it be all around you. And do you know why, Jonathon?"

"Because He is with me," said Jonathon, smiling through his tears.

"Exactly," said Jesus, whose smile mirrored Jonathon's. "He will lead you."

"So what should I do now?" asked Jonathon.

"You already know," said Jesus. "You go back to Christopher and Jerry and prepare for the battle to come. Stop doubting yourself. Make your decisions, decide what you are going to do, and do it. Christopher was right. Do or do not…there is no try."

"Yoda," said Jonathon.

"No, George Lucas," Jesus responded. "And he was right."

"Are You coming with me?" asked Jonathon.

"No," said Jesus. "This is your mission. You're the leader this time. You'd best hurry. You're running out of time."

Jonathon took several steps forward, then turned around. Jesus was gone. He shook his head and then smiled. "Thank You, Lord," he said. He continued down the canyon with renewed resolve, faith, and courage. He had a mission to complete.

The position that Lilly found herself locked into was becoming most uncomfortable. Although her toe had fully regenerated, and the pain associated with the loss was now but a memory, she remained troubled. She had experienced only a taste of the torments of Hell. But it had given her a heightened sense of the fate of those sentenced to that terrible realm.

During the past several hours, she had come to know her cellmates better. Clearly, two of them were guilty of the crimes that the demons had accused them of, but the rest were only guilty by association or guilty of being in the wrong place at the wrong time. Zachary, the young man who hung from the wall directly across from her, fell into that category. He was only 20 years of age, and had been taken by the demons for simply living next door to a home in the City of Zion where particle rifles for the resistance were being made.

Nevertheless, guilty or innocent of participating in the revolt, they were all children of God. The demons had no right and no authority to treat them as they had.

After their deliverance from those horrible rats, the group had more hope than ever before. Yet as the hours passed, Lilly became increasingly concerned. She had hoped that her stay here would have been a brief one. She still exuded hope on the outside, yet deep within her soul her fears were growing. Those fears were multiplied when she heard footfalls coming down the steps beyond the door. She heard someone grab the slide over the cell door window. A moment later it slipped to one side, and she was looking into the face of a demon.

The demon scanned the room. He seemed shocked to discover the condition of the four dozen or so rats, whose bodies lay bloodied, crushed, and contorted throughout the cell. His eyes passed from prisoner to prisoner until they focused on Lilly. Their eyes met and locked. It was only then that Lilly realized just who this demon was—Zurel. The tension within the room was almost unbearable. If he sounded the alarm, the entire operation was compromised. Lilly was surprised when the slightest of smiles came to his face.

"I've seen you before," he said in a soft, calm tone. "You are Jonathon's friend, are you not?"

There it was. Should she tell the truth? "Yes, I am," she finally said.

Again Zurel scanned the harvest of death before him. "Very good, little one."

Zurel closed the slide. A moment later Lilly heard his footfalls fade into the distance.

"What now?" asked Zachary. "He'll certainly tell the other demons what he saw in here." He pulled on his shackles with only too predictable results.

"He almost seemed amused by what he saw, not angry," noted Christa. "How do you explain that?"

"I don't know," replied Lilly. "We've dealt with him before. I truly don't know what will happen next."

Twenty minutes passed. The group listened intently for any noises from beyond the metal door, but there were none. All was quiet.

"I would have thought that something would have happened by now," said Christa.

"I would too," agreed Lilly, "unless he didn't tell anyone."

"Why would he do that?" objected Cindi, the young woman on the far side of Christa.

"I'm not sure," admitted Lilly. "Unless…" she stopped in mid-sentence.

Suddenly, all eyes were upon her. Her expression seemed so far away. In the back of her mind she heard a voice, a calm and reassuring voice. A smile slowly came to her face.

"My knight in shining armor has arrived," she said, in a voice that almost seemed dreamy.

Less than ten seconds later a blue mist filled with sparkling stars formed in the middle of the room. From it stepped Lilly's three knights in shining armor.

Jonathon scanned the room, then turned to Lilly. "You were right when you said that you'd made a mess." He walked over to her and attempted to free her right wrist.

Christopher took up a position at the cell door, while Jerry picked up a small communications device from his belt.

"We're in," Jerry spoke into the device, before returning it to his belt.

All the while Jonathon worked with the shackle around Lilly's wrist. Then it released.

"Oh, that's it," said Jonathon. "It doesn't need a key. It's easy enough to open, so long as you're not wearing it."

Jonathon released Lilly's left wrist in a matter of just a few seconds. Within a minute, she was free. Lilly collapsed into his arms. She started to cry.

"I was afraid I'd never see any of you again," she wept.

"Come on, Lilly, be strong," said Jonathon in a quiet tone. "We're here now, and we're going to get out of here. Just have faith."

"I have faith," she said. "I wish they hadn't taken my shoes."

"No problem," said Jerry, focusing his attention upon the floor in front of Lilly. It took less than ten seconds before a pair of very sensible shoes materialized.

"Thank you," said Lilly, wiping the tears from her eyes.

Jonathon and Jerry set to work releasing the others, while Lilly turned to help Christa out of her restraints. Inside of two minutes they were all free, and thanks to Jerry, equipped with new shoes.

Jonathon opened a large satchel filled with particle rifles and pistols. "Does anyone here know how to use one of these?"

"I do," said Christa, picking up one of the rifles.

The three men quickly followed suit.

"I didn't make the weapons, but I did learn how to use them," said Zachary. "Now what do we do...fight our way out of here?"

"If we have to," said Jonathon, "but we're not going alone. We're leaving no one behind."

The others agreed. It took about ten minutes to bring the former prisoners up to speed on the plan. They were ready to go. The group moved to either side of the door. Jonathon nodded to Christopher who reached for the handle. Miraculously, it wasn't locked. Then again, it didn't need to be locked, did it?

Jonathon scanned the stairs and saw a figure standing at the very top. It was Zurel. Zurel quickly placed a finger to his lips to warn the group to be silent.

"Don't fire," said Jonathon to the others.

Zurel looked up and down the corridor before coming down the stairs. "I suspected that something like this was going to happen. I assume that you'll want to free all of the prisoners."

Jonathon only nodded.

"Yes, I suspected as much," said Zurel. "That is why I asked for this duty tonight. Rank has its privileges."

"You knew that we were planning this?" asked Jonathon.

"Yes," replied Zurel, "at least I suspected it from our conversation. I gave you all of the information that you'd need."

Jonathon looked on in stunned amazement. "You're helping us?"

"Yes, my friend," confirmed Zurel. "My fight was with the angels of Michael and Gabriel, not with the children of God, and not with the Father. I will be a party to Satan's plan no longer. I will not raise my sword against the Father or His children. I am not so foolish. You may find it hard to believe, but I still love the Father. And how can I love the Father but hate His children? It is I who unlocked the cell door for you."

"I'm glad to have you with us," said Jonathon.

"You're actually trusting him?" asked Christa.

"I am," said Lilly. "He could have sounded the alarm when he saw all of the dead rats in the cell, but he didn't."

"Based on what my friend Jonathon told me yesterday, I assumed that you were searching for a way to gate into this place," continued Zurel. "That could only have been accomplished if the ring were active." Zurel paused, then smiled slightly. "Yes, Jonathon, I too knew the only weakness in the hall's defenses. Most of my fellows did not. I found an excuse to activate the ring for a sufficient period of time to allow you to enter. I assumed that you had determined a method of detecting when that occurred. That is how you are here."

The group looked at each other in astonishment. To be befriended by a demon seemed an impossible concept, yet the evidence was before them.

"There are few guards on this level," continued Zurel. "I can distract them long enough for you to make good your escape. Wait here."

Zurel headed up the steps and gazed into the corridor. Then he headed off to the right, out of sight. The group waited in silence, not knowing what to expect. After about a minute he returned and motioned for the others to follow. Jonathon started down the steps to the cell on the far side of the corridor, yet Zurel stopped him.

"That one is empty; only the six of you were deemed so vile as to deserve the rats. I've sent the other sentries off on a meaningless task. It will be some period of time before they return. Indeed, they are unlikely to return before the changing of the guard. Follow me."

The group followed Zurel down the corridor to the place where all of the other human prisoners were kept. The presence of armed human resistance fighters accompanied by a demon lieutenant drew more than a few amazed looks.

Zurel pulled a small, black cylinder with a small, green crystal embedded in the end from a pocket in his leather armor. "This will unlock the cell doors," he said, handing the key to Jonathon. "Just pass it over the crystal in the lock from left to right. I assume that you already know how to release their manacles. I'll take up a position at the end of the corridor and detour any of my kind that happen this way. You'd best make haste—we are less than one of your hours from a changing of the guard."

Jonathon nodded and Zurel made his way to the end of the corridor some 70 feet away. Jonathon wasted no time in opening the first cell. The lock disengaged with a resounding clunk when he passed the crystal across it. The sound was a bit too loud for his taste, but there was nothing that could be done about that. He went from cell to cell as the others proceeded to release the captives within.

All the while, Jonathon weighed his options. He was only too aware of the passing of time as he made his way along the corridors, which took the shape of an X. Three legs of the X led to dead ends; only one leg of the X led to another corridor and inevitably to the exit. That would be their escape route of last resort. Their best route would be to gate the entire group to the Ion Desert. If the ring were used again, the window of opportunity would open.

But that window would close once the ring shut down. It would take time to get all of the captives through the gate they formed between here and the Ion Desert. Only he, Christopher, and Jerry could open the gate; the others would have to follow behind them. Suppose the ring shut down while people were in transit? What would happen to them? Jonathon wasn't sure. There were just so many unanswered questions.

There were 124 cells in this cell block—124 cells and 327 prisoners, including Lilly. Jonathon counted them all as he unlocked them. Zurel had been right. The releasing of the prisoners was occurring at an ever-accelerating rate as the number of freed humans increased.

Jonathon was shocked to discover just how many children were among the captives. Some were certainly no older than 6 or 7. The barbaric nature of their imprisonment was bringing his anger to the boiling point. These demons had to be made to pay. No, that was wrong thinking. He had to be practical. An out-and-out battle against the demons within their own fortress was a very bad idea. The humans were ill-equipped for a fight. The available weapons, eighteen particle rifles and six pistols, had been distributed to those prisoners who already had experience using them. That wasn't very many weapons if Zurel's estimation of demon strength was accurate. Of the 330 humans, only 27 of them were armed.

"We've got everyone loose," said Christopher, rushing toward Jonathon. "What now?"

Good question. Jonathon recalled a story of the Earth conflict known as World War II. "Christopher, did you ever hear of the World War Two Battle for Stalingrad?"

Christopher had to think on that one. "I think so. It was the turning point of the war, or something like that."

"It was the turning point on the eastern front," confirmed Jonathon, "but that wasn't exactly what I was referring to. During that battle, rifles were in such short supply on the Russian side that not every soldier could be issued one. Although all of the soldiers were supplied with ammunition, during an advance against the German lines only the first few rows of men in an advancing column were actually equipped with weapons.

"As those soldiers fell, it was the responsibility of the men in the columns behind them to pick up those weapons and continue fighting. Perhaps we will need to resort to a similar strategy here. In these narrow hallways, fighting in close quarters, it just might work. At least it would have the effect of evening up the odds."

Christopher looked at Jonathon incredulously. "You're kidding, right? I mean…that isn't a solution."

"I sure hope it's not necessary," said Jonathon, heading back toward the growing crowd in the corridor.

Jonathon turned to the first and best option. He focused on forming a gate back to the Ion Desert. It didn't work. The ring was not active and the field of force, the nerloft as Zurel called it, was still in place. They'd have to wait. Jonathon left the group and approached Zurel, who stood at the junction of the corridors.

"You don't have very much time," warned Zurel. "I don't believe that the ring is scheduled to be used again tonight, certainly not between now and the time of the changing of the guard."

"I was afraid of that," lamented Jonathon.

"I could attempt to activate the ring again," said Zurel.

"How long could you keep it active?" asked Jonathon, glancing back at the rest of the crowd in the corridor.

"Not long," Zurel replied, "perhaps twenty of your seconds, perhaps a bit more."

"That's not long enough to get all of these people out," said Jonathon. "Couldn't you stall for time, stretch it out a bit?"

"Not likely," said Zurel. "The master expects us to conserve energy, and that means swift as possible transportation from one ring to another. I would be pushing it at twenty seconds."

"What would happen if other people were in the midst of gating when the ring shut down?"

Zurel shrugged. "I don't know. I thought that would be your area of expertise."

Jonathon shook his head. "I've never tried it."

Zurel paused to think. "You might get bounced back to your starting point. You might end up adrift in the ether. You might even be ripped apart. Personally, I wouldn't want to be in transit when it happened. I'm not even sure that I could make it to the ring before the change of the guard. Even if I did, it would seem awfully suspicious that I needed to use the ring twice in one night."

"Then that's no good," replied Jonathon.

Zurel seemed surprised. "Are you telling me that you embarked upon this mission without a clear escape plan?"

"I have an escape plan," objected Jonathon. "I'm just not that confident that it will succeed."

"Fortune favors the foolish," said Christopher, stepping up to Jonathon. "Perhaps it favors the faithful as well."

"If you are going to resort to some backup plan…now is the time to execute it," noted Zurel.

"I suppose so," said Jonathon, turning away.

"Wait a minute," said Christopher, "maybe we're going about this all wrong. We don't need to escape the same way we got here. Our problem is this force field crystal, right?"

"Yeah, right," confirmed Jonathon.

"But the crystal is heavily guarded," objected Zurel.

"Yeah, but we could gate right up to it, couldn't we?" asked Christopher. "We could blow it away before anyone realized that we were there."

"I doubt that you could gate closer than a hundred feet from it," said Zurel. "The nerloft that surrounds it would probably prevent you from getting any closer."

"And none of us have ever been there," said Jonathon. "Gating around in the close quarters of this building would require that we have at least have some knowledge of it, more than we've gained from just a rough floor plan."

"But Zurel has that knowledge," said Christopher.

"I do," replied Zurel, "but I'm not human—I can't gate."

"But I could," said Jonathon, turning to Zurel. "Look, I don't have time to explain it all to you, but if you know it, focus your mind on it; then I can know it."

Zurel looked at Jonathon. "Yes, it is all becoming clear to me now. Very well...I'm picturing it in my mind at this very moment."

Jonathon took several steps toward Zurel and their eyes met. He focused on this peculiar being. What he saw this time was not some weak-willed creature whose mind could be bent to his whims. He saw an entity whose thoughts were as clear as a pool of deep, fresh water, a being full of dreams and aspirations. It hardly seemed like the mind of a demon.

Jonathon linked onto Zurel's vision of the corridors above almost instantly. He saw the guard posts and the passageways, the cubicles and the side chambers, and he understood what needed to be done. The only problem with the plan was that it would alert the demons to their presence. Still, if they struck quickly and decisively enough, it should work.

"I figure it will take about twelve of us, thirteen counting Zurel," said Jonathon looking about at the others. He then focused once more on Zurel, the only demon he had ever met that he could truly call his friend. "That is, if you wish to come on this mission."

"I would insist on it," replied Zurel. "I believe I could be of help to you."

"It would almost certainly involve firing on your own kind," cautioned Jonathon. "Do you think you could handle that?"

"Yes," Zurel replied. There was not the slightest hesitation in his answer.

"OK," said Jonathon. "In my mind's eye, I see a small room that the demons don't use much. It is fairly close to the field generator. We could gate in there and make for the generator. Still, we don't know what the security looks like right around the generator itself. Zurel has never been there. The longer it takes, the more difficult this whole mission will become. If we don't take it out in about five minutes, I don't think we ever will."

"In that case, we'd have to fight our way out," deduced Christopher.

"That's about right," confirmed Jonathon.

By this time, Jerry and Lilly had joined the gathering at the junction of the corridors. They'd heard enough to catch the general game plan.

"I think I need to go with the group that takes out the field generator," said Jerry.

"Right," confirmed Jonathon. "Christopher and Lilly will stay here and hold this junction of the corridors." Jonathon turned to Christopher. "I suspect that it won't take too long before the demons get around to checking on their prisoners. When they do, you and the others will need to hold them right here. You can't let them get into this corridor because then they'll be able to split your forces."

"I understand," confirmed Christopher. "No retreat, no surrender."

Then Jonathon turned to Lilly. "You'll need to stay in contact with me. I'll try to reach out to you. I'll let you know if our mission has failed. In that case you'll need to get these people on the move toward the only exit. Do you feel strong enough to bring up that barrier of yours, the one you created in the battle in the forest?"

"Yes," said Lilly, "and I know how to get to that exit from here."

"If we can't take out that generator, we'll retreat and take up a position behind you. Then we'll cover you from the rear."

Lilly nodded.

It took a few minutes to bring the rest of the group up to speed on what they were about to attempt. Many of the former prisoners volunteered to go along with Jonathon, Jerry, and Zurel. In the end, they selected the best qualified. Six of them were former Marines. Indeed, they had all fought in combat before, but not quite like this.

"In about fifteen minutes, my relief sentries will arrive," noted Zurel. "We can delay no longer."

Jonathon turned to Lilly and smiled. "You take care of yourself while I'm gone. I want to take you out surfing tomorrow."

"I'd like that," said Lilly.

"OK," said Jonathon, taking a deep breath, "we're on our way."

The mists formed before Jonathon and his team and they stepped in. The others watched with trepidation as the last of them vanished into the mists. It would be a waiting game now, but not for too long. This fight would be determined one way or the other within the next five minutes.

CHAPTER 8

JONATHON GATED INTO THE DARKNESS, illuminated only by the glow of the glimmering stars of the portal through which he had just passed. Almost immediately the illumination increased. He looked behind him to see that Jerry had materialized some sort of glowing crystal in his hand to light the way. He continued forward to the wall eight feet in front of him. Within 10 or 12 seconds, the entire group was within this otherwise empty 18-by-18 foot room. Jonathon identified a heavy metal door behind him. "So far so good."

"The corridor beyond this room is not frequently traveled," noted Zurel. "I will go first."

Zurel moved to the door and drew his demonic sword. The rest of the team powered up their weapons. Zurel swung the door open to behold nothing except a dimly lit empty corridor that led to a T-shaped junction about 30 feet down. The light in the corridor beyond was far brighter.

"We will need to proceed to the right," said Zurel. "If we are fortunate, the corridor will be clear."

Zurel led the way into a wide corridor. The others followed two at a time behind him. The last two soldiers to reach the junction covered their advance, their weapons trained on the corridor behind them.

"We will need to proceed up to that junction," said Zurel. "Then we bear to the left, then immediately to the right. There we will most assuredly encounter resistance. There is a checkpoint there. It will be helpful if we do not have to fire our weapons before then. If we do…we lose the element of surprise."

They cautiously advanced to the first turn. Zurel, Jonathon, and Jerry had already made the turn when they heard a high-pitched scream followed by two loud particle beam blasts. The advantage of surprise had evaporated like an ice cube in a blast furnace.

"Forward!" hollered Zurel. He turned the next corner to see three confused demon sentries at the end of the corridor. "Come this way, quickly!" he yelled, in the common language of demons.

The demons acted impulsively, running toward Zurel. Within five seconds they had been engulfed by a fireball from Zurel's sword and then blasted apart by particle beam blasts from Jonathon's and Jerry's rifles.

At the rear of the column another firefight had arisen. A large group of demons had been surprised by the human invaders. The first two had been blasted into a scattered mass of bubbling blood, bone, and tissue. The rest had taken shelter beyond a turn in the corridor 40 feet back.

The last two human soldiers in the column took up positions at the turn in the corridor in an attempt to pin down the demons at the far end of the passageway, while the others proceeded with caution toward the field generator.

"The generator is not far," said Zurel to Jonathon. "It lies beyond the four-way junction straight ahead. It is perhaps fifty feet straight ahead and to the right..." He hesitated. "I think."

"You think?" asked Jonathon. "I sure wish you'd been there before."

"However, that is not the case," said Zurel. "I am relatively confident about the information I gave you."

Jonathon and the strike team arrived at the four-way junction only to discover a demon army converging on them from both the left and right passageways, weapons drawn.

"Oh crap!" Jonathon exclaimed, swinging to his left and opening fire at the demons scarcely 20 feet away. His first several shots were fired straight down the corridor. The corridor turned red with vaporized blood. Jerry swung around to the right and opened up on the demons coming in from that side. The eight comrades behind them joined in the firefight.

"The target is straight ahead?" asked one of the soldiers who now stood in the middle of the junction.

"Yes," confirmed Zurel.

The soldier directed his fire into the ceiling about 30 feet down the corridor to the left. The five shots were well placed, bringing a sizable portion of the ceiling crashing down into the corridor, partially blocking it. Unfortunately it also had the effect of blowing a hole in the floor of the level directly above them, offering another point of entry for the demon defenders. This mission was falling apart fast.

Everyone was looking to Jonathon for guidance. He quickly assembled one last-ditch plan. He turned to his soldiers. "The six of you will need to hold this junction," he said to one group, then turned to the others. "Zurel, Jerry, and you two follow me. We're going for the field generator."

They covered the remaining 30 feet to the split in the passageway only to find themselves facing a column of demons closing in from both sides. They were surrounded.

"Hold this junction," said Jonathon to the former captives by his side. He, Zurel, and Jerry rushed at the demon force approaching them from the right passageway, particle rifles blazing. The weapons cut the demons down like wheat before the scythe. Within seconds they were wading through a stream of boiling blood, engulfed within a fog of the same.

They turned a corner to see a kaleidoscopic range of color emanating from a corridor to their left. It was the field generator—it had to be. But between here and there was a span of some 40 feet, and it was rapidly filling with armed and angry demons.

The three opened fire, shooting into the growing mob. The flashes of high energy particles and plasma meeting normal matter lit up the corridor with a brilliance that was well beyond that of normal daylight. Yet this time the fire was coming in both directions. Their beam blasts were returned in the form of super hot fireballs emitted by a dozen demon swords. The three attackers were forced to take cover. Even at that, they were all severely burned by the heat.

Still, despite the pain and shock, they didn't withdraw. They opened fire again in an attempt to clear the wide corridor of the enemy. But it was no good; there were just too many of them and their numbers were growing by the second. They had lost. Jonathon fired several shots into the ceiling 30 feet in front of him. Jerry followed with shots of his own, bringing a large portion of the ceiling down between them and the demons. It gave them the time they needed to withdraw.

They pulled back to the junction where their two fellows had resorted to a similar strategy of bringing down the ceiling in an attempt to delay a vast number of attackers. The whole group withdrew to the next junction. Here they encountered relative calm, for the demons had temporarily withdrawn—no doubt to regroup for a new assault.

Jonathon searched for a plan. He came up with one. He turned to the wall beyond the three-way junction from which they had just come. Could the field generator be just beyond that wall? Perhaps enough firepower could blast through that wall and destroy the generator. It was a long shot, but it was all that he had left. He opened fire. Apparently, some of the others got the message, for they followed his lead. The results of their efforts were impossible to immediately gauge, as the smoke, heat, and intense brilliance hid what lay beyond their view.

"Cease fire!" yelled Jonathon.

The group viewed the results of their concentrated attack. In the end, the results had not been what they'd hoped for. The corridor's walls, floor, and ceiling had been reduced to a mass of red-hot molten rock and metal, yet the power of the nerloft remained. The generator was still intact; all they'd managed to do was cut themselves off from it. However, they had also shut off that avenue of attack.

Jonathon turned to see his two rear guards retreating in his direction. Apparently, they too had been overwhelmed. He reached out with his mind to Lilly, to tell her of the news. They would be gating back. He quickly gathered his forces and tried to open a wormhole. It didn't work.

"You are too close to the generator," said Zurel.

Again they withdrew. Jonathon could hear the commotion in the corridor ahead of them. Things were going from bad to worse. Again he tried to form a wormhole. This time it worked. The group stepped into the mists just seconds before a contingent of demons saturated the entire corridor with fireballs.

The weary fighters emerged into the relative calm of the dungeon. Lilly ran to Jonathon and Jerry.

"You've been hurt!" she cried.

"We'll be OK," said Jonathon, "but we're going to have to fight our way out of here, and we've got to start now. Have you had any trouble here?"

"We've only had two demons come our way," said Christopher. "It was just a minute ago. We took them out. I don't think their leaders have figured it all out yet."

"But they will," said Zurel. "We must withdraw."

"We can't make it all the way to the entrance from here," objected Jonathon, "it's just too far. The four of us are going to have to gate this group somewhere closer to the entrance of this building, somewhere there aren't likely to be demons waiting for us."

"But where?" objected Zurel. "By now, probably all of the demons within this facility will be at arms, combing every hall and cubicle in search of you. They know that you still have to be in the building."

"On my way in I saw a bunch of rooms not far from the entrance that didn't look like they were being used," said Lilly.

"The contemplation and rest cubicles along the main corridor," said Zurel. "There are about twelve of them. But they're all filled with supplies from top to bottom. No, there isn't enough room to gate into them. I don't see any other option…you're going to have to fight your way out of this place."

The four children looked at each other in bewilderment. They had foreseen this as a possibility, yet they'd pushed it into a dark corner in the back of their minds. They could do that no longer.

Another two minutes of planning and they were all set. Jonathon reached for his communicator. As with the first time, the message was short. "We're moving out, plan three, two minutes."

The four children led the way. Christopher couldn't help but draw an analogy between their group advancing into the corridor and Moses leading of the children of Israel out of bondage in Egypt. Their column had a few fighters leading an even larger group of unarmed civilians. Their strategy was to place most of the armed fighters up front, with a smaller number stationed in the back of the procession to defend against attack from the rear.

None of the children were in the mood to compute their odds. From a natural perspective they were not good, even when one took into account their superior weapons. Yes, they had a few tricks up their sleeves, but would they be enough? Time would tell.

They heard weapons firing at the rear of the column. They could only hope that it was their rear guard following their instructions and bringing down the ceiling in the corridor behind them, the corridor that represented the only other access route to their makeshift prison. With

Kenneth Zeigler

it totally collapsed, they would only have to focus on a demon assault from the front—for the moment.

They had only proceeded about 50 feet when a small demon scouting party appeared, running down the spiral stairway before them. They opened fire. Most of the demons were shredded to scattered flesh and bone within a matter of seconds. The group picked up their pace. Heavier resistance was surely only a minute away. They had to make as much forward progress as they could.

They reached the wide, spiral, stone stairway and began the long trip upward. They had gone scarcely 30 feet when they encountered heavy resistance. Apparently, their location had been discovered. They were at a disadvantage. The demons had the high ground. Still, for the moment, the demons couldn't get a clear shot at them. But that wouldn't last, Jonathon was sure of it. Within a few minutes the demons' numbers would grow to sufficient strength that they could step out into the corridor and launch a fireball attack. Then the demons would storm them, overwhelming the humans by sheer force of numbers. The demons had virtually unlimited reinforcements.

Christopher moved to Jonathon's side. "You were speaking of the Battle of Stalingrad."

"I was," confirmed Jonathon. "But as you said, that really isn't an option."

Christopher gazed up the stairway. "We only have about sixty or seventy feet to the ground floor, right?"

"Right," confirmed Jonathon.

"Did you ever hear of the Battle of Anzio?" asked Christopher. "It was the same war, a few months later."

Yes, Jonathon had heard of that battle. It took place in Italy. The allies had been stalemated by the German defenders for months. They decided to go around them and make an amphibious landing to their rear. It had worked—sort of. "You want to bring in men behind them?"

"Yes," confirmed Christopher.

"There are all kinds of rooms along the corridor up there. I saw them," said Lilly. "A group could gate into one or two of those rooms and attack them from the rear. Then you could advance. We could trap and destroy them."

"Whoever went up there would be cut to ribbons," objected Jonathon. "You'd be surrounded by demons."

"It wouldn't matter," assured Lilly. "I'd go in first. You've seen the power of the shield I can project. It can stop a fireball or a sword. Christopher and I would go in there along with the rear guard. We'd tear them up."

"You can't go in there," objected Jonathon.

"I'm not arguing with you again," said Lilly. "We're a team. You'll need to charge when you hear the weapons fire."

There was no time for argument—Lilly wouldn't have it. She and Christopher gated out. Jonathon quickly sensed that they had moved to the rear of the column. He looked up the stairway, which had grown strangely quiet. The calm before the storm? He waited. Then he heard it: massive particle weapon fire from up ahead. In his mind he heard Lilly's voice saying, "Not yet." Then she repeated it.

"Get ready to move!" hollered Jonathon. Then he heard her voice again. "Now, charge!" he yelled.

Jonathon, Jerry, and the rest stormed up the stairway to find the demon forces in disarray. The corridor was ablaze with particle weapon fire and fireballs. Surely the temperature was nearly 200 degrees.

A fireball barely missed Jerry and Jonathon, striking the wall some distance behind them. Yet from the cries of pain that emanated from below, Jonathon knew that many of the former prisoners had been burned by its heat. The thought made him ill.

Jonathon was amazed when he discovered that Jerry had put away his rifle and held a sword. How had he materialized it so fast? He engaged a nearby demon in brutal hand-to-hand combat. Jonathon was even more amazed when Jerry lobbed off the demon's head.

Particle weapons were never intended to be used in such close quarters. Besides the heat and splashes of boiling blood, they were turning bones into high-speed projectiles, which were flying everywhere. Time became a meaningless blur.

Then Jonathon saw Lilly. She held a particle pistol in one hand. The other hand projected a powerful force field, red with the impacts of so many fireballs upon it. Then he saw a demon that appeared different from the others, caught between the forces led by Lilly and Christopher and his own column. Lilly focused upon it.

"You should have listened to me," she cried, pulling back on the trigger.

The demon was blown apart from its midsection. The two parts of the demon writhed in pain, but not for long. Two more shots from Lilly's pistol destroyed both halves.

Twenty seconds later the two forces met.

"What kept you?" asked Lilly, who was still focusing a large part of her might on maintaining the force field.

Lilly moved forward, as did they all, protected by the might of her force field. Many demons discovered the hard way that this field was a potent weapon. To simply come in contact with it was a virtual death sentence. They fled before it, firing what seemed to be futile fireballs into it.

For the better part of a minute the group advanced. Yet the look on Lilly's face spoke of her growing pain and exhaustion. Jonathon was very concerned. Her force field was the only thing standing between their meager complement of humans and a demon force that by now numbered in the tens of thousands.

They reached the broad main corridor. In the distance, still 150 yards away, was the exit and freedom. It was a straight shot. Just beyond that exit Jonathon could see the flashes of particle beams. His great-grandfather and about 100 men and women of the resistance had opened up a second front somewhere just beyond the Hall of Angels.

It was time to break radio silence. Jonathon reached for the communicator. "Grampa, we're fighting our way toward the exit. We're in the main corridor."

There followed a long silence. Jonathon was becoming concerned when he finally heard his great-grandfather's voice.

"Hang in there, Jonathon," said Grampa Bud. "We're in a real nasty fight out here. It isn't the duck shoot I'd hoped it would be. The demons are swarming everywhere. Thousands of them are emerging from the top of the building. We're being forced to pull back; we're taking heavy casualties. We'll draw as many of those demons as we can away from you. I'm sorry, Jonathon, but…"

The connection was abruptly lost. So much for a rescue. Indeed, now Jonathon was concerned for his great-grandfather. Jonathon looked over at Lilly. He saw tears in her eyes; she was crying. It was clear that she was near the end of her endurance. Then one of the things Grampa said echoed again in his mind. There were thousands of demons emerging from the roof? He turned to Christopher, "Try to create a gate to the Ion Desert."

Christopher reached out. To everyone's amazement, a cloud of stars appeared before him. They had a stable wormhole!

"The field is down! Join hands," yelled Jonathon. "Follow Christopher into the gate, unarmed civilians first. Hurry!"

The people didn't have to be told twice. They rushed to Christopher, forming a human chain, and headed into the mists. More and more people joined the beautiful chain that would lead them to freedom.

Jonathon turned to Jerry. "We need a second gate. You'll need to lead them through."

"I'm needed here," objected Jerry.

"I don't have time to argue," said Jonathon. "Do it!"

Jerry nodded, and a second gate opened. He reached out to a woman nearby. She took his hand, then someone else took hers. Within seconds they were on their way out.

Again Jonathon turned to Lilly. The events occurring around her had renewed her spirit. But there was something else: she was crying tears of blood. He could hardly imagine her pain.

"Go," she said, "I've got to stay here and hold them off."

"I'm not going anywhere without you," replied Jonathon. "We're a team, remember?"

Lilly only nodded. All the while, the former captives vanished into the mists. Jonathon watched nervously.

Jonathon grabbed his communicator, hoping that Grampa was listening. "The door is open, we're gating out." He repeated the message three times. Then he put the communicator away and turned to Lilly. Only a few people remained to evacuate. It was time. Jonathon formed a gate to the Ion Desert just a few feet behind Lilly. As the last of their group disappeared into the mists, he took Lilly into his arms and carried her to safety. The mists vanished even as the corridor was filled by a barrage of fireballs.

Jonathon carried Lilly through the mists. She held on tightly. A moment later they stepped into a cheering crowd in the darkened Ion Desert. The four children came together once more. They hugged each other. They had really done it.

Jonathon turned to the others. "Now you are free to go wherever you like. Let's win this war!"

Slowly, the people departed, but not before they gave thanks to their rescuers. Over 20 minutes later, when nearly everyone had gated out, Christa stepped up to the four children.

"I need to leave, but I had to thank you before I did," she said. "I still don't understand exactly how you did it, but I'm forever in your debt." Christa paused. "Why don't you come with me? I'm sure General Washington and the others would enjoy meeting you."

"Thanks, but I think we need to be heading on home," said Jonathon, who still had an arm around Lilly. He looked around to see the others nod in agreement. "You just get that information to the general. Maybe we'll see you a bit later."

"This conflict is almost over," said Lilly in a weak voice. "The battle that you are preparing for will be the final conflict—the defeat of Satan and his armies is certain. Very soon Heaven will be in the hands of the children of God once more."

For a moment Christa seemed confused.

"She's like that," said Christopher. "I, for one, believe her."

"So do I," said Jerry.

Christa smiled. "I'll be sure to include that in my report to the committee." A moment later she vanished into the mists.

"Mission accomplished," said Zurel, stepping out of the darkness. "And what of me?"

"Oh, you're coming with us," said Jonathon. "I'm sure my great-grandparents wouldn't mind if you stayed at their home for a while."

Zurel cocked his head in surprise. "Really?"

"Really," confirmed Lilly, "we wouldn't have it any other way."

"No, you need to stay with us, at least for a while," said Christopher. "We could use a guardian angel."

"They're right," said a Voice out of the darkness.

The group turned to see a Man in a long, white robe walking toward them. It was Jesus. Zurel immediately responded by dropping to his knees before the Son of God. Jesus walked up to him and drew Zurel to his feet.

"Remarkable," Jesus said. "In the end, even after all that you have been through, you chose a path worthy of an angel of God."

"I could do nothing less," replied Zurel. "I will not lift my sword against the children of God any more than I would lift my sword against my Creator. My fight was with Michael, Gabriel, and their minions..." He hesitated, "I suppose that now I am at war with my former master, Satan, as well. I have no place to lay my head."

Jesus placed His hand on the fallen angel's shoulder. "You're wrong, Zurel. Go with them, you will be welcomed in their home. They are your friends; you aren't alone. You may even count Me as your Friend. I tell you this: when the day of your judgment comes, and it is near at hand for all of the angels, these children will stand at your side, as will I."

Jesus then turned to the children. "Well done, all of you. You showed exemplary faith, stepping into the Valley of the Shadow of Death, knowing that you might not find a way out. The four of you have been faithful in this thing, and our Father will, in time, put you in charge of even greater things, things you cannot yet imagine. But for now, go home and rest. For you, the war is over."

Jesus turned again to Zurel. He placed His hand upon the fallen angel's shoulder once more. Almost immediately, a wondrous transformation occurred. Zurel glowed all over in a soft, blue light. In that moment, he was transformed. His bat wings melted away to be replaced with white-feathered wings, and his raiments became as those of an angel of light. "This is the appearance that you should assume hence-forth. Now go with the children. For now, you shall be their guardian angel."

Zurel looked upon himself in wonder. "Thank You, Lord, for the kindness You have shown to me."

Jesus smiled but said nothing.

The children gathered around Jesus and gave Him a big hug. Their Lord's smile grew even more.

"Thank You, Lord," said each of the children as they gated home. Jonathon was the last to leave, taking Zurel's hand and vanishing into the mists.

Jesus stood there alone for a few seconds. His smile never dimmed. "Blessed are the children," He said, "for it is they who shall bring the words and blessings of our Father to the universe."

With those words Jesus too stepped into the mists. Quiet and solitude returned to the Ion Desert.

The children emerged from the mists, arriving once more at the place where this whole adventure had begun. The sound of the pounding surf was overwhelmed by the sounds of cheers. Grampa Bud and Grandma Gladys emerged from the darkness to welcome the children home. They were followed by more than 100 men and women of the resistance.

"They're all safe," said Jonathon to his great-grandmother.

"It was the hand of God that saved you," said Grandma Gladys.

She got no disagreement from any of those present. It was a time for celebration, and that celebration continued into the morning light. To many, the presence of Zurel was a concern, at least initially. Yet the words of Jesus resonated in their hearts. He had spoken of this strange being as a friend. None would be so foolish as to question it. So Zurel would also be accepted as a friend in their midst. After all, he was an angel of God.

Grandma and Grampa even found a room for their new guardian angel. For them, the war was now over.

It was morning as the children finally got into bed. The next three days passed very uneventfully. Neither demons nor angels crossed their skies. The children did what most children do when they're happy—they played. They wandered through the forest without fear and spent many happy hours on the beach with their new angelic friend.

For the first time in his existence, Zurel found time to relax. He even managed to become moderately proficient on a surfboard. There was something strangely incongruous about an angel riding a surfboard. *Wipeout* was not a term in his vocabulary. When the board got away from him, he simply took to the sky. Then he'd land in the shallows to retrieve his board. Somehow that didn't seem quite fair, but no one was about to say anything about it. They were just happy to see him having fun.

At the end of the third day the news came: the war was over. Human and angelic forces had decisively defeated the armies of Satan. Satan and a few survivors of his once-great army had fled through the gate in the City of Zion to Earth. Most of the other demons had either been physically destroyed or captured and imprisoned.

What they had accomplished in the City of Sarel had set the stage for that victory. Their mission had been successfully accomplished. But what now? What would the Father have them do next? There was only one way to find out, wasn't there? It was time to return to Zion, to visit with the Father once more.

The following day, the children and their newfound friend and guardian angel, Zurel, set out for the Holy City of Zion, not quite knowing what to expect. They materialized at the great city's eastern gate. They were amazed to discover that a state of calm had returned to the great metropolis. People were coming and going as they always had. All around them blue mists were fading and materializing, as citizens of Heaven passed into and out from them. Even the sections of the wall that had been damaged had been restored to their former glory.

Yet they sensed a strange mixture of spirits in the air that was hard to explain. There was a spirit of joy that was somehow more wonderful than they had ever felt before. Yet they felt a spirit of mourning as well. The children were at a total loss to explain it.

They passed through the magnificent archway and into the walled city beyond. They marveled to discover that the rubble that had littered the streets but a couple weeks earlier had been cleared. Indeed, there was no damage visible as far as the eye could see.

The streets were much as they had been before the conflict. People stopped to talk, browsed the shops where wonderful things were given and traded but never sold, and made their way into and out of the great libraries. People seemed to be interested in catching up on the latest news—and there was a lot of it.

The children were particularly interested in reaching the Holy Place. Many people around them seemed to be of like mind and were heading in that direction. The tense excitement within them seemed to magnify the distance.

Slowly but surely a story of incredible bravery was emerging. It had been one woman's entry into the city at the height of the battle that had turned the tide. She had set free humans and angels captured by the demons and awaiting transport to their prison by breaking the shackles that had bound them. She had traveled all the way to the Holy Place to bring the children of God a message—that the power to defeat Satan and his angels was theirs. And they had latched onto that hope and discovered the power within her words. In the end, they had manifested the same gifts that the children had known these past few weeks. With those gifts came the end of Satan's hopes of victory.

Yet, as always, with great power came great responsibility. The sons and daughters of God were children no longer. There were many things that their Father, in His love, had shielded them from. For one, He had shielded them from the hurtful things of their lives on Earth. For the most part, they could not remember the people or events that may have brought sadness to their hearts. They could not remember those who had been with them on Earth but would never be part of their existence again; they had no recollection of their loved ones in Hell.

But as the partaking of the fruit of the knowledge of good and evil had opened the eyes of Adam and Eve to that aspect of existence, so had the Father opened the eyes of His children to all of the events of their own existence. He offered it to all who would accept it, and many did. His Firstborn had such knowledge. The time had come for His other children to leave childhood behind and become adult sons and daughters.

For these four children of Heaven, the granting of such knowledge was not necessary. Jerry and Jonathon had no experiences on Earth to remember. Christopher and Lilly had lived on Earth, but strangely had always had full recollection of that experience. Still, they could comprehend the magnitude of the burden that so many of the citizens of Heaven were now accepting.

As they approached the Holy Place, Zurel came to a stop. "It is not for me to enter into this place," he said, gazing out at the millions of humans before him. "This place is for the children of the Father, not for His servants. I shall await your return here."

"That may be awhile," cautioned Jonathon.

"Time means little to angels," Zurel replied with a smile. "Take whatever time you need. When you return, I will still be here."

The children moved on into the Holy Place. Although the great crisis had passed, the number of people here in the presence of God had not diminished. If anything, that number had grown. But there was more to it than that: the atmosphere of this place had changed. There was so much weeping in Heaven today. And the children knew only too well the cause of that sadness.

They only traveled a short distance into the Holy Place before they came to a halt. They sat in a circle upon the glistening floor. They didn't say a word to each other, but closed their eyes and opened their hearts. Then they waited. They didn't have to wait long. Within seconds, the din of voices of those around them faded, as did the light.

Jonathon opened his eyes first. The group still sat in a circle, though now they sat in that long, familiar hallway within the home of the Father. "Hey, we're here!" he announced, rising to his feet.

Lilly opened her eyes and reached out to Jonathon. He drew her gently to her feet. The others opened their eyes and gazed around in wonder. A smile came to every face.

"I was really hoping that the Father would bring us back here," said Christopher, who quickly joined Jonathon and Lilly.

"So was I," said Jerry, who made his way first to the window, ten feet away. "Hey, take a look."

The others walked to the window. Below them, as far as the eye could see, was a world, a darkened planet of clouds, which was almost continually being illuminated by strikes of lightning dancing between the mists. The storms stretched out to the distant, curved limb of this mighty world. To the left was a great bow of light, where night met day. Beyond, the clouds took on hues ranging from white to pale yellow below a narrow bow of blue sky that gradually faded into the blackness of space.

"It's a gas giant planet, I think," noted Jonathon. "My Grandma Gladys has told me all about these. There is no land under those clouds, only more clouds."

"Interesting," said Christopher, scanning the vista below. "I guess Father moves His house around a lot. It's sort of like a big RV in the sky."

Jonathon looked over at Jerry and smiled. Yep, it was the kind of comment that only Christopher would come up with. He turned his gaze to the open double door down the hallway on the right. Bright light was streaming from that room. "I think the Father is probably waiting for us."

"We shouldn't keep Him waiting," suggested Lilly.

With those words, the group made their way toward the partially open door. Reaching it, Jonathon looked in. He was astounded to discover not the library he remembered from the previous trip, but an alpine meadow filled with yellow flowers, cloaked here and there with thin wisps of morning mist. In the background were tall snow-covered peaks; beyond, a forest of tall pine trees.

The sun hung not far above the distant mountains, and in terrestrial skies above it was a crescent world many times the size of the moon. It was a world of white and faint yellow banded clouds intermixed with zones of blue. Still higher in the sky was another much smaller crescent and then another, all perfectly aligned. The lower of the two crescents had a yellowish hue while the smaller, higher one was light gray.

Standing in the meadow some 50 feet away was the Father, dressed in a white shirt, white trousers, and white shoes.

"Come in, My beloved children, I've been expecting you," He said. Upon His countenance was a radiant smile. "You have all done very well, and I am most proud of you."

The children stepped into the meadow. Turning around, Jonathon saw a most unusual sight. He could clearly see the double door through which they had just passed hanging in midair among the flowers of the meadow. Beyond the door he could still see the corridor of the home. A few seconds later, the door closed on its own and then vanished from sight.

"Wow," remarked Christopher, looking around at the wondrous scene, "it's like the moon of Yadith."

"The moon of Yadith?" asked Lilly, gazing about.

"I suspect that it has something to do with the movie *Star Wars*," deduced Jerry, "it usually does."

The Father laughed. "You are very close to the truth, Christopher. As you have surmised, we are no longer in Heaven, nor are we on Earth." He stretched out His arms. "This humble world is a moon circling a giant planet, which in turn circles a star not so far from Earth." The Father motioned toward the great crescent in the sky. "Scientists on Earth know of this world. They call it Forty-seven Ursae Majoris b, but the people of this world call it Sedron."

"There are people on this world?" asked Christopher, perking up. "Father, please...tell me what they're like."

Again the Father laughed. "Why, they're like you, Christopher, bright and inquisitive, formed in My image. They too are My children, for I breathed the breath of life into them as well. They are your brothers and sisters, your younger brothers and sisters. They are not nearly so advanced as you are. They are still quite primitive in their ways. They are just now learning how to farm this rich land. I have sent My angels to look over them, to protect them, as I did with your ancestors."

"Hopefully, the angels do a better job this time," said Christopher. "The last time they made a bit of a mess of it. I mean, they got sort of fresh with the girls."

"Christopher!" said Jonathon in frustration. He was surprised to see the Father nod in agreement.

"Very true," said the Father, whose smile never dimmed. "That mistake will not be repeated. Still, hard as it may be to believe, even that was necessary. You see, I have plans for those angels, those dark angels that made that mistake. They too have a part to play in My plan."

"But why are we here?" asked Jonathon.

"Because I am going to tell you the answer to a great mystery," replied the Father. "It is a wonderful thing that I have told no others beyond My firstborn Son, and He in turn was instructed to do the same. That secret, in part, has to do with this place. For the moment, it must remain a secret among us. Are you able to keep a secret for a while?"

"Oh yes," replied Christopher.

The others quickly agreed.

Again God laughed. "Very well then, here is the secret. It is the answer to this question: What is the ultimate purpose of humankind? Wise ones have sought the answer to this question for thousands of years." He looked to Christopher. "You spoke wisdom beyond your years when you said that Heaven is not a rest home in the sky—it isn't.

"First, Heaven is a place where you can be perfected, a place where you can become as My firstborn Son. It will take time, much time, but you will attain that goal. On that day, your spirit will become very much attuned to Mine, and those who see you shall see Me within you. That is what My Son meant when He said that those who have seen Him have seen Me. The day is coming when those who see you shall see Me."

The children were speechless—with the exception of Christopher.

"Oh, Father, I want to be like Jesus so much! I want people to be able to see You in me."

The Father placed His loving hand upon Christopher. "I know you do, and it makes Me very happy. The day will come when that will be true."

"I know that we all feel that way. I do," confirmed Jerry.

"Nothing would make me happier," said Lilly.

Jonathon nodded in agreement.

"Well, you have already started the journey," announced the Father, "and it is a good start. In freeing the hostages taken by the demons, you became agents of My will, as did Zurel. I assure you that on the day of his judgment, that act shall be taken into account. But let us focus on the four of you. There will be obstacles for each of you to overcome along the way, but you shall overcome them.

"You see, your adventure hasn't ended; it is only beginning. The final adventure of your journey will be had in this place, with these people. They know that I exist—their hearts tell them that. Many of them truly love Me. They also know the difference between good and evil, but they will need guidance that My angels cannot provide them. Only My elder sons and daughters can."

"Oh please…send us," begged Christopher.

"Yes, Father, we want to do it," confirmed Jonathon.

"Those are My intentions," confirmed the Father. "When you are ready, I will send you here to teach them." The Father paused. "But neither you nor they are ready just yet. I will send you here when the moment is right, as I sent My Son to your world. You see, you, the children of Earth, were the first, but My children are more numerous than the grains of sand upon all of the beaches of your Earth. I shall send you, the elder brothers and sisters, to teach all of My other children scattered across the universe. It is a great responsibility, and, in time, you shall be up to the challenge. This is the destiny of My children—to spread the good news across the universe."

"It's wonderful," said Jonathon.

"It is," confirmed the Father, "but you must prepare yourselves first. Each of you will know what it is that you must do. For the moment you will be parting company with the others, but when the time is right you will come together once more."

"Father, look," said Lilly, pointing to the edge of the forest.

The group looked to see about a dozen animal skin-clad people gathered there, staring at the mysterious visitors. Though the children were the better part of 100 yards away, with their heavenly vision they could see these people in remarkable detail. They appeared just as human as the young people did. They were not some sort of stooped primitives but stood upright, gazing at the wondrous people in white before them. They appeared to be no older than the four friends—little more than children.

Lilly hesitated, and then waved to them. All of the children of Heaven did. They were a bit surprised when the group at the edge of the forest exchanged the greeting.

The Father smiled. "Now you know what these people look like."

"Can we go over and meet them?" asked Christopher.

"Not today," said the Father. "It is time for you to go back. You have a journey to begin, but I promise you that it will lead back here."

Before the children a blue mist filled with sparkling stars appeared. The Father motioned toward it as He vanished from view. It was time to go. The group gave a final wave to the children at the edge of the forest. It was too bad that they couldn't get to know them yet. Then they stepped into the mists and vanished.

CHAPTER 9

WHEN THE CHILDREN OPENED THEIR eyes, they were in the Holy Place once more. They rose to their feet.

"So what now?" asked Christopher.

"You go to study with Professor Faraday," said Jerry. "You learn all about the universe around us and the rules that make it work. Am I right?"

"Yes, I guess so," replied Christopher, "and you?"

"I really don't know," admitted Jerry. "Maybe I'll go home." He hesitated. "No, home will never be the same. I can't go back to fishing—not now, not after all that we've been through. There has to be more to my life than that."

"There is," said Lilly, "but there is something that you must do first, something that you must know."

"Like what?" objected Jerry.

"I don't know," admitted Lilly, "but I think you do."

Jerry was silent for some time. All eyes were on him. "Yes, I think I do. I think there is someone I need to forgive."

The others looked at Jerry. Apparently, they didn't understand. Only Christopher nodded in approval.

"And what about you, Jonathon?" asked Jerry. "Where will you go now?"

Jonathon shook his head. "I don't know."

"You will," said Lilly, placing her arm around him.

"Yeah, eventually," said Jonathon, "but for the moment, I suppose I'll continue living with Grandma and Grampa. They still have a lot to teach me." He looked to Lilly. "Maybe you could live with us, at least for a while."

Lilly hesitated. "I'd like to, Jonathon; really, I would. But I'm confused."

Jonathon looked at Lilly in amazement. "You...confused?"

"Yes," confirmed Lilly. "I know that there is a woman, one I've never met except in my dreams, who has things to teach me. I know it. She calls to me. I feel like she is very close, and I know I have to follow her."

"If anyone else had told me that, I'd think they were a little bit touched," said Jonathon, looking into Lilly's eyes, "but coming from you...well, that's different."

Lilly giggled and squeezed Jonathon tight. "I'll take that as a compliment, noble knight."

Jonathon blushed slightly but said nothing more.

It was time to move on. The group moved toward the edge of the Holy Place. They agreed to return to the mansion by the sea. In the morning, Christopher would gather up his things and go to the home of Professor Faraday. In reality, he would be arriving there almost two weeks late. Still, he was certain that Professor Faraday and his wife would understand.

They were almost to the edge of the Holy Place when Lilly heard someone calling her name. She turned to see a slender, dark-haired woman in a long, frilly dress.

"It's you!" exclaimed Lilly. "I know you—you're Elizabeth!"

"Hello, Lilly," said Elizabeth, taking Lilly by the hand. "It is delightful to at last meet you in person. The Father told me that I would find you here."

"Bless you, Sister Elizabeth," said a young man, approaching the group. "What you have done for us has been a true inspiration."

"Tis the Father and our Lord Jesus who are to be blessed," said Elizabeth.

The young man nodded and moved on. Elizabeth turned once more to Lilly.

"I have heard of the contribution that the four of you made in saving so many of our brothers and sisters," said Elizabeth. "It was an act of great bravery."

At that moment Christopher put it all together. "You're the one I've heard so much about, the one who made her way through the battle lines, setting the prisoners free. You showed the people how to harness the power of the Father's Holy Spirit to defeat the demons."

"I may have been the one who used the power, but the source of that power was not within me," replied Elizabeth. She gazed into Christopher's eyes and smiled. "But you too have harnessed that power. I am not so sure that you didn't discover it before me. That was an act of great faith and courage."

"You seem to know a great deal about us," noted Jerry.

"One of your number possesses the same gift," replied Elizabeth, turning to Jonathon.

"That may be," replied Jonathon, "but you yourself seem to possess all of the abilities that we possess as a group."

"That is why the Father told you that you must act as a group," said Elizabeth.

"And I am to learn from you all of these things," deduced Lilly. "I am to become your student. That is, if you will accept me."

"That is the will of the Father," replied Elizabeth. "I gladly accept you, little sister. I have lived alone for far too long. I have already made room in my home for you. Once we leave the city, that is where we shall go. The Father would have me tutor you and teach you those things that I have learned during the many centuries that I have been here."

Lilly nodded and then turned to Jonathon. "I'm afraid that I will be leaving you, at least for the time being. I'll need to gather up my things from your great-grandparents' home, and then I'll be on my way."

"But we will get to see each other from time to time," replied Christopher, "at least I hope so."

"Of course," replied Elizabeth. "The four of you are still a team, even though, for now, you will be studying in far-flung places. You will always be welcome in my home."

The group departed the Holy Place, met up again with Zurel, and traveled through the city. They spoke of what had already happened and what was to come. They spoke of the goodness of the Father. When they reached the Great Hall of Records, Jerry stopped.

"You go on," he said, looking to the great crystal structure. "I have something to do here, and it may take me awhile."

"Do you need help?" asked Jonathon. "I am most familiar with the cataloging structure of the books here. I'd be happy to assist you."

Jerry smiled. "Thank you, Jonathon, but this is a personal thing. It's something that I sort of have to do on my own. I have to do this before I take another step."

Christopher nodded. "Let me know how it all turns out."

"I will," said Jerry. "I'll try to catch up with the rest of you a bit later."

As the rest of the group headed on down the avenue, Jerry took a deep breath and made his way toward the main door of the Hall of Records. Jonathon had been right: he did know this library far better than Jerry did. He might have been of great help to him. Jerry thought back. He had a lesson on how to use this place a long time ago. Did he still remember enough to make use of it?

Jerry stepped through the great doors. This place was almost empty. Not too many people visited this place. Even now that the eyes of the people of Heaven had been opened, they seemed reluctant to come here. Jerry cleared his mind. He focused upon his birth mother. He didn't even know her name—that was, until now. The name came into his mind as if it had always been there: Leona Stahl. Her book was on the third level, aisle 34, section 7. He was on the move up the spiral stairway.

One idea after another rushed through his mind. He had always assumed that he would never see her here in Heaven and that her life was none of his concern, but he didn't think that way anymore. He had forgiven her, and now he was searching for a way to rescue her from herself, to bring her into the family of God. There just had to be something that he could do for her. She couldn't be that old, perhaps in her early to mid-40s. Every day middle-aged people gave their hearts to the Lord. Why couldn't she?

He would look into her book. Yes, that is what he would do. He would first evaluate her life situation, then go from there. He could go to the Father, perhaps speak to a guardian angel. There had to be options.

He reached the third level and made his way toward aisle 34. All the while his mind was working. Here was aisle 34. He turned. He found section 7, then row 3. He scanned the bindings. Then he found her book. *Leona Stahl* was printed in bold white letters upon its coal black binding. No, perhaps he wasn't remembering the system properly—that must be it. But he *was* remembering it properly. This was a *black* book. His birth mother was already dead and in Hell.

In his most terrible dreams he hadn't expected this. The Father had wanted him to find this book; he was sure of it. But why? If his birth mother was beyond all hope, beyond all redemption, why did he have to know this?

He hesitated, then pulled the book from its place in the shelf. He sat down on the floor and opened it to the first page. Almost immediately the words printed upon that page were transformed into an image. He was witnessing his own mother's birth in a hospital in Ottawa, Canada. For the first time he saw his grandmother and her newborn child.

He moved ahead to try and understand the life of the mother he had never known. He became witness to his mother's first steps and her first words. He watched as the family moved to Ohio. He saw his mother's first day in school. She was so cute with her red hair and freckles. It explained a lot about him.

His grandparents weren't particularly religious. They belonged to a church but rarely attended. He watched his mother grow from a child who was fair of face, to a pretty girl, to a beautiful young woman. She was a good student and a member of a thing called the student council. She was a very popular girl.

But all was not well in the Stahl home. His mother's father was a truck driver and was on the road sometimes for weeks at a time. There were rumors and suspicions about his extramarital affairs when he was away from home. Then one day he simply left, abandoning his wife and his teenage daughter. Leona's home life, which on the surface had seemed stable, began to crumble. Her parents' divorce gave closure and child support gave some financial stability, but the lives of Leona and her mother were on the rocks. Leona's mother struggled to keep their home, but her daytime job as a secretary and her evening job as a waitress barely paid the bills. Leona tried to help too, working after school at the local supermarket, but they were losing ground.

That was when Leona met Tom. Tom was a salesman at his father's large and very successful new car dealership. He was 22 and she was barely 17, but it didn't matter. She was swept off of her feet with talk of love and romance. Tom had the resources to take her out on expensive and elaborate dates. Even Leona's mother approved. After all, Tom came from an affluent and well-respected family. He had the wherewithal to take good care of Leona.

One thing led to another. Four months after their relationship started, Leona found herself pregnant. Still, she wasn't concerned. After all, the father of her child was Tom. She would become Mrs. Tom Sanderson and live happily ever after. Sadly, it wasn't to be. Only too late she discovered that all she was to him was some action on the side. He had other more serious interests—a fiancée who was more his age and social class. He could hardly afford to have his life ruined by an underage teenager from the wrong side of the tracks.

Still, he had been playing with fire. Leona was an underage minor, and her mother had every intention of bringing this little fact to the attention of the authorities. His little fling could well earn him a conviction as a sex offender and some time in the gray bar hotel. Clearly, an arrangement, a financial one, had to be made.

Tom's parents agreed to fork out a considerable sum of money to Leona's family in compensation for their son's indiscretion. However, there was a condition. Tom Sanderson could ill afford to have Leona coming back to him at some future point demanding child support. His affair with her had to remain a secret from his fiancée. True, there could be a clause in their legal agreement that would forbid Leona's mother from doing this, but that wouldn't prevent Leona from doing it herself when she turned 18. There was really only one solution: the child would have to become a nonentity; it would have to be aborted and soon. After all, Leona was already well into her fourth month.

Leona was devastated by the prospects of sweeping this first child out of her life. But at her mother's urging, she relented. The settlement would pay off the mortgage and the credit cards and give Leona a start toward college, a chance at a new life.

Leona was promised that it would be a simple procedure. It was called partial birth abortion, a new procedure that was often used in the case of a late-term pregnancy. Jerry witnessed it all in that sterile operating room within the federally funded abortion clinic. The doctor and nurse were so comforting to his mother even as they proceeded to kill him. He witnessed his mother's own grief as the procedure was concluded.

Yet there was something else. For the first time, he remembered the terrible pain of the procedure, a pain beyond imagination. He remembered the confusion. It had been a new sensation for him. Up until then, all that he had known was a sort of bliss, a sense of quiet awakening, a sense of becoming something new. Yet as quickly as the pain began, it had ended. In that moment, he had been born into a new life, the life he knew now.

The procedure ended, and after an hour or so, Leona was on her way home. She cried almost the entire way.

The intense pain and fever began some time late that night. Leona was rushed by her mother to the emergency room. Then she was placed in the intensive care unit. By noon the following day, Leona had joined him in death. Yet they would never be together. Even as her spirit rose from her body, a dark violet vortex formed within the hospital room before her—an ethereal corridor to another realm.

The nurses couldn't see his mother's spirit and her perilous plight as she tried to escape the vortex that was in the process of drawing her into its dark depths. They were too busy trying to resuscitate the young patient before them.

A few seconds later, Leona vanished into the swirling clouds of the vortex. Jerry followed her helpless, ethereal plunge as she hurtled through the growing darkness. He could almost feel her pain as the surging electricity coursed all around her.

A moment later she seemed to materialize in a stone corridor, her back to the wall. Before her was the brightness of what appeared to be a great arena. Leona was terrified—Jerry could feel her fear—yet she began to walk forward; indeed, she couldn't seem to resist. She stepped into the vast, white marble arena. A wall that was perhaps ten feet high separated her from a vast number of spectators all robed in white who sat in ever-ascending rows of seats beyond the wall. They must surely have numbered in the tens of thousands.

Beyond the spectators was a series of tall, white columns that encircled the arena and towered toward the stormy sky. Yet the most spectacular sight here was the radiant Being who sat upon a great white throne before her. He was a true giant robed in white, and His eyes were focused upon her. Dressed only in her hospital gown, Leona was hardly prepared for such a grand meeting. An angel approached Leona and quickly took her by the arm.

"Come, child," he urged, drawing her toward the great Being before her.

All the while Jerry walked by her side. Yes, he knew this place; he had been here once. This was the Great Judgment Hall. It was in this place that he had officially proclaimed his love for the Father and His Son. He had been so happy that day. On that glorious day he had truly entered into the Kingdom of Heaven. He recognized the Being before him all right: He was the Father. Yet on this day He seemed different. He was stern, even sad.

"Let the book be opened," He said in a thundering voice.

And it was. Leona saw her entire life unfold before her. Throughout most of it she remained silent. It wasn't until the end, when she saw the birth and immediate death of her son, that she broke down into tears.

"Does Leona Stahl's name appear in the Lamb's Book of Life?" asked the Father, turning to an angel who stood at a crystal podium, upon which sat a thick book.

It took only a few seconds before the response came. "No, Lord, her name is not here."

The Father turned to Leona. "Why did you not turn to My Son? He was there for you if only you had asked. Now I must cast you from My sight into outer darkness and into the hands of Satan and his angels."

"I deserve it!" cried Leona. "I have killed my own son."

"Do not cry on his account," said the Father in a kind voice. "Before you are cast out into that place, I wish you to know that your son is safe and in Heaven. He will grow up in a good home with loving parents, who shall train him in My ways. He will grow up to become a fine young man. He shall set the captives free and bring hope to the hopeless, for he is special, a child of Heaven, and you had a part in bringing him to be. He is your hope." There was a pause. "Now go, child—to meet your own destiny."

Leona wiped the tears from her eyes. "Thank You for looking after my son."

The Father didn't reply. Leona was escorted by the angel toward an arching passageway that led out of the arena. The passageway ended in a sort of circular portal framed by a silvery ring of metal. The portal emptied into a void of darkness.

"Take my hand," said the angel.

Leona did as she was told. A moment later the angel took her in his arms and flew into the abyss, plunging ever downward. Jerry remained behind. He peered into the darkness. The angel and his mother were nowhere to be seen.

"I thought I'd find you here," said a voice from behind him.

Jerry turned to see Christopher standing there. "I thought you left with the others."

"I did," confirmed Christopher. "That was two days ago."

Jerry looked at Christopher incredulously. He quickly wiped the tears from his eyes. "Two days? It doesn't seem like it's been that long."

"You sort of lose track of time when you get into these books," said Christopher. "Some people even lose control. They can't figure out where the books end and their reality begins. They lose their way and find that they can't get out. When you didn't come back I sort of figured that was what happened."

"Thank you for coming back for me," said Jerry.

Christopher stepped forward and looked into the portal. "I didn't think you'd want to go beyond this point, Jerry. You don't really want to know what happened to her. That's why I stopped you. Actually, I stopped the flow of time in the book." Christopher paused. "I guess she wasn't the way you thought she was."

Jerry shook his head. "No, she wasn't. I'll never forget her. I feel so sorry for her."

"Life on Earth is tough, tougher than we realize," said Christopher. "Are you ready to go home?"

Jerry gazed into the darkness of the portal. Then he turned to Christopher. "I probably should, but I can't, not yet. I have to know what happened to her."

Christopher looked at his friend in shock. "Why would you want to do that? There's nothing you can do for her. You know that."

"But I have to know," insisted Jerry.

Christopher nodded. "Then I'm going with you. You shouldn't do this alone."

"I appreciate you going with me," said Jerry.

"I'm taking control of this," said Christopher. "She could have ended up stuck in a holding cell for days before they finally got around to dealing with her. It's just the way things work down there. So we're not going in there in real time. There is no point in you waiting there with her for days. It would only upset you needlessly. We're going in there to find out exactly what happened. So we're just going in there long enough to get the facts."

"Sounds like you've done this before," observed Jerry.

"I have," confirmed Christopher. "Now you know. The angels didn't know about it. They wouldn't have allowed it, but I did it anyway. You see, I had to know what it was like in Hell."

"That's why you took so much interest in the story of Chris and Serena Davis," said Jerry.

"Not exactly," replied Christopher. "It was the story of Chris and Serena that got me thinking. It led me to go on my first journey to Hell using the books. I'm probably the best guide you're going to find. But understand, I'm in control; we leave when I say we leave."

"OK, fine," confirmed Jerry. "When do we start?"

"We start now," replied Christopher.

Within a second, they found themselves plunging into a netherworld of darkness. They were swept through what looked like a huge rocky tunnel in space, which led to the fiery world of Hell—the lone planet of the red star Kordor. Within another few seconds they stood before a tiny 8-by-8 foot cell, one of apparently thousands of cells along a dismal and musty stone corridor. The entrance to the cell was guarded by a crude set of heavy, metal bars, and within that cell was Jerry's mother, still dressed in her hospital gown. She stood with her hands firmly gripping the bars, gazing out into the corridor. Her dusty cell contained no furniture, not even a bed, and the air was filled with the cries and moans of the prisoners of this terrible realm. The corridor in which they stood was illuminated by a series of huge crystals imbedded in the ceiling that glowed with sallow amber light.

"It looks like most of the cells in this block are already filled," noted Christopher, looking about. "It won't be long before the demons arrive to harvest them."

"Harvest them?" asked Jerry.

"Yes," said Christopher. "The angels bring the condemned souls to this place and lock them into the cells. When all of the cells of a block are filled, the demons come to harvest them. They first prepare them, dressing and shackling them appropriately. Then they may take a soul off to Satan himself, if the case of that particular individual interests him. But more often they are taken to their eternal fate, and that is determined by their crimes."

"Their crimes?" asked Jerry. "My mother is not a criminal."

"Anyone who sins falls short of the glory of God. You know that," replied Christopher. "I saw some of your mother's life. Yes, terrible things happened to her; she was treated very badly, but sin is sin. Without Jesus we're all lost."

Jerry only nodded.

"We need to move forward in time," announced Christopher.

Again Jerry nodded silently.

The scene around them changed. The vast dungeon itself was engulfed in dense mists. Only Leona's cell was visible. Leona was surrounded by three demons. Her eyes were damp with tears and her wrists had been shackled behind her back. She no longer wore the hospital gown, but rather a skimpy, ragged, gray top and a sort of loincloth, which was narrow at the sides and somewhat longer in front and back. Its tattered fabric barely covered her more intimate areas. The demons roughly escorted the barefoot woman from her cell and into a dark vortex that had formed in what used to be the corridor. Christopher and Jerry followed.

Within seconds they were transported to a hot, barren plain. The boys had a momentary sense of disorienting vertigo, but it passed quickly. They scanned their surroundings; they were alone, at least they appeared to be. Yet all about them they beheld an astonishing sight: thousands upon thousands of 6-foot-tall metal statues arranged with geometric precision as far as the eye could see. Each sat upon a light gray marble base and was set about 20 feet from the next.

The bloated, red sun hung rather low in the sky over the distant hills. The dry air was filled with the odor of sulfur and what smelled like hot tar, and it reverberated with the sound of crashing waves. The boys quickly identified the source of the loud sound and offending odor. They stood near the edge of a high cliff overlooking a turbulent, stormy sea. But this was no sea of water—it was a sea of black, shiny oil smashing again and again into the rocks of the cliff below them. Flames of yellow and blue fire roared across the heaving surface of the sea, surging into tall, raging pillars of fire in some places. The statues continued right to the edge of the cliff. Indeed, some seemed as if they were on the threshold of tumbling off.

"The Great Sea of Fire," said Christopher, turning to his friend. "It covers nearly half of the surface of this world called Hell. Mostly it covers the dark side. You see, Hell is a planet circling a small red star in the midst of outer darkness. One side of Hell has perpetual day; the other side lies in eternal night. This place is in a sort of moderate zone between the intense cold of the dark side and the terrible heat of the light side.

"At least that is a break for your mother. Under the midday sun, the temperature of Hell is over three hundred degrees. On the dark side it could easily be a hundred degrees below. It seems to be about ninety here." Christopher continued to survey their surroundings. "But these statues…this is something I never saw before. I have no idea what these are about."

"Where are the demons and my birth mother?" asked Jerry, looking around.

Christopher said, "I thought we may need a little time to sort things out, so I did a little trick with the book. Most people don't realize that you can do it. You felt the dizziness when we arrived? I brought us here about five minutes before the demons will arrive with your mother. It will give us a moment to figure out where we are before things get crazy."

"Good idea," said Jerry, walking away from the cliff and toward one of the nearby statues. To say the least, the metal statue was crude, lacking any detailed facial or body features beyond the basic curves. Based upon that observation, Jerry figured that this was a representation of a woman. The next one in the row looked like a male figure, at least from where he was standing. They had no arms. He assumed that these statues depicted persons with their arms behind their backs. The legs were represented as a single column and flared out at the bottom where the legs met the stone pedestal, like an old style chess piece.

One of the stranger features of these statues was the large circular stone basin attached to the front of the base upon which they sat. A trough cut into the stone base ran from a hole in the front of the metal statue to the basin. What was this for?

Jerry knocked on the side of the statue; it resounded with a dull, hollow ring. It wasn't solid, but what was inside? This statue reminded Jerry of a sarcophagus, a coffin, somewhat similar to those of Egyptian pharaohs of old. He walked around it. It had three sets of heavy hinges on one side and a barely visible seam that appeared to divide the statue vertically in two. Clearly, this thing was intended to open up, but how? He followed the seam to the other side of the statue. Here he saw some sort of odd metal dial just behind the seam. There were strange markings on it. "What do you make of this?" asked Jerry.

"I don't know," replied Christopher, walking up to the statue. He glanced at the hinges, then turned his attention to the dial. "Those symbols are angelic. I believe it is the dialect of the demons. Jonathon is the real expert on this stuff." He paused and then pointed at the inscribed symbols. "I believe this word means *open*, and this one is *close*."

Once more he hesitated as his finger moved on to the third word, a word inscribed deeper into the metal than the others. "I'm not sure about this one. The written demonic language is different from the angelic in so many ways. I just don't know, but I wouldn't mess with that dial. Actually, it probably wouldn't move anyway."

Christopher moved on to the next statue, while Jerry continued to examine this one. About half a minute passed. Jerry scanned the scene more carefully. Some of the statues depicted men. But now that he took a closer look, most of them were crude depictions of women. He was at a loss to explain that inequity.

"Jerry, come over here, quick!"

Jerry practically ran to the statue Christopher was pointing at to find a trickle of blood flowing from the base of the statue and into the trough. The basin at the end of the trough was lined with dried and clotted blood that had apparently entered it through the trough. Apparently the statue had been dripping blood off and on for a long time. Jerry looked to his left to discover a large blackbird drinking what appeared to be blood from one of the nearby basins. Then Jerry heard a muffled moan from within the metal statue before him.

He discovered that the dial of this statue had been turned to the third setting, the one that Christopher couldn't translate. More than that, the dial seemed to have been partially melted to the statue. Clearly, it would never be able to be turned again. The seam itself seemed to have been welded shut the whole way around. Even the hinges had been ruined.

He rushed over to the statue he had observed previously. After a moment's hesitation, he turned the dial to the open setting. The hinges creaked and groaned as the statue began to slowly open by itself.

A wave of trapped heat from within startled him. This thing was indeed hollow. The interior of the back side of the statue was smooth enough, but the interior of the front side was quite another matter. It was lined with over three dozen long, sharp metal spikes, the purpose of which became only too clear. The back half of the device was equipped with five heavy lengths of chain connected to one side, apparently to wrap around and tightly secure the victim. This was no statue.

It was then that the demons arrived through the portal with Jerry's birth mother in tow.

"Remember, they can't see you or hurt you," said Christopher, stepping to Jerry's side. "These are only shadows of the past, a record of things that happened a long time ago. Just stand out of the way and watch."

"We've prepared a very special place for you, wench," snarled the demon leading the precession, the one who seemed to be the leader. "You killed the life that was within you. You gave it so much pain as it died. We thought that it was only fitting that you be placed within a thing that in turn will grant you pain untold, pain eternal. It is a thing created by the mind of man for just such a purpose as this. Your people had a name for it: they called it the virgin or the iron maiden. But call it what you will, it shall become your eternal home, your eternal nightmare."

The demon looked toward the device and seemed surprised to find that it was already open.

"Oh my God!" gasped Leona, gazing at the terrible instrument before her.

"I didn't leave it open," objected the demon on Leona's right.

"It matters not," growled the demonic leader. "It saves me the trouble of opening it. Prepare her!"

The other two demons roughly escorted Leona toward the iron maiden. She struggled with them, but it was to no avail.

"Don't get involved," repeated Christopher. "It's a great way to lose your way within the book."

With her arms shackled behind her back, Leona was forced into the maiden. It was a tight squeeze.

One of the demons pulled and tightened the chain around her waist, thereby restraining her within the maiden, while the other restrained her at her ankles. They then proceeded to place additional lengths of chain around her throat, thighs, and knees. The end of each chain was stretched across her body and fed into a metal slot on the opposite side of the sarcophagus. It was then ratcheted tightly around her, securing her body in place. Following this, the demons stepped back.

The demon leader looked on approvingly, then stepped forward. It became abundantly clear that this creature loved its work. "When this lid closes upon you, these spikes will be slowly driven into your tender flesh. You may find it interesting to learn that the predecessor of this device did not grant even its mortal occupant a quick death. Oh no, they were not nearly so fortunate." The demon caressed one of the spikes with its gaunt hand. "The smooth, tapered nature of these spikes seals the deep wounds they produce. The struggling of the victim, even their breathing, wiggles the spikes within those wounds and causes the person to slowly bleed to death.

"Even at that, it may take a day or more for the victim to expire. It's all a matter of making the spikes just the right length and placing them in the right places to optimize the effect. I can assure you that we have done an expert job on that score, and this device was designed specifically with this place in mind."

"This has to be a dream," gasped Leona. "You can't be real."

"Oh, I assure you that we are very real," replied the demon. "So is this place. If anything, it was your life on Earth that was the dream. But allow me to continue." The demon pointed to the two rows of spikes that would be driven into her legs once the lid closed. "These spikes were designed specifically to penetrate the muscles of your legs right to the bone. With even the slightest of movement on your part, their sharp tips scratch those bones, producing agonizing pain."

The demon pointed to another pair of spikes farther up. "These penetrate your kidneys, creating their own unique pain. This one drives into your liver and this one into your spleen. These penetrate your intestines, and these your stomach." There was another pause. "On Earth, a device such as this would not have a spike that drove itself into your heart. No, that would ruin the entire effect, bringing about a premature death. However, the rules here are slightly different."

Leona was weeping bitterly now, and her tears were ripping apart Jerry's very soul. Yes, this was the woman who had denied him a life on Earth, yet she was also the woman who had given him an existence. She was his mother, and he felt a bond there even now.

Then the demon pointed toward the last two spikes, which were somewhat smaller and shorter than the others—the only ones located within the head of the maiden. "Ah, but these are special. You humans are so sensitive about your eyes. If we are going to desecrate your other organs, we can hardly neglect those blue beauties, can we?"

Leona's eyes grew wide with terror. She tried to turn her head, but she couldn't move.

"No, you cannot move your eyes out of the path of these spikes. You shall spend the rest of your eternity blind, suffocating, and in intense agony," continued the demon, placing its hand upon the dial and turning it one notch.

The hinges of the device creaked and groaned as the lid slowly began to close. Leona cried and struggled wildly, yet she could hardly move. It took the better part of a minute for the lid to close. The last few seconds were the worst as the spikes slowly dimpled her flesh and then broke through. The lid closed tightly amid Leona's muffled screams.

Then the demon turned the dial another notch and stepped back as the seam that separated the terrible device began to glow with bright orange heat. Lastly, the dial itself seemed to ignite into bright luminance. Within another minute the task was complete. The demons reentered the vortex and it vanished once more. All that remained was the sound of crashing waves and the faint muffled screams of Leona. Another few seconds saw the first few drops of her blood ooze from beneath the terrible device on their way to the basin.

Jerry fell to his knees weeping even as the vision faded and was replaced by the quiet of the library. Christopher took his hand.

"Now you know," said Christopher. "I'm sorry."

It was a minute before Jerry responded. "Now I know what I have to do."

"Rescue her?" deduced Christopher.

"Yes—I have to," confirmed Jerry.

Christopher didn't respond. He knew that there would be no changing the mind of his closest friend. He only hoped that his determination would not be his downfall. They walked together from the Hall of Records. Jerry hardly said a word as they made their way from the city.

Two days later, Christopher stood side by side with Jerry at Professor Faraday's science complex on the first level of Heaven. They gazed with wonder at the magnificent craft before them. Over 180 feet across, the saucer-shaped craft was still little more than a framework of substructure sitting upon its four spidery legs.

"This is the culmination of my life's work," announced Michael Faraday as he pointed at the great vehicle, "mine and that of about a hundred other scientists and engineers. Thankfully it wasn't damaged during the war. We've built upon the pioneering work of Dr. Kepler, Nikola Tesla, and others. However, we've overcome the limitations of size. This vehicle will carry three hundred people on a journey of exploration, or in the defense of our way of life."

He turned to Christopher. "My staff and I look forward to completing your education in physics and engineering. I'm sure you will become a valuable member of our science team."

Then he turned to Jerry. "And I must say that I am most impressed with your abilities in the art of physical materialization. We will teach you to become even better as you work with our team to create the complex components that will one day make that thing fly through the universe."

"I would like to think that I might one day pilot crafts that can explore the universe as well," replied Jerry.

"That too is possible," confirmed Faraday. "It will be a competitive field, but you are welcome to try."

Jerry smiled. "Professor Faraday, the way I see it is that I can do it or do it not...there is no try. I will do it, sir."

Faraday chuckled slightly. "Yes, Jerry, I think you will. Let's get you situated. My wife and I have made room for you in our home. Our home will become your home. We have much to do in the coming months and years. I look forward to hearing good things about both of you."

As Christopher and Jerry made their way to the beautiful mansion, they both knew that they had their work cut out for them. This was just the beginning for the four children who had grown so much during the past couple of months. The Father had told them that their task was not yet complete, and they had no doubt of that.

Perhaps Christopher put it best when he said that the children of eternity would ride again. Jerry had to think about that one for a time. He didn't exactly understand the vernacular. When it came to Christopher, he often didn't, but he was certain that Christopher was probably right.

PART II

THE LEONA STAHL INCIDENT

CHAPTER 1

RILLIANT SUNLIGHT GLISTENED OBLIQUELY OFF the snow and ice of the gently rolling terrain of this vast arctic valley. In the distance, high mountains covered from top to bottom in a mantle of white reached toward the crystal blue heavens. It was a scene of magnificent desolation—and total isolation.

Bedillia Farnsworth planted her ski poles firmly into the snow and gazed out across this land through her dark snow goggles. She wore a heavy down parka, an arctic snow suit, and thick snow boots as protection against the cold. She was certainly no stranger to the cold. She had spent much of the last ten years living and working in a far harsher environment than this. To her, today was a very mild day with its still air and brilliant sunlight.

She turned to gaze into the sunlight again. She pulled the woolen scarf from her face to soak in all of the energy this brilliant orb had to offer. How wonderful it felt. The sun hung just a few degrees above the distant horizon, and it wouldn't be getting much higher than this, not at this time of the year. Indeed, this day would be scarcely four hours long.

When she was last here, three weeks ago, the sun wasn't visible at all. It remained below the horizon during the entire day, and bright aurora played amid the stars in a realm of twilight. Aurora and stars together— how very beautiful it all was. She recalled a realm of eternal night where shimmering aurora danced against a charcoal sky devoid of stars, a realm beyond the universe of humanity. In that place, a single mistake, one careless step, could lead to consequences beyond comprehension.

Why did her mind always wander back to those days? Wasn't it best to put that all behind her?

Bedillia had seen and experienced a lot in her lifetime of 67 years—far more than most. Was that all…just 67? It seemed like so many more years had passed. Still, she had weathered them well, at least on the surface. To the casual observer, she was a truly beautiful woman, appearing to be no more than 30, and she didn't even have to work at it. Still, one had only to look deep into her eyes to see her true age. There one could see the pain, the fear, and yes, the wonder of her existence. She was the rarest of beings in Heaven, one who had also experienced, firsthand, the horrors of Hell. It was an experience that she would gladly have done without. Even as other children of God sought knowledge of the realm beyond Heaven, including the knowledge of their loved ones in Hell, Bedillia wished only that she could forget.

Even here, in Heaven, the memories of those terrible years still haunted her dreams. God the Father had forgiven her. He had made that quite clear when she stood before Him in the Great Hall of Judgment. He had given her that rarest of commodities: a second chance, and that chance had been granted to her on the very day of the rapture of the saints. Yet in granting her entrance into paradise, He had also bestowed something else upon her—notoriety. It was a notoriety that she would just as soon have lived without. Everyone here knew who she was and how she had come to be here.

People around her tried to be pleasant, of course, yet she was absolutely convinced that to them she was a second-class citizen of Heaven. They weren't about to question the decision of the Father in granting her entrance into their realm of course, but she could sense their uneasiness around her.

Hadn't she paid for her transgressions during the nearly ten years that she had spent hanging from a chain within that terrible furnace, broiling like a dark, sizzling, yet never-quite-done flank of meat? And that meat that had once been a human being felt the agony of the flames. The physical laws that governed Hell were different from those of Earth.

There was no death, no slipping into a state of shock or unconsciousness, but there was pain—endless pain. No matter how much damage was done to the bodies of the damned, they always regenerated. No injury was terminal and no disfigurement permanent.

The devil knew this well, and he used it against the multitude of humans condemned to his realm. The trick was to inflict brutal damage to the spiritual bodies of his victims at approximately the same rate at which they were capable of healing. Such an act of sadistic torture could be perpetuated almost indefinitely.

No, the saints of Heaven could not even conceive of such an ordeal. How could they possibly know what it was like to have the eternal nature of their spiritual bodies turned against them?

Had it not been for the act of kindness of the dark angel Abaddon, she might be there still. He had delivered her from her suffering; and during the ten years that followed, she did the same for so many others. They had become a thorn in Satan's side—angels of mercy operating in the heart of Satan's domain from a hidden fortress known only as Refuge. It was during just such a rescue mission, the most dangerous and selfless one of all, that her deliverance had come.

Now she was safe, beyond Satan's grasp. Still, she felt like a woman without a country. She didn't feel welcome in Heaven. So she lived alone, retired. The woman who had stood at the very center of the greatest of all struggles—the fight between good and evil—now sat on the sidelines. No, not even that. She wasn't even in the arena. Her mansion stood amid the pine forest of a lonely northern valley, not 1,000 miles due south of this very wilderness. Periodically, she journeyed to the great City of Zion to commune with the Father, but otherwise she kept to herself.

Her mind returned to the present. She focused on a cloud of steam rising from the valley about a mile away. It was the hot springs, her destination.

"A penny for your thoughts," said a voice to her right.

Bedillia looked over at her daughter and smiled. "Oh nothing, Serena. I was just daydreaming, that's all."

"About the Dark Continent, about Refuge?" asked Serena.

"Yeah, mostly," replied Bedillia.

Though Serena was Bedillia's daughter, they could well have been mistaken for sisters. Both had the appearance of women in their late-20s or perhaps 30.

"I only spent a day on the Dark Continent, a long time ago," noted Serena, shivering slightly. "A very cold day. That was enough for me—more than enough really. Here we're what, about seven hundred miles short of the North Pole?"

"About that," replied Bedillia. "But within a couple of months this valley will undergo an almost magical transformation. The snows will melt away, retreating to the mountains. This frozen wasteland will be transformed into a rocky, green meadow carpeted with all manners of wild flowers."

Serena laughed. "Now Mom, how would you know that? You weren't here last spring."

"I have it on good authority," assured Bedillia. "You're right. I've never seen it firsthand. Still, this is one of Aaron's favorite haunts. He told me all about it, and angels don't lie."

"I guess they don't, certainly not Aaron," said Serena, who was shivering again. She was dressed every bit as warmly as Bedillia was, but in her case it didn't seem to help.

"Are you OK, Serena?" Bedillia asked.

"Oh sure, Mom, I'm fine," she replied. "I think I'm starting to get the knack of extreme cross country skiing."

"Why do you call it extreme, dear?" asked Bedillia.

"Well, look at this place," said Serena. "It's got to be twenty or thirty below zero."

"Eleven below, dear," corrected Bedillia.

"I'd never imagined that there were places in Heaven this cold," continued Serena. "Oh Mom, I've wanted to spend quality time with you for so very long, but you choose some pretty strange places to spend it. You know, there are some beautiful beaches on the shore of the Crystal Sea. The water is fresh water, not salt, and there is this wonderful sea breeze. It is so nice there…nice and warm."

"You can have your tropical beaches," said Bedillia, smiling broadly. "But this…this is the land where the true wonder of the Father's creative hand shines forth. Every spring the miracle of life rises anew in shades of green, yellow, blue, and red. Then in the fall the snows sweep back in and the land sleeps once more. The story of creation is repeated again and again. And it is so quiet here, Serena. This is the place where I feel closest to the wonders of the Father's hand…where I can think, contemplate."

"That's it, isn't it, Mom?" said Serena. "You want solitude."

Bedillia hesitated. "Yes, I guess I do."

"You spend too much time alone," continued Serena. "You need to get out more."

"And go where?" asked Bedillia.

"Why don't you visit Chris and me more often?" asked Serena. "We'd love to have you over. I know you don't like warm climates, but we have such wonderful evenings."

"I've been there," replied Bedillia. "Your place is beautiful. I just want you young people to have time to yourselves. You've been through a terrible ordeal."

"An ordeal that you rescued me from," said Serena. "I need to have you with me now."

Bedillia took Serena's hand. "I *am* with you right now. I'm here whenever you need me."

"Oh Mom," gasped Serena, "you've gone and retired. The resistance still needs you."

"They need me to do what?" asked Bedillia.

"To get back in the fight," said Serena. "You've been to see Dr. Kepler and the others, what…one time? Your knowledge of the conflict in Hell makes you a valuable asset as an advisor, and they're going to need plenty of advice during the next few months."

"A valuable asset?" asked Bedillia. "Is that what I am now?"

Serena was absolutely flustered. "I just don't understand why you're being this way."

"I'm being this way because I need time to heal too," replied Bedillia. "You need to be patient—give me that time."

Serena said no more. Bedillia could sense her frustration. She only hoped that it would pass. She so treasured this time she had with her daughter. She didn't want anything to spoil it.

Several minutes of silence passed before Bedillia pointed toward the pillar of clouds rising from the snow and ice of the valley a couple miles away. "It looks like the hot spring is very active today. Oh, you've just got to see it, Serena, it's breathtaking. It will only take about another hour to get there from here."

"Why didn't we just gate straight there?" asked Serena. "Why the long walk?"

Bedillia laughed. "Because, my dear daughter, much of the point of the sojourn is in the sojourn itself."

"I suppose," replied Serena, shivering once more. The journey continued.

The sun was sinking lower as they ascended the final low, rocky ridge and beheld the geyser field. It lay in a valley between two low, gently sloping ridges about half a mile apart. It wasn't a large field of geysers—there were only three of them. A trace of snow was clinging to the top of the ridge on either side of the valley, but otherwise the valley itself was snow-free for about half a mile in either direction.

Between the many rocks and boulders, large amounts of green grass with an occasional yellow or blue wildflower could be seen. There were even a few small trees in their spring foliage dotting the landscape. Caribou, snowshoe rabbits, and other small animals grazed upon the plentiful grass. The land here seemed most incongruous amid the surrounding snowy terrain. Parts of the valley were occasionally enshrouded in mists that leaked from the three geysers at the valley's barren, rocky center. A narrow, steaming stream led from there and flowed off to the west, leading to a frozen lake about a mile away. The air was noticeably warmer here, a fact that seemed to bode well with Serena.

"Was it worth the trip?" asked Bedillia, scanning the valley before them.

"Oh yeah," said Serena, her smile beaming. "I've never seen anything like it outside of Yellowstone." At that moment Serena caught sight of something that didn't seem to quite belong. Two people were standing by the steamy stream, just to the west of the geyser field. She pointed.

"Yes," confirmed Bedillia, "I see them too. Apparently, I'm not the only person who appreciates this place."

The two individuals seem to have noticed Bedillia and Serena because they were now waving at them and moving in their direction. Bedillia and Serena returned the greeting.

"I wonder who they are," said Serena.

"I suppose we'll find out soon enough," said Bedillia, removing her skis and beginning to walk in their direction.

A minute later the two individuals stepped into a column of blue mists, and then they materialized about 50 yards in front of the women a few seconds later. One appeared to be a man in his early 20s, while the other looked like a boy in his early teens. Wearing only light jackets, they didn't seem particularly well-prepared for these arctic latitudes. They wore hiking boots and long trousers but no snow shoes. Apparently this island of warmth had been their only destination.

As the women approached, one of the two young men materialized a pair of hats for them to wear.

"Nice trick," said Serena. "I want to learn how to do that."

"Materialization isn't easy," cautioned Bedillia. "There were only a few people in Refuge who could do it, and that was with the help of a machine. I think these boys are improvising this arctic adventure as they go. That's not such a great idea."

As the two youths approached, Bedillia could discern their names—Christopher and Jerry. No, she was certain that she had not met either of them before.

"Bedillia Farnsworth and Serena Davis," said the younger of the two, the one named Christopher. "Oh wow…this is really just such an honor to at last meet the two of you. I'm Christopher and I'm your biggest fan. You are both just so famous…legends really."

How did one respond to that? Both youths extended their hands in friendship, and Bedillia and Serena accepted them.

"Mrs. Farnsworth, you rescued so many people from the torments of Hell," continued Christopher. "You even rescued your daughter from Satan himself. I feel so honored to meet you."

Serena looked over at her mother and smiled. "Mom, you are loved and appreciated here in Heaven."

"Absolutely," said Jerry. "We're sorry to be disturbing you way out here, but we just had to meet you. Both of you have been such inspirations to us. Mrs. Davis, years ago when I was just a kid, I got to know your husband, Chris. He and his mother lived only a few miles away from me and my folks."

"Oh yes!" exclaimed Serena. "You're *that* Jerry. Chris told me all about you, the great fisherman. You would catch the fish when everyone else went home empty-handed." Serena laughed. "Oh, he told me all of those fish stories. He will be so thrilled when I tell him that I ran into you out here."

"We were both in the Great Judgment Hall when you came through," continued Christopher. "I was waiting for my parents. They were both caught up in the rapture, and the Father said I could be there when they arrived. The two of you came through right before they did. We were so excited to finally see you, even if it was at a distance. Remember the standing ovation you both got when you arrived? Well, I'll tell you we were more than standing—we were jumping up and down."

"We were," confirmed Jerry. I'm not too sure that very many people have done that in the Great Judgment Hall." He hesitated. "But we did it anyway."

"Mrs. Farnsworth, we followed what was going on when you were on that island, when you rescued Serena," said Christopher. "We had your book open. We were rooting for you all the way."

"It was standing room only in the Great Hall of Records," confirmed Jerry. "We were there with our friends Jonathon and Lilly, and the great Dr. Kepler, and my friend David, and gosh, twenty or thirty others at least. Just as many were watching using your book, Mrs. Davis."

"OK," said Bedillia, "first of all, I'm Bedillia, not Mrs. Farnsworth."

"Please call me Serena," said Serena. "I feel like we're almost family here."

"Thanks," said Jerry.

Serena paused. "It seems to me that I heard a story. It was about four young people who rescued hundreds of the saints held prisoner by Satan's forces in the Hall of Angels in the City of Sarel. They saved them from what might have become a trip to Hell."

"That would be us," confirmed Jerry, "us and our friends Jonathon and Lilly."

"Then it is we who should feel honored," said Serena.

Serena's comment was followed by a round of laughter from all. "What are the odds?" she said.

Jerry looked over at Christopher, then back at Bedillia and Serena. Then he turned to Christopher. "Should I be the spokesman?"

Christopher nodded.

Jerry turned to Bedellia. "We have a problem, a big problem…and we really need your help."

"I'll do whatever I can," promised Bedillia.

And so the story began. Jerry spoke a bit about their adventure in Sarel, but mostly he spoke of his birth mother and their journey to Hell through her book. He spoke of her terrible fate and his determination to rescue her. In the years since, he had traveled back there several times using the book, gathering more information and determining exactly where in Hell she had been sentenced.

"About two years ago I finally thought I had all of the information that would be needed to perform a rescue," said Jerry, "so I went to see Dr. Kepler. I explained what had happened and where she was. I knew that the people of Refuge had rescued many deserving people from their tortures in Hell.

"He told me of the thousands upon thousands of requests just like mine that he had received since the eyes of so many of the children of God had been opened. He tried to pass some of the names along to Abaddon, but he explained that you folks had limited resources and even more limited power. He also told me that the politics of Hell was, well…complicated."

"It is that," confirmed Bedillia. "But two years ago we were in the midst of a real power crisis. I knew that those requests were coming in, but we couldn't do anything about them. I'm really sorry, Jerry."

"It's not your fault," said Jerry. "I guess I figured that what I and the others had done at Sarel would count for something—that my request might get moved to the front of the line."

"I don't think that we were able to honor any of the requests," said Bedillia. "More recently our power problems have been solved, but our political situation has become even more difficult. You could say that, for a time, we had friends in high places when it came to the demons of Hell, but that is no longer the case. For all I know, Satan may be in full control once more."

"I guess what I'm asking is…could you talk to Abaddon on my behalf, see if he might be able to rescue my birth mother?" asked Jerry. "I know that you have some influence."

Bedillia nodded. "Yes, but influence may not be enough. Still, I will try."

Jerry handed Bedillia a sheet of paper. "This gives the coordinates of my mother's sarcophagus. There is one more problem I didn't mention. We don't have much time left. Every day that terrible Sea of Fire hammers at the base of that cliff. It is very rapidly eroding it. Large chunks of it are falling into the sea and with it go the sarcophaguses. The demons make no effort to relocate them. They simply allow them to fall. For a time, the spiked sarcophaguses are tossed about on the surface of that rough sea, as they are heated well beyond the boiling point. Imagine the tormented souls within, having those spikes thrust in and out of them with every crashing wave even as the heat within builds.

"The sarcophaguses eventually float out into the sea, into deeper oil, with only about their top quarter exposed. All the while, oil slowly leaks into them. Eventually they sink to the bottom, pulled down by the weight of their stone bases. And there they are forever. For the helpless occupants, matters are now much worse. I've measured the rate of erosion. If we don't act within the next six to eight months, my mother's sarcophagus will end up at the bottom of the sea."

"That's unimaginable," gasped Serena. "I know what that sea is like. To be floating on the surface is horrible beyond imagining—I experienced it. But to be trapped in one of those spiked boxes on the bottom… well…I can't even imagine what that would be like."

Serena turned to Bedillia. "Mom, you've got to do something. *We* have to do something. Maybe if we both asked, something could be done."

"We'll do it today," vowed Bedillia. "We'll go to see Dr. Kepler and use his telesphere to contact Abaddon. I'll propose a special rescue mission. Do you know where my mansion is?"

"Yes," confirmed Jerry.

"Meet me there in three days," replied Bedillia. "I should know more by then."

The young men quickly agreed. After a few minutes they gated away, leaving Bedillia and Serena alone once more.

"I think your retirement is over," noted Serena.

"Yes," confirmed Bedillia. "Our visit to the geysers will have to wait. We need to be off to Dr. Kepler's laboratory. I'll need to stop off briefly at my own home first; then we can go from there."

Serena nodded.

The blue mists formed before them, and Bedillia and Serena vanished. The quiet isolation of this arctic wilderness returned.

Late the following day, Christopher joined several other scientists and engineers at Pad B of Dr. Faraday's launch complex. They were looking toward the sky. After over three and a half years of study here, Christopher was still considered an apprentice in the trades of starship propulsion and electromagnetic manipulation, but he had moved to the very top of the roster. He could easily make journeyman in the next few months.

His gaze shifted from the sky to the 180-foot-diameter metallic saucer 400 yards away, which was glistening in the late afternoon sun. It was named the *Intrepid,* and over the years he had watched as it slowly transformed from a skeletal substructure to a completed vessel. He never tired of gazing at it. *Intrepid* was a thing of beauty. Next week it would take to the skies for the very first time.

Only 50 feet away stood the smaller crafts—the daggers. The three crafts looked not so different from small earthly fighter jets with exceptionally short wings. Each of the twin engine, 35-foot-long crafts seated two crewmembers, one in front of the other, beneath a clear crystalline canopy, and each bore a number and the insignia of a brown cross superimposed against the background of a golden crown. It was the emblem found on all of the vehicles here—an emblem to honor the One who made this bold enterprise beyond life possible.

Yet the daggers were not typical jets in the earthly sense. Each was equipped with two distinctly different forms of propulsion. For flight within the atmosphere, they utilized a form of jet propulsion, but these were no ordinary jet engines. These engines tapped the power of the Father's own Spirit, a power that permeated the entire universe to generate a powerful electric current, which in turn drove the engine. For propulsion in the very high atmosphere and in space, the vessels used an electromagnetic-drive, wormhole-generating hybrid, which was capable of speeds approaching that of light in normal space and far beyond it in hyperspace. These crafts were designed to fit into four independent launch bays built into the belly of the *Intrepid,* and they had both exploratory and military application, with an array of sensors and twin particle cannons.

Christopher again gazed up into the clear blue skies. He could hear the faint whine of the twin engines of Dagger 1, and that whine was growing ever louder—yet the craft was nowhere to be seen.

"Very nice," said a young engineer to his right. "Very impressive."

Christopher continued to scan the skies. Then he saw it. It looked like a distortion in the sky, a slight ripple that took the form of Dagger 1. The ripple became a translucent form; then the dagger materialized in all of its glory about 100 feet away. "You gotta love it," he said.

Less than ten seconds later, Dagger 1 set down on the pad beside the others, and the whine dropped swiftly in pitch. The canopy opened, and Jerry stepped out dressed in his tan flight suit. He was followed quickly by his flight engineer, John Caroway.

"That is the closest to invisible we've been," said one of the engineers. "You were virtually undetectable to the eye and on high frequency radar. I don't think we can do much better than that."

"But we need to try," said Jerry, approaching the group. "I'd like to think that it's possible to make this bird totally invisible, totally undetectable."

"There is always going to be a residual signature," said another engineer.

Jerry seemed prepared to make another comment, yet he didn't.

"Good job people," said the group leader, a 117-year-old engineer by the name of Mitch Headlands, who appeared only about 35. "Let's spend the rest of the afternoon crunching the data and meet in the conference room at ten tomorrow."

The others nodded and went their separate ways. Jerry walked with Christopher.

"It was really very effective," said Christopher.

"Yeah, but demons have very good eyesight, especially in the infra-red," countered Jerry. "About the only way I could hide my engine signature from them would be to come in low over the Sea of Fire and then put her down right on the edge of the cliff in that small open area we've seen." He paused. "I've been to the Hall of Records again and I looked into her book. Another big piece of the cliff tumbled into the sea yesterday, and there is a crack forming about two feet behind her sarcophagus.

"The Sea of Fire has been unusually violent of late. It took a bunch of those sarcophaguses with it last time. We thought she might have six months. I don't think she has anywhere near that long. We may only have a matter of days. If we have another collapse like the last one, it could take her with it. Then we might never recover her."

Christopher nodded. He could sense Jerry's pain. He had been planning this rescue for so long. They had thought they had more time.

"She was praying, Christopher," continued Jerry, "I heard her. She prayed for mercy from God, but she also prayed for me. How I wanted to say something to her, to comfort her, but I couldn't." Jerry paused. "But there are other times, times when she howls like a crazed animal. She struggles wildly within that awful sarcophagus, struggles until the blood just pours out of that thing. If we don't get to her soon, there may not be any part of her humanity left.

"I've started to study what the torments of Hell do to people, especially ones like that. In the Sea of Fire, the victims eventually go totally nuts. I don't want her to get like that. If Bedillia isn't able to convince Abaddon to help us, I'll have to go in there myself. We'll have to go through with our own plan...with or without their help."

Christopher shook his head. "Jerry, we're not ready. I looked at your temporal capacitor data from the last flight. It isn't carrying enough power to get you there and back. Once you pass into outer darkness, your dagger won't be able to tap the Father's Holy Spirit for power—you'll be relying on that capacitor for everything.

"The cloaking field, those two engines, and your navigation system all draw power. Just getting there will drain you down to about fifty-five percent. Once you maneuver in, land, get her out, and set course for Refuge, you'll be down to forty-five percent power or less. That's assuming that you don't have to work those weapons repelling a demon attack."

"I could override the safeguards, charge the capacitor to one hundred and ten percent," countered Jerry.

"And potentially blow the capacitor and the ship apart, and you along with it," objected Christopher.

"I'm willing to accept that risk," replied Jerry.

"But I'm not," replied Christopher. "Your heart is in the right place, Jerry, it always is...but there are bigger things to consider. Suppose you were shot down and captured? Suppose you were seen entering and exiting Refuge? The blame for our actions might fall on Abaddon and his people. They could end up paying the price for our mistake.

"Abaddon and the others in Refuge are in a difficult situation. I don't think we can appreciate how difficult. They are isolated, surrounded by demons, and hopelessly outnumbered. Yes, they have superior weapons, but I don't think that's going to help them if they end up in an out-and-out war. Our interference could trigger that war. Do you want all of those lives on your conscience?"

"No, of course not," replied Jerry.

"You're right," said Christopher, "the cloaking field isn't good enough yet. If it were, you could go in there, free your mother, knock her empty sarcophagus into the sea, and then basically disappear. No one could prove a thing. For all the demons would know, her sarcophagus tumbled into the sea due to natural forces. It's only a couple of feet from the edge. They would write her off. They wouldn't search the bottom of that black sea looking for her. There would be no need for it. That was the plan, wasn't it? You go off half-cocked now, and we could have real problems—bigger than us probably being kicked out of this program."

Jerry nodded but said nothing.

"Then we stick to the plan," said Christopher. "I truly believe that she's going to be rescued, but we don't change the plan now, OK? Give Bedillia a chance."

Jerry nodded. "Sure, Christopher, we stick to the plan."

Jerry headed toward the locker room to get out of his flight suit. Christopher watched him leave. Christopher had a bad feeling about this. If Bedillia couldn't get Abaddon to go along with a rescue, there would be no stopping Jerry. He prayed for guidance.

The snow was falling once more as Bedillia led Jerry and Christopher into the large living room of her home, which took the form of a rather spacious Swiss-type chalet. A small fire burned within her stone fireplace, yet the room was distinctly chilly. Within the room the young men encountered both Chris and Serena. It had been a very long time since Jerry had seen Chris, and they certainly had a lot to discuss, yet right now only one thing weighed on Jerry's mind.

Everyone but Bedillia sat near the fire for its warmth. Bedillia seemed hesitant to approach it. It didn't take much deduction for Christopher to figure out why. Her experience in Hell must have been ghastly.

"My daughter and I both talked to Abaddon at length," began Bedillia. "There was a brief time when the fallen angel Cordon ruled over the demons of Hell. Note that I call him a fallen angel and not a demon. That is the way we all thought of him. He was reasonable, even noble. He ruled over Hell for some time in Satan's absence. I can tell you that he wouldn't have been Satan's first choice.

"After the War in Heaven isolated Satan from his followers in Hell, we of Refuge were able to negotiate a non-aggression pact with Cordon. In those days it was possible to rescue a limited number of loved ones from their torments. Yet, some months ago, Cordon was replaced by a demon by the name of Krell, the former head of Satan's military. Krell spoke of continuing many of the policies of Cordon. He spoke of allowing even more tormented souls to be released. Krell even appointed Cordon as his liaison between himself and the people of Refuge. We were all hopeful. But things didn't turn out as well as we had hoped.

"Abaddon speaks of a recent turn for the worse, of a tightening of Krell's policies. Abaddon is certain that Satan himself is pulling Krell's strings. It is even rumored that Satan has found a method by which he can travel freely between Earth and Hell. If that is true—and I think it is—he is the true master of Hell once more, and Krell is just a puppet. About a week ago, Cordon was forced to flee into exile. Apparently, he was about to be arrested, and I think Satan was behind it. No one has seen or heard from Cordon since."

"And this all affects the mission to rescue my mother," deduced Jerry.

"Very much so," said Bedillia. "Satan would like nothing better than to wipe Refuge off of the map, but he'd rather not be the first one to break the treaty. The day following Cordon's disappearance, Krell sent a messenger to Refuge. He stated that under no conditions was Abaddon to free any more of the damned souls from their torment. This point was not negotiable. The rescue of your mother would be seen as a violation of that order. I'm sorry."

Well, there it was. Silence ruled the room for half a minute. Not surprisingly, Jerry was the one who broke that silence.

"Not if her sarcophagus was assumed to have fallen into the sea," interjected Jerry. "It is on the threshold of doing just that. Suppose that I rescue her?"

"You rescue her?" asked Bedillia. "How would you do that?"

Jerry told the group the plan by which he would rescue his mother and then lead the demons to believe that her sarcophagus had simply plunged into the sea. He assured them that it would be easy enough to do.

"But what if you were seen?" objected Serena.

"I wouldn't be," responded Jerry, describing the new cloaking field that would surround the dagger. Jerry made an impassioned argument. Still, his term *almost invisible* drew some concerns, as did the distance from his landing point to her sarcophagus. It was over 50 yards. There wasn't any place closer to land. A lot could go wrong in the transit.

"Suppose you were discovered by demons?" asked Chris.

"I would be forced to terminate the demons using my particle rifle and toss the remains over the cliff—what few remains there would be," replied Jerry.

Chris seemed a bit doubtful. "It would be difficult to remove all of the evidence. A particle rifle makes quite a mess, believe me, I know." There was a pause. "Look, I know how much this means to you, Jerry, I more than anyone. I'm the last one to lecture you about not going. But it's just so risky. Would the Father even approve of you doing this?"

"I've spoken to Him," replied Jerry. "He told me that He would allow it, but I would be on my own. If something happened, I couldn't expect a band of angels to come and rescue me. Still, I know that I could pull this off."

Again there was an uncomfortable silence.

"I may be able to do something about the almost invisible situation," said Christopher. "It involves only a small adjustment to the field generator. I've thought the problem out, and I proposed the modification yesterday in the engineering meeting. It will take only a few hours to make the adjustments. Actually, they're being made as I speak. Personally, I'm very optimistic about it."

"But suppose that you were seen entering Refuge?" asked Bedillia. "The demons have been keeping a close eye on whatever enters and leaves. Can you be sure that this ship of yours would be totally invisible to them, totally quiet?"

"No," replied Christopher.

"Mom, maybe they don't need to take Leona to Refuge," suggested Serena. "Maybe Refuge could come out to meet her. The transfer from Jerry's ship could be made somewhere else, at some very remote location. From there, representatives from Refuge could gate his mother directly to the ring in Refuge unseen. It would work."

There was a moment of silence.

"Sounds reasonable," said Chris.

Bedillia seemed deep in thought. "Maybe, we'll need to bring this to Abaddon."

"When could you do that?" asked Jerry, who seemed a bit nervous.

"How about right now?" replied Bedillia. "Follow me."

The group followed Bedillia down a short hallway and into a small room on the left. It had the appearance of a bedroom with bookshelves and a few books on the left, a large, finely crafted, wooden desk directly before them, and a nice brass bed on their right. Beyond the desk was a window that gave the group a panoramic view of the snowy valley below the house. But what seemed most peculiar about the room was the small crystal ball sitting on a black base in the middle of the desk.

"A telesphere," said Serena, surprise in her voice. "Mom, I didn't know that you had a telesphere in your own home. I mean, when we contacted Abaddon we used the telesphere in Dr. Kepler's laboratory."

"Yes dear, I know," Bedillia replied, walking over to the telesphere and waving her hand across a small panel on the base. "I've wanted to keep this a secret. I mean...I have an unlisted number." She paused.

No one said a word.

"OK, I'm not so good with the jokes," Bedillia continued. "I use this quite a bit, really, talking to old friends back in Refuge. It allows me to keep up with the goings-on there without tying up someone else's telesphere."

"But why didn't you want me to know about it?" objected Serena.

Bedillia hesitated. "Because I didn't want you to become upset. I want you to be happy."

"Upset about what?" asked Serena. "Mother, what's going on?"

Bedillia heaved a sigh. "OK, Serena. Things aren't going well in Refuge. In reality, they are going more poorly than I've led you to believe. Even if we managed to get Jerry's mother there, we may only be delaying the inevitable. Four days ago, just before we set off to the arctic, I got a message from Abaddon. Krell had issued to him what amounts to an ultimatum. Krell said that he couldn't risk having armed humans within his realm. He was willing to extend the treaty between his people and the people of Refuge only if they agreed to turn over every weapon they had to him. He gave them two weeks to comply with his demand.

"If they refused, they would be subject to attack anytime after that. When we left the geyser fields I said that we needed to come here first, remember? I told you that I needed to change clothes, but that was only part of the reason. I contacted Abaddon on the telesphere and asked him not to tell you about these recent developments. He agreed. We knew that it would only upset you."

Serena nearly went ballistic. "Mother, how could you? I'm not a child anymore!"

"Serena, calm down," urged Chris, who turned to Bedillia. "How many people know this?"

"Everyone in Refuge, of course," she answered. "Dr. Kepler and some of his staff know." Bedillia turned to Chris and Jerry. "I think your Professor Faraday knows."

"What's being done?" asked Chris.

"Everything that can be," replied Bedillia. She turned to Jerry. "With what you now know, do you still want to risk your own eternity to save your mother?"

There was not so much as a second's hesitation in Jerry's response. "Yes."

"OK, then I guess we contact Abaddon," Bedillia said.

She made an adjustment to the telesphere and the crystal globe vanished. It was replaced by a much larger sphere of static, not unlike the snow seen in an old-style television set, only this static was three-dimensional. Within a few seconds, the static vanished to be replaced by the image of a pretty young woman. She smiled.

"Hi, Bedillia," she said in a pleasant voice.

"Hi, Julie," replied Bedillia. "Is Abaddon anywhere nearby?"

Julie nodded. "Yes, he figured that you may be calling."

The group saw movement in the background. A few seconds later, a being cloaked in black approached the telesphere. He had a well-trimmed, dark beard and dark, piercing eyes; from his shoulders, two great black wings like those of a crow arched to either side. He was very handsome and appeared not unlike a man in his early 40s.

"They already know," said Bedillia.

"I see," said Abaddon.

"They still want to go through with the rescue of Leona Stahl," continued Bedillia. "They have a plan. I personally feel that it has a high probability of success." Bedillia turned to Jerry. "This is Abaddon, administrator of Refuge. Without him, Serena and I would probably still be in Hell. Tell him about your plan."

Jerry had heard of this amazing angel many times. He was practically awestruck to at last meet him. He presented his plan as directly and concisely as he could. Abaddon listened in silence. When the plan was told, Abaddon seemed deep in thought.

"You humans have a saying," began Abaddon. "I don't know if I can quote it perfectly. It has something to do with jumping from a frying pan into a fire. That may well be what you are subjecting your mother to."

"I'm taking her from hopelessness to hope," said Jerry. "I think it's worth it."

"Then my answer to you is yes," said Abaddon. "If you are willing to risk your own eternity, I'm willing to support you. Let us make our plans."

For the next three hours, those plans were made. Abaddon called in his head of security and even Nikola Tesla, his ambassador from Heaven, to counsel him. In the end, they developed a workable plan.

"I will need to talk to Professor Faraday before I can set off in the dagger," said Jerry. "I'd thought about just taking it, but I realize that I can't do that."

"I seriously doubt that Professor Faraday will oppose your plan," said Abaddon. "Several days ago he offered me any assistance he could provide. He even spoke of dispatching his starship, the *Intrepid,* to support our cause. We may indeed lose this war, but we will not go down easily."

"You will have my support," vowed Jerry.

"And mine," said Christopher.

"Do you think for one minute that I would abandon you in your hour of need?" asked Serena. "I owe you more than my life. I will stand with you."

"So will I," said Chris.

"Make that unanimous," said Bedillia, smiling. "You aren't getting rid of me that easily."

Abaddon smiled. "I stand in amazement that I have such wonderful old and new friends."

"You're going to win this war," said Christopher. "You can take that as a prophecy if you wish."

"I shall," said Abaddon. "Let us begin the journey."

CHAPTER 2

THREE DAYS LATER, EVEN AS dawn was breaking over Professor Faraday's launch complex, a group of several dozen gathered to see Jerry off on his bold mission. Jerry had donned his flight suit and prepared to pilot Dagger 1 alone into the abyss. Upon the nose of the craft was its new name—*Hope*. Christopher had come up with it. It seemed appropriate enough.

Professor Faraday and his wife stood at Jerry's side.

"I sure wish that you weren't going alone," lamented Faraday.

"This is a mission for one man," said Jerry. "There's no point in risking anyone else's eternity."

"I remember when you came here," continued Faraday. "It's been nearly four years now. You told me that you would become a pilot. You were so certain. Now you have become the finest. I cannot think of a better pilot for this mission."

"Remember, don't charge the capacitor beyond one hundred percent," warned Christopher. "Don't go into hyperdrive until you reach point ninety-eight of light speed. The faster you're going when you engage it the better. You'll be surprised how much fuel it will save you."

"I will," promised Jerry, climbing into the cockpit. He took his seat and buckled in. It was time to go. He paused. "I'll see you this evening."

Christopher nodded. "You bet."

The group pulled back as the canopy closed and sealed. Jerry engaged power. He went over the checklist; everything was a go. A minute later the ship lifted off the pad in a cloud of dust, steadily gaining speed and altitude. At 90,000 feet, he switched from jet to electromagnetic propulsion. Less than six minutes found him in the blackness of space. He brought the capacitor to full charge. He resisted the temptation to take the capacitor to 102 percent. He would stick with the plan.

Jerry pushed the throttle of the electromagnetic drive forward. His status display hung like a phantom before him. He watched his speed build. Under normal conditions, he would not go to the trouble of achieving such incredible speeds before engaging the hyperdrive. Still, the science team was convinced that it would buy him valuable power. He would stick to the plan.

It took over half an hour of his time to achieve the required speed, which was closer to 45 minutes in ground time. Most of that time was used in getting from 90 to 98 percent of light speed. To get to 99 percent of light speed could easily require another hour. It was just the nature of relativistic travel. Again he checked his instruments; he was ready to engage the hyperdrive.

The jump to hyperdrive was accompanied with a dizzying sense of acceleration as the stars of normal space seemed to evaporate. They were replaced by clouds of colored vapor, high energy plasma really, rushing past him, contrasted against a velvet sky. They looked like the mare's tail cirrus clouds one might see on a warm summer's day—clouds touching the edge of the stratosphere.

This was nothing new to him. He'd made hyperdrive jumps dozens of times, yet never had he seen them sweep past him at such a speed as this. He plummeted ever deeper into the ether. The clouds around him faded in both brightness and color as he headed toward outer darkness. Within seconds the source of power that this vessel depended on would start to fade. At that point he would have to augment it with power from the capacitor. But as the seconds passed and his surroundings faded to black, it didn't happen. His engines were still drawing power from somewhere—that much was clear.

Christopher had said something about such high speed creating a narrow tunnel of normal space in its wake. Through that tunnel the power of the Father's Holy Spirit still flowed, feeding the engines. It was another minute before that power began to fade and the engines were compelled to draw on the power stored in the capacitor.

Jerry prepared for his entry into outer darkness. There was one critical maneuver still remaining: a four-second, full reverse power to the hyperdrive. Without it he would enter outer darkness at incredible speed, overshooting Planet Hell by 100 million miles—or worse, crashing into it at nearly the speed of light. So critical was this maneuver that it had been left to the onboard computer to initiate. All Jerry needed to do at this point was to sit back and enjoy the ride.

The maneuver was anything but a pleasant experience. Even with the inertial dampeners at full, it felt like he had just plowed into a wall. Bright amber light filled the cockpit, followed by a sudden jolt. Ahead, the nearly full disk of Planet Hell was hurtling toward him at breakneck speed. He applied full reverse thrust to the electromagnetic drive to reduce his forward velocity. It worked. A minute later, his speed had been reduced to 10,000 miles per hour, just as planned.

What Jerry beheld was a vast desert world that took up a fifth of the sky. It was painted in shades of brown, red, and black. Yellow storm clouds filled with bolts of powerful blue lightning hid portions of the planet's surface from view. These were the firestorms. Below them a mixture of flaming sulfur and powerful sulfuric acid rained down upon this barren world and its hapless inhabitants.

In other places, volcanoes spewed out poisonous gases and red-hot lava. The sulfur within these eruptions was what provided the raw materials for the great firestorms. Even from here it was not a planet that would entice a passing space traveler, yet it was one of the most traveled-to destinations in the universe.

Before him was the daylight side of the planet where temperatures could soar past 300 degrees. Jerry turned to his navigation display. It was highlighting a region of the planet to the far left, not far from the place where eternal day met eternal night. Here, a vast tan-colored desert met a black, fiery sea. He was right on course.

A firestorm could be seen some distance to the south, but it would pose no obstacle to his approach or rescue. All was proceeding as planned. Jerry glanced at his power readings. He was amazed to discover that he still had nearly 71 percent power in the capacitor. He breathed a sigh of relief. Fuel for the trip home would be no problem. This mission was going very well so far.

Yet there was something here that he had not anticipated: a sense of isolation, of loneliness. He tried to shake it, but he couldn't. It was the absence of the Spirit of God. The reality of God's Spirit was something he had taken for granted for so very long—a comforting Presence that was conspicuously absent here. He had read about this effect, but he hadn't expected it to make his heart feel this heavy. Jerry concentrated on the mission. He was 63 minutes from touchdown; he would have to focus.

The flight in continued uneventfully. As seen from the surface, he was coming in straight out of this world's huge red sun. It would obscure his approach, at least in the beginning. Now at an altitude of 200 miles, he engaged the cloaking device. It was a power consumption hog, but a necessary evil. He applied reverse thrust to bleed off speed. His entry into the atmosphere would need to be relatively slow—Mach 3—and it would slow rapidly from there. This would generate relatively little heat and no sonic boom.

Only a few minutes passed before Jerry could hear the rushing of the highly rarified air across the dagger's airfoil as he slipped through the ever-thickening atmosphere some 30 miles up. He got a much closer view of that sulfur firestorm to his south. Its billowing, yellow clouds towered over 12 miles above the surface, and the clouds were alive with powerful bolts of blue lightning. Below it, the sulfuric acid rain came down in gray sheets, mixed here and there with a rain of sulfur fire. It was an awesome yet ghastly spectacle.

Right now Jerry was crossing a range of barren mountains just to the east of the target zone. He switched from electromagnetic to jet propulsion. He would overshoot the zone and then swing around and approach it from the fiery sea. He glanced over at the mission clock; it was just over 12 minutes to touchdown.

"Hold on, Mom," he said, "I'm almost there."

Around him the sky was undergoing a transformation from the blackness of space to a sort of dark blue and now to a more tan color. Ten thousand feet altitude came and went as he passed over the landing zone. He was still too high up to see any detail. He only hoped that his mother's sarcophagus had not fallen into that black sea.

Six thousand feet over the black, fiery sea Jerry began to experience rough air, and it only got rougher as he descended. The intense heat of the sea was causing powerful thermals that buffeted the dagger. This would make his approach all the more difficult. At 3,000 feet he made a hard bank to the left, reversing his course. He had dropped to a mere 1,500 feet when he rolled out of the turn. The sea was coming toward him awfully fast. He had dropped to less than 200 feet when he finally increased power and leveled off. He scanned his high frequency radar: no contacts other than the cliff two miles ahead. That, at least, was a break.

Two minutes later Jerry was in hover mode just beyond the cliff. Again he scanned his surroundings—nothing. He identified the landing site; everything was just as it appeared in the book. Before him he saw his mother's sarcophagus, still undisturbed. He was in time. He extended the landing gear and made a soft touchdown on the rocky plains just 15 feet from the cliff's edge. The engines shut down. Only the cloaking device and high frequency radar remained active.

Now time was of the essence. Every minute here on the ground increased the probability of detection. Jerry grabbed his rifle and the tool kit and popped the canopy. He climbed down the ladder. He felt as if ants were crawling all over his body as he stepped through the force field of the cloaking device. He turned to look back.

Sadly the ship was still almost invisible, a rippling outline against the background. Still, from a distance of 100 yards or so, it probably was invisible. He moved on, walking amid the shining, metal coffins.

This place was just as it appeared in his mother's book. However, the heat and smell of crude oil and sulfur were far more noticeable. Occasionally he heard a muffled moan emanate from one of the coffins, but mostly he heard the relentless crashing of the waves upon the cliff below. It took less than a minute to get to his mother's sarcophagus. He looked down to discover that the crack in the ground appeared no wider. That was a relief.

It was unusually quiet within the sarcophagus. Jerry didn't know if that was good or bad. He sat his kit on the ground and opened it. He pulled from it a high energy plasma cutter and a remote scanner. He sat the scanner, which linked to the radar in the dagger, where he could monitor the screen as he worked. He engaged the plasma cutter, and it came to life with a low hum. He moved it toward the metal seam and began his work.

He was relieved to discover just how quickly the stream of high energy plasma sliced into the metal. Within just a few seconds he had cut several inches. Already the heat and stench emanating from within that awful tomb was almost overwhelming. He had cut nearly two feet when he heard a gasp from within the sarcophagus, followed by several rapid breaths.

"Ohhh!" came the cry from within. It seemed so full of agony. Then came the rapid breathing, one gasp after another. "Air," muttered a woman's voice from within, "air."

"Please, be still," said Jerry, in as calm a voice as he could. "I'm here to rescue you."

For a moment there was no response, just more rapid breathing. "Rescue?" came the disoriented cry. "I'm really being rescued?"

"Yes," confirmed Jerry, who continued to cut through the metal at approximately waist level.

"I feel air, there's air," groaned Leona. "I can breathe."

"Yes," confirmed Jerry, "and there's going to be more. I'm cutting through the metal. I'll have you out of there in just a few minutes."

"You're a hallucination, you've got to be," moaned Leona. "I'm going out of my mind. I know it." Leona began to cry between her gasps.

"No, you're not going out of your mind," said Jerry. "I'm not a hallucination. Please don't cry. You're going to be OK. Please trust me."

She was talking to him, and she was making sense. It gave Jerry new hope as he carefully cut along the neck of the sarcophagus.

"Ohh!" cried Leona. "Oh, God, that burns."

"I'm sorry," said Jerry. "I'm cutting you out of there with a plasma beam. I'm trying not to hurt you. I'm sorry."

"Don't stop, please don't stop. Please, get me out of here. For the love of God, please," urged Leona. Again she went silent. Her breaths seemed less labored now. "You're not a hallucination; you're real. I know it now. How did you get here? Who are you?"

That was the question that Jerry didn't want to answer, not right now at least. He needed to have her calm. To tell her that he was her aborted son wouldn't sit too well with her in her current state of mind.

"I'm a friend," he said. "I've been planning this rescue for years. I'm sorry that it has taken so long."

"I don't have any friends…not anymore," gasped Leona. "They told me that no one would remember me, that I'd suffer here for all eternity forgotten by everyone who ever loved me. The demons told me that."

"You can't believe demons," said Jerry, who was now stretching to cut the shell open over her head. "I remembered you."

"But who are you?" asked Leona.

There was a moment of hesitation. "My name is Jerry."

"Jerry?" said Leona. She said it so slowly. "I don't remember you. I don't know who you are. I don't know anything anymore. All I know is the pain of these spikes, the pain of not being able to breathe, the pain of not being able to die…" There was a pause. Leona was breathing regularly now, though she occasionally moaned in pain.

"It hurts so much every time I breathe, every time I move, even a little bit. But breathing feels so good too. I haven't breathed in a long time, Jerry." Again she paused. "Please, keep talking to me, Jerry. I just want to hear another human voice, a voice that's real, not in my head. How long have I been here, Jerry? Do you know?"

"Yes I do," said Jerry. "You've been here for over twenty-three years."

"Twenty-three!" gasped Leona. "It seems so much longer than that. The pain makes it that way. It feels like a hundred years…a thousand."

"I reckon it would," said Jerry. "I can't imagine what you've been through—but it ends today. There'll be no more pain. You've had enough pain for one eternity."

"I've dreamed of being rescued," cried Leona. "I've dreamed of it so long, but I was giving up hope."

"Hope has been reborn," said Jerry. "It may seem strange, but that is the name of my ship, the ship that will carry you out of here—*Hope*. I'm taking you to a place where no one will ever hurt you again, where there will be people to take care of you. I think you'll like it."

"What place is that?" asked Leona. "It sounds so wonderful. I can hardly imagine a life without pain."

"It is wonderful," confirmed Jerry. "The people there are very nice. They call it Refuge. There are people just like you there, people who have been rescued from the torments of Hell. Now they work to help free others. There are even angels there, very special and loving angels."

"Is that where you're from?" asked Leona.

"No," replied Jerry.

"Where are you from?" she asked.

"That's a little hard to explain right now," said Jerry, "but I'm from Heaven. I know how that must sound, but it's true."

"Why would anyone in Heaven care about me?" gasped Leona. "I'm a dark soul damned to Hell. I killed my first child, my first son, and God threw me away for it. I deserve to be here. But I'm sorry that I did it. I wish I could take it back. I've begged God for forgiveness." Again Leona was panting for air. A strange gurgling sound arose from within the sarcophagus.

"But why would anyone from Heaven rescue me?" There was another pause. "Unless, unless…no, that couldn't be." Again Leona was crying.

"Please don't cry," said Jerry, who had begun to cry himself. "Oh, please don't cry. I care for you, I love you."

Jerry was now cutting the shell down the other side. He'd come to the first hinge. It looked like it might still swing. He bypassed it.

"I don't understand," wept Leona. "How could you love me? Who are you, Jerry? I've got to know." There was a moment's hesitation. "Is it you?"

Jerry hesitated. He wasn't quite sure what she meant, but he had to tell her the truth. "I love you…you're my mother. You brought me into existence, and I'm getting you out of here."

"My son!" gasped Leona. "It *is* you! How can you love me? I killed you."

"Life on Earth is overrated; you sent me to Heaven," said Jerry, who could think of no other way to respond. "I grew up as a child of Heaven. I've had a wonderful life there. But my life won't be complete until I've rescued you. I can't live knowing that you are suffering in this awful place."

"I'm so sorry for what I did," wept Leona. "Oh, please forgive me, Jerry...please forgive me."

"I forgave you a long time ago," said Jerry, trying to focus on the task at hand. He'd reached the second hinge, a mass of melted metal. He sliced it away. Occasionally he glanced at the scanner sitting on top of his case. They were still alone.

"And you've done great things," said Leona, her voice a little stronger. "You've set the captives free, right? God told me that you would."

Jerry laughed through his tears. "Yeah, I guess I did. I rescued over three hundred people held captive by the devil and his minions during the War in Heaven. People tell me I'm a hero, but I'm not...not really. I was pretty scared the whole time I was rescuing them. I did it because I love people, and I love God. I think you'd be proud of your son."

"I am already," said Leona. "I wish I could see you, but I'm blind. I have no eyes."

"You will," promised Jerry. "Your eyes will be restored, you'll see. I have one more captive to set free."

Jerry's attention was drawn by a beeping of the scanner. They had company. By the sounds of it, that company was still distant. He kept working. He had less than two feet to go. He glanced at the screen. Three blips very close together were displayed on the screen. He couldn't quite tell, but they appeared to be about 300 yards away—not too close. They were hardly moving. Perhaps they were delivering a new victim to this terrible cemetery of the damned. He'd try to pry the sarcophagus open, yet leave the hinges intact, rather than slicing away the front completely. Demons had very good ears and they might hear it when the front of the sarcophagus hit the ground. Then he reached the end—he'd sliced the shell in two.

"OK, Mom, listen carefully," said Jerry. "I'm going to try and open this thing. I know it's going to hurt. It will be difficult, but try not to scream. There are demons nearby. I don't want them to hear."

"Oh please, go," pleaded Leona. "I don't want them to get you too. I'm not worth it."

"You are worth it, Mom," said Jerry. "Are you ready?"

There was a pause. "Yes."

Jerry reached for the gap in the shell and tried to pull it apart. He tried with every ounce of strength within him. It didn't budge. He went for the hinges and cut them loose. Then he pulled once more. Slowly the front of the sarcophagus began to fall forward. Jerry did his best to lessen its impact with the ground. It must have weighed better than a quarter of a ton. He heard his mother gasp in pain, yet she didn't scream. The lid of the sarcophagus hit the ground, but it made relatively little noise.

Jerry looked up to behold his mother. It was a ghastly sight to behold. She was so very pale, covered in places with clumps of dried blood, and there were two gaping holes where her eyes should have been. In addition, she must have had three dozen deep puncture wounds all over her body. She was still tightly chained into the coffin, her hands shackled behind her back. She was gasping at the air as pus flowed from the puncture wounds in each of her lungs. Had she not been immortal, these wounds would surely have been fatal the first day the lid closed upon her. Immediately Jerry began to cut through her chains.

"To breathe again is so wonderful," said Leona, starting to cry again.

"Just be still," said Jerry. "I'll have you out of there in no time."

The last chain severed, Jerry helped his mother from that terrible coffin. Then he used the plasma beam to cut the chain joining her wrist manacles.

"I'll remove the manacles themselves later," he promised. They sat for a moment on the base of the sarcophagus. Leona was shivering.

"I'm so thirsty," she gasped.

Jerry reached into the pack and retrieved his canteen. "I've got water here for you. I'm bringing the canteen to your lips. Just drink slowly. Don't gulp."

Leona opened her mouth. Her tongue was dry and cracked from a lack of water. She began to drink. At first she coughed. Taking in water was something she hadn't done in 23 years. But slowly she adjusted. She drank nearly half of the water in the canteen before she at last stopped. "I never thought I'd drink water again," she said in a soft voice. Again, she shivered. "I'm so cold."

Jerry knew that he had to get her out of these horrible clothes, but there just wasn't time now. He stowed the plasma cutter and glanced at the portable scanner. The news wasn't good: the demons were coming this way. He had to get his mother out of here. "Can you walk?"

"I don't think so," gasped Leona.

Jerry weighed his options. He'd spoken almost jokingly about a shootout with the demons. Now it was starting to look like that just might happen. If they were going to make a run for it, his mother would need shoes. He focused his thoughts to materialize them. It didn't work. There was no Holy Spirit in Hell, no well of power to draw upon. That was why his particle rifle had its own auxiliary power supply. It could fire anywhere from 8 to 32 times, depending upon the power setting. Then he would need to reload. He only had three cartridges in his case. Right now he wished that he'd packed more.

"Something's wrong, isn't it?" asked Leona, still shivering.

"Demons…three of them," said Jerry. "I can't see them, but I have them on the sensors."

"I don't understand," said Leona.

"That's OK," replied Jerry. "You're going to stay right here for a while. It will give you time to heal. I won't be far away."

"Take my hand, Jerry," said Leona.

Jerry placed his hand in his mother's hand. She squeezed it slightly.

"I had to do that," she said. "I just had to hold your hand. On that terrible night after you died, I cried. I cried because I would never get to do this."

Jerry placed his arm around his mother. "It's OK, I'm here now, and I'm going to be here for you from now on. This is all going to work out, you'll see."

"You have things to do," said Leona. "You go and do them. I'm not going anywhere."

Jerry rose to his feet. His mother had placed her hands over her face. He was certain that she was crying again. He wanted to stay with her— she needed him—yet he couldn't. First and foremost he had to get her out of here. He had to get her to safety. He stepped away.

Jerry cautiously advanced toward the demons. Hiding behind a sarcophagus about 50 feet away, he pulled a set of electronic binoculars from his pack and scanned his surroundings carefully. At first he didn't see them; then he zoomed in. There they were: three demons walking between the living tombs. They were coming in his general direction. "What are you doing?" he asked, almost under his breath.

The demons were walking from one sarcophagus to another, apparently inspecting each one. They were still about 200 yards away. He watched for several minutes. Then they abruptly turned to the left. Now they were actually walking away from him. He watched carefully as they continued their inspection.

What should he do? He considered making the first move—attacking. If he could only get close enough unseen, he could whack these demons before they knew what was happening. The problem was: How close could he get before they saw him? Demons had exceptionally keen senses. If only Jonathon were here. He probably could have convinced these demons to turn on each other.

In the final analysis, Jerry decided to withdraw. He didn't want to leave his mother alone any longer. He headed back.

Upon his return, he discovered that an amazing transformation was underway. Leona's skin had taken on a more natural hue. She gazed upon him with blue, tearful eyes. Her regeneration was well underway. A smile slowly came to her face.

"So handsome," she whispered.

"I take after you," said Jerry, smiling. He looked to see that his mother's wounds were barely half the depth that they had been.

"What about the demons?" asked Leona.

"They're moving away," said Jerry. "I don't quite understand what they're doing. They stop and linger at one of the coffins for a moment and then they move on to another."

"They're tormenting them," said Leona. "They talked to me once in a while. They taunted me, said horrible things, and then they moved on."

"We're going to hold up here for a little while longer," said Jerry. "They can't see us right now, but they may when we climb into my ship. I'd rather get out of here without incident."

Leona nodded. "How did you find me?"

Jerry told his mother about the Great Hall of Records, about her book. He told her a lot about Heaven—even the war. Through it all, Leona listened quietly, gazing into the face of her son. Occasionally, Jerry checked the radar; the demons were still moving away from them. He looked at his mother's wounds again. They were almost gone. "Do you think you can walk if I help you?"

"I'll try," said Leona.

Jerry reached into his pack and pulled out a power cell. He grasped it firmly in his hand and concentrated. Before Leona, a pair of shoes materialized. "You'll need these," he said, placing them upon her feet.

"You just made those shoes appear by thinking about them?" asked Leona.

"Yeah," said Jerry. "Actually, people tell me I'm pretty good at it. I'm one of the best, really."

"I'm so proud of you," repeated Leona.

"Ready?" asked Jerry.

"Ready," said Leona.

Jerry helped his mother to her feet. She took a step but quickly stumbled. Jerry caught her.

"I'm sort of dizzy," said Leona. "Let me try again."

Leona took several faltering steps. Jerry was with her all the way.

"I'm so tired," admitted Leona. "I feel like I could sleep for a year."

"You probably won't sleep for a year, but you may sleep for several days," said Jerry. "I've been told that people who have gone through what you've been through have sort of a rough time for a while. So much pain for so long takes its toll. But it will pass, and there will be people to get you through it."

"You'll be there for me, won't you?" asked Leona.

"Not right away," said Jerry. "I've got to go back. But I'll return as soon as I can. I may be there when you wake up."

"I hope so," said Leona, whose steps seemed to be getting a bit more certain. "Where is your ship?"

"Straight ahead," said Jerry. "We're nearly a third of the way there. You can't see it, but it's there."

They continued on through the heat. Jerry checked the scanner frequently. Then he breathed a sigh of relief. "The demons just vanished from my screen. I think we got it made."

Half a minute later they stood just beyond the cloaking field. Leona looked on in wonder.

"I can see the outline of your ship," she gasped. "It's like a ghost ship."

Jerry laughed. "No, it's not a ghost ship. It's surrounded by a field that makes it nearly invisible. I warn you: it will feel real weird as we pass through the field. Are you ready, Mom?"

"Yes, I'm ready," said Leona.

They stepped through the field. A second later they could both see the ship clearly. Jerry helped his mother climb up the back ladder to the rear seat of the ship. He strapped her in and got ready to go.

"I'll be sitting right in front of you," he said. "We have about a two-hour flight to our rendezvous point. From there you'll be taken to Refuge by people who will be taking care of you until you get well."

"OK, son," said Leona.

Jerry was on his way back down the ladder when the sensor started beeping wildly. A second later there was a loud explosion. Jerry turned to see three demons only about 100 feet away. One had directed a fireball toward the ship. It had barely missed.

"Jerry!" cried Leona.

"Mom, stay in the cockpit!" yelled Jerry.

Jerry jumped to the ground and engaged his rifle. He fired at the demons. His first shot was a clean miss. He took aim again.

By this time the demons were scattering for cover. He hit the one on the left. The demon exploded in a cloud of vaporized blood. The weapon was set at 100 percent—way too high. He dialed back to 50. Jerry targeted another, but he didn't have a clear shot. The demon had taken cover behind a sarcophagus. Should he blow it away to get at the demon? There may be a human being in there. He took the shot, directing his fire at the stone base. There was an explosion and a ballistic scattering of debris. The sarcophagus itself was sent flying, landing about five feet away.

The demon stumbled back, then directed its sword in Jerry's direction. A fireball erupted from its tip. The shot was wide, missing Jerry, but it did hit the ship near the tail.

The other demon stepped from behind another sarcophagus and took a shot. Again it missed Jerry but hit the hull of the ship. There was a flash and a bang. The ship fully materialized. The cloaking device had been put out of commission.

Jerry took a shot at the demon that had fired the first fireball. The demon exploded on the spot. He turned his weapon on the second, but it was too late. It had vanished into a sort of purple vortex.

"Great," said Jerry shouldering his weapon and sprinting up the ladder. He stowed his gear and jumped into the cockpit. The fact that the display panel was dark filled him with trepidation. One thought weighed on his mind more than any other: *Would the ship still fly?*

He hit the main power—nothing. His mind searched for ideas. He hit the breaker reset switch. Then he hit the main power again. The heads-up display came on, but with half a dozen red caution and warning lights. It didn't look good.

"What happened, Jerry?" asked Leona.

"We took two hits, Mom," he replied. "I'm not sure how bad. I've got power, but I'm not certain if I have engines. The cloaking device is gone. Normally I wouldn't take off with so many warning lights, but this isn't a normal situation."

Jerry closed and locked the canopy. He scanned the display again. He put power to the port engine and prayed. The growing whine of the engine was music to his ears. He engaged the starboard engine. All he got was an alarm and a set of flashing red lights. He shut it down. He did a quick diagnostic. He shook his head.

"The heat from that fireball fried the ignition circuits," he said.

"Can you still fly?" asked Leona.

The hesitation was not encouraging. Jerry searched his mind for a solution. That demon would be back, and it would be bringing friends, lots of friends. Jerry entered some commands into the floating display. "If I can just get that engine to work for half a minute we could take off. We could limp to the rendezvous point on one engine. I'm going to try to crosswire the circuits, to start the starboard engine using the port ignition system."

"Have you ever done that before?" asked Leona.

"No, I haven't," replied Jerry. "I'm just trying to be creative."

It took about 30 seconds to command the ship to redirect a portion of the port ignition system power to starboard. All the while, Jerry awaited the coming attack. The computer displayed a confirmation of the reroute along with a warning that it was not recommended. They were ready.

"Hold on, Mom. This is likely to be a rough take off," warned Jerry.

A second later, the starboard engine roared to life. Immediately, Jerry went to full vertical thrust. The dagger leapt off of the dusty plane in a cloud of dust. They had climbed to about 100 feet when two fireballs passed directly underneath them. Jerry engaged forward thrust and banked hard over the sea as three more fireballs lit up the sky around him.

The horizon seemed to turn on its side as the dagger lurched forward and to the right. For a second, the fiery sea dominated their horizon. Jerry yanked the stick left. His mother gasped, but she didn't scream. They could both feel the acceleration as the nose of the ship came up. A few seconds later they were flying straight and level, a mere 30 feet above the heaving waves. Jerry eased back on the yoke, bringing the nose up still farther. The dagger climbed.

Then what he had been expecting happened: the starboard engine cut out. Jerry corrected for the loss as best he could. They continued to climb at a considerably reduced rate. He brought up the landing gear to reduce the drag, and their rate of speed and climb increased. Several more fireballs hurtled past them, but they were very wide of their target. Jerry and his mother had escaped—at least for the moment.

The immediate crisis over, Jerry glanced at his radar. They were already better than two miles past the coastline and there was no immediate sign of pursuit. He glanced at his other instruments: 500 feet altitude and climbing, speed 280 miles per hour and increasing. This dagger flew pretty well on only one engine.

"We're out of danger," said Jerry.

"Thank You, Lord," said Leona. "Thank You, Lord, for sending my son to rescue me."

Jerry only nodded. It sounded good to hear his mother talking that way. He changed course to southwest, following the coastline. He also began a more detailed study of the damage. There'd be no safe way to restart the starboard engine, not in flight anyway. It didn't look like the crosswiring job had done any damage to the port ignition system. That was a break. But the cloaking system was fried, and both the electromagnetic drive and the hyperdrive were questionable. In addition, he'd lost the inertial stabilizer.

Could he reach 75,000 feet on one engine? He wasn't sure. He'd never tried it. Two things were certain: he didn't dare engage the electromagnetic drive short of 75,000 feet, and he couldn't engage hyperdrive within the atmosphere. It would take the electromagnetic drive to get him out of the atmosphere and into space. Added to that, flight through hyperspace without a fully functioning inertial stabilizer could be hazardous to his constitution—as in crushed beyond recognition. Not a pleasant thought. All in all, things were a mess, but he wasn't about to tell his mother that. Right now she was too full of hope. He would need to weigh his options.

The flight became significantly smoother as the dagger crossed 10,000 feet. The clouds of the firestorm he had seen from space were now towering above them. He seriously doubted that he would be able to climb over that hellish maelstrom. Jerry turned a bit to the east; he'd have to go around it. He was evaluating one system after another as they climbed past 12,000. He extended the airfoils to their full extent in order to get maximum lift. From the feel of the ship, several options were already off the table. Getting this ship back into space without making some serious repairs first was out of the question. That also meant there would be no return trip, at least not immediately.

Landing would also be a tricky proposition. A vertical landing would require restarting the starboard engine, which would require another crosswire, jeopardizing his only remaining ignition cell. There would be only one landing in their immediate future, and hopefully that would be at the rendezvous point. But getting to the rendezvous point would be dicey.

They had climbed to 30,000 feet when Jerry brought the dagger into level flight. It seemed unlikely that he'd encounter any demons at this altitude. He glanced at the airspeed indicator—480 miles per hour. That wasn't so good. He would be very late reaching the rendezvous point. That point was over 8,000 miles away, much of which would be flown over the Sea of Fire. That fact in itself caused him concern. Right now the port engine display read green, but he had no way of knowing if that engine had taken some damage that just wasn't showing up yet. Suppose they lost it over the sea? Ditching in the Sea of Fire was not an option, and there were no large islands along their flight path.

He glanced back toward his mother. She had fallen asleep. He wasn't quite sure whether that was good or bad. Bedillia had explained to him what happened when people in Hell were freed from their torments. For a while they were fine, but eventually a sort of strange withdrawal set in. After years of having their senses bombarded by continual and intense pain, their bodies became used to sensory extremes. Once those were removed, they slipped into a sort of sensory deprivation that was total agony for them.

The analogy that Bedillia had drawn about it being similar to withdrawal from drugs was a totally alien concept to Jerry. He simply understood that it was a bad thing. She said that it usually set in between 12 and 24 hours after a person's rescue. His mother would need professional care during that period. He needed to get her to Refuge. At best it would take 17 hours to reach the rendezvous point. That was cutting it kind of close. There was no choice—he had to break telesphere silence. Perhaps he could set up an alternate rendezvous point, one a bit closer.

He tried to engage the telesphere link to Refuge. The telesphere didn't activate. The fireball must have created a system-wide power surge. It was difficult to tell what other systems may have been affected. At least the navigation and radar systems still worked. He also had a handheld communicator not dissimilar to those used in Refuge. The problem was that it only had a range of about 80 miles. He glanced at his navigation system, then out at the towering clouds of the firestorm about six miles to the west. He would be around it in another ten minutes, and then he could resume course. He'd be following the coast for nearly another two hours before the long trek over the sea began. He'd try to sort things out in the meantime.

CHAPTER 3

"HOW LONG HAVE I BEEN asleep? Where are we?" asked Leona, looking through the clear canopy into a crystal blue sky above the brown, dusty land below.

Jerry glanced back and smiled. "You've been asleep for about three hours. As to where we are, we're currently at an altitude of thirty-three thousand feet on a heading of one hundred ninety-two degrees. We're almost fifteen hundred miles from where you've spent the past twenty-three years."

Leona looked about. There was not a cloud to be seen across the horizon. The sky up here was a deep blue that slowly transitioned to a hazy salmon color as she looked downward. The land below her was predominantly brown and overall very rough, dominated by jagged hills. There was not a trace of green anywhere. It could have been a scene from an earthly desert, perhaps the Sahara or the Gobi, but it wasn't—this was Hell. "Do you know where you're going?"

"Actually, yes, I do," confirmed Jerry. "I finally came up with a plan, and I think that it's a good one. I didn't want to risk a long flight over the Sea of Fire on one engine—an engine that, even as it is, is running a bit hotter than I'd like. If we lost that engine...well, it would be like going from the frying pan into the fire. So we have a new destination. It is called the Valley of Noak. It lies another eleven hundred miles along this course.

"There is a place there not unlike Refuge. It has come to be called Monrovia, after its founder, Tim Monroe. Apparently he fought a battle against his demon tormentors and won with the help of tiny flying creatures called Abaddon's children. Despite their size, in great numbers they are very dangerous—and very powerful allies. I suppose you could call them scorpions with wings. Right now, Earth is infested with them too."

"They sound disgusting," said Leona.

"I've never seen one," admitted Jerry, "but apparently they aren't as repulsive as you might think. They are highly intelligent, and I've heard that they can see into a person's soul and discern whether what is there is good or evil. Those determined to be evil are likely to be attacked. It is said that there are ten million of these creatures under Tim Monroe's command. The demons have made peace with him. I think they're a little afraid of him. He has been called 'the Alexander the Great of Hell.'"

"How wonderful," said Leona. "Do you think he can be trusted?"

"My friend Bedillia Farnsworth thinks so, but I'm not so sure. Still, he is our best option. From Monrovia we can get you to Refuge. Apparently, Tim Monroe and Abaddon are willing to work together and they do," said Jerry.

Jerry made a few entries into the computer. An image of a desert scene was displayed on a monitor in front of Leona. He continued, "But this is what interests me: it's a cave, a very large one. The Valley of Noak is loaded with them. I think I could maneuver the dagger into this one and out of sight. It would give me an opportunity to make repairs..." Jerry hesitated. "The problem though...it's a good twelve miles over rugged terrain from this cave to Monrovia."

"I can do that," said Leona, "I have to."

Jerry hesitated. "Mom, it's not that simple. I've been sort of hesitant to tell you, but you're likely to get pretty sick and soon. It's all part of the recovery process. I told you a little about it before, but I didn't tell you just how sick you're likely to get. It could get real bad."

Jerry told his mother about the withdrawal symptoms that she would soon experience, symptoms that included delirium and terrible hallucinations.

"Then I guess we'll have to hurry, won't we?" said Leona, determination in her voice. "I won't be a burden on you. I'll make it there somehow."

Jerry nodded. Now he knew where his dogged determination came from. He could only hope that her determination would see her through.

The flight continued. Jerry remained ever alert in the event of trouble, yet trouble didn't materialize. This dagger he called *Hope* lived up to her name. She was flying well now, and the port engine continued to perform faithfully. It gave him quality time with his mother. From her book, he had learned a lot about her. Now she was learning about him. He told her of his life in Heaven, how he grew up in the forest by the stream and about the family that had adopted him. He spoke of the War in Heaven, his three closest friends, and of the present situation on Earth.

"I wish I could tell you more about that world," said Leona. "The problem is, my world ended where those spikes and the inside of that metal shell began. Once in a while I could hear the rain falling on it and hear the thunder rumbling. I had no way of knowing that it was sulfuric acid and not water."

"How did you survive it with your sanity intact?" asked Jerry, but then he continued. "Mom, I know that's probably a very personal question. When I looked in on you from the Great Hall of Records, I sometimes heard you praying. But you had your bad times too. I was so afraid that when I finally opened that sarcophagus that it would be… well, too late…that you would be out of your mind after so many years of pain and horror."

There was a moment of silence. Jerry was afraid that he might just have said the wrong thing.

"At first I was totally terrified," said Leona. "I mean, imagine going through all of that. I think those two spikes going through my eyes was the most horrible thing. I tried to turn my head just a little bit so that they would miss, but I couldn't. Feeling that one spike drive into my heart was the other thing. Every time I moved, I could feel those spikes in me. I was sure that I was going to die, but I didn't. I went wild. I would scream for hours, but when it was all over I was still there; it hadn't done any good.

"I'd wiggle around in those chains. I'd try to free my hands. But nothing worked, it just made the pain worse. After a while I sort of gave up. Once in a while a kind of madness would overcome me and I'd bounce around for a time, but like I said, that didn't do any good. Then I began to focus on something God had said at my judgment. Maybe I was reading more into it than I should have. I became convinced that in time I'd be rescued. I became convinced that it was you who would rescue me."

"It looks like you were right," said Jerry, scanning the ship's display. "And that's what kept you going?"

"Yes," replied Leona. "I learned that I didn't need to breathe. My body insisted that I did, but I didn't. Breathing only made the pain worse. It pushed the spikes into and out of my lungs. If I remained totally still, the pain faded. I could even sleep for a few minutes at a time. But I would slump just a little bit and the pain would wake me up. It just went on and on. It was always the same. Just another day, just one more. But I was beginning to lose faith."

"I'm glad you didn't," said Jerry, starting to pull back on the power. "We have a hundred twenty miles to go. I'm going to start taking us on down. I figure we'll be landing in about half an hour."

The dagger *Hope* slowly descended toward the rugged landscape. All the while, Jerry kept his eyes on the radar for any sign of demons. Here and there he picked up a fleeting signature close to the ground. It gave him reason for concern. He knew that he was not leaving any sort of vapor trail behind, but his ship was visible. Not so much from this altitude—but once he got to lower altitudes that would change.

His attention was drawn to a dust storm not far ahead. It didn't look like it would seriously impact his landing, but it might help obscure his approach. He turned his attention again to the cloaking device. He tried to run a diagnostics test. Jerry was surprised when the diagnostics program actually ran. Perhaps some of the circuitry had simply been knocked off line temporarily. After a minute, the diagnostics results were displayed before him.

"The power coupling," said Jerry.

"What did you say?" asked Leona.

"I think I can bring the cloaking device back on line," said Jerry, "the thing that makes the ship almost invisible. All I need to do is transfer power from another compatible power coupling." For a moment, Jerry seemed deep in thought. "The high frequency radar and the navigation system power couplings are the same. I just have to reroute power from one of them."

"I don't think I understand," admitted Leona, "but wouldn't you lose one of them if you did?"

"Yeah," said Jerry, "but I won't need the radar, not really. Once I land I can materialize a replacement coupling."

"Like you did the shoes," deduced Leona.

"Right," confirmed Jerry.

They were passing through 20,000 feet when Jerry rerouted the power. His radar screen went blank as the ship's cloaking device went active. At least the instruments indicated that it was active. He hoped that the readings were reliable.

The sky around them gradually transformed from deep blue to light blue to the dusty salmon color as the ship passed 5,000 feet altitude. Jerry added half flaps and slowed their speed and descent. He reached into his pack and pulled from it a device that had the appearance of an old-style flip phone. He opened it.

"You have a cell phone?" asked Leona. "I mean, do people use cell phones in Heaven?"

Jerry looked back in puzzlement. "What's a cell phone?"

"That thing in your hand."

"Oh, it's a communicator," said Jerry, extending its small antenna. "The people of Refuge use these things to stay in contact with each other at a distance. We use them too at our research facility. They have a range of about eighty miles. I was hoping that the officials in Monrovia could also use them. We should be within range now."

"A cell phone," said Leona.

"If you say so," said Jerry, bringing the phone to his lips. "This is Jerry Anderson on one twenty-two point four calling any station, come in."

There was no reply.

"This is Jerry Anderson, calling any station in Monrovia. I'm approaching you from the north. Please respond."

Still nothing.

"No signal," deduced Leona.

"I guess not," said Jerry. "We should be in range. Maybe no one is listening."

"I guess not," replied Leona.

"The cave is in a sort of narrow canyon," said Jerry, putting the communicator in his flight suit. "I'll do a flyover or two to get the lay of the land, and then I'll try to land. Get ready."

"I know," confirmed Leona, "seat backs and tray tables in the full upright and locked position."

"What tray tables?" asked Jerry.

His mother smiled slightly. "Never mind, dear, it's an Earth thing."

Jerry kept his full attention on the skies around him, looking out for any demons, as his altitude dropped. He identified the target and pulled back on the power. He knew that he'd need to be careful; this dagger would have less than half of its climbing power if he had to pull up suddenly. He placed the *Hope* on a course right down the center of the valley about 500 feet above the valley floor. He pulled back his speed to 180 miles an hour and added full flaps.

The mountains on either side of the Valley of Noak rose about 2,000 feet above the valley itself and now towered above him, while the valley itself was about three miles wide at this point. The canyon in which the cave was found was a side canyon on the steep southern slopes of the wide Valley of Noak. At its mouth it was about 300 yards wide, but it became ever narrower farther south. The cave was located on the shadowy east face of the canyon about a mile up, while the canyon itself dead-ended in a sheer 500 foot rock face only a mile above that. Adding to that the almost certainly unpredictable canyon air currents, the landing was a perfect example of threading the needle. This was not going to be easy.

"Mom, look for the cave. It's going to be on your left once we enter the canyon. I'm going to be pretty busy just flying this thing."

"OK," said Leona.

Jerry swung the *Hope* hard to the south and lined up with the canyon. "I'll take us in just above the canyon rim. See what the canyon floor looks like, whether it's rocky or smooth."

"Right," confirmed Leona.

The *Hope* entered the narrow canyon right at rim height. Jerry's heart was pounding as he maneuvered through this narrow passage. He dropped a bit lower to afford his mother a better look.

"I see it!" exclaimed Leona. "Wow, is that cave big!"

The *Hope* navigated around a slight turn in the canyon. The end of the canyon almost immediately loomed before them. Jerry added power and pulled back on the yoke. They hurtled over the rim with all too little space to spare.

"What did the canyon floor look like around the cave?" asked Jerry.

"There were some rocks along the edges," said Leona, "but it was mostly sand, I'm sure of it. But that cave was so big. I never saw a bigger cave. I'm sure you could fit this jet in there."

Jerry pondered the situation once more. He was swinging the *Hope* back around toward the valley. He'd gone over this in his mind a half a dozen times on the flight here. He would have to keep both engines running on the port ignition system by doing another crosswire, but it would be an awful strain on the hardware. If the unit failed, he'd lose both engines in a really bad place. But he really didn't have a choice on this one, did he? This was the only way to do it.

He really didn't want to fly through this narrow canyon again unless he was going to land. He'd have to cross the circuits just before he entered the canyon. He'd have to trust his mother's evaluation of the site. If the landing zone was too rough and he had to execute a go-around, he wasn't all that sure he'd be able to pull out before he reached the end of the canyon, in which case...scratch one dagger.

"OK, this is likely to get a bit rough," said Jerry. "Mom, make sure you're braced for a crash."

"You're not going to crash," said Leona. "You've got to think positively. You've done wonderful things with your life. This is just going to be one more. This is going to be a great landing. I have faith in you, my son."

Jerry swung the *Hope* around and lined up on the canyon once more—only this time he was coming in right on the deck. He instructed the computer to initiate the cross just before they entered the canyon.

Again he got a warning message, actually two of them. He overrode the safety protocol. This had worked the last time. It only had to work one more time.

"Full flaps, gear down," said Jerry, as the canyon seemed to hurtle toward him. He remembered that day almost four years ago when he told Professor Faraday that he would be the best pilot in the program. Well, here was his chance to prove it.

He pulled the power back as he brought the nose up in an attempt to bleed off a little more speed. This was it; there was no turning back now.

He swept into the canyon only 40 feet above the deck. He was relieved to hear and feel the starboard engine roar to life. He pulled the nose up still farther. The stall horn sounded. He scanned the canyon wall for the cave. The canyon floor was fairly smooth—his mother had been right.

"Just another few seconds, we're almost there," warned Leona.

Then he saw it. Just another three seconds. Now!

Jerry reversed power while at the same time applying vertical thrust.

It almost felt as if the dagger had slammed into the ground, so hard was the deceleration. Then he cut the power. The dagger fell for a total of less than 3 feet to the canyon floor. Its landing gear contacted the soft sand with little more than a dull thud. Then there was silence.

Jerry gazed about in wonder. They were on the ground only about 80 feet from the cave. In his wildest expectations he hadn't expected to get the ship so close. Better still, there were no large boulders blocking their way. The dagger could nose right on into the cave and even turn around. Jerry brought power to the port engine back on line and taxied very slowly toward the cave.

The sand was not as soft as he had at first thought. The tracks made by the three landing gears were scarcely an inch deep as he slowly maneuvered the *Hope* toward the cave. He switched on the landing lights to see his way. The cave wasn't quite as deep as Jerry might have hoped. It penetrated the nearly vertical canyon wall for maybe 120 feet before branching off into several smaller tunnels. He gingerly nosed the *Hope* into the cave, traveling as far as he dared go, and then he slowly swung it around. The whine of the engines faded away. He'd done it.

"Jerry, you are some pilot," said Leona.

Jerry nodded. "I reckon I won't argue that one—good, or just lucky."

"Try, blessed by God," said Leona.

"That sounds better," replied Jerry, shutting the systems down with the exception of the cloaking field. "Are you ready to go explore?"

"Sure," said Leona. "I guess we need to get moving."

Jerry slid the canopy open. The cave had a dry, musty odor to it, but it was also rather cool. It would make a more than adequate hangar from which he could make repairs. He grabbed his kit and a duffle bag and made his way down the ladder to the ground. Leona quickly followed. Sufficient light entered the cave to allow them to see their way around, at least here, 60 feet from the entrance. It became much darker farther back.

"First things first," said Jerry. "I'd have taken care of this earlier, but we were in a bit of a rush." Jerry pulled from the duffle bag a new set of clothing for his mother. "These should fit you. I'd like to dress you in something nicer; but for what we need to do, this is more practical. It is a flight suit like mine. It has lots of pockets; it is real utilitarian. My mother is not going to run around this place wearing a loincloth. Everything you'll need is there."

Leona picked up the flight suit. It even had the name *L. Stahl* on it. "I think it's a wonderful gift." She kissed Jerry on the cheek. "Thank you, Jerry."

"You can change back there by the tail of the *Hope*. I'll step outside of the cloaking field to give you some privacy."

"Thank you, kind sir," said Leona walking toward the back of the ship.

Jerry smiled and stepped through the cloaking field. He walked about 20 feet before turning around. He was impressed. In the semi-darkness he couldn't see the *Hope* at all. He did some calculating in his head. Could he afford to keep the cloaking field on for days at a time? Did he even need to? He stepped from the cave and into the open canyon, his particle rifle slung over his shoulder.

A slight but rather warm breeze blew up the canyon, but there wasn't a soul around. Sunlight didn't seem to reach the canyon floor here at all. It was perpetually in shadows. That was fine by him. Already he was figuring out the best route to Monrovia. It was a completely underground city. He had studied what information he had about it on the computer during the flight here. The hike wouldn't be particularly difficult. It would be over pretty level terrain really. If all went well, they could make it in six hours—but there were some awfully big maybes in that estimate.

Jerry pulled his communicating device from his pocket. He scanned the narrow canyon as he raised the antenna. "Probably a dead zone," he said. He switched it on. "Jerry Anderson calling any station in Monrovia, come in."

There was still no reply. Maybe the powers that be in Monrovia didn't monitor the airwaves. Jerry heard footsteps behind him. He turned to see his mother dressed in her flight suit. She did a little spin.

"The latest fashion," she said. "Next spring all of the fashion conscious women in America will be wearing a flight suit."

His mother's levity made Jerry laugh. It felt good to see her smile. He could hardly believe how well she had bounced back from her ordeal. It was a true miracle.

"One more thing," said Jerry, "let's get those shackles off of you."

"That would be nice," said Leona. "They are still biting into my wrists."

Jerry took an abrasive wheel tool from his pack. He had his mother sit down on a nearby boulder and went to work. He worked as carefully as he could. This metal was stronger than steel. It took the better part of ten minutes just to cut through the left shackle. He was shocked to actually see how it was fashioned. Although it was smooth on the outside, it was rough and barbed on the inside. It took a little less time to remove the second one.

"Oh, that feels so good," said Leona, hugging her son. "Thank you."

"We need to get started," said Jerry. "There is some survival gear back in the ship. We'll need to pick it up before we go."

"Fair enough," said Leona.

The two headed back into the cave. Jerry had already made a decision. The cloaking device running constantly would completely drain his capacitor in about four days. The repairs were likely to take much longer than that. He'd have to risk shutting it down. He climbed back into the cockpit and started to unload the gear they would need. In the process, he shut the ship completely down.

All the while, Leona stood watching him. A moment later she looked around. "Jerry, I thought I heard something. Do you think there are bats in this cave?"

"Bats...in Hell?" asked Jerry.

"Yeah," said Leona. "On Earth we had a saying: 'Flying as fast as a bat out of Hell.'"

Jerry laughed. "I've never heard of any bats in Hell. Anywhere in Hell you go it's either perpetual night or day. I don't think that bats would like that much."

"Maybe not," said Leona, who now seemed nervous, "but there's something flying around in here."

Jerry closed and locked the canopy and descended the ladder. He stood by his mother and listened.

"There it is again," said Leona, taking Jerry's hand.

"Yeah, I heard it too that time," confirmed Jerry. He handed his mother a pistol in a holster. "Here, you may need this. I'll show you how to use it in a minute."

Jerry pulled out his flashlight and turned it on. Its incredibly bright beam penetrated the darkness like a searchlight. He slowly directed it at the ceiling. The ceiling was crawling with small, winged creatures—thousands of them. Their eyes reflected the illumination of his flashlight.

"Jerry…" said Leona in a trembling voice.

"Be calm," said Jerry. "If they were going to attack us, they'd have done it awhile back."

"What are they?"

"I'm not sure," said Jerry, turning off his light. "I think what we need to do is slowly back toward the entrance of the cave. Don't make any sudden moves."

The two stepped cautiously backward toward the light. What happened next was unexpected.

"Welcome, son of the Most High God," said a voice out of the darkness. It was a soft, kind voice; the voice of a woman.

"Hello," said Jerry awkwardly.

"Don't be afraid," said the voice. "You are indeed welcome among us. You and your mother are both welcome. We are honored by your presence, son of God."

"Thanks," replied Jerry. "It's good to be welcomed…and you can call me Jerry."

Leona seemed perplexed. "Jerry, who are you talking to?"

Jerry turned to his mother in surprise. "Well, don't you hear her?"

"Jerry, I don't hear anyone," said Leona.

"This is incredible," said Jerry. "I've heard stories about this, but I never dreamed that I'd experience it myself. Mom, those things in the cave, they're Abaddon's children."

"The local people call us ACs for short," said the voice. "My name is Chloressa. May I come down to meet you, Jerry?"

"Sure, Chloressa," replied Jerry, "I'd love to meet you."

"OK," said Chloressa, "here I come."

There was a sound of wings as one of the creatures swept in from the ceiling. It circled Jerry several times before coming to rest on his left shoulder. Jerry found himself gazing at a being that may have been all of four inches long. It was almost insect-like in its shape with two pairs of translucent wings. Yet it was covered with light brown fur. At its scorpion-like tail was a menacing looking stinger, yet its face was very much like that of a woman with unusually large brown eyes. And the creature was smiling at him.

"Hello, Jerry," she said.

Jerry returned her smile. "Hello, Chloressa, I'm very pleased to meet you."

"I too am pleased to meet you," replied Chloressa. "I and my family are at your service."

"Chloressa, this is my mother, Leona," said Jerry.

"Hi...Chloressa," said Leona, in a tentative voice.

"Tell your mother that I send greetings to her as well," said Chloressa. "Her spirit is contrite and very repentant. You can tell her that she need not fear us. Indeed, in us she has found a friend, many friends."

Jerry conveyed the message to his mother. She seemed very relieved.

"We're trying to get to Monrovia," said Jerry.

"Yes, we sensed that," replied Chloressa. "We are all in the service of Sir Tim Monroe. I am sure that he will be pleased to meet you. I and several of my clan shall see you safely there. The rest shall remain here guarding your ship."

"I'm grateful for your help," said Jerry.

"It is only our reasonable service to a son of God," said Chloressa.

A few minutes later, Jerry, Leona, and about 20 ACs were on their way to Monrovia. Leona still seemed to be doing fine, easily keeping up with her son's brisk pace.

"It is good that you are traveling swiftly," said Chloressa. "We are some distance beyond the boundary of our master's territory. Demons patrol these parts and do not tolerate trespassers."

"That's good to know," said Jerry. "The way I feel about it, I'm a child of God. God created the entire universe, including this place. I have as much right to be here as any demon. If he prefers to argue that point, all the worse for him."

Leona smiled slightly at Jerry's comment.

"A noble attitude," noted Chloressa, "but it is my experience that it is usually the stronger entity, the one with the most resources, that makes such decisions."

"Just my point," said Jerry. "If God is for us, who is there that can be against us?"

This time Leona laughed outright. "That's my son," she said proudly.

"I hope that your strength will not need to be tested on this day," said Chloressa.

After 20 minutes, the party cleared the narrow canyon and made their way down into the Valley of Noak. It was considerably hotter, near 90 degrees, and a definite tenseness could be felt in the air. Yes, Jerry had spoken bravely, but his words had mainly been for his mother's sake—not to impress her, but to ease her fears. Along the way, Jerry showed his mother how to use and load the particle pistol.

"You need to be careful with that weapon," warned Jerry. "It's only about half as powerful as a particle rifle, but it still packs a real punch. It also goes through its somewhat smaller power cells rather quickly. Each cell is good for about six rounds of fire, and then you need to reload. You've got to make every round count."

They continued for nearly two hours without incident. Yet Leona seemed to be slowing down.

"You OK, Mom?" asked Jerry.

"I'm not sure," admitted Leona. "I'm starting to feel sick…dizzy."

"She is coming down with the sickness," said Chloressa. "I have seen this before. You only today took her from her torment, a very severe torment."

"Yes," confirmed Jerry.

"You must get her to Monrovia quickly," warned Chloressa. "She will soon need great help."

"What are you two talking about?" asked Leona in a tired voice.

"Chloressa is concerned about you," said Jerry.

"Don't worry," said Leona. "I've survived for more than twenty years in that spike-lined coffin, I'll make it to Monrovia."

They continued through the heat across the rocky terrain of the valley. Leona stumbled more frequently. Her eyes were taking on an ever-more glassy appearance. The first symptoms of withdrawal were materializing. They had nearly reached the boundary of Monrovia when they spotted several dark silhouettes against the dusty sky. Jerry pulled out his binoculars to get a better look.

"Now what do we have here?" he said, zooming in. "Three demons in flight—range three hundred fifty yards and closing." Jerry powered up his rifle.

Leona looked toward the approaching figures. Her eyes seemed to come into sharp focus. She unbuttoned the holster and caressed the pistol. Jerry heard the unmistakable sound of the capacitor charging.

"Mom, no itchy trigger fingers," warned Jerry. "If we can talk our way out of this one, that's what we need to do."

"OK, Jerry," said Leona.

The demons were coming straight toward them. They hadn't drawn their swords, so, for the moment, Jerry made no aggressive moves.

The three demons landed 50 feet in front of Jerry and his mother. Jerry motioned to his mother to stop. "Don't make any aggressive moves. Best let me do the talking."

The demons advanced, halving the distance between the two parties. "Who are you?" snarled the one in the middle.

"My name is Jerry, and this is my mother." Jerry showed no emotion whatsoever.

"You are trespassers," accused the demon. "Humans do not walk free in this part of Hell."

"We do," replied Jerry, "and we are not trespassing. We are children of the Father. The Father made all that you see around us. We walk upon that which our Father created. We are not trespassing."

"Don't think to anger me, boy," said the demon. "I am a great warrior and not to be trifled with. I am a veteran of the War in Heaven."

"As am I," replied Jerry. "Need I remind you who won that conflict?"

The demon reached for its sword. "I tire of your insolence, boy."

"Don't even think about it," said Jerry, taking his rifle in hand. "You'd never even get it out of its scabbard." Jerry looked at his mother. She'd already drawn her weapon and the safety was off. "Calm," he whispered.

The demon's hand pulled back. "So, child of Heaven, why are you here?"

"I'm a tourist," said Jerry. "I just had to see what this place was really like."

The demon glared at him. Jerry realized that his explanation held water like a sieve.

"There was an incident at Mathris Los not so many hours ago," said the demon. "A soul was taken from the master. You fit the description of the thief. You are in violation of the Treaty of Sardon."

Jerry had done his homework. He knew well the terms of that treaty between the demons and the people of Refuge. "I am no thief, neither was I a signatory of the Treaty of Sardon. That treaty was between the dark angels, the lost souls, and the fallen angels—I am not a member of any of these parties. I am a son of God. I am not bound by this treaty's terms. I am well within my rights to reclaim a soul that was created by my Father. That soul was never yours to begin with."

"There are six demons approaching from the northwest," warned Chloressa. "They are trying to outflank you."

Jerry nodded but said nothing verbally. He hoped that Chloressa was able to discern his thoughts.

"I shall do as you ask," confirmed Chloressa.

"Let us pass," commanded Jerry.

"I will not," replied the demon.

"I won't go back to that spiked coffin," said Leona, who now trained her weapon at the demon.

"It doesn't matter what you want," said the demon. "You belong to the master."

"Jerry…" said Chloressa.

I already know, said Jerry, in a voice heard only by the mind.

A few seconds later, Jerry and his mother found themselves surrounded as the other six demons joined the original three.

"Do you propose to shoot down all of us with your weapon?" asked the demon.

"He doesn't have to," said a bald-headed man who had just stepped out from behind a large outcropping of rocks some 60 feet to their right. In his hand was a particle rifle similar to the one Jerry held. He wore a brown uniform that allowed him to blend in with his surroundings.

"There are six weapons trained on your compatriots. I assure you… this young man is right: your weapons would never clear your scabbards before we cut you down."

The demon scanned its surroundings. Its eyes focused on two figures on the ridgeline above him, both of which held rifles trained upon his party.

"It's your move," said the mysterious stranger, "but be advised that you are currently trespassing on Monrovian territory." He pointed to a rock about 60 feet behind the demon. "That is the boundary line back there. So, it is you that stand in violation of the Treaty of Noak. I'm sure that your master would be most displeased if you started something here."

"Very well," said the demon, "but I will report this."

"Yack, yack, yack," said the man. "That's all you demons ever do. Now go."

The demons took to the air. Jerry and his mother both breathed a sigh of relief.

The man in brown put away his weapon and walked toward them. "I would guess that you are Jerry Anderson."

"Yes," replied Jerry. "And this is my mother, Leona."

"We've been expecting you," said the man in brown. "I'm Karl Howard, commander of our security forces." He extended his hand and Jerry accepted it. "When you came up late at your rendezvous point, we got a call from the governing council at Refuge to keep an eye out for you should you decide to come our way. We've been briefed on your mission. When we got your first message, we went on high alert. Then we began to track an object too large and too high to be a demon on our radar."

"You have radar?" asked Jerry in amazement.

"Certainly," said Karl, "surface to air missiles too. Then we heard from the ACs that you had landed. We've been waiting for you for over an hour."

"Mr. Howard, you have no idea how glad we are to see you," said Jerry.

"I can imagine," said Karl. "But I'm sure your mother will need some assistance."

Karl drew from his belt a communicator not unlike Jerry's and spoke into it, "We have them. We're bringing them back. Be advised that we have one in need of medical attention."

"How far is it to your base?" asked Jerry.

"About three miles, not far," was the response. "It is not a difficult walk, and there will be people coming to help you with your mother. Our sovereign is most interested to meet you."

"I'm interested to meet him too," said Jerry. "I've heard a lot of very good things about him from Bedillia Farnsworth."

Karl nodded approvingly. "A good woman, that Bedillia Farnsworth. We were sad to see her go. She was the one who sealed the alliance between the honorable people of Refuge and ourselves. Still, we were overjoyed that she has achieved Heaven. Perhaps one day we shall do likewise."

"I hope so," said Jerry.

The three continued walking up the valley. Occasionally they spotted a demon flying overhead, observing their progress.

"We see a lot of them now," said Karl, looking up. "They're fixing for a fight all right, and if that's what they want...that's what they'll get. We'll make their lives hell—no pun intended. Then, when it's all over, we'll ask for ten times the land we have now, and they'll give it to us. Lord Monroe will drive a hard bargain, of that you can be sure."

Jerry was astounded at the confidence of this man. Lord Monroe? This Tim Monroe must be some leader to instill such confidence and reverence in his people. Jerry was very much looking forward to meeting him.

During the journey, Jerry told Karl of the state of his ship and the need to repair it. Karl nodded.

"You can be sure that we shall provide you every courtesy in the repair of your vessel," assured Karl. "I'm sure we have several engineers and mechanics able to assist you in your efforts."

At last they arrived at another canyon leading off to the south. Karl drew Jerry's attention to a vertical cliff to their right that rose 500 feet above the rocky valley floor. "That was once known as the 'plunge of desolation.' For thousands of years, a procession of thousands of poor ragtag souls was led shackled and barefoot up this narrow canyon, under the cruel whips of their demon taskmasters. They were then driven up a winding trail that climbed the west side of the canyon to a ridge and inevitably to this cliff.

"Here they were compelled to throw themselves from the precipice onto the rocks below. Then they were forced to drag their broken bodies back up the trail that led into the canyon...and the journey was repeated again and again. This was the fate that Lord Monroe delivered us from. Now we are eternally in his debt."

"The only successful rebellion against the demons led by a human in the history of Hell," noted Jerry.

"Ah, you know our history," said Karl.

"A bit," said Jerry.

"What was their crime that such a terrible thing was done to them?" asked Leona.

"Homosexuality," replied Karl, "at least mostly. There were also transsexuals, bisexuals, and the like in our midst. We saw it as the way we were, the way we were made; there was nothing unnatural about it to us. We loved and were in turn loved."

Jerry only nodded. In Heaven, people were neither married nor given in marriage, though many, like his adoptive parents, chose to stay together. Sexuality was rather a bit of a mystery to him, and that was fine. On Earth it seemed to be an issue that created much confusion. Crimes of passion and cruelty were as surely results of it as were matrimonial bliss and happiness. He would surely cast no stones at these people.

They entered the canyon. Even after years, the trail of dried blood was still discernable. They passed the sloping trail that led inevitably to the top of the cliff. In the background they could hear a throbbing sound. It grew louder and louder until in the midst of the canyon they beheld a marvelous thing: a field of green. Here, irrigated by wells driven deep into the bedrock, were fields of corn and wheat, tomatoes and onions, set out in neat rows and carefully cared for by the people of Monrovia.

"It's wonderful," said Leona, gazing through tired eyes.

Four individuals, two men and two women, waited for them with a stretcher for Leona. They helped her onto the stretcher.

"You can ride the rest of the way," said one of the women. "We know what you are going through, and we shall see you through it...no matter how long it takes."

"Thank you," said Leona.

"It would be better not to move her to Refuge in her current state," said another of the women. "We can see to her needs just as well here."

Jerry nodded. They were probably right. Why carry her through a wormhole to Refuge in her current state? Anyway, he would need to stay here while seeing to the repairs of the *Hope*. This way he could be closer to her. Perhaps he could even be with her when she awoke.

They proceeded, following a road that led through the fields. Due to the presence of the irrigation and the lush green plants, the air was more moist here and a good 8 to 10 degrees cooler. Many people were laboring hard in the fields, yet they seemed so happy. Small trees were even growing here in the canyon.

"There are orange, peach, and grapefruit trees right now," said Karl. "The trees are new. The seeds all came from Heaven, but they seem to grow fairly well in our soil. We don't have to eat to sustain our lives, of course. But it does make life more pleasant."

"So beautiful," said Leona. Her voice was soft. It was the voice of one on the threshold of falling asleep.

At last they came to a cave entrance on the right canyon wall, which was bathed in sunlight. It was an impressive stone arch entrance guarded by about a dozen armed soldiers.

"We are always on our guard," explained Karl. "At the first sign of a demon attack we can have our military ready within minutes, long before they arrive." He paused. "I'm sure that Lord Monroe will want to speak to you on this subject, but I wanted to have a few words with you first."

"About what?" asked Jerry.

"About technology," said Karl. "We will need all of the high technology we can get in our coming fight with the demons—and it is coming, I assure you. The demons even now plot an attack on Refuge. That, of course, we cannot allow. We will help them. Our treaty is very clear on that issue. We would like the opportunity to examine your ship, to learn from it."

"I would be happy to help you," said Jerry. "It is the very least I can do for you after the kindness you have shown us."

They passed through the arch and into the cavern. It wasn't at all what Jerry had expected. It had smooth, almost polished arching walls with glowing crystals in the ceiling to light the way.

Chloressa, who had been flying about the group during most of their journey, alighted upon Jerry's shoulder. "I want to go with you."

Jerry turned to Karl, who smiled broadly. "You are most blessed, my friend," he said. "To have one of our guardians bond to you upon your arrival is a most fortunate happenstance. This female will be yours for life. She will defend you with her very life and help you communicate with others of her kind. A person who finds his or her own guardian finds a good thing. Of course she may travel with you, even to the throne room."

Jerry smiled, turning to Chloressa. "You may come with me, little one."

Chloressa rubbed her fur against Jerry's neck. It sort of tickled. He petted her. He was rather surprised when she started to purr like a tiny cat.

"We'll need to leave you now," said one of the women at his mother's side. "We will be taking your mother to our care center where we can help her through the difficult days ahead. I think Lord Monroe will want to see you immediately."

"Of course," said Jerry. He leaned down to his mother, who looked up at him with weary eyes. "These women are going to take care of you. I'll be back to see you as soon as I can."

"OK, Jerry," said his mother in a voice barely above a whisper.

Then his mother was taken down a tunnel to the left. For a moment Jerry just stood there.

"She'll be fine," assured Karl. "Those gals are the best, let me tell you. Your mother will be well again."

"I'm sure of that," said Jerry. "She's strong."

"Well, are you ready to meet our leader?" asked Karl.

"Ready as I'll ever be," replied Jerry.

The two men headed down the right passageway. Jerry hadn't really planned on meeting a head of state today. He prayed for the right words.

CHAPTER 4

"NO WORD YET?" ASKED BEDILLIA as she gazed into the telesphere in her home.

"Nothing," said Abaddon. "Your friend Jerry is now eleven hours late to the rendezvous point. I'm afraid that we must assume the worst. I even contacted Tim Monroe in the hopes that Jerry might try to reach his settlement, but I haven't heard anything from him either."

"Chris has traveled to the Hall of Records to look into Jerry's book," said Serena. "We should know something soon."

"If he has fallen into Satan's hands, we are in serious trouble," said Abaddon. "It just might be the excuse that he uses to launch a full-scale invasion against us."

"But that was going to happen anyway," noted Bedillia. "What sort of defense plans have you mounted?"

"Everyone has been armed," noted Abaddon, "and all of my children that I still control here in Hell are ready to fight."

"How many is that?" asked Serena.

"About six million," replied Abaddon. "There should be far more than that, but I've been unable to contact the rest."

"Can't you recall some from Earth?" asked Serena.

"I can't do that," replied Abaddon. "They are busy doing the Father's work."

"I can tell you that you aren't in this alone," said Bedillia. "Many of the saints intend to stand by your side. If necessary, they will gate straight into Refuge so as to fight at your side."

"I'd not want to have their lives on my conscience," said Abaddon. "We're just not ready for this attack, not yet."

"We'll contact you again in about four hours," said Bedillia. "Hopefully we'll know more by then."

Abaddon nodded and the telesphere went blank.

Bedillia looked about the room. "Where is Christopher?"

"He left a few minutes ago," replied Serena. "He said something about having some contacts to make. He didn't say anything more than that."

"I'm sure he must feel terrible," noted Bedillia. "Jerry was his best friend. To think of him maybe being in Satan's hands is not a pleasant thought." Bedillia shook her head. "I had the opportunity. I had Satan right there in my sights. For a moment I thought that particle beam blast had taken him out. But it didn't."

"It wasn't to be," said Serena.

"I suppose," lamented Bedillia. "Still, it was a nice thought."

"Yeah," said Serena. "I'm just glad that you were there for me. You saved my life that night."

Bedillia placed her arm around her daughter. "How about I make you some nice mint tea while we wait?"

"That sounds good," said Serena, following her mother toward the kitchen.

The sun had already set and it was snowing again. It was going to be a long, cold night.

Christopher stepped into the grassy forest meadow to find Lilly sitting in the lotus position, her arms outstretched and her eyes closed. He quietly approached her. It had been over a year since he had last seen her. This 17-year-old young woman seemed so very beautiful, almost angelic.

"Hello, Christopher," she said, without even opening her eyes or changing her position. "I've been expecting you."

"I shouldn't be surprised by that," said Christopher. "Elizabeth told me that I'd find you here."

"There's been trouble," continued Lilly. "Don't worry, Jerry is safe, as is his mother, at least for the moment."

Christopher was tempted to ask her how she knew that, but he resisted. He sat down on the grass beside her.

"We're needed again," continued Lilly. This time she lowered her arms and looked to Christopher. "There is another storm coming," she continued, "and the four of us must stand in the midst of it."

"You're amazing," admitted Christopher. "I suppose you know what's been going on."

"Yes," confirmed Lilly. "You and Jerry have attempted to rescue his mother from her torments in Hell." Lilly paused, then she smiled. "It doesn't take a seer to figure that out. The two of you have been talking about it for years. You talked about it the last time I saw you."

"I'm sorry I haven't been around," said Christopher.

"I understand," said Lilly, "you've had a lot on your mind. It was very bold for the two of you to undertake this mission—bold and foolhardy."

"Well, you know Jerry. Once he sets his mind on something there's no turning him around," said Christopher.

"Who is more foolish," asked Lilly, "the fool or the fool who follows him?"

Christopher laughed openly. "I guess you have me on that one."

"It's OK, this was meant to happen," replied Lilly.

"Hello, hello, never fear, Jonathon is here."

The two looked up to see Jonathon walking toward them, the mists of the gate fading behind him. Both Christopher and Lilly laughed. Yep, same old Jonathon—he always did know how to make a dramatic entrance.

"We have a problem," said Christopher.

"Jerry," deduced Jonathon.

"You and Lilly have been in contact," deduced Christopher.

"Lilly and I are always in contact," replied Jonathon. "I sense her thoughts every day. I come here once in a while, but we are in communication almost all of the time."

Christopher looked to Lilly. "That's got to be annoying," he said, almost under his breath.

"Your attitude is noted," replied Jonathon, whose smile told him that he had taken no offense. "But seriously, Lilly knows a lot about what is going on in Monrovia, and some of it is rather disturbing. I think you'll need to hear her out."

"I'm listening," said Christopher.

"It's about Tim Monroe," began Lilly. "He has created his own little empire in Hell, and he is getting support from right here in Heaven."

"Yes, I know," confirmed Christopher. "Dr. Kepler and his team support the efforts of Abaddon in Refuge, and he in turn supports Tim Monroe. For all I know there is probably direct dialog between Dr. Kepler's team and Tim Monroe."

"There is," confirmed Lilly, "but that's not the support I am speaking of. There are other parties here in Heaven supporting Monroe. It all started not too long after the War in Heaven. Many people here in Heaven sought to know all that they could know. They sought the restoration of all of their memories of Earth, even those of lost loved ones.

"As you know, some of these people went to Dr. Kepler and his team, pleading with them to approach Abbadon regarding the rescue of their loved ones. Still, Abaddon was not free to act on their behalf. He had a treaty with Cordon, the demon leader of Hell, to uphold, and it severely limited the number of souls he could rescue from their torments. He had his own people to think about. That fragile treaty was all that stood between his people and annihilation. When that failed, these saints sought other avenues of rescue for their loved ones. It was then that they found out about Tim Monroe."

Christopher was stunned by this revelation. "Yeah, but how would they have contacted him? The only way they could have done it was by angelic courier or telesphere. I think angels are currently banned from making the trip to Hell, and telesphere technology has been shared with only a few people here in Heaven. It has remained a carefully guarded secret."

"How are any carefully guarded secrets obtained? Industrial espionage," replied Jonathon. "All it would take was one disgruntled member of Kepler's or Faraday's science or engineering team to leak the information to parties unknown. Perhaps this person had a loved one suffering in Hell whom they wanted to rescue, but they knew that Abaddon's hands were tied."

"Who tied Abaddon's hands?" asked Christopher.

Jonathon just shook his head. "Some things never change."

"He means that the treaty didn't allow Abaddon the latitude to act in a timely manner," said Lilly.

"Oh," replied Christopher, "you could have said that in the first place."

"Tim Monroe had a telesphere," continued Lilly. "It was given to him by Abaddon. As to how a citizen of Heaven could obtain a telesphere, it wasn't necessarily an act of espionage. Keep in mind that there are no secrets in Heaven. All one would have to do was go to the Great Hall of Records and look into the book of Nikola Tesla or Johannes Kepler. Eventually you could piece together how to build any of their mechanical creations, assuming that you have advanced knowledge in building such things."

"There are plenty of people in Heaven who do," interjected Jonathon.

"I don't know how it happened, and it really isn't important," continued Lilly. "The point is, someone managed to do it. They contacted Tim Monroe and appealed to him to rescue their loved ones."

"Yeah, but what could they possibly offer him?" objected Christopher. "From what I've read about Monroe, he wasn't likely to do it out of the goodness of his heart."

"He didn't," confirmed Lilly. "They gave him what he wanted—weapons and technology. He in turn rescued their loved ones. He must have a teleportation ring. How he got it, I cannot say. But I can tell you that he has rescued many—perhaps thousands. Each one he rescues adds one more soldier to his own army. At this point, I believe that he would welcome a war with Satan's forces. He is confident of victory. In his mind, it would bring him all the more power. People have called him 'the Alexander the Great of Hell,' and he views himself as such—and the comparison is accurate. His goal is to become the sole master of Hell."

"Well, he's got to be preferable to the current one," noted Christopher.

"I'm not so sure," said Jonathon, "but we could always hope."

"But how could he defeat Satan?" objected Christopher. "It's a nice dream, but he has to be outnumbered thousands to one."

"He has a reason for his confidence," said Lilly. "What it is, I cannot say."

"But you don't know who is supporting him?" asked Christopher.

"No, I don't," said Lilly.

Christopher turned to Jonathon.

"I don't know either," admitted Jonathon, "but I suspect that we could find out, eventually. A logical and systematic search of selected books of the Hall of Records could give us the information we need."

"That would take too long," objected Lilly. "We have less time than you think."

"But regarding Jerry, you have concerns about his being there," said Christopher.

"Yes," confirmed Lilly. "Tim Monroe is rapidly growing drunk with power. There are things that he wants from Jerry. I doubt that he will allow him to leave until he has them."

"Like the dagger," deduced Christopher.

"For one thing," said Lilly. "From my understanding, few people know that craft better than Jerry. Then there is his ability in matter manipulation. I doubt that they have anyone in Monrovia with that level of mastery. Given time, he could probably build more daggers for Monroe."

"Big trouble in River City," said Jonathon.

Christopher had to think about that one for a moment. He got the meaning. "So we need to rescue him."

"No," said Lilly, "at least not yet."

Christopher was puzzled. "So what is there that we can do?"

"For now, nothing," said Lilly. "It isn't time. But the time is coming when we must stand with him."

"But against who?" asked Christopher, "Against Tim Monroe?"

"Not necessarily," said Lilly. "What is happening must happen. But we will be there to…how shall I put it? Adjust the course of events."

"You're suggesting that we go to Hell?" asked Jonathon, who seemed genuinely surprised.

"If it comes to that," confirmed Lilly. "There is another war coming, and it will have as far-reaching implications as did the War in Heaven. Hell cannot remain as it is; it must change, evolve."

"And we're going to change it…the four of us?" asked Jonathon.

"No," said Lilly, "but we are going to guide the direction of those changes…influence those who will."

"And the Father will guide us," deduced Christopher.

"Yes," replied Lilly. "As I said, Hell must change."

"You wouldn't care to elaborate on that, would you?" asked Jonathon.

Lilly turned to him and smiled. "No, not at this time, and no, you're not going to discover what it is through the Jedi mind trick."

Again there was a round of laughter, which eased the building tension. Christopher was glad to be back together with these two friends, but he wouldn't feel complete until they were a foursome again.

They spent a little bit of time catching up on each other's lives. Apparently, time had honed their skills. Christopher could now proudly boast that he could levitate several tons, perhaps even a dagger if it came to that. He also spoke of his precious reunion with his parents. Now, at last, his life was almost complete.

Jonathon, of course, spoke more about surfing with his great-grandmother than of any new skills he may have learned. In addition, he now had his grandparents to keep him company. They had arrived out of the tribulation along with the rest of the saints just a few months ago. They hadn't been at all surprised to find him in Heaven. Indeed, they knew of his exploits before he even told them.

That was especially true of his grandfather, whose abilities as a prophet rivaled Lilly's. And Jonathon's grandfather had his own stories to tell too. He spoke of the discovery of the comet that dealt so crippling a blow to Earth. Indeed, he had been present on the night of its discovery. He was the one who had urged Jonathon to come here today, saying that it was part of God's plan. He also mentioned something about adventure. If it was to be an adventure, you could count Jonathon in.

Lilly spoke of the honor of studying with one of the greatest spiritual figures in all of Heaven, but she spoke little of herself beyond her joy of being reunited with her own mother and uncle. It was so much like her. She hadn't changed.

"Well," said Christopher, "I think I should head back to Bedillia's home. I really need to tell her what we've discovered."

"Tell her what we've learned about Jerry, but not about what we know about Tim Monroe," said Lilly. "That must remain between us for the time being."

Christopher shook his head. "I don't know if I'm comfortable with that."

"It is important," assured Lilly. "For things to go as the Father would wish, this is the way it must be." Lilly paused. "You disagree?"

"It's being deceptive," objected Christopher. "After all, we're all on the same side."

"You've done it before," continued Lilly, "during the War in Heaven, remember? You had a word for it: plausible deniability. It is the same thing here."

Christopher felt as if the tables had been turned on him, and he didn't particularly like it. "OK, Lilly, I'll go along with it."

"You will understand why…and soon," assured Lilly.

Christopher said his goodbyes and gated back to the far north. Hopefully Chris would be back and they would know more of what had transpired. It would be difficult to keep this secret, but he would do it.

Jerry walked with Karl down long, rocky corridors so nearly rectangular in form and so very smooth that they didn't look like subterranean tunnels at all. Large and very regular shaped crystals imbedded in the ceiling that glowed with a steady white light provided the illumination. Additionally, metal ducts along the ceiling with large vents kept the fresh air circulating. There were also conduits that looked like electrical cables. In the background Jerry could hear the distant sound of machines running.

"After serving as a U.S. Marine in the Pacific during World War Two, I was a mechanical engineer back on Earth," explained Karl. "Believe it or not, this excavation work was all done without the use of machines and with relatively little manual labor. Our small creatures, the ACs, have teeth with surfaces rivaling the hardness of diamond. Thousands of them cut the existing tunnels to a regular but rough shape. Then teams of workers took the rock dust they left behind and made it into a sort of plaster to fill in the low spots.

"Finally, we use a technology we borrowed—or if you like, stole—from the demons: the ability to produce small and precisely directed fireballs. These fireballs fuse the wall's surface, making it perfectly smooth and very hard. We currently have nearly eighteen miles of tunnels, all constructed in this manner."

"Remarkable," said Jerry, as they made their way through the rather busy passageway. He noticed that intersecting corridors had numbers, not names, and along them were doors, which were all labeled.

"We derive our power from a reactor that converts the energy within power spheres that we imported from Heaven into usable electricity. That energy is derived directly from the Father's own Holy Spirit. It is an energy that pervades the entire universe, except for here. That is why we are dependent upon our supporters in Heaven to provide it to us. It is a technology we borrowed from our good friends in Refuge. It drives the fans that circulate the air and generates the radio frequency that excites the crystals in the ceiling to glow," said Karl.

They passed a pair of armed sentries and made a turn to the left into a corridor of glistening walls. They passed through a great dome-shaped cavern room and into another great hallway. At the end of the hallway stood a pair of massive metal doors the color of brass guarded by two more sentries.

The sentries opened the doors for Jerry and Karl, and they entered into what may best be described as a fantastic throne room. Rectangular in shape, the room had walls adorned with great tapestries depicting all manner of natural scenes, including tranquil forests, mighty rivers, and peaceful meadows. The floors were so smooth that they glistened. Here and there, Jerry saw small porticoes built into the walls, and around and within them numerous ACs gazed at the approaching visitors. From the small size of some of the creatures, Jerry figured them to be juveniles. On the far wall was another closed metal door, which was also guarded. Near the middle of the chamber, on an elevated circular stone platform, were two stone thrones adorned with gold and jewels.

Upon the left throne sat a brown-haired young man in a purple robe who appeared to be no older than Jerry, perhaps even younger. Jerry noticed that an AC was perched on his shoulder as well. The young man's brown eyes scanned the pair as they walked toward him.

To his left was a young, blond-haired woman dressed in a white, Grecian-style dress, who also had one of the tiny creatures on her shoulder. Her blue eyes also followed their visitors with interest.

"Lord Monroe, here is our visitor from Heaven," said Karl. "His name is Jerry Anderson. His mother has been taken to the recovery center. It may be some days before she is able to meet with you."

Tim rose to his feet, a beaming smile on his face. "Oh yes!" he exclaimed. "Welcome to my home, Jerry. I so rarely get to entertain guests, especially ones from the Father's realm."

"Thank you for your hospitality, Lord Monroe," said Jerry.

"Oh, no, no, not Lord Monroe. Let's forget the stuffy titles. My name is Tim. You are welcome to this island of sanity and reason amid the craziness and pain of this dismal world." There was a pause. "Oh, but where are my manners? Allow me to introduce you to my queen, my wife, Megan. She makes my life make sense; she keeps me focused."

Megan rose to her feet. "Welcome, Jerry," she said in a distinctly Australian accent. "We rejoice with you at the rescue of your mother—a very brave and selfless act."

"Thank you, you're very kind," said Jerry.

"Oh, and allow me to introduce you to another member of my immediate family," said Tim, motioning to the AC on his shoulder. "Without him I would still be groveling in a dark cave, shivering and frightened. His name is Goliath, like the giant. He may seem small, but he is a giant in my eyes."

Jerry was surprised when Goliath did a sort of bow to him.

"And this is Cindy," said Megan, motioning to the AC on her shoulder.

"It is so very wonderful," said Tim. "Cindy was the second of our guardians to enter my life. She is the mate of Goliath and has bonded telepathically to my beautiful wife. Together we make quite a family."

"Yes," agreed Jerry. "You can see the hand of the Father in it all."

There was a momentary pause in the conversation. Jerry wondered if he had just made a serious blunder.

"Perhaps," replied Tim. "One can never know about such things." Again there was a pause. "Yes, but you must be hungry and thirsty after your long voyage. I want to hear about all of it, Jerry. Let us get better acquainted. I've taken the liberty of having a meal prepared in your honor…" Again there was a pause. "Karl, I'd like it if you could join us, if you have the time."

"Yes," replied Karl, "thank you."

The group retreated through the door at the far end of the throne room and into a dining room. To say the least, Jerry was amazed at what he saw. He had expected to find some sort of stone dining room table and stone chairs. After all, stone was Hell's primary building material. Instead, his eyes fell upon a long and finely crafted wooden table and wooden chairs with velvet upholstery. An ornate glass chandelier hung above the table, while the floors were composed of the finest tiles.

Upon the table were fine china dishes and crystal glasses. The courses included oranges, apples, and a variety of vegetables.

"You will need to excuse the nature of our diet," said Tim. "We are all vegetarians here. Taking the life of any animal, after what we have been through, is simply not appropriate."

"No, that's fine," said Jerry. "It's just that I wasn't expecting to see a dining room like this here."

"Oh," chuckled Tim, "well, I have quite a number of supporters and benefactors in Heaven. Many of these things come from there. However, we are slowly growing an ever-greater percentage of our food right here. Of course we are not required to eat, but old habits are tough to break. I lived on Earth for fifteen years before coming here. But I understand that you never lived on Earth at all."

"Yes, that's right," confirmed Jerry, "I've lived all of my life in Heaven."

Tim motioned toward several chairs with plates and glasses already set on the table before them. "But please, make yourself comfortable, eat and drink. Then tell me about your life. I do want to hear of your adventures. I understand that you were very involved in the War in Heaven. I want to know all about it."

It seemed to Jerry that this Tim Monroe already knew an awful lot about him—more than he had expected, and more than he should. Something wasn't quite right here.

During the dinner Jerry seemed to do most of the talking, answering one question after another, but he did get Tim Monroe to give him a little bit of information between questions. Tim spoke of the settlement of Monrovia and how it had developed. He also spoke of his fight for freedom. Still, he spoke in generalities, shying away from any specifics. He talked a lot, but he didn't say very much. It was when Jerry asked a few questions about the nature of Tim's benefactors that Tim finally opened up. This seemed to be a matter of pride with him.

"I have an entrepreneurial spirit," began Tim, "nothing wrong with that. On Earth it is considered a good trait. Specifically, I provide a needed service that no one else in Hell is currently willing or able to provide. Since the War in Heaven, there has been an awakening in Heaven. I suppose you know about all of that.

"All of a sudden people were becoming aware of their nameless loved ones in Hell. It was nice to have one's existence acknowledged for a change. It is so depressing to be suffering for all eternity only to realize that not a single soul realizes it or even knows that you exist. Those in Heaven knew that they would be separated from these husbands and wives, sons and daughters, mothers and fathers forever. This they could not change. But the thought of them being tortured, in pain forever, was unbearable. That could be changed, and I'm the one who could change it…" Tim paused.

"Look, Jerry, Abaddon is a real nice guy. I like him a lot, OK? Any bad blood between us has been gone for a long time. But he fears the demons way too much. He has stopped reaching out to the lost beyond those who are loved ones of his own people in Refuge. But I'm different—I take risks."

Jerry listened carefully to Tim's words. Actually, it was more the way he said them than what he said. Could there be a trace of madness hidden deep within them? He realized that he would have to exercise great care in dealing with this guy.

"People in Heaven pleaded with Abaddon to rescue their loved ones," continued Tim, "but he wouldn't. He was unwilling to take the risk. Then they found out about me. When I was first approached about freeing these poor souls, I jumped at the chance. But like any good entrepreneur, I had a price. It was a very reasonable one really. I rescued their loved ones, saw that they were well-cared for, and they provided me with things that I needed. It is all done very much on the q.t. of course, but there are no losers here. It's a win-win situation."

Jerry was stunned. "Yes, I suppose it is."

"Of course it is," continued Tim. "Everyone who comes here to Monrovia is very grateful to be here. You can understand that. First, we see them over the initial shock that comes with their release. Bedillia explained it all to me—something about the mind's response to being in such great pain for so long and then suddenly having that pain removed. It creates a sort of vacuum in their souls. They get over it, but it takes time."

"I've seen it firsthand," interjected Megan. "It's one of my jobs to help people get over that horrible hump. It's a rough job, but it's very rewarding to see them finally get up, free at last."

"Megan is a real angel of mercy," said Tim, taking her hand. "I'm very proud of her."

"Tim saw me through my rough days," said Megan. "He was wonderful."

There was a moment's silence. Tim and Megan gazed into each other's eyes. They seemed so serene.

A moment later, Tim refocused his thoughts. "Well, as you may imagine, our new citizens dread the prospects of returning to the torments that had driven them to the edge of insanity. They really want to make it here. Consequently, they are great workers and soldiers. This is the perfect society."

Jerry nodded in approval. "Offhand, do you know just how many souls you've rescued?"

"Over twelve thousand," was the reply. "By the way, our population is about four times that of Refuge."

"I know that Abaddon takes great care in getting each soul out of Satan's hands," said Jerry. "He generally relies on stealth to free them. How have you taken so many and not gotten caught?"

Tim laughed openly. "Because, my friend, I don't use stealth; I use deception. Years ago Abaddon released millions of his tiny children into Hell to prey upon the demons."

He turned to the creature on his shoulder. He stroked him gently. "Goliath here was the eldest of Abaddon's children. My biology teacher back in high school used to call such a creature of a family grouping an alpha male. And make no mistake about it, the ACs are collectively one large family. As the alpha male, he has considerable authority. When I found him out there in the canyon, he had been injured by a demon in battle and was dying. I hid him away, nursed him back to health.

"As fortune would have it, we share a telepathic link. Abaddon could never understand why he was unable to control over a third of the children he sent out into Hell. That was because I controlled them. Now most of the ones he controls are on Earth, doing battle with the allies of Satan. Most of the ones I control are still here. They usually travel in packs and obey my commands.

"When I get a contract to rescue a specific victim of Satan from his or her torments, I first send in a pack of tens of thousands of my little friends. They overwhelm the demons and clear the area for me. Then I use my teleportation ring to go in and rescue that individual, as well as any others in the area who may be of use to me.

"We often leave a scattering of human or demon remains behind. This gives the demons the illusion that the ACs are capable of reducing a damned soul or one of their own kind to bones that do not regenerate, utterly destroying them. It hides what we are really doing and it breeds fear among the demons." He laughed. "They ought to be afraid, very afraid."

Jerry nodded. He would never have thought of such a plan. Still, Tim was playing a very dangerous game. If Tim were discovered, the demons would probably declare open war against him.

"The demons can't be trusted," interjected Megan. "We all know that here. Eventually they're going to come after us, no matter what we do. Just last week, one of their emissaries stood before us and demanded that we give them all of our weapons. He gave us two weeks to comply—or else. We didn't tell him yes or no, but I know this: I'd rather have a large army with real weapons when they come back than to be groveling helplessly in these caverns."

"Right on!" said Tim. "You just gotta love her."

"Jerry, things have to change in Hell," continued Megan. "I don't believe that God intended for us to be tortured here. I don't think that's His way. I think that our punishment was to be separated from Him and His love. It was Satan and his demons who decided to torture us. I accept God's judgment, but I won't accept Satan's."

"Now you see why I love her so," said Tim.

Megan smiled but said nothing more.

"So, what are you going to do when they come for your weapons?" asked Jerry.

His question was followed by a long pause. Tim seemed deep in thought. "Yes, I'll tell you," he finally said. "Why not? When the demons come back, we're going to tell them no."

Again there was silence.

"And then?" asked Jerry.

"I'm moving most of our guardians, our ACs, back to us here. They will reach us in time, over twenty million of them. Come, come with me."

Tim led Jerry to what appeared to be a black framed table with a sheet of clear glass on the surface. The glass immediately took on a milky appearance and then the form of a three-dimensional map of the area, which showed the boundaries of Tim's tiny empire. He moved his hand in a circle.

"Most of my guardians shall take up positions in the caves around this place, about five miles out on all sides, hidden from the enemy's sight. When the demons come sufficiently close, we shall open fire on them using our pulse cannons," Tim said.

"Pulse cannons?" asked Jerry. "I've never heard of such a thing."

"Oh," replied Tim, "you're in for a real show. A pulse cannon fires a shell through the air, like a cannon. It detonates some distance out with quite a bang. You've just gotta love it. It's like a particle weapon overload. We've got hidden pulse cannon batteries surrounding our fortress.

"Then we bring in the guardians and our ground troops. They attack what is left of the demon force after our pulse batteries are finished with them. Then we turn the tide on them; we go on the offensive. By the time this is all over, they'll do almost anything to get us to stop."

Jerry looked at Tim skeptically, then at Megan. He could tell that they were serious about this thing. Then a thought hit him. "Why are you telling me all of these things?" he asked.

Tim smiled like a Cheshire cat. "Oh, bravo, I was wondering when you would ask that question. You know that it is very unlikely that your mother will be ready to be moved before the demons attack. She'd be no better off in Refuge—worse actually. In the meantime, you're sort of stuck here. You want to be here when she wakes up, right? You want to be a good son, right? Well, while you're waiting, there is something that I need from you."

Then Jerry got it. How could he have been so dense? "You want the dagger."

Tim laughed loudly. "Oh no, you're wrong on that one. You think I would take your ship? You misjudge me, sir…I would never do that."

"He wouldn't," said Megan. "My husband isn't that sort of man at all. He is a great man, an honorable man, and he will, in the end, change the very face of Hell. People will one day come to call him Tim the Great."

Tim stretched out his hands, smiling broadly. "Like I said, you gotta love her. But come, my friend, allow me to put your mind to ease."

The four departed by a side door that led 50 feet through a wide but empty corridor to another door, which was closed and guarded. Beyond that door was another room that housed a silvery, eight-foot ring mounted upon a large, black marble base. Nearby, a sort of control console sat at about waist level atop a crystalline stand. A man in a brown uniform standing before the console bowed slightly before his sovereign.

"To the hangar, Wyatt," said Tim.

A few entries into the console brought a blue mist filled with sparkling stars into the midst of the ring.

Tim looked toward Jerry. "Follow me, if you please." Tim stepped into the mists. The others followed.

Only a few steps brought them through another somewhat larger ring near the wall of a huge cavern room that was well over 100 feet across and better than 50 feet high. The clearly subterranean room was almost perfectly dome-shaped. But it was neither the shape nor the size of the room that brought a sense of astonishment to Jerry. Here, illuminated by 12 bright crystal lights in the ceiling, were three dagger fighters virtually identical to the *Hope*. Scattered on the floor about the fighters were tools and maintenance equipment not unlike that used in Heaven.

"How?" asked Jerry. He stepped forward to get a closer look at these marvels of engineering.

"As I said, I have my methods," said Tim. "Getting the plans and having the parts fabricated was not so tough. One of your own engineers provided us with those plans. In turn, we rescued both his mother and his father. Another man, the head of a materializer's guild who was highly skilled in the art of materialization, saw to the fabrication of most of the parts. For him, we saved his wife from a…well…I'd rather not say.

"Most of the parts easily fit through the ten-foot ring. Some of the parts were made right here. The problem is that these ships don't work properly—not one of them. The artisans who built them did their best, but they weren't up to the challenge. Mechanically, the ships fit together fine; the complex electronics are another matter. Apparently, we're doing something wrong. We don't know what."

"That's what you need me for," deduced Jerry.

"Yes," confirmed Tim. "My people are very good at assembling the parts. They could do the heavy work of repairing your ship. They know how your ship works and where all of the parts go. We need someone to get our electronics right. We also need someone to teach our pilots."

"How long do we have?" asked Jerry.

"Eight days," said Megan.

"That's not enough time," objected Jerry. "Assuming that I could figure out all of the bugs in these ships in eight days—and I doubt it—we'd still have to train pilots to fly them."

"We have pilots for you," replied Tim. "We've got the best. We have anything you need—just name it. When it's all done, we can even teleport you back to Heaven. These teleportation rings can send you safely home, although I and my people would perish if we made the attempt. It has something to do with the nuclear density of our atoms or something like that. I'm not a scientist."

Jerry looked over at Tim, then at the three ships. He noticed a long, wide tunnel that led toward an opening 100 or so yards away. It looked like a launch tunnel.

"We have thought of everything," assured Tim. "When the first desperate people of Heaven came to me, I was thinking organization. We organized them so that they could work together to save their loved ones. I am the key element of that organization. I put those people in Heaven in contact with each other. I turned them from individuals with a dream into an organization with a purpose." Tim paused.

"But your mission, your purpose, still puzzles me, Jerry. Surely you knew what the situation was here and in Refuge when you set out to rescue your mother. Abaddon must have told you that we would soon be under attack. You knew that your mother might only find safety there for a short time, yet you still came. Man, that just doesn't make any sense. Is there something I'm missing here?"

"No, you're not missing anything," said Jerry. "I just knew that I had to come. I acted on faith."

Karl spoke up: "You knew that we'd be outnumbered ten thousand to one by the demons, yet you came anyway. Jerry, there's no sense in that unless you know that we can win this."

"Yes, you know we can," echoed Megan.

"But we need your help," said Tim. "You're supposed to be here. Call it God's will if you wish, but you know it's true…" Tim paused. "You can make the difference…" There was another pause. "You probably think I'm crazy, a little bit nuts—fine. But you're also asking yourself: What if he's right? What if he really can pull this off? Think of it. Think of what we could accomplish."

"I am," admitted Jerry.

"There is no real danger to you," continued Tim. "You can teleport out of here anytime you want. I'm not stopping you." Tim pointed to the ring. "There's the door. Leave if you wish. We'll take care of your mother if you leave…at least for as long as we can."

"Jerry, we need you," said Megan. "We just want the opportunity to relieve the suffering of so many others. All we ask is for the opportunity to continue our work. If Satan destroys us, if we are gone…who is going to do it? All hope will be gone."

Jerry was indeed confused. He hadn't set out to do this. In very fact, he was wondering what he had intended to do even if his plan had gone flawlessly. Tim was right: this rescue mission of his didn't make any sense unless he was willing to do this.

He scanned the faces looking at him so hopefully. "I'll need the schematics from my ship," he began. "I'll also need power modules—lots of them. If you have anyone with a good knowledge of basic matter materialization, I'll need them working with me."

"Then you'll do it?" asked Megan.

"Yes, I'll do it," confirmed Jerry.

"You'll have everything you ask for," promised Tim, "and getting back and forth from your ship will be easy with the ring."

"Then I guess it's time to get started," said Jerry.

"You're making the right decision," assured Tim, shaking Jerry's hand. "My wife speaks of changing the nature of Hell. I'll never doubt her again."

Jerry knew that he had just taken a big step on faith. He only hoped that he could deliver.

CHAPTER 5

CHRISTOPHER ARRIVED AT BEDILLIA'S MANSION to find Bedillia, Serena, and Chris discussing what Chris had discovered at the Hall of Records in the City of Zion. Chris had looked through both Jerry's book and Leona's book and obtained a detailed account of the happenings in Hell.

"I'm surprised that Tim Monroe hasn't contacted Abaddon about the arrival of Jerry and his mother," admitted Serena.

"I'm not," said Chris. "Monroe needs Jerry. He doesn't want to take the chance of losing him to Abaddon. He wanted to make his own pitch to Jerry first."

"I fear that all this positioning is going to mean very little in the long run," said Bedillia. "Very soon this is all going to fall apart. Satan will attack both Refuge and Monrovia. Then there will be only suffering for the damned souls of Hell. I can't stand by and allow that to happen. If all I can do is pick up a particle rifle and go through Dr. Kepler's portal to Refuge—that is what I'll have to do."

"Mother!" exclaimed Serena. "No, you can't do that! I won't allow you to do that."

"You can't stop me," said Bedillia. "I need to be there, fighting at their side. They're my people, Serena, I need to be with them."

"No," objected Serena, tears coming to her eyes. "I've finally got you back. I don't want to lose you again."

"We don't go off half-cocked and act emotionally," objected Chris. "We can't allow this to happen—you're right. We've got to do something, but not that."

"Now wait a second," said Christopher. "I read in history once that before the United States entered World War Two and during the Cold War, the U.S. got involved in foreign conflicts by shipping war supplies to the nations they wanted to support. They gave those nations technology that they couldn't possibly have developed on their own. They also sent in advisors to help those people with that advanced technology."

"It's all very nice that you remember your history," said Chris, "but remember, we only have eight days. Those things happened over the course of many years."

"Look," said Christopher, "I may be young, but I helped design and build those daggers. They could turn the tide of the battle if we equipped the people of Refuge and Monrovia with our latest technology. I could go to Monrovia and get those three daggers running in a day or two. We may even be able to build them more."

"Going to Hell?" objected Serena. "You can't be serious. You can't even begin to realize what it's like there."

"Look, I know how you feel," said Christopher. "I can't even imagine what you or your mother experienced there as victims of Satan. But I'm talking about going there as an advisor. I get those daggers up and running and I'm out."

"Can't you help Jerry from here?" objected Chris.

"No, I can't," replied Christopher. "He is good at matter materialization—he may be the best—but he doesn't know these systems like I do."

"The whole issue is academic anyway," said Bedillia, turning toward the others. "The only person I know who has a ring capable of dialing into any location in Hell is Dr. Kepler, and he absolutely won't permit you to go. Your parents would probably go ballistic over that idea. For the first time in eleven years you are finally getting to be with them.

Now you want to go off on this reckless mission. Think, Christopher… this isn't the way to do it."

"I guess you're right," lamented Christopher.

"If you come up with some ideas, you can talk to Jerry directly over my telesphere," continued Bedillia. "I'm sure we can make a connection. Tie it up for days if you wish, I don't care. I have a great long distance plan—unlimited minutes."

"Dr. Kepler will come up with some way that we can help," said Chris.

"I'm sure he will," continued Serena.

The group continued to throw ideas back and forth during the next hour or so. They came up with some pretty good ones. They agreed to approach Dr. Kepler with them in the morning.

As Christopher left the meeting, he already had a plan, and not one that they had discussed. First he would be visiting Jonathon, and then they would both be heading for the Great Hall of Records. They needed to do a little bit of detective work. He only hoped that they had enough time.

For over 12 straight hours Jerry had focused on the problem of the daggers. During the past five hours, Jerry had been materializing the components he would need to repair the *Hope.* He was using one of the matter materializers in a workroom adjacent to the hangar. These units provided a steady stream of power, allowing him to work at nearly the speed he might have in Heaven. He'd also decided to trust Tim's technicians in the installing of the components. They seemed to know what they were doing. It was best if he focused on this, and on the task of unraveling the sources of the problems of the daggers—the most mentally challenging jobs.

All the while his small guardian watched him from the other side of the table. She hadn't said anything for hours, apparently sensing Jerry's need for full concentration, at least until now. "That is the last one?" she asked.

"I hope so, Chloressa," he said.

"You have a great gift," she said.

"I only hope that it's great enough," lamented Jerry.

Yeah, he had his work cut out for him all right. He'd had the opportunity to hop into the cockpit of one of Tim's daggers about eight hours ago. It was amazing; it looked just like any of the daggers on the line at Pad B of Professor Faraday's research facility. One minor variant was that these daggers sported a symbol of a blue lightning bolt against the background of an orange disk rather than a brown cross superimposed against the background of a golden crown. To each his own. The daggers were also numbered—one through three.

The canopy of the dagger had slid back smoothly and the interior layout was identical to the ones on Pad B. But, unfortunately, the similarities stopped there. The heads-up display was blurry and dull, and the computer diagnostics failed to even recognize entire flight systems. The engines came on line, but only in manual mode. This thing would probably get off the ground, but it might not stay in the air very long. It would almost certainly be unstable and hazardous to fly even at low speeds. Jerry wasn't about to attempt that. This thing would not be effective in battle. It needed a lot of work.

Jerry determined to get the *Hope* back into shape first, then he would focus his attention on the other ships. Still, he had his doubts about ever getting these other three in shape, at least in the time allotted. Right now he had several technicians replacing some of the old components on one of Tim's daggers with the new ones he had just fabricated. Would it do any good? He was just about to find out. Jerry headed back into the hangar as three technicians were replacing the service panel on the dagger.

"She's ready," said one of the technicians. "Oh, and the team working on your dagger said they're ready for the next set of parts."

"They're in the workroom," said Jerry, climbing up the ladder to the cockpit. He sat down in the seat and prepared to check the new components. A second later, Chloressa alighted on his shoulder. She scanned the cockpit carefully. Jerry looked over at her with some amusement. He'd gotten used to her presence surprisingly fast.

"Your mother is resting comfortably," said a voice from below.

Jerry looked down to see Megan looking up at him.

"I've been with her personally," continued Megan. "She may sleep for days, there's no telling. I didn't mean to bother you. I just thought you'd want to know."

"I did," replied Jerry. "Thank you."

"I can't begin to tell you how much we appreciate what you're doing for us," continued Megan. "I know that my husband must seem a bit strange to you, but you've got to consider what he's been through…what we've all been through."

"I can hardly imagine," admitted Jerry.

"You should get some sleep," suggested Megan. "My husband has seen to it that you are provided with sleeping accommodations while you are our guest. They may not be much by heavenly standards, but it is the best we have to offer."

"You've been very kind," said Jerry.

"I know you have work to do," said Megan, taking a step backward. "I should be going."

"I have a question," Jerry said hesitantly. "You may find it rather personal."

"Ask whatever you like," replied Megan.

"You spoke of a vision of a future Hell during dinner," said Jerry. "I was just curious…what do you see?"

Megan smiled. "It is really rather strange. You see, I have these dreams, very real dreams. I see a world partially ruled by the demons, but only partially. It is a world of nations, not unlike Earth, and of competing philosophies and ideas. In it there are struggles, just like there were on Earth. The sun even rises and sets upon it."

Megan chuckled. "That's sort of strange, isn't it? I mean, the sun neither rises nor sets here; it pretty much stays in the same place all of the time. Oh, how I miss night! How I'd love to see a sunset. I really missed the night during my years in the procession of the plunge of desolation. How I longed for the coolness of night. In the world of my dreams there are clouds, even rain. In a way, it's sort of dismal. But within it, men and women make their own destinies, and Tim and I are part of it. It's funny, you know? I'm fighting to create that dismal world."

Jerry nodded. "I like it. You remind me of a very special friend back in Heaven. She dreams of the future too. Keep on dreaming, Megan."

Megan smiled and departed. Jerry watched as she stepped into the teleportation ring and vanished into the mists. Jerry's mind focused once more on the business at hand. He engaged the heads-up display. It came up crisp and clear. He scanned the readouts. There were so many cautions and warnings showing, but the good news was that all of the systems did display. He rubbed his tired eyes. Megan was right: he needed to get some sleep.

He left instructions with the technicians. They'd be busy installing the new components for hours. There was nothing that he could do here for a while. Jerry shut down the power and descended the ladder. An aide escorted him to his quarters, which were down a short hallway leading from the hangar.

He was relieved to find real wooden chairs and a bed—not a slab of rock—and real blankets and pillows. This place wasn't bad at all. It was comfortable and quiet. A few hours of sleep might give him an entirely new outlook on the problem. His head hit the pillow; he was asleep within minutes. Chloressa alighted near his feet. She would watch over him as he slept.

Christopher closed the white book and placed it back into its place on the shelf. He'd been so sure that it had been this one. It wasn't.

"Are you having any luck?" asked Jonathon, coming up the aisle toward Christopher.

"No, not yet," replied Christopher as he moved again. "Level four, section D, row twenty-two. That's my next stop."

The two youths made their way down the aisle. They'd been at this for four hours now, and the sense of urgency grew with each passing minute.

"I was so sure about this one," lamented Christopher. "We know that one of the technicians I worked with gave the dagger plans to Tim Monroe. But which one? There are over thirty of them. What about you? Finding anything?"

"I'm making some progress," Jonathon replied. "I now know that Tim Monroe got the plans to the dagger five months ago."

"The daggers were just entering the flight testing stages then," said Christopher, turning toward the main stairs. "If those daggers were built based on plans from that time, I have an idea as to where we'll need to start with the modifications."

"I was hoping that Tim Monroe might have been given more information as to who actually provided the plans in the first place," Jerry responded, "but he wasn't. He does a lot of delegating in his colony. I did, however, run across the name of an organization that I have never heard of. It is the organization that funds and supplies him. It was formed shortly after the War in Heaven by individuals desperate to free their loved ones from the cruel clutches of Satan. They called themselves the Knights of Zion."

"That's original," replied Christopher, just a bit of sarcasm in his voice.

"No, it's not original," replied Jonathon, "neither in name nor the goal. Chris Davis attempted a very similar thing a number of years back, as we both know. But this time it was launched on a massive scale, and I'm here to tell you that they became organized. They appointed a president, a board of directors, and tons of committees. They were formed as a rather shadowy organization really, made up mostly of veterans of the War in Heaven. Over a thousand individuals joined the Knights of Zion.

"Their original goal was to petition Abaddon and to work with him on the mission to free their loved ones. When that deal fell through, they turned to Tim Monroe. By this time they had several working telespheres and were attempting to assemble their own teleportation ring—one capable of teleporting supplies, and maybe even people, back and forth between Heaven and Hell."

"Yes, we knew that before," said Christopher, who was now on the steps and heading down to the fourth level.

"But did you know that they had the permission of the Father to proceed with their plan?" Jonathon asked.

That revelation stopped Christopher right in his tracks.

"Ahh, you didn't know that," said Jonathon, amusement in his voice. "Their president, a certain Don Kelly, and several of the board members went to the Father shortly after their organization had been formed to petition Him for His support. He gave them His blessing on certain conditions: One, they were not to attempt to bring any of the lost souls back to Heaven or to Earth—those souls had to remain in Hell. Two, they could not become directly involved in the rescue effort themselves. They could supply support to any partisan agency in Hell they wished.

They could even travel there as advisors, but they could not go on the rescue missions themselves.

"Third and last, if they did travel to Hell, they were on their own. They could not expect to receive aid from the Father or His angels. Over the three years that they have been involved in this effort, I cannot find a single incident where they have violated their covenant with the Father. Shadowy as they may be, they do have the blessing of God."

"I think I've heard of Don Kelly," said Christopher. "Didn't he lead the famous Via Norte charge during the War in Heaven?"

"The very same," said Jonathon. "Saved General Washington's regiment, he did. Now he leads the Knights of Zion."

"Wait a minute, now I remember. Colonel Kelly's battalion was called the Knights of Zion," said Christopher.

"Yes," replied Jonathon. "That was what led me to Colonel Kelly."

"You don't happen to know where his organization's headquarters are, do you?" asked Christopher.

"Yes, I do," confirmed Jonathon. "They are right here in the City of Zion, less than three miles from this very spot."

"You have been busy," said Christopher, a growing smile on his face.

"Hey, I've been doing this Hall of Records detective work for a while now," replied Jonathon. "I'm good."

Christopher nodded. Yep, Jonathon was as self-confident as ever. There was nothing more to do here. They were on their way to meet Don Kelly.

On the way, Jonathon filled Christopher in on some of the details. Colonel Don Kelly had been a British army officer, a lieutenant colonel, who had been killed in Korea in 1951. He'd also been an officer in the War in Heaven, serving under General Washington. He'd gone to Tim Monroe to seek the rescue of his own father, who had served in World

War I. He was just one of a long line of military men from a proud military family.

Colonel Kelly's home was like most any other in the densely populated city. It was just another of the brownstones on the busy Via de Gloria.

"I sure hope he's home," said Christopher, knocking on the front door.

It was only a few seconds before a fair-faced young woman came to greet them. She smiled at the two young men. "Christopher, Jonathon, so nice to meet you. The colonel has been expecting you. Please, follow me."

"Expecting us?" said Christopher to Jonathon. "I wasn't expecting that."

"Neither was I," admitted Jonathon.

They were led down a grand hallway to the colonel's study. Christopher heard laughter coming from the study. It was an all-too-familiar voice. Entering the grand study, Christopher came face to face with Colonel Kelly, and at his side was the ever gleeful Lilly.

The colonel seemed to be one of those people who preferred to take on the appearance of a slightly older man. He looked to be about 50, with reddish hair graying at his temples, and a long mustache. His brown eyes were full of life and upon his lips was a grand smile. He was, all in all, quite handsome.

"What kept you?" asked Lilly.

"Traffic," replied Jonathon.

"Oh," giggled Lilly. "Guys, this is my good friend Colonel Don Kelly, president of the Knights of Zion."

"I've been hearing a lot about you," said the colonel. "You've had quite the adventure these past few years. I'm glad that I've finally gotten to meet you."

"And we've heard a lot about you," replied Christopher. "Your brilliant combat strategy during the Battle for Zion is legendary."

"I wouldn't call it legendary," laughed the colonel, "brilliant, perhaps."

That comment elicited another round of good-natured laughter from all.

"I was actually withdrawing in the face of a vastly superior demon army when I ran into Washington's regiment under siege," explained the colonel. "We surprised his demon attackers when they just happened to be along our own retreat route. Between the two of us, we pretty much wiped them out. And between the two of us, we were finally able to make a stand. That's the long and the short of it. It was more good fortune than anything else." He paused. "But my friend Lilly tells me that you have a bit of a problem."

"I've given the colonel all of the details," continued Lilly. "I saw, in my mind's eye, all that Jonathon saw as he scanned the books."

"What you propose to do is very dangerous," said the colonel. "But after talking to Lilly, I realize that I won't be able to talk you out of it, neither should I attempt to. Clearly, you are on the Father's business." The colonel hesitated before continuing. "I want to send an armed escort in with you to see to your safety. They may come in handy."

"Thank you," said Lilly, "but we have to go alone. I'm sure you understand."

"I do," confirmed the colonel, "but I'm still sending an escort. Those terms are not negotiable. If you are using my teleportation ring, you have to abide by my rules. I would never forgive myself if something happened to you—so, you see, I am doing this as much for myself as for you."

"Of course," replied Lilly, "I understand. I think I can speak for all of us in saying that we accept your terms. We thank you for your concern."

"I assure you that the knights that I send along with you will not get in the way of what you need to do," said the colonel. "Indeed, they will be at your service."

"Actually, I think it's a good idea that they come along," said Christopher. "I for one will appreciate their help."

"I'll make sure to send knights who have useful technical skills that may benefit your work," assured the colonel. "In addition, my organization will stay in touch with you by telesphere and send you anything you may need."

He paused. "I think you need to know one more thing before you head out. We've developed a somewhat more sophisticated telesphere technology than the one Dr. Kepler employs. We've used it to monitor the telesphere frequencies—eavesdropping as it were—on communications between Abaddon and the good doctor. From what we've gathered, there is going to be a big push to defend Refuge when Satan's attack finally comes—and it will come.

"They have many thousands of volunteers, perhaps tens of thousands, prepared to journey to their aid. They are determined to do whatever it takes to keep Refuge from falling. However, they have given little consideration to the people of Monrovia. I suppose they consider them expendable."

"I hope that's not the case," said Lilly.

"So do I," said the colonel. "I have over six hundred volunteers ready to go in if called upon. Our loved ones are there; we can do little else. If bad things happen, we'll need to be ready to get you out of there."

"I don't think you'll need to do that," said Christopher. "Like you said, it seems like Monrovia has been forgotten by the other people of Heaven. That is why we are going there."

Lilly looked at Christopher and smiled. "Yes, that is why we are going."

The colonel looked at the three youths in amazement. "You really think that the three of you and your friend Jerry can make a difference?"

"Yes," confirmed Lilly, "and it won't be the four of us who make the difference; it will be six. Together as a team, and with the Holy Spirit within us, we will defeat the armies of Satan."

Jonathon seemed surprised by Lilly's comment, yet he remained silent. He looked over at Christopher, who nodded in agreement. "Is the teleportation ring here?" asked Jonathon.

"No," replied the colonel. "It is on the first level of Heaven, in the middle of a high, mountainous wilderness. It is indeed a remote location with few prying eyes. Lilly knows where it is. I will meet you there tomorrow at noon."

The colonel paused. "But before we part today, would you care to join me in a cup of tea? It's my teatime and I prefer to have company, if you don't mind. One should never drink alone. Anyway, I'd like to hear more of your adventures. In return, I'll share with you some adventures of my own."

And so the three children visited with the colonel for a while longer. They spoke of the War in Heaven. They even listened to a few of the colonel's old war stories—tales of the war in Korea mostly. They were stories of particular interest to Lilly.

He also told them what he knew of Hell. He had actually been there on several occasions, visiting with his father. He was one of the few knights who had undertaken the perilous journey. He had walked the dusty plains of that most terrible world himself. He spoke of the emptiness one felt in a place devoid of the presence of God. Still, try as he might, he couldn't dissuade the children from their quest. He would see that all of the arrangements were made.

Jerry, with Chloressa on his shoulder, walked quietly into the care center, a large and dimly lit room containing about two dozen beds separated by floor-length curtains. Once again, the beds were not what Jerry had expected. They were not slabs of rock, but real wooden and metal-framed beds. The stone walls had been painted a light blue color and were adorned with beautiful paintings and tapestries.

On this day only four beds were actually occupied. One of the patients seemed to be in a delirium. He thrashed back and forth, moaning and crying softly. Two people, a man and a woman, were with him, trying to keep him calm. The other three patients seemed to be sleeping.

Jerry quickly located his mother, who was apparently sound asleep. She had been dressed in a long white nightgown and was being attended by a young woman sitting in a chair by her side. Jerry immediately recognized her as Megan. Megan looked up and smiled as Jerry approached. She too had her AC, Cindy, upon her shoulder. Jerry sat down by her side.

"She's resting quietly for now," she said in a whispery voice. "She was having a pretty rough time about an hour ago. I think she thought she was still in that terrible coffin. It didn't last very long, and she went back to sleep after just a few minutes. This is totally normal. She's really doing very well."

"How long have you been here with her?" asked Jerry.

"About seven hours," replied Megan.

Jerry shook his head. "When do you get any sleep?"

"When your mother finally recovers," replied Megan. "When someone new comes to us, we assign only two people to watch over them. It allows us to draw close to them, to feel their pain and try to pull them away from it. We all know what it's like. When she finally wakes up, I'll be here for her, to pull her away from the nightmare that was her life."

"You're very kind," said Jerry. "I can't begin to tell you how grateful I am for what you and your husband have done for her. I am greatly in your debt."

"No," corrected Megan, "we are in yours. We are so grateful to all of those in Heaven who have helped us out of the goodness of their hearts. God's love shines through you and lights up our world. You give us hope." Megan hesitated. "How is your work coming?"

"The *Hope* is fully repaired," replied Jerry. "Your technicians did a good job putting her back together. As for your three daggers—I'm still working on them. I'm making some progress, but it's slow. I'm just not an engineer."

Jerry heard footsteps behind him, then he felt a soft hand on his shoulder. Quite suddenly, Megan's eyes were full of wonder.

"Your mother is such a beautiful woman," said the female voice behind him. "She is almost angelic."

Jerry turned around to see a familiar face; it was Lilly. He began to tear up. "Is it really you?" he asked.

Lilly dropped to her knees and hugged Jerry. "Yes, it's me."

"But how did you get here?" asked Jerry.

"I have a friend with a teleportation ring. He let me use it," said Lilly. "Oh, don't worry…Christopher is in the hangar running a diagnostics check on one of the daggers. I think that's what he called it. He claims that he can have all three up and running in two days, at the most. Jonathon is up there with him."

Lilly paused and gazed upon Chloressa. Chloressa in turn bowed before her. "Looks like you found a friend."

"Yeah," confirmed Jerry, "she's quite protective of me."

"I can see that," replied Lilly, giggling.

"But it was dangerous for you to come here," objected Jerry.

"Not really," assured Lilly. "When all four of us are together, the Father's Holy Spirit is with us also. We're a team, Jerry. Next time you travel into outer darkness, keep that in mind."

Then Lilly's eyes focused upon Megan, whose eyes were still focused on her. "You have a beautiful spirit, Megan," she said as she rose to her feet and walked toward Megan.

"It's you!" said Megan, tears rolling down her cheeks. "But I'm awake, this isn't a dream."

"You're awake," confirmed Lilly. "I've come to help you find that pure spirit within you. I tell you that the Father is not finished with you, nor has He abandoned you. You have a work to do here. Very soon you shall stand with the four of us against the minions of Satan, you and your husband. On that day, the fate of your empire shall be determined."

"Our empire?" asked Megan.

"Yes," confirmed Lilly. "Follow the commands of the Father and the two of you shall rule over a great people who shall change the face of this world."

"But we, my husband and I, are damned souls," said Megan.

Lilly's expression grew very serious. "With God nothing is impossible. There is coming a day when there shall be a great judgment before the white throne of God. On that day, the books shall be opened and all humankind—both living and dead—shall be judged. Will you be ready?"

"I will," said Megan.

Lilly nodded. "We shall see. The coming days shall try your resolve." She turned to Jerry. "I believe that Christopher may need your assistance in the hangar. I will remain here with Megan."

Jerry hesitated then made his way toward the door.

"Is there really hope for Tim and me?" asked Megan.

"I cannot say," replied Lilly. "That the Father has not revealed to me…but opportunity lies before you. Don't pass it by. The alternative is far less pleasant."

Megan nodded. She realized what was at stake.

Jerry stepped through the ring and was immediately transported to the hangar. Here he saw a great flurry of activity. At least a dozen men he had not seen before were busy working on the three daggers. Access panels were opened everywhere, and directing the activity was Christopher.

"Nice of you to join us," said Jonathon, placing his arm around his old friend. Then he looked at the creature on Jerry's other shoulder. It smiled at him. "Hello," said Jonathon. To Jerry he said, "You make friends everywhere you go, don't you?"

"I guess," chuckled Jerry.

"Oh," said Jonathon, "Christopher has a long list of components that he needs you to materialize. I think you've got your work cut out for you. Remember the Ford assembly line concept my great-grandfather Bud used to talk about? Well, that's what we're up to. Christopher diagnoses the problems these ships have; you materialize the intricate components; the technicians materialize the larger, simpler stuff; and the mechanics assemble it all. We even managed to steal another dagger pilot from Professor Faraday. We'll extend our apologies later. For now, we need you to materialize parts. Christopher has them prioritized."

"And you?" asked Jerry.

"I'm working with Tim Monroe in an attempt to sharpen up his defenses," replied Jonathon. "We've got to think out of the box here."

Jerry nodded and made his way toward the workroom. Along the way he got a quick wave from Christopher who was sitting in the cockpit of

Dagger 2. Christopher's attention quickly returned to what he had been working on. Heading into the workroom, Jerry found two unfamiliar technicians materializing parts for the daggers. Upon his worktable was a list of parts and a stack of schematics. Jonathon was right: he had his work cut out for him. He got to work on the first component on the list.

Over the next many hours, Jerry had a chance to chat a bit with the technicians in the workroom. Both were master materializers from the matter materialization guild. They were members of the Knights of Zion and had gated in from Heaven to assist in this project. Slowly the story of the knights unfolded before him. It felt really good to have so many good people behind him. For the first time in days, he didn't feel alone. He even got a chance to talk with Christopher, though those conversations were indeed fleeting.

Rarely had Jerry worked so long, or so hard, at his craft of matter materialization. Here in Hell he tired far more easily. He had to keep totally focused on his work. He had been at it for nine hours when a mechanic burst into the room.

"Dagger Three has a green board!" he said excitedly. "She is ready to fly!"

"Does it have a cloaking field?" asked Jerry.

"She's got everything," said the mechanic. "We've almost got number one on line—just a few more tweaks."

"Incredible," said Jerry, who turned back to the task at hand. It sure seemed like he was making a lot of extra parts.

After another four hours of constant work, he reached the bottom of the list. Jerry now knew a new sensation: a headache. He practically stumbled for the door and out into the hangar. He was surprised to discover that even more men had joined the work detail. He also noticed that the three daggers had been moved about.

He noticed Christopher talking with several technicians at the far end of the hangar and headed toward him. He casually glanced up at the nearest dagger—number five. Number five! He moved onto the next one, which was numbered four.

"What the...?" gasped Jerry. Then he looked into the launch tunnel to see two additional daggers lined up one behind the other, numbers one and three. There were five daggers here. He ran to Christopher.

"You got all of the parts materialized?" asked Christopher, looking up from the diagnostics scanner in his hand.

"There are five daggers here!" exclaimed Jerry.

"Yes," said Christopher, in a calm tone, "six including the *Hope*. There'll be more. We're bringing the parts through the ring. There are another six on the other side. Now that we know what's wrong with them, we're bringing them through and assembling them here, making the adjustments on site.

"Oh, you can take a break for a while. I've got another master matter materializer set to relieve you. He is one of the knights. He is not quite as fast as you are, but he does good work. We're going to run out of room soon. We'll park a couple in the cave beside the *Hope*."

Christopher paused. "Oh, Megan said that your mother appears to be regaining consciousness. I was about to come and get you. I think she'd like it if you were there when she woke up."

Jerry still had a ton of questions, but they'd have to wait. He made his way toward the teleportation ring. He had to hold up for over a minute while two wings and a tail section came through the ring from Heaven. Then he was off.

The nearest ring to the care center was less than 50 yards away. Jerry sprinted from the ring to the center. He was amazed at what he saw upon entering. About 50 people had gathered within the care center, and the lighting was at full. There was real excitement as Lilly laid her hand upon one person after another, praying for each one. Some people were on their knees weeping, while others had their hands raised in the air. Stranger still, Megan was following Lilly's lead, praying for one after another. More and more people were entering the room asking for prayer.

Then Jerry's attention turned to his mother's bed. He was amazed to find her sitting there wide awake, her hands lifted unto God. She turned to see her son enter the room. She rose to her feet and ran to his arms; they embraced.

"I've found peace," she said, tears in her eyes. "No matter what happens now, I've found peace."

At the far end of the room, Lilly motioned for silence. A hush fell upon the growing crowd.

"I'm looking out at a people who are just beginning to find new hope," she began. "I bring a word to you from the Father. Know this: You are cast out but not forgotten. You are loved, that I can assure you. Each of you lived once upon the good Earth—you lived your lives and, as must come to all men and women, your lives ceased. All have sinned and fallen short of the glory of God. That is why the Father sent His Son into the world—that humanity might not perish, that they could have life, and have it more abundantly.

"None of you accepted that free gift from the Father, granted by His Son. You failed to accept it for reasons that only you know. For that cause you were cast out of God's presence—sent here. I do not need to know how you have suffered here, for I know all of you have. But understand this: your suffering is not from the Father. The Father is not a torturer. His sentence upon you was separation from Him, nothing more. That in itself is reason for wailing and gnashing of teeth, for you have all lost paradise."

"But Satan rules here," cried out one. "Hasn't the Father thrown us to the wolves?"

Lilly raised her hands as she looked about at the swelling crowd. "Where is he, this Satan? I don't see him, do you? He doesn't rule here; *you* do. By the courage of one young man, little more than a boy, you have been delivered from Satan's power. Look at what you have accomplished with your own hands. I marvel at it." Lilly paused.

"Now that same Satan, whose sins are far greater than any of yours, that usurper, seeks to take away what you have created. What gives him the right to torture you?"

"His demons," cried out another. "They tortured us until we were nearly mad. He put us in chains and threw us in terrible pits where horrible things happened to us. There are so many of them…and they are so strong. Now they're coming to take us back."

"If you let them!" yelled Lilly. "Your leader Tim Monroe speaks of defeating them. He says it with confidence—and I tell you now, he is far from foolish. They will not defeat you—no, you will defeat yourselves. Is that what you want?"

The group roared a defiant, "NO!" Lilly nodded approvingly.

"I cannot tell you what the future holds for you," continued Lilly. "I cannot promise you that the Father will accept you into paradise. I do not know the mind of the Father in that regard. What is within your control is your future here. If it is to be your eternal destiny to remain in this place, then you—not Satan—must write that destiny.

"In five days you will need to fight for the right to shape it. I and my friends will stand with you, come what may. There are others in Heaven who will stand with you as well. Your future is in your hands. Now it is up to you."

The crowd roared in approval as Lilly walked over to Megan and raised her hand into the air. Failing hope was reborn—the people were ready to fight. Through it all, Jerry stood there in amazement, holding his mother's hand.

The care center slowly emptied. All of the recovering souls who had been there were now healed. More than that, healing was spreading throughout Monrovia. The minds of the people were no longer on the odds against them, but on the power within them.

In the days that followed, the productivity of the people nearly doubled. The number of dagger fighters grew from 6 to 9, and then to 16. Jerry led the fledgling pilots and their navigators on one training mission after another. All of them had previous flight experience, yet now they were becoming part of the most amazing flying machine they had ever flown. They were learning quickly. Jerry was convinced that they would be ready.

They also kept in touch with the people of Refuge. They too were mobilizing for the attack that could be but two days away. It became abundantly clear that they would be sharing tactical information and strategy; but in the final analysis, both needed to stand on their own.

The children stayed in regular contact with their friends in Heaven and in Refuge. Spirits were not as high in Heaven or Refuge as they were here. Then again, they didn't have Lilly. With less than 24 hours to go until the deadline, all anyone could do was watch and wait.

CHAPTER 6

Just 12 hours before the deadline, Tim Monroe and his advisors met in his makeshift war room—formerly his dining room. Outwardly he'd kept a positive outlook, but the stress was beginning to show on him.

"We currently have about fifty percent of our guardians back in the valley," said Karl. "We should have better than sixty percent of them back by the deadline. Most of the others are still a day or two away."

"I'd really counted on them," lamented Tim. "I need all of them."

"We currently have twenty-two dagger fighters and pilots to fly them," said Jerry.

"Better than I'd dared to hope," said Tim, looking around the table at his special guests from Heaven. "I am very indebted to you."

"We have met or exceeded all of our other goals," noted Megan. "We are ready."

At that moment the technician monitoring the radar made a grim proclamation. "We have demons on radar—millions of them—approaching out of the northwest, distance eighty miles. They'll be here within the hour."

"They're early," said Tim, placing his face in his hands.

For a minute, silence ruled the room. All eyes were upon Tim, who didn't move. Megan looked upon him with concern. She turned to Lilly as if seeking guidance. Lilly shook her head. Megan waited.

Then, abruptly, Tim looked up. "All right, Jerry, in a few minutes I want you to get your pilots ready for takeoff. Hold for my order."

Then he turned to Karl. "Charge the pulse cannon batteries to full, but don't fire upon the demons unless they stray into our territory. Even then, give them about half a mile of leeway before you open up on them. Get all noncombatants inside and place our army on standby. If we have to fight, we fight."

Megan breathed a sigh of relief. She looked at her husband with a sense of pride in her eyes.

"OK, everyone," said Tim, "let's get to our stations."

The group broke up as Tim rose to his feet. "Now we wait," he said. "If they do attack, let's hope they show that all-too-familiar demon arrogance. Let's hope they underestimate us." He looked to Lilly as if seeking a response. She said nothing.

Tim and several of the others walked over to his holographic map that showed the approaching demon hordes as a huge, orange blob that dominated the northwest quadrant of the map. They watched for several minutes as the orange blob grew like some sort of horrible cancer on the screen.

"Thirty miles," noted the technician. "I don't know that I could even begin to guess the numbers—perhaps twenty or thirty million."

"Are they reporting anything like this at Refuge?" asked Tim.

"Not yet," replied an aide. "Then again, they don't have this sort of radar."

"When they get into range, train the pulse cannons on them—but do not fire," said Tim. "I want them to make the first move."

The group watched the legions of demons grow ever closer. They were nearly at the border when they began to land, slowly filling in the northern half of the valley all the way to the mountains.

Tim watched in puzzlement. "What are they up to?"

Soon the entire flight of demons was on the ground. As the group watched them, a lone blip separated from the mass and headed toward the entrance to the canyon.

"What do you make of that?" asked one of Tim's advisors.

"A lone demon," replied Tim.

"Perhaps it is an emissary," suggested another advisor.

"Perhaps," replied Tim. "Send someone out to meet it. I don't want anyone getting trigger happy. If they want to meet with us, we'll go along with it."

"It was about an hour later that the demon lieutenant was brought before Tim in his throne room. Tim and his wife sat on their respective thrones, wearing their formal robes of state. Around them were three of their closest advisors, Lilly, Christopher, and Jonathon, and half a dozen guards.

The demon had chosen to take the form of a darkly handsome man with jet black bat wings. In his hand he held a white flag. He looked to Tim Monroe and bowed ever so slightly. "My master, General Kang, and his council request an audience with the great Tim Monroe, king of Monrovia."

Tim smiled, though slightly. "Your master and his entourage are welcome in my court. I can personally guarantee their safety."

"My master respectfully declines," replied the demon. "He would like to meet with you at a neutral location, perhaps at our border."

"I wouldn't recommend that," said Tim's nearest advisor. "Such a location would place you in a vulnerable position."

"No," said Lilly, turning to Tim. "My lord, I recommend that we accept this emissary's kind offer in the interest of mutual trust. I also recommend that your closest advisors accompany you so as to give you counsel during your meeting."

"That would be acceptable to us," confirmed the demon emissary.

Tim's other advisors looked on with obvious concern, yet they held their peace.

Tim looked at Lilly for several seconds, then back toward the emissary. "Tell your master that we accept his terms and shall be out to meet him presently."

The demon bowed once more. "Very good, your majesty. With your permission, I shall depart to inform my master."

"Of course," said Tim, smiling. He looked to his guards. "Please see our honored guest safely to the border."

The emissary and his escorts departed. Tim turned to Lilly.

"I request that you allow me, Jonathon, Christopher, and your lovely wife to accompany you to the meeting," said Lilly. "It should only be the five of us. I suspect that Jerry will be joining us later."

"You realize that this is almost certainly a trap," said Tim.

"Of course," confirmed Lilly, "but a trap for whom?"

Tim chuckled. "Pretty lady, I just don't understand you sometimes."

"That's good," replied Lilly. "That means that the demons probably won't either. Let's prepare ourselves. There are a few things that we must see to before we set off for the meeting."

Over an hour later, Tim and his entourage set off from the underground city's main entrance and headed off down the road that ran between the farming fields. It seemed strange to see no one out here minding them.

Each of the travelers hardly seemed dressed for conflict if it came. The children of Heaven were each dressed in the white robes that they may have worn if they were traveling to Zion to visit with the Father. Even Tim and Megan, following the urging of Lilly, were similarly dressed.

"I'm doing this your way, Lilly," said Tim, scanning the skies around them. Occasionally he caught sight of some of the guardians hiding among the rocks of the towering cliffs on either side. Even Goliath, who, as always, sat upon his left shoulder, seemed nervous.

"That is good," replied Lilly. "It shows great faith on your part."

"Great faith…or stupidity," noted Tim. He glanced over at his wife, who walked by his side. He noticed her mouthing the word *faith*. "Faith is a word that hasn't much been part of my vocabulary," continued Tim. "I don't place much of it on invisible higher powers."

Lilly laughed openly. "You say that and yet I see faith all around me in Monrovia. You are the author of much of that faith." Lilly paused. "Doesn't it seem strange to you that your efforts in Monrovia have met with such success, against all odds?"

"Not really," replied Tim. "That is the result of hard work."

"Hard work driven by faith," insisted Lilly.

"I don't see why we are walking this distance," complained Tim. "We could simply have teleported to the meeting point by going through the ring."

"Oh," replied Lilly, "are you in a hurry?"

"No, not particularly," replied Tim.

"Good," said Lilly. "It turns out that time is on our side, not theirs. So we make them wait, yet without making it seem like we're making them wait. Demons don't have a lot of patience. That has always surprised me, as angels do. If this General Kang is made to wait, he may become impatient. That in turn may lead to him making a mistake."

"There was still no sign of an attack at Refuge when we set off," noted Christopher. "I wonder if the demons are attacking here first—testing the waters, as it were."

"I'm not sure," admitted Tim. "I would have expected them to attack both places simultaneously."

"Don't allow your mind to be distracted by what might or might not be happening at Refuge," cautioned Lilly. "Our focus must be upon what is going on here and now."

It took the better part of 40 minutes to reach the place where the narrow canyon met the wide Valley of Noak. From here they could finally see the demons. Their black wings darkened the entire northern half of the valley. They quickly pinpointed the place where the demon commanders awaited their arrival.

"You're right," confirmed Jonathon, smiling slightly. "The demons are becoming very annoyed at us. General Kang is not accustomed to being kept waiting."

"They'll become more annoyed still," assured Lilly.

"They are on a strict schedule," continued Jonathon. "I can sense it even from here. We're inconveniencing them."

"Right again," replied Lilly, whose eyes remained focused on the demons.

Tim picked up the communicator from his pocket and spoke into it. No one was able to discern what he was saying.

It took nearly an hour before the group stood before the demon general. He was unremarkable in appearance. His armor was studded with gold rather than brass, and he assumed the physical features of a man who was perhaps in his 50s. Behind him were three of his lieutenants and several hundred large metal chests. His dark eyes scanned the approaching delegation.

"I do not appreciate being kept waiting," he said in an unemotional voice.

Tim glanced up at the red sun and then back to the general. "Why? Do you have somewhere else you need to be?"

The entire delegation could see the growing anger in the demon's eyes. Jonathon caressed the particle pistol beneath his cloak, as if to verify that it was still there.

"I see no pile of weapons out here in the valley," continued the general, gazing about. "You were instructed to bring them to this place. You were supposed to have disarmed yourselves."

"Oh," said Tim, his tone calm, almost cavalier. "I thought we still had ten hours before the deadline. You're early."

"Well, it matters not. Those were our old terms," continued the general. "My master has set forth new terms. They are very simple. You will assemble your people and send them out to this place, single file."

The general nodded to two of his lieutenants who made their way to the stack of chests. From one of them, the lieutenant produced a handful of ankle and wrist shackles. He cast them on the ground, even as the other lieutenant opened another pair of chests. Both were brimming with gray, tattered rags.

"Loincloths," said the lieutenant as he pointed. "These are for the men, and these over here are for the women."

"Once your people arrive in this place, they will disrobe and pile their clothes over there to be burned. Then they will put on these clothes, which are more appropriate for the humans condemned to Hell. After that, they shall put on their ankle and wrist shackles. Thus fettered, they shall be taken away one at a time by my soldiers to their new home.

"But don't worry, your people will not be separated for long. We will be taking all of you to the same place, a very appropriate place where you will cause the master no further problems."

Tim surprised the general by laughing out loud. "You disappoint me, general. I thought you were going to propose something more original, more interesting."

"My terms are not negotiable," said the general. "You will begin to comply with my requests immediately, starting with you and your lovely female. Take a good look at her beauty now—she will not remain beautiful for very much longer."

The demon lieutenant pulled from the chest a tattered gray loincloth and a top. "These are for you, my dear," he said, glaring at Megan. "Disrobe yourself and put them on."

He was surprised when Megan didn't show the slightest sign of emotion.

"They're not my color," she replied. "Do you happen to have anything in a nice shade of beige?"

Some of the others in the delegation chuckled mildly, which further angered the general.

"Counterproposal," said Tim. "If you apologize to my wife and leave now, I'll forgive your little indiscretion. You demons still don't get it, do you? The days of torturing people for your own pleasure are coming to an end. We have as much right to live free of fear and pain as you do. If you insist on wiping us out, then I must insist upon expanding our domain.

"Leave now or face those consequences. After all, your master wouldn't be pleased if your actions here today lost for you the graveyard at Katlisa, the altars of Vendikar, and the plunge at Sarai. These are the things that I will take from you if you do not back down."

"I've heard enough!" roared the general. "I'll teach you some manners." The general reached for his sword.

Tim smiled. "Oh, is that the way you want it to play? So be it."

The demonic general seemed surprised when Tim drew out his own sword from beneath his cloak. "How about you and I do battle? You win, and these people are yours. I win, and you surrender to us the places I just mentioned and the lost souls imprisoned there."

The rest of the delegation looked on in utter shock. They looked around at each other as if seeking guidance. Only Lilly seemed unfazed by Tim's wild challenge.

However, no one was quite as surprised as General Kang. He glared at this human who was surely no more than half of his size. "I would vanquish you within twenty of your seconds."

"Do you want to add that to the terms?" asked Tim. "I survive in a fight against you for twenty seconds and I win?"

Kang took two steps forward, his sword drawn.

Tim looked to Goliath. No words were exchanged. Goliath then jumped over to Megan's shoulder beside her guardian, Cindy. Then Tim calmly removed his cloak and handed it to his wife. "Hold this for me, would you? I'll only be a few minutes." He kissed her on the cheek. She was trembling. "Don't worry," he whispered, "have faith in me."

"I do," she said, a tear coming to her eye.

"Be strong for me," Tim said as he stepped away from the group. "No one interferes," he added, looking about at the others, "not on either side."

The demon general smiled an evil smile. "This will be so easy."

Tim didn't reply. He simply motioned with his hand for the general to step up, which he did.

The general thrust his sword forward at lightning speed, as if to end this fight with a quick kill. Tim slid out of the way, never so much as losing his balance.

Kang swung around. There was fire in his eyes. He advanced again, his sword swung low and swift, yet Tim leaped above the hurtling blade. Then their swords clashed three times in rapid succession. The sheer force of the blows drove Tim back several steps. A fourth blow from Kang's sword found only empty air.

"Oh, you'll have to do better than that," taunted Tim. "I'm not some shackled and helpless human whom you can strike down without fear of reprisal. I'm your worst nightmare."

Kang let out a yell of rage as he thrust forward toward his adversary once more. Megan gasped as the blade swept within an inch of her husband. Yet Tim was quick to pivot about and drive his blade through Kang's right wing, drawing blood. The demon hoards gasped in collective amazement.

Kang roared in rage, turning his sword on the human in a fit of total demonic power. Five times the blades clashed amid bright blue sparks. Each time Tim was driven back. He seemed off balance as Kang continued his mighty offensive. Tim retreated to the right, only to come under still more attacks. Then Tim was on the ground struggling to get up. Kang moved in for the kill. Tim tumbled out of the way and found his way back onto his feet as Kang's sword struck the ground.

"Twenty seconds," cried Tim. "I win!"

"You win nothing, you human worm!" yelled Kang. His sword was thrust down upon Tim. There was a splash of blood, then a scream. It all happened so fast. The demon was on top of Tim. Then he rolled to the side—Tim's blade clean through his heart.

Tim stumbled to his feet and thrust his blade into the general a second time. "That's for threatening my wife," he said. He gazed out at a million demon faces. "Who's next?" he demanded. Only silence answered his challenge.

He looked to one of the demon lieutenants, "Take your boss with you and leave." He sheathed his sword and walked back toward the human delegation. "Too bad there's no real death in Hell."

Several of Kang's lieutenants rushed toward their commander. After a moment they helped him to his feet. The dazed and bloody demon looked at the human in amazement.

By now Tim was arm in arm with his wife and had turned once more toward the general. "Now, leave—all of you. We'll discuss the new territorial arrangements at a later time."

"No!" roared Kang. "Do you think that I would honor the whims of one such as you?"

"No, I didn't," said Tim, "I just thought that I'd give you one more chance. It was the human thing to do. This negotiation session is over."

Tim took his communicator in hand and spoke into it. "Plan A. Now."

A strange whining sound that echoed off the canyon walls all around them commenced, as a dark cloud began to rise out of both the east and west. The children of eternity formed a tight circle in the midst of this valley of death.

"Take them!" ordered Kang, his voice full of pain. "Destroy their city—bring these people low!"

The demon army advanced on the ground and took to the air, rapidly outflanking the children. Yet the children showed no fear.

"This is what we came here for," said Jonathon, gazing out at the encroaching demons. He focused on a group of six demons that was closer than the others. A few seconds later, one of the demons was attacking the others. Then another joined him.

A second later, a rock that surely weighed two tons was hurtling through the air into the demon ranks, scattering many and crushing others. Christopher looked to Jonathon. "May the force be with you," he said.

Jonathon only smiled as he focused his thoughts on yet another group of demons. They too began to fight among themselves.

A fireball cast by a demon's sword and then another hurtled toward the children. The balls were deflected by a sphere of force, 20 feet across, which now surrounded the humans.

From the canyons more than 20 daggers roared out of their hiding places, visible only as faint distortions against the canyon walls. They fired their particle cannons into the ranks of the demons, destroying and scattering them across the valley, even as clouds of millions of ACs attacked the demons' flanks.

The pulse cannon ground batteries hammered at the flying demons, filling the skies with blinding flashes of light and the crashing of thunder, which shook the very ground they stood on.

"Begin to make your way back toward the canyon," said Lilly, as one fireball after another struck their protective sphere. "We are too exposed out here."

"There is war in Hell," said Christopher, stretching out his hand and turning a flying demon into a trailing ball of fire that vanished into a cloud of dust before hitting the ground.

"And this is only the beginning," promised Lilly. "Blood will flow and go on flowing, for there is no death to stop it. As long as hate and vengeance rule this place, blood shall flow."

By now particle weapon fire from the cliffs to the south erupted as the ground forces from both Heaven and Hell emerged from their hiding places and joined the fight. The daggers roared overhead. The children were no longer the primary focus of the demons' attention. The evil hordes had bigger issues now.

Nevertheless, large numbers of demons were closing in around the children. Lilly's field of protection continued to deflect all projectiles and all enemies who came against them, but clearly that protection was limited.

Quite abruptly, beams of intense power seemed to emanate out of nowhere and ripped a path of destruction through the advancing demon ranks. A loud whining sound with no visible source thundered overhead. Less than ten seconds later it returned, only this time coming from the other direction. Again it ripped a path of destruction through the demon ranks that stood between the children and the entrance to the canyon.

"Only one person I know could turn a dagger around that fast at that altitude," said Christopher.

As if confirming his suspicion, a familiar voice came over the communicator attached to his belt. "Just looking out for you, little brother," said the voice. "I'll plow the road between you and the canyon entrance… you folks just keep moving."

Christopher picked up his communicator, a broad smile on his face. "Got you, Jerry. Thanks for the help."

"No problem," said Jerry. "I just wanted to let you know that I'm here for you."

An army of several thousand human defenders emerged from the canyon before them and into the valley, joining the fray and moving toward the children. The sound of the battle had become deafening.

Christopher looked up in alarm as a shattered dagger, its cloaking device destroyed, plunged toward the demon ranks not far away. He focused all of his Holy Spirit-born power upon that battered ship. It nosed up and was carried as if in a child's hand to another part of the valley where it gently touched down. He was relieved to see the pilot and the navigator escape safely from the craft and reach an advancing column of the Monrovian military. Thankfully it wasn't Jerry's dagger.

The battle was complex and confusing; thousands upon thousands of individual struggles were overlapping into a montage of chaos and destruction. Still, the initial momentum of Tim's army was slowing. Hordes of demons swarmed into the valley and focused fireball barrages against their pulse cannon emplacements, one of their most effective weapons. One by one these powerful batteries were going silent. In other places demon fireballs were directed at the clouds of ACs sent against them, sending thousands of the tiny creatures plunging to the ground in flames.

Swarms of demons so dense as to block out the sun were descending upon the valley. Half a million fireballs rained down from the sky, directed at the 2,000 or so human defenders near the mouth of the canyon. The fireballs were met with thousands of particle beam blasts, which unfortunately detonated only a small fraction of the incoming rain of fire.

The entire area exploded with the intense heat, leaving parts of the canyon floor and walls glowing with radiant energy. Christopher, Jonathon, and Lilly looked on in horror. Even from here—hundreds of yards away and through their shield—they could feel the searing heat. In the middle of that firestorm, human bodies would surely have been reduced to little more than bones. Despair filled the hearts of the children of Heaven.

Then the glare and smoke cleared to reveal the army unit a bit singed but still intact. Each member was surrounded by a glowing, blue bubble. The children looked on in amazement, and then they turned to Tim. Strangely enough, he nodded in approval.

"I guess those personal shields work well enough," Tim said. He paused, looking at the others. "What? Do you think you have the only shield technology in town? These were a gift from the Knights of Zion. They developed them a bit too late to be used in the War in Heaven, but just in time for us. I'll need to send Don Kelly a thank you card."

"We need to keep moving," urged Lilly.

Tim looked at Lilly and nodded. "Generating this shield around us is a real effort for you, isn't it?"

"Yes," replied Lilly, her tone of voice a bit strained.

"Yeah, I can understand that," confirmed Tim. "That's the whole problem. Shields like these require huge amounts of power to maintain. Those shields over there are the only thing protecting my troops from the raging heat all around them. I'm very much afraid that those shields may not stand up to another attack."

Tim continued to observe the troops within the demon-created hot zone. Several people dropped their shields in order to return fire. Yet those who did paid for their mistake by being baked by the radiant heat around them. Tim turned away in frustration.

"Blast it!" he cursed. "I hadn't figured on such a huge fireball bombardment. My troops in the canyon are caught in a catch-twenty-two."

"Catch-twenty-two?" asked Christopher.

"Yeah," confirmed Tim. "They can't fire at the demons unless they drop the shields first. But if they drop their shields, the heat around them will just about bake them, so they won't be able to get off more than one shot. But if they don't drop the shields and fire, the demons will. In the end their shields will be depleted, and they will suffer the consequences."

Tim was on his communicator again, barking order after order.

From the ridge, soldiers concentrated their fire upon the demons that had launched the original volley of fireballs, which now had his soldiers in the canyon pinned down. The problem was that there were so many of them.

The two remaining pulse cannons also concentrated their fire upon that hoard of demons in an attempt to break their attack. A second volley of fireballs was launched at the troops in the canyon, though not as powerful a volley as the first. Then that demon contingent scattered.

Still, it became clear that the situation was deteriorating. Whole legions of demons had turned their fire upon the ACs, the one element of Tim's defense on which he had placed so much hope.

The pulse cannons went silent as the demons took out the last one with a massive fireball volley. The daggers continued their attacks; yet under the weight of such overwhelming numerical odds, even they were slowly succumbing as more and more demon reinforcements streamed in.

As for the children of Heaven, they had become trapped. The intense heat surrounding the mouth of the canyon prevented a ground retreat to Monrovia, and they were surrounded on the other three sides by the demons. It might be possible to teleport back to one of the rings within the city, but then what? Most of Tim's forces would be unable to follow them, as they would eventually be captured by the demons. Those few who did make it back would end up in a fighting retreat through the tunnels. Eventually, there would be no place left to run.

They had come so far. Tim's radar operator had estimated the strength of the demon army at nearly 30 million. They had, perhaps, destroyed half of that army—an astounding feat—but now the other half would destroy them.

"It can't end this way," lamented Tim. "There has to be a way to win this."

Megan took her husband's hand. "It isn't over yet. I know...I feel that there is still hope."

A mighty roar came from the salmon sky as a luminescent column of red, shimmering light 200 yards wide descended to the far side of the valley, then vanished. It generated a mighty blast wave radiating out in all directions amid a high speed cloud of dust.

"What the...?" exclaimed Tim, as a second column like the first hit the ground half a mile farther up the valley.

A third and a fourth column quickly followed, both hitting the demon-occupied side of the valley. The shock waves were bearing down on the children at frightening speed. In a few seconds, Tim was once more on his communicator.

"Everyone, find cover, get your shields up!" yelled Tim, even as the first shock wave reached the force field surrounding them.

The visibility reached zero as 100-mile-an-hour winds swept around them. Still, the force field held.

The airwaves were filled with overlapping communications between Tim's troops, yet they quickly vanished into the growing static. Again and again the children heard the thunderous roar. For three minutes it continued. They could only assume that still more attacks from on high were under way. What was happening? Would these beams of destruction soon be falling upon them?

Silence fell upon the valley. It was then that the communicator on Christopher's belt became active once more.

"This is Captain Smith of the *Intrepid* calling any ground station, come in."

Christopher picked up the communicator. "This is apprentice first class Christopher Pace calling *Intrepid*, I read you."

"Good to hear from you, Mr. Pace," replied the captain. "Can you confirm that our plasma cannon barrage was on target?"

"The first few shots were right on," confirmed Christopher. "After that, visibility dropped to zero."

"I'm sorry that we had to fire so close to your position without warning, but we had no choice," continued the captain. "Between your troops and the daggers, targeting the demon forces without hitting friendly forces was like threading a needle in the dark—but we did it. We're showing the demon forces in full retreat."

By now the dust all around them was settling to reveal the troops at the entrance to the canyon rushing away from the still very hot ground. Some had received pretty serious burns in the process, but they remained an effective fighting force.

In the distance, the rain of plasma energy from space continued to pound the retreating demon forces. It was clear that the battle had been won.

"When it became clear that the forces of Satan were concentrating their full force on Monrovia and not on Refuge, we moved the *Intrepid* over to this side of Hell," continued the captain. "I'm here to tell you, it was one hectic ride to get over here in time."

While Tim listened intently to the conversation, he seemed deep in thought. Then he acted. He spoke into his own communicator. "Come on, folks, let's get organized. I need a 'go' or 'no go' for Plan C within twenty minutes."

"Plan C?" asked Jonathon. "What's that?"

"Someone once told me that the best defense was a good offense," replied Tim. "I warned the demons about this, but they wouldn't listen. Now they're going to pay. If things look good, we're going on the offensive. We're going on the attack, starting with the great city of altars at Vendikar. It's a place where helpless men and women are chained to horrible black altars, and they become a meal for huge birds of prey bred to feed specifically upon human flesh.

"The birds reduce their victims to little more than bones and indigestible organs, only to watch them regenerate and then feed on them all over again. That is worse than what happened to us here. It is relatively close—about five miles. We're going to defeat their demon sentries and set the captives free. There must be over ten thousand people there."

Both Christopher and Jonathon looked at Tim skeptically. This guy had to be kidding.

"We barely got out of this battle with our skins intact," objected Jonathon. "Now you want to step out on a limb and attack?"

"Sure," confirmed Tim. "We've got them on the run. There'll never be a better time."

"We never discussed anything like this," objected Christopher.

"You never asked," countered Tim. "Look, we've got to expand, spread out. This means more soldiers and workers. The next time Satan moves against us we'll be ten times stronger."

"Smith to Pace," said the voice over the communicator.

"Pace here," replied Christopher.

"Look, we've drained our capacitors to nearly the limit," replied the captain. "I think you'll be able to handle things from here. We should be back within a few days. Stay in touch with us by telesphere; we'll keep the line open."

"Roger," confirmed Christopher, "and thank you."

"Glad to help," replied the captain. The channel went silent.

The airborne dust within the valley continued to clear. The demons that remained were grounded and badly wounded. Already the ACs had begun their assault upon them. Another radio dispatch order from Tim sent several thousand of his people into the valley to seek out the wounded demons.

"What will you do with them?" asked Christopher.

"What we've done to all of the other demons in the past," was the response.

Now Christopher was really confused. "I don't understand."

Tim seemed increasingly frustrated. "I really don't think that this is the time for an explanation."

"I disagree," said Jonathon. "I'm also curious. Do you haul them in front of a particle rifle firing squad and destroy them utterly?"

Tim only laughed. "OK, let's discuss it then. That may work in Heaven, but it doesn't work here. If you destroy a demon's body in Heaven, it may not reconstitute there, but the sewer flows downhill. You destroy the body of a demon in Hell, and you're already at the bottom of the hill. Its spirit has nowhere to go, so it wanders about for a time. Eventually it comes to rest and begins to reconstitute somewhere else.

"They're like cockroaches; you never seem to be able to get rid of them. All of these demons we fought today will be back—just give them some time. Similarly, all of my people will be back too. It's just the way it works. In Hell there is no birth and no death; you just get recycled. But I have a way around that."

"Which is?" asked Christopher.

"I keep them in Monrovia," replied Tim.

"Wait a minute," objected Christopher, "I didn't see any demons wandering around in Monrovia." Christopher glanced over at Megan, who quickly looked away. Then Christopher turned back to Tim. "What have you done?"

"Nothing more than they have done to us," snapped Tim. "There is a place in the very deepest depths of Monrovia, a dungeon, cut off from the rest of our great city by hundreds of feet of rock. It's a dungeon from which there is no escape. The only way in or out is through a single tele-portation ring. There I've imprisoned them—hundreds of them—bound in chains.

"And to keep them company, my guardians, my ACs if you will, visit them on a regular basis." A slight smile came to Tim's face. It was strangely disquieting. "ACs have to eat to survive. In Refuge, Abaddon keeps millions of them in a sort of hibernation, so that they don't eat him out of house and home. I have a more practical solution. Need I say more?"

"You feed the demons to your ACs?" deduced Jonathon.

"Very good," replied Tim. "My guardians know where the food is, and since the demons continually regenerate, the food supply is endless. Still, I will need more demons if I am to grow my army of guardians even bigger." Tim looked over at Goliath, who sat upon his shoulder once more. "Isn't that right, my dear friend?"

Goliath nodded.

"This is nuts," objected Christopher. "In doing this, how are you any different from the demons?"

"Because they did it to us first," objected Tim. For the first time there was anger in his voice. "I watched them do it to my beautiful wife. They did it to me. They are the lowest creatures in God's creation, lower than the foulest beast that swims or crawls on Earth. You've never experienced their cruelty. Don't lecture me on morality."

"I have experienced their cruelty," objected Lilly, turning to Tim even as she discontinued the field of protection surrounding them. "I experienced it during the War in Heaven. You accomplish nothing by descending to their level."

"Except revenge," said Megan, in a voice barely above a whisper.

"Then hear these words from the Lord of Hosts," said Lilly. "Your vision and struggles shall in time make you and your people into a mighty nation. Word of your victories shall spread across this globe. The demons will tremble at the sound of your name. Whether that nation shall be a great nation or not depends upon you. Mighty nations fall, but great nations endure."

Tim crossed his arms and glared at Lilly. "What is that supposed to mean, child of Heaven?"

"That is for you to determine," said Lilly. "Understand and embrace its meaning, and your empire may yet endure. Ignore it, and you shall stumble and fall. There is a new Hell coming, Tim Monroe. It is up to you what form it shall take."

"Up to me?" asked Tim.

Lilly only nodded.

"OK, then answer me this," asked Tim. "Will I win at Vendikar?"

"Yes," replied Lilly. "You'll be victorious at Katlisa and Sarai as well. You will set the captives free. You will in time become Timothy the Great."

"Timothy the Great," laughed Tim. "I love that; it has such a nice ring to it." He turned to Megan, yet she looked away.

A few seconds later Karl's voice was heard over Tim's communicator. "Lord Monroe, your army is intact and ready. I'm here to tell you that the people are really psyched. We'll follow you wherever you lead. God is surely with you."

Tim hesitated, then he replied. "Then let us proceed. We shall do it just the way we planned. We begin in five minutes."

"Yes, my lord," confirmed Karl.

"It's time for us to leave," Lilly said in a soft voice.

"Yes, I suppose it is," said Tim. "I do thank you all for what you've done. Perhaps we do not see eye to eye on all things, but I do assure you that I hold each of you in the highest regard." With those words Tim walked away toward a group of his soldiers heading in his direction.

"Goodbye," said Megan, following her husband.

Christopher just shook his head. "What did we just do?"

"What we had to do," said Lilly.

"Hey guys," Jerry said over Christopher's communicator, "the other daggers are bugging out; I don't know to where."

"Let them go," said Christopher. Head back to the hangar. We'll meet you there as soon as we can."

"Roger that," said Jerry.

"So this is it?" asked Jonathon.

"This is it," confirmed Lilly.

The three headed back toward the canyon. The area at the mouth of the canyon was still incredibly hot. The heat had converted the sand into glass in some places. The children managed to skirt around the hottest regions and proceeded into the shadowy chasm.

Armed soldiers raced past them, but no one paid any attention to them. They might just as well have been invisible. No one said very much.

"Tim disappointed me," admitted Christopher. "I really thought that we were getting through to him." Christopher turned to Lilly. "He could make such a difference here, but he's going to make a mess of this, isn't he?"

"I really don't know," admitted Lilly. "There is a lot of anger in him. There was anger in him while he still lived on Earth. He was angry about the way people treated him, just because he was different. When he came here, the demons and what they did to him only reinforced that anger."

For a moment Lilly seemed deep in thought. "But there is Megan. The love between them may yet save him from himself, but I don't know. That is something that the Father hasn't revealed to me. I will tell you this: he is going to make a difference here. Hell will be changed because of his presence. In that respect, he is doing the will of the Father."

Not too far up the canyon where it began to widen out, Christopher was surprised to discover one of Tim Monroe's daggers—number 11. Apparently, it had been forced to make an emergency landing during the battle. It had hit the ground pretty hard. Its main gear had folded under the force of the impact and its starboard thruster had been virtually decimated. Skid marks in the sand revealed that it had slid for several hundred yards before coming to a stop. The open cockpit and the two pairs of footsteps in the sand leading away from the craft seemed to indicate that the crew had gotten out unharmed.

Christopher took a moment to survey the wreckage. They'd have a heck of a time salvaging this one. The hull was covered with burn marks. Apparently, it had taken a whole lot of fireballs, maybe 20 or so. Well, it wasn't his problem—not anymore. They moved on.

They traveled past the farming fields. Remarkably, the canyon itself had largely sheltered them. There was some damage but not much.

"Scenes like this will become more common," continued Lilly, "swaths of green upon this barren landscape. One of Tim's great aspirations is to change the face of Hell, to bring it back to life. Abaddon has similar goals. They will see these things come to pass, but it will be a struggle."

"I don't think Satan will be too happy about that," deduced Christopher.

"He won't have much say in the matter," continued Lilly. "His reign is swiftly coming to an end. He very soon will find himself in a dark and dismal place, alone, and bound in chains. He will have no contact with humankind or even with his own people for a thousand years."

"He isn't going to end up in Tim Monroe's little dungeon is he?" asked Jonathon.

"I'm not certain," admitted Lilly. "I'm sure that Tim would like that, but I don't think so."

"It must be depressing to have the gift of prophecy," observed Jonathon, "to know what is going to happen and be unable to do anything about it."

"It can be," confirmed Lilly, "but I can't look at it that way. Elizabeth, my mentor, explained it to me like this: All that a prophet is really seeing is the perfect will of God. To try to alter it is to say that God doesn't know what He is doing and that He is in need of our advice. Do you want to be the Father's advisor?"

Christopher laughed openly. "I don't think I'm up to that one."

"Neither am I," agreed Jonathon.

"I guess Satan, in his pride, figured that he was up to the challenge a long time ago," noted Christopher. "We can all see where it got him."

"And us," said Jonathon. "It bought us a week in Hell. I didn't even get around to seeing the sights."

"I'm sure Jerry would take you up in the dagger to give you a bird's eye view of this beautiful vacation spot," noted Christopher.

"I think I'll pass on that one," said Jonathon. "What I have on my mind right now is a pretty, white surfboard with a red stripe and a beautiful stretch of beach along the north shore of the Crystal Sea."

Jonathon paused for a moment. "Hey, why don't we all go? It's been years since all of us have been there together. We could go surfing, take in some rays, take in some of Grandma Gladys's wonderful food…it would be cool. And now my grandparents are there too, in a mansion not a mile farther up the coast. They can be a blast."

"I'll have to take a rain check on that one," said Lilly. "I need to get back to my studies. The past week has shown me how much I still have to learn."

"I'll be busy for months studying the telemetry data from the *Hope*," said Christopher. "This was her first time in actual combat. We need to analyze her strengths and weaknesses to be ready for next time. There is a lot to learn. Maybe we can get together later."

"Yes, maybe later," agreed Lilly.

"I never imagined that eternity would be so busy," said Jonathon.

By the time they arrived at the hangar, Jerry and his mother were waiting there for them, and on Jerry's shoulder was Chloressa. The hangar itself was empty with the exception of the *Hope*. The rest of the daggers were either plowed into the sand somewhere or fighting the Battle of Vendikar.

"I'm taking my mother to Refuge," announced Jerry. "It's all arranged. I just don't feel all that comfortable about her staying here. Did you folks want to come along?"

"That could be interesting," noted Christopher. Jonathon and Lilly nodded in agreement.

"Then Refuge it is," said Jerry walking hand in hand with his mother toward the ring.

"Refuge ring control, this is Monrovia, prepare to accept transport," said the technician, turning to the telesphere by his side.

"Refuge ready, go ahead," was the reply.

The four stepped into the blue mists and vanished from the hangar.

CHAPTER 7

THE FIVE HUMAN TRAVELERS STEPPED out of the mists and into the ring room in Refuge. They were met by Abaddon himself, accompanied by Bedillia, Serena, and Chris.

"From what we've been hearing, it sounds like you've had quite the adventure," said Bedillia.

Jerry and Christopher quickly introduced their friends, Lilly and Jonathon. Then Jerry introduced his mother.

Bedillia turned to Leona. "You must be very proud of your son."

"And very grateful to him," said Leona. "I don't think a mother ever owed so great a debt of gratitude to her son."

"I know there is one who owes a similar debt of gratitude to her daughter," said Bedillia, turning to Serena. "I truly believe that children can be a mother's greatest gift from God. In the Bible, Paul talks about a mother's salvation through her children. It is almost as if he was thinking about us."

"How long have you been here?" asked Christopher.

"About four days," said Serena. "My mother was determined to come here. Chris and I couldn't let her come here alone. Abaddon is our friend too—we're going to stand with him."

"An angel never had such good friends," said Abaddon. He bid his visitors welcome and invited them to visit with him in his audience chamber where they could all sit down and talk. The great dark angel was very interested in learning about what happened in Monrovia a few hours ago. The story told by the children was incredible.

"When we realized that Satan planned on concentrating his forces against Monrovia," Abaddon explained, "the *Intrepid* was stationed directly over us. The *Intrepid* was quickly dispatched to see if they could lend aid to the people of Monrovia.

"Still, I don't believe Satan realized just how powerful a fortress Monrovia was. He does now. I myself didn't realize their military potential..." Abaddon paused. "We offered to send over eight hundred of our best soldiers to help in the fight when it became clear that the demons intended to attack Monrovia and not us. Tim Monroe declined our offer. I could hardly believe it."

"Eight hundred soldiers more or less wouldn't have had much of an effect on the battle," noted Jerry. "As best as I can tell, he had over eight thousand troops in the field, not including those defending Monrovia itself."

"Yes," continued Abaddon, "that explains much. Indeed, he has been very reluctant to allow us anything but very limited access to his colony for nearly two years now. When our representatives do visit him, they are always escorted and where they can travel is restricted. At one time his people lived like cavemen and women, hiding away within the depths of their caverns. Now the technology, sophistication, and population of his colony probably exceeds that of our own."

"He gained powerful allies in Heaven because he took risks that you and your council hesitated to take," observed Jerry. "No offense meant."

"None taken," assured Abaddon. "However, under the present conditions, we may need to consider changing our philosophy."

"I think we can help you on that score," Jerry said, as he removed a book from his flight suit and placed it on the table before him. "In here you will find detailed construction plans for most of the marvels he has been supplied with by his supporters in Heaven. Christopher and I put this thing together over the past few days. I believe these devices will be useful."

Abaddon picked up the book and opened it. "Remarkable. But I fear that your actions will do little to endear you with Tim Monroe and his people."

"I'm sure it won't," interjected Christopher. "Still, we had to do it. We had to be certain that the playing field was kept level. Anyway, I doubt that we'll be visiting Monrovia again after this."

"We won't be," confirmed Lilly. "Our job is done. It takes but a gentle push from one small child to start the journey of a snowball down a long slope. After that, the snowball grows in size and continues on its own to where it will go. It could become a nearly unstoppable force, gathering up all of the fallen snow in its path. The child does not determine its path, nor does he or she determine what snow it does or doesn't pick up. That is determined by other things that the child does not yet see.

"And other forces are arising in this world, forces we do not as yet see. Persons you have lost sight of and may presume are gone shall one day return in power. They shall usher in a new world in outer darkness, a world different from the one you know. The wind blows from all points of the compass. Some winds will be cool and benign, while others will be hot and torrid. Some will blow for but a season and others for a millennium.

"In the end, the Father will gather up all of the winds and weigh what they have brought with them in the balance. On that day, the books shall all be opened. On that day, this world will pass away."

Silence ruled the table for half a minute before Jonathon finally spoke. "These also are the words of the Lord of Hosts: In the end, judgment will fall on this place. All who are here will meet the fate that they have forged with their own hands."

Jonathon turned to Abaddon. "You are the guardian of this place—you, not Tim Monroe, and not Satan. In the end, you are the one who will control the master of lies, defeating him in mortal combat and then binding him in chains for a thousand years."

Abaddon nodded. "I thank the Father for the honor of serving Him. I thank the children of Heaven for opening the door to a new age."

"I'm thankful that you've agreed to give my mother a home," said Jerry. "I just didn't feel right having her remain in Monrovia."

"It is my pleasure," assured Abaddon. "She will be welcome among us."

"Abaddon has taken in other lost mothers," said Bedillia. "I'll be here to help your mother make the adjustments that are ahead. It will be my privilege."

"Then you're staying?" asked Christopher.

"Yes," confirmed Bedillia. "I'm needed here. I know that the gates of Heaven are open, and I'll return there from time to time…but my mission, my calling, is here."

"As is mine," said Serena. "I've had a terrible fear of this place for so very long. Now I know that if the people here are to have a chance, they are going to need teachers. I need to be here beside my mother."

"If they stay, so do I," said Chris. "I think Serena and I are going to be doing a lot of traveling. We have been for years. I suppose that's our job."

"Remarkable humans," said Abaddon. "These are truly the sons and daughters of God." There was a pause. "I know that you need to be on your way, but allow me to give you a little tour of Refuge. It is not as large as Monrovia, yet I feel in many ways it is more inviting. There is a closer and warmer sense of community here. These caves, hidden amid the eternal night of this Dark Continent, represent the first and best hope of the repentant humans of Hell. I still believe that."

Abaddon took his guests through his world, from the modern laboratories to the rather Spartan living quarters of his people. Toward the end of the tour, Leona was shown the quarters she would occupy here in Refuge. It was little more than a small, rocky room hewn into the side of a natural cavern. Only a set of brown drapes separated it from the passageway. The bed was made of rock with a simple mattress and single blanket. Yet it would be home.

"My place is just a little ways up this same corridor," Bedillia said to Leona. "It's nothing like my grand mansion in Heaven, but it is more of a home. I'll be here for you if you need me."

"And I plan to visit you often," promised Jerry. "It is only a short trip through a teleporter ring to here. I really want to get to know you better."

"I'd really like that," said Leona. "I'm starting to get the feel of being a mother, and I really love it."

"I'm sorry, but we need to be getting back," said Lilly.

"Yes, I guess so," said Jonathon. "We need to be going."

The children returned to the ring room where they said their goodbyes.

"We can send you straight back to any of the rings in Heaven," said Abaddon.

"I suppose we should return to the ring controlled by the Knights of Zion," said Jonathon. "It's where this journey started."

"I think I'll ride home with Jerry on the *Hope*," said Christopher. "I didn't want him to have to make the trip alone."

Lilly turned to Jerry and Christopher. Her expression had become suddenly very serious. "Why not come with us?"

"I can't just leave the *Hope* there in Monrovia," objected Jerry. "It's the property of Faraday Enterprises. Anyway, it's in perfect condition, I ran a complete diagnostics. It will make the flight home just fine."

"OK," continued Lilly, "I can see I'm not going to talk you out of this. Go get your ship, but get out of there as quickly as you can. Understand, the two of you can't stay here."

"OK…" said Jerry very slowly. "Is there a specific reason?"

"You need to accept things on faith," continued Lilly. "I'm not sure of the reason. I only know that this is very important."

"I'll see to it that he doesn't stay," promised Christopher. "We'll only be over there long enough to load up and get out."

Lilly shook her head but said nothing more. Jerry didn't seem concerned, but Christopher was another matter. He had suddenly begun to feel very uneasy. They couldn't go with Lilly and Jonathon because they needed to retrieve the dagger, but they'd best do it as quickly as possible.

After final goodbyes, Lilly and Jonathon stepped into the ring on their way back to Heaven. They vanished into the glowing blue vapors. Then the vapors themselves vanished.

"Jerry, you are welcome to visit your mother whenever you wish," promised Abaddon.

Leona stepped up to Jerry and kissed him on the cheek. "I hope to see you soon, my son."

"You will, Mom," promised Jerry.

At that moment Chloressa jumped from Jerry's shoulder over to his mother's. She looked back at Jerry with sad eyes. "Where you go, Chloressa can't go."

Jerry hadn't considered that. "It's OK, Chloressa," he said. "I'll be seeing you every time I come to see my mother. Now you need to watch after her, OK?"

"OK," said Chloressa. "Come and visit me soon."

Jerry agreed.

"We really need to be going," said Christopher.

Abaddon nodded to the ring operator. He turned to the telesphere to his left. "Monrovia, this is Refuge, ready to transport two to Hangar One."

"Roger, Refuge," came the reply, "transport when ready."

A few seconds later the ring was once more filled with mists. Jerry and Christopher stepped into them and vanished as had the others.

"Well," said Abaddon, as the ring cleared once more, "I think we have a world to change."

The four humans and the dark angel filed out of the room. They had a job to do.

Jerry and Christopher emerged from the ring and into the hangar. They discovered two of Tim Monroe's daggers sitting beside the *Hope*. One appeared to have taken some damage.

"Welcome back, gentlemen," said a security officer standing nearby. "Our daggers are returning. Several of them have been damaged."

"How badly?" asked Jerry.

"Not too bad," replied the officer. "Lord Monroe asked that you delay your departure until he returns. He wishes to discuss with you a contract to build dagger parts here in Monrovia. We lost six daggers in the fight today. Most of them probably won't be worth much more than a few spare parts. Another three won't be flyable until we make some repairs. That leaves us with only thirteen that are flyable. If Satan's forces counterattack, we'll be in trouble."

Jerry walked over to the damaged dagger. He did a quick walk around. "It looks like we'll need to replace the starboard engine cowling assembly. You'll need to do a diagnostics on the port engine too."

"The dagger that crashed in the canyon still has a good cowling assembly," noted Christopher, "you could cannibalize one from it. I suspect that the port engine is good too. It would be quicker to do that than to materialize an entire new one."

Jerry nodded in agreement. "I materialized literally dozens of spare parts for the daggers. They're in storeroom three."

"The thing is, we need to return to Heaven," continued Christopher.

"But we'll see that your parts are delivered," interjected Jerry. "It will be my top priority."

"We need you here, both of you," insisted the security officer.

There was a moment of silence. Then Jerry said, "OK. We're going to need the technical support staff in here as well as the mechanics. You just see that we get those parts off of that dagger in the canyon. Strip it; we will need all of the salvageable components."

Christopher looked toward Jerry in disbelief. He couldn't be serious.

"We can do that," confirmed the officer.

"We're going to start with my dagger, the *Hope*," said Jerry. "It took a fireball hit starboard. The starboard engine has been running hot ever since. I'm probably going to need a replacement thermal manifold." Jerry turned to Christopher. "I'm going to need your help. I'll fire up the starboard engine. I'll need you to run a diagnostics from the navigator's station. I'm not so sure I can trust the readings I'm getting from up front."

"Makes sense," replied Christopher, who now saw where Jerry was going with this. He hoped that the security officer didn't.

"A lot of the people you need may still be at Vendikar," said the guard. "We've had a glorious victory. We're trying to get as many of the people we rescued teleported over here as soon as possible. That project has our resources all tied up right now. But I'll do what I can."

The officer got on his communicator and started to make the arrangements. Jerry's attention turned toward a stack of materials on the floor not far from the *Hope*.

"Come on, Christopher, let's move it," urged Jerry. "We need to get this dagger up and running. If the demons counterattack, I want it in top flight condition."

Jerry and Christopher made their way over to the dagger and climbed the ladder into the cockpit. A moment later the canopy closed.

"You were kidding about the starboard engine, right?" asked Christopher.

"Of course," said Jerry. "I just needed an excuse to get us into the cockpit. You won't be able to go back and get any of your stuff from your room. I hope there wasn't anything important there."

"Nothing I can't live without," said Christopher. "That was some pretty quick thinking back there. You even had me fooled for a moment."

"I took Lilly's warning seriously," said Jerry. "I always do. But we're not out of the woods yet—not by a long shot."

Jerry brought up his heads-up display and fired up the starboard engine. He glanced over at the security guard who was still talking on his communicator. The whine of the engine increased in pitch and volume. Then he brought the port engine on line very slowly. He didn't want the guard to realize that both engines were running.

"Have you ever played navigator on a dagger?" asked Jerry.

"In simulations," replied Christopher. "But I had a role in the design of most of these systems and in the layout of the panel. I know where everything is and how it works—theoretically."

"That's encouraging," said Jerry. "Strap in, things are about to get a little loud and bumpy."

Jerry reached for the throttle. Suddenly the starboard engine's roar increased by a factor of two. It was running very rough. Then he activated another system.

"Warning, activation of the electromagnetic…" The computer's automatic warning system was suddenly silenced.

Christopher immediately realized what Jerry was up to. "You can't be serious!" he gasped.

"I sure am," confirmed Jerry.

There was a sudden jolt. A large drum on the floor of the hangar was literally thrown into the wall. Then the hot exhaust from the engines ignited its contents. There was a loud detonation as the hangar began to fill up with billowing black smoke.

"Three, two, one, blast off," said Jerry, in an incredibly calm tone.

The dagger lurched forward, throwing Christopher back into the seat before the inertial dampeners engaged. Half a second later, the *Hope* was hurtling through the launch tunnel; and three seconds later, they had cleared the mountainside. There was a rumbling as the gear came up. The ship swung sharply upward and to the right. Christopher was looking at the swiftly tilting horizon and then into the dusty, amber sky.

"Up, up, and away," said Jerry, as the engine thrust increased.

Only about a minute later, a voice came blaring over the telesphere. "What are you doing, Jerry? I need you back here." Jerry recognized the voice as that of Tim Monroe.

"I'm sorry, Tim," replied Jerry. "I was starting to realize that this was the only way I was going to get out of there. Sorry about the mess in the hangar. There shouldn't be any real damage."

"I've changed my mind, I still need you here—both of you," replied Tim. "Come back at once!"

"I'm sorry," replied Jerry, "I can't do that. You'll get along fine without me. The Knights of Zion will be able to help you rebuild your fleet. You don't need me."

"This is not a request—it is an order!" retorted Tim. "I'll shoot you out of the sky!"

"With what?" replied Jerry.

"I'll do it," said another voice. "This is Karen Harbison, Dagger Twenty-two. I'm right on your tail."

"I wouldn't do that, Karen," said Jerry, pulling back on the yoke and placing the *Hope* on a course for space. "You're a good pilot, and I'd hate to see you hurt when that dagger crashes. Break off."

"I'm sorry, Jerry, I can't do that," replied Karen. "Throttle back and return with me to Monrovia."

"I can't see her," said Jerry to Christopher. "That dagger was the last one we built."

"I know," said Christopher. "It has a better cloaking device and improved engines. I designed them." Christopher made adjustments to the high frequency radar settings. He scanned the screen before him intently. "I've got her—she's sixteen hundred yards behind us and closing. She's locking onto us with her particle cannons."

"Oh, crap," cursed Jerry, pushing the throttle forward to full power. They were passing through 15,000 feet. It was a long way to the point where they could engage their more powerful electromagnetic drive. Karen would have a good shot at him long before that.

"She's still closing," announced Christopher, "fourteen hundred yards."

They were pushing through the sound barrier now, but it was no good—Karen was still closing. Jerry shook his head. Again he was on the telesphere.

"Call her off, Tim," warned Jerry. "I'll plant her in the ground for sure. Neither you nor I want that."

"She has her orders," replied Tim. "It will be you who loses this engagement. Give in, return."

Jerry glanced again at his altimeter. They were just passing 36,000 feet. Just another minute and they could engage the electromagnetic drive and leave Karen eating their ion exhaust.

"A thousand yards and closing," warned Christopher. "Even with our cloaking device on, she'll have a shot in another few seconds.

"OK," said Jerry. "Hold on, I'm breaking left. When I do, I want you to take a shot at her with the aft cannon. You can do that, right?"

"Yeah," confirmed Christopher, "I can do that, but you're asking me to fire at another human being."

"It's her or us, Christopher—choose," replied Jerry.

Christopher sighed and activated the cannon. He did his best to get a lock on the virtually invisible target. The computer wouldn't lock. This would have to be a guess.

The *Hope* swung sharply to the left and dropped into level flight. Its speed rapidly increased, passing Mach 2 in a matter of just a few seconds. In those seconds Christopher took his shot, two of them.

"Missed," said Christopher.

"That was what I was hoping for," said Jerry, banking hard to the right and then left again. On the horizon he spotted a towering sulfur firestorm. He headed straight for it.

"Mach three and accelerating," said Christopher. "What are you trying to do? That's a firestorm out there."

"You noticed," replied Jerry.

Three particle beams shot around the *Hope*. Two were very wide, one only ten yards off. They felt a strong jolt in its wake. Again Jerry made an evasive turn.

"She's good," he said. "I taught her well."

"A bit too well," noted Christopher. "Do you want me to return fire?"

"No," replied Jerry, "you'll give away our position."

"Mach four!" said Christopher. "Jerry, these engines weren't designed to maintain this level of RPM."

"These are the kind of problems I have when there's an engineer in the backseat," said Jerry. "Nag, nag, nag, telling me what this ship can't do. Let me show you what it *can* do."

Jerry followed a swaying course toward the storm that was giving Christopher a very uneasy stomach. The storm was coming up fast. Below they could see the coastline of the Sea of Fire rapidly coming up.

"Mach five," said Christopher, trying to remain calm. "I just thought you ought to know."

"I know," replied Jerry, "it's a new atmosphere speed record for a dagger. We'll call Guinness later."

"Guinness?" asked Christopher.

"Never mind," replied Jerry, whose eyes were on the engine temperature gauges, which were rising into the red.

"Jerry, I can't see Karen's dagger on the radar," said Christopher. "Do you think we may have lost her?"

"I wouldn't count on it," replied Jerry. "I wish it was anyone else but Karen back there. She was the best of the students I had this past week, a former Israeli fighter pilot. She has real heart and uncanny senses when it comes to flying."

Christopher looked at the radar screen, then at their airspeed indicator. "At this speed, we're less than one minute from the cloud boundary. Jerry, those are concentrated sulfuric acid droplets out there, mixed with liquid sulfur. If you hit the boundary at this speed I can't guarantee that the engines will survive, to say nothing of the hull."

"We aren't going to hit it at this speed," said Jerry. "About fifteen seconds from impact I'm putting her in full reverse. Then we're shutting down the engines and closing the engine manifolds. From there…just hold on."

Two particle beams shot past the *Hope*. Both were uncomfortably close.

"She's been riding in our wake all this time," said Christopher. "That's why I couldn't see her."

Abruptly Christopher felt the sudden deceleration. Even with the inertial stabilizers on, it threw him forward. There was a sudden roar and severe turbulence as Dagger 22 shot past them, missing them by a matter of only a dozen or so yards. They were still doing better than Mach 2 when they entered the cloud. They were instantly engulfed in the deadly mists, which were illuminated irregularly by powerful bolts of lightning.

Jerry banked hard to the right. By this point Christopher was totally disoriented. Even his instruments were giving conflicting readings. Then the mists broke and they were free of the cloud. The engines roared to life once more as they hurtled toward space.

"Nice, Jerry," said Christopher, "but I think I'm going to be sick."

"Just direct the radar aft," said Jerry. "Let me know when you see Karen come out of those clouds."

It was better than twenty seconds before Christopher saw the blip on the screen. "There she is," he said. "Looks like her cloaking device is down." There was a momentary pause. "Jerry, she's dropping awfully fast. I think she's lost power."

"Monrovia flight control, this is Dagger Twenty-two," said Karen in an amazingly calm tone. "I've experienced double engine failure and am losing altitude. I'm going down over the Sea of Fire. There's no way I'll be able to reach the coastline. I'm sorry, I've lost them. Express my apologies to Lord Monroe."

It was not flight control but Lord Monroe who responded. "Karen, hold on. I'm sending three daggers to your location. Hang on, girl, we'll get you out of there somehow, I promise."

"No, my lord," insisted Karen. "There's nothing you can do for me. I'm sorry about the dagger."

"Hang the dagger," replied Tim, "it's you I'm concerned about. Three daggers are on their way."

A silence followed. "Jerry, if you can hear me, it looks like you won this one," said Karen. "I salute you—you are the superior pilot."

Jerry pushed the nose of the *Hope* forward. "I've got you on my radar, Karen. I'm coming."

"To do what?" asked Karen. "There's nothing you can do for me."

"Karen, shut down power to your engines and attempt a restart," said Jerry.

"What engines?" objected Karen. "My turbines are a mass of melted metal. They're frozen in place. My intakes must have sucked in about fifty pounds of molten sulfur. I guess I should have been smarter than to fly into that cloud."

"Extend your wings to full," said Jerry. "Get all of the glide out of her you can."

"I have," replied Karen. "I'm just passing twenty-eight thousand feet. The coast is about fifty miles away. Do the math, Jerry. This thing isn't a glider. I'm going to fall short by twenty-some miles. Ditching this bird over the Sea of Fire wouldn't be my first choice of emergency landing spots. At least it won't kill me, though I wish it would."

I'm just five miles above you," said Jerry. "I'll be there in a minute."

"So you can do what?" asked Karen. "Watch me go into the Sea of Fire?"

Jerry shook his head. He didn't reply.

"Jerry, can you get us within fifty yards of her and hold a parallel course?" asked Christopher.

"Sure," said Jerry, "for a few minutes, until she hits the sea."

"Then do it," said Christopher. "Give me a chance to try one last thing."

The *Hope* was passing 14,000 feet as it came into a parallel course with Dagger 22, about 100 feet off of its wing. The dagger was pretty beaten up, barely flying, and descending rapidly.

"Hold this position for as long as you can," said Christopher.

"That would be about three minutes," said Jerry.

Christopher offered a silent prayer and focused his thoughts on the dagger. Yes, he had done this before, but it had been taxing. This time he would have to do it for a far longer period of time.

"What do you think you're doing?" objected Karen.

"Rescuing you," replied Jerry. "Just hold course."

For a time nothing seemed to be happening. Then gradually the dagger's rate of descent began to slow. A minute later they were flying straight and level at just over 10,000 feet.

"What's happening?" asked Karen. "I'm showing straight and level flight. Whatever you're doing, keep doing it."

"You just have to believe in miracles," said Jerry. He glanced back at Christopher, whose total focus was on the dagger. "Keep it up, buddy, you're doing it."

Christopher continued to focus. He thought about the fishing lure he had levitated four years ago. He imagined the dagger to be that lure. It wasn't heavy; it was so light, easy to pick up. He imagined holding it in his hand.

"We're losing altitude again," said Jerry. "We've still got twenty-eight miles to the coast."

"I can't keep this up," said Christopher. "It's too heavy."

The dagger's rate of descent was still increasing. Jerry looked over the *Hope's* nose to see the Sea of Fire coming up fast. Their previous rate of descent had resumed.

"Hey guys, I need some help here," said Karen. "We're still a bit too far out to begin our descent."

Jerry looked back at Christopher. "You've got to carry her farther, just a bit farther."

"That ship is so heavy," gasped Christopher.

"Come on, Christopher, just a little bit farther," said Jerry.

"I'll try," said Christopher.

"No," objected Jerry, "do or do not…there is no try. You told me that once. Now do it, Christopher."

Christopher looked out at the dagger once more. He remembered his grand meetings with the Father. "It's not by might, it's not by power, but by My Spirit says the Lord."

They were down to 3,500 feet when the dagger nearly leveled once more. They were still descending, though slowly.

"Keep it coming," said Karen, "just keep it coming."

"Twelve miles," said Jerry, "just twelve more miles."

Christopher put his heart and soul into it. For the very first time, he felt truly challenged—perhaps facing a task that he could not accomplish.

They had dropped to less than 300 feet when the one-mile mark was reached. No, he couldn't lose it now, not now.

They crossed above the high cliffs at the edge of the Sea of Fire with only 20 feet to spare. Karen's dagger slammed into the loose earth beyond the cliff pretty hard. The impact collapsed the landing gear within seconds, and the craft slid through the rocky terrain for 200 yards before coming to a stop.

The *Hope* hovered about 50 yards off while Karen emerged from the cockpit, a bit banged up but OK. She waved to Jerry that she was fine. On the radar Jerry noted the approach of the three daggers sent on the rescue mission. It was time to go.

The *Hope* was once more on its way home, climbing at a steep angle through the atmosphere, ever accelerating. Jerry watched his radar as the daggers landed around Karen's ship and picked her up—mission accomplished. Jerry glanced back to find Christopher sound asleep. He wondered if he would sleep the whole way home.

An hour later and 8,000 miles into space, Christopher finally awoke. He gazed about at the starless, velvety darkness. "Did she make it?" he asked in a drowsy voice.

"Yeah, she made it," confirmed Jerry, "thanks to you. We're about two minutes from a hyperspace jump. You may find it interesting."

"Sounds nice," said Christopher.

"I spoke to Professor Faraday a few minutes ago," continued Jerry. "They'll be expecting us. I think the two of us will be answering questions and completing reports for some days to come. I suspect that we'll be home inside of ninety minutes."

There was no response to Jerry's comment. He looked back to see that Christopher had faded off to sleep again. Jerry smiled. "You're not much company," he said, more to himself than to Christopher. "At least it's a short flight."

Christopher awoke to a familiar face. That face had a beaming smile. "Hi, Mom," he said in a weak voice.

"Hi, Christopher," she said. "Did you have a nice nap?"

"Where am I?" asked Christopher.

"You're home—in our home anyway. Your friend Jerry thought to bring you here rather than taking you back to your apartment at the facility. I'm glad he did. He told us about your adventure, the whole thing. Your father and I are just so proud of you. If you'd have told me where you were going, I'd probably have been frightened to death. I guess it was best that you didn't."

"How long have I been asleep?" asked Christopher.

"Almost two days here," said his mother. "I've just been waiting for you to wake up. Jerry told us that it could take a few days. We've wanted to spend time with you. We've missed you so much these past fourteen years. Being with you is…well, sort of special."

Christopher reached out and took her hand. "I've missed you too. I've looked in on you from time to time using your book in the Hall of Records. I've seen all of the wonderful things you and Dad did to spread the Gospel on Earth, especially toward the end. I'm proud to be your son." Christopher paused.

"You know, I've learned a lot about mothers and sons and their love during the past few months. There were so many reunions after Jesus brought His people home. But you know, I just saw what I think is the most incredible reunion of them all. I saw what ends a son would go to in order to rescue his mother. I've also come to realize just how good we have it here. The Father's love is so special, and I guess that is His greatest gift to us. There is so much of it that it overflows, and we in turn give it to others."

"Well said," replied Christie, his mother. "Your father and I were wondering if you'd mind spending a little time with us. We've so wanted to have time with you. Jerry said that Professor Faraday wouldn't be expecting you back for at least a week. Why not spend that week with us?"

With his mother's help, Christopher got up to a sitting position. "I think I'd like that."

"Your friend Jerry said that we ought to take you fishing," continued Christie. "He materialized all of the stuff the three of us would need. He said that you'd probably enjoy it."

Christopher laughed openly. That was Jerry. "Yeah, I think I'd like that too."

Christopher spent that week and then some with his parents. They had missed out on so much of his life growing up. During those precious days they spent together, they gave the term *quality time* new meaning. They couldn't recover the years when they were apart, but they could start creating fond memories from this day forth. By the time Christopher returned to his responsibilities at the research facility, he was feeling better than he had for a long time.

Three weeks later journeyman third class Christopher Pace was pondering a new engine cooling design for the starship *Messiah*. He leaned back in his chair and looked out the window to gaze once more at the still skeletal craft sitting alongside the *Intrepid*.

The *Intrepid* itself hadn't seen any battle action in nearly four weeks, though Captain Smith and his crew had taken her out on several shakedown cruises to work out the bugs. Its raw power made it one heck of a deterrent. The demons weren't likely to bring down the wrath of that silvery avenger upon themselves again. There was even word of a ceasefire between Satan's legions and the people of the now much larger and more powerful Monrovia.

Apparently, Satan wished to concentrate upon his expanding earthly kingdom rather than bother with internal affairs in Hell. That was probably a mistake, for his internal difficulties weren't going away. It was estimated that Tim Monroe and his forces had liberated nearly 50,000 souls. He was rapidly becoming a force to be reckoned with.

Christopher looked up to consider the design that seemed to float just above the white table before him. Yes, he had an idea now. That idea was laid aside as Jerry entered the room with a man in a blue cloak at his side. Under the man's arm was a large and very ornate black box. Christopher immediately recognized the insignia of the Knights of Zion upon it. The handsome, dark-skinned man bowed slightly before Christopher, who immediately rose to his feet.

"I hope I'm not interrupting something important," said the knight, looking at the transparent engine displayed before him. "A hyperdrive engine, if I'm not mistaken."

Christopher was impressed. "No, you're not mistaken."

"I too study FTL drive systems," said the knight. "My name is Barasuka Collins, knight of the order of the Knights of Zion. I have been entrusted with a gift for you and for Jerry Anderson from Lord Timothy Monroe. Lord Monroe sends his greetings and his eternal thanks. He has sent both of you a very special gift. He said that it will certainly be unique, the only two of their kind in all of Heaven."

The knight sat the box on the floor and opened it. Within were two finely crafted swords with gem-encrusted scabbards. The knight then personally presented one to Christopher and the other to Jerry.

"These swords are a Monrovian variation on the demonic sword. Yet they are essentially unique, designed for the human hand," said Barasuka. "The blade is composed of angelic metal. It is one of the very few materials found in Hell that can survive teleportation to Heaven. This weapon has very unique properties. Lord Monroe has included a personal letter that expresses his gratitude to you and describes the proper use of the sword."

Christopher drew the sword from its scabbard. Never had he seen a blade that glistened as this one did. "I had the honor of witnessing Lord Monroe do battle with a demon general armed only with a sword like this. Never have I seen such exceptional swordsmanship. I cannot imagine a more wonderful gift. Please extend my thanks to him. I will treasure it."

"As will I," said Jerry. "Please tell him that I too will treasure this gift as a memory of the time that we worked together to defeat the armies of Satan."

The knight smiled broadly. "I will indeed pass these words on to Lord Monroe. I'm sure that he will be pleased." There was a pause. "He is going to change the face of Hell. He will bring relief to the captives."

"Of that I have no doubt," said Christopher. Jerry quickly agreed.

The knight bowed once more and took his leave, vanishing into the blue mists.

"I have a feeling that we will be hearing from Tim Monroe again," noted Jerry.

Christopher shook his head. "Of that I also have no doubt…" He paused. "I wonder if we'll ever go back there."

"I don't know," admitted Jerry. "I visit my mother in Refuge once every week. She is doing much better. Interestingly enough, she has a gift of materialization and she has come a long way with it."

"Like son, like mother," said Christopher.

They both had a good laugh over that one. Then they opened the letter from Tim Monroe.

Christopher read through it. It wasn't very long, only a few paragraphs. "Tim says that he is very sorry for the way that we were treated that last day. He says that he was only thinking about his people."

"And his own ambitions," said Jerry. "Tim couldn't bear the thought of not being Lord Monroe."

"Yeah, that too," noted Christopher. "He thanks us for coming back and rescuing Karen." Christopher chuckled. "He says here that he is interested in the tractor beam technology we used to save her and her dagger—and that if we were prepared to share it, he would make it worth our while."

"That's Tim," laughed Jerry, "the eternal entrepreneur."

"He goes on to say that he now has three people sufficiently skilled in the art of materialization to fabricate even the most intricate components, and two of them are his own people. He now has twenty-eight daggers in his air force, and he's building two new, much larger hangars in which to store and maintain them. He's training pilots to fly them, and your friend Karen is in charge of his flight school."

"That doesn't surprise me a bit," said Jerry. "She was a good student—she will make a good teacher."

"I guess they've found some caves in the Vendikar region in which to build a second underground city," Christopher continued. "He is also starting to build some homes for the farmers on the surface. He claims a population of over fifty-six thousand people now.

"He says also that he has just signed a new treaty with the demons, one that concedes a huge amount of land to him. It enlarges his kingdom by a factor of nearly thirty. Now, for the first time, he has to give serious thought as to the form of government his new enlarged empire will take. That's about all he has to say." Christopher handed the letter to Jerry.

"I doubt that Tim will be satisfied with what he has for long," said Jerry, scanning the one page letter. "I don't think Satan will honor the treaty for very long either. In the end there will be another war, a far longer and more devastating one."

Christopher nodded. "I suppose it is the nature of empires."

The two young men got back to work. There was plenty to do if they wanted to get the *Messiah* off the pad in four months. Tomorrow they would be traveling into Zion together to commune with the Father. They both had some deep questions to ask. They hoped that He would grant them some answers.

Epilogue

THE HOLY PLACE WAS INDEED busy today. It was full of singing and praising saints. Christopher and Jerry made their way through the joyful crowd in search of a good place to sit.

"Since the rapture of the saints, this place has been so crowded," observed Jerry. "I think the day of sitting down within a mile of the presence of the Father is long gone."

"We've gotten a lot closer than that a couple of times," said Christopher as they moved through the crowd.

"Yeah, I remember," said Jerry. "That was so cool."

"You're really going to ask the Father that question today?" asked Christopher.

"I am," confirmed Jerry. "I mean…I have to know."

"Here's a place," said Christopher, pulling Jerry toward an open spot. They immediately sat down and began to clear their minds. Christopher noticed that the voices around them were fading. "Oh yes, please let it happen," he whispered. A moment later, he opened his eyes. Yes, he had been here before, but this time it was different. Bright sunlight streamed through the large window at the end of the long hallway. Beside him, Jerry too had opened his eyes.

"I was hoping that the Father would bring us back here," said Jerry.

"Hey guys, long time," said a voice from behind them.

Christopher turned to discover both Jonathon and Lilly standing there. "The four children of eternity are together again," he said.

"You gotta love it," said Jonathon, giving his friends a thumbs-up.

Christopher and Jerry rose to their feet and looked out the window across a great plain of tall grass with large oak trees scattered about. It appeared to be about midday.

"The Father does get around," said Christopher.

"Well, speaking of the Father, let's not keep Him waiting," said Lilly, leading the way to the Father's study.

They quickly made their way down the hall and into the study. The Father stood by the great window. He stretched out His hands to them.

"Well done, children, well done indeed."

The four ran to the Father to hug Him. Hugging the Creator of the universe was a wonderful feeling.

The Father turned to Lilly. "Elizabeth tells me how wonderful a time you have been having with your mother. Your mother is very glad to be reunited with you. Do not feel that you are neglecting your studies when you are with her. She needs you now. Love must sometimes take precedence over matters of duty, even such an important duty as the one you have been given."

"Thank You, Father," replied Lilly.

Then the Father turned to Jonathon. "I love a cheerful son, and you are certainly that. You have walked through the Valley of the Shadow of Death and you have triumphed. Now I give you a new commission. Learn all that you can from the family elders around you. Profit from what they teach you. The day is coming when the unity of your family will be of utmost importance, for I am sending all of you on a mission."

"A mission?" said Jonathon.

"Yes," confirmed the Father. "As Lilly has already learned, you will not always be granted the knowledge of what is to come. It is for your own protection that this is so. What you need to have is faith—faith in My plan, faith in Me. I will never leave or forsake you."

Jonathon nodded.

"Christopher," said the Father. "On your most recent journey you learned the true meaning of sacrifice. You reached out with all of your being to someone you didn't even know, someone who intended you harm. In doing so, you have changed her life and her outlook. That one selfless act will reap great dividends. You will see them."

"I understand," said Christopher.

"For now, take a rest. Get to know your parents better, for they love you more than you can imagine. They have just come through the great tribulation. They do have things to teach you."

"Like how to fish?" asked Christopher.

That comment brought laughter to the Father. "For one thing. Your earthly father may make a fisherman of you yet."

The whole group laughed.

Then the Father looked at Jerry. He was silent for some time. Jerry was unsure what to say.

"You had a question," said the Father. "Don't be afraid. I will answer it."

"I was concerned about my mother," said Jerry. "She is so sorry for what she has done. I've more than forgiven her; I guess I've come to love her very much. Will she always be in Hell?"

"That is not an easy question to answer," said the Father. "I shall put it this way: Hell was intended to be a place of separation from Me. Its inhabitants feel that emptiness. They didn't recognize the place in their being that I filled until My presence was gone. They didn't seek out My

Son and the salvation He offered because they didn't understand what it was.

"Persons like your mother do realize that now. They look back upon their lives with regret. I tell you this: there are many people in Hell who still don't understand that. They prefer the darkness, though they dread the pain that has come with it for so long. I sentenced them to that place, and the angels delivered them there, but it is Satan who torments them. That is about to end.

"The Hell you've known is already changing. You are in no small way responsible for that change. In the end, the Hell in which your mother lives will not be the same Hell to which she was sentenced. It will become less a place of torment and more a place of pandemonium— a realm that will try the determination of those who seek to make it a better place. It will become a place of ceaseless war as a variety of chairmen and presidents, emperors and warlords vie to become its ultimate ruler. In the end, they will rule over nothing."

Jerry nodded, yet he still had a question.

"So why did I allow Satan to rule for so long?" asked the Father, apparently anticipating Jerry's next question. "He ruled because it was essential to My plans for humanity. He became the refining fire of Hell—and yes, often that fire was only too real. But the mastery of that domain is slipping through his fingers. His days are numbered. If you must know how many days, the number is one thousand ninety-seven.

"And when his rule has come to an end, Hell shall continue to change for a thousand years. During that time Satan shall find himself bound in chains in a dark place where no one shall hear his screams. At the end of those years Satan will escape, but his freedom will be brief. He will try to reestablish his kingdom, but he will fail. Then all of the books will be opened, and the people of Hell will be judged, as will those who sleep in their graves."

"It's a judgment," deduced Jerry, "so there is hope for my mother and the others."

"There is hope," confirmed the Father. "That is the answer that you have sought. However, the day that hope is realized is yet a long way off."

"Their own children shall be the ones who are the source of their salvation," said Lilly.

"Yes," confirmed the Father. "Now you know. But I tell you this: few shall find it. That fact makes Me sad…" The Father paused. "But today is your day, My children, and a beautiful day it is. Go out with Me and feel the breeze through your hair and the sun on your face. Know that I hold the universe in My hands, and small as you are, you are loved; you are significant. You are My sons and daughters. Know that I love to watch My children play."

A door by the windows swung open wide, letting in the odor of grass and flowers. And God walked hand in hand with the children into the fields of grass and tarried with them. For a time, they felt as if they were the center of the universe, at the center of the Father's love—and they were.

About the Author:

Kenneth Zeigler was born in Harrisburg, Pennsylvania, in 1954. His life underwent a dramatic transformation following his near-death experience in 1972, when this young teenage atheist became a born-again Christian. He studied chemistry at Shippensburg University and graduated with a master's degree in chemistry education in 1982, having done his graduate thesis on quantum mechanical modeling of the hydrogen atom. He has taught chemistry and astronomy at both the high school and college level, and has conducted research into the nature of main belt and near-Earth asteroids at both Lowell and Palomar Observatories. He has also been an educational consultant for NASA, working on the Messenger Mercury mission. He currently teaches advanced chemistry at La Joya Community High School in Avondale, Arizona. He and his wife, Mary, have two grown children, Rob and Beth, and two grandchildren, Kindra and Kristen.

Get more information about The Tears of Heaven book series, including blogs, images, and a schedule of upcoming book events at the Tears of Heaven webpage: www. thetearsofheaven.com. Also check out Kenneth Zeigler's free online book, *Lilly of the Valley*, available at the website.

IN THE RIGHT HANDS, THIS BOOK WILL CHANGE LIVES!

Most of the people who need this message will not be looking for this book. To change their lives, you need to put a copy of this book in their hands.

> *But others (seeds) fell into good ground, and brought forth fruit, some a hundred-fold, some sixty-fold, some thirty-fold* (Matthew 13:8).

Our ministry is constantly seeking methods to find the good ground, the people who need this anointed message to change their lives. Will you help us reach these people?

> *Remember this—a farmer who plants only a few seeds will get a small crop. But the one who plants generously will get a generous crop* (2 Corinthians 9:6).

EXTEND THIS MINISTRY BY SOWING
3 BOOKS, 5 BOOKS, 10 BOOKS, **OR MORE TODAY,**
AND BECOME A LIFE CHANGER!

Thank you,

Don Nori Sr., Founder
Destiny Image
Since 1982

DESTINY IMAGE PUBLISHERS, INC.

"Promoting Inspired Lives."

VISIT OUR NEW SITE HOME AT
WWW.DESTINYIMAGE.COM

FREE SUBSCRIPTION TO DI NEWSLETTER

Receive free unpublished articles by top DI authors, exclusive
discounts, and free downloads from our best and newest books.
Visit www.destinyimage.com to subscribe.

Write to: Destiny Image
              P.O. Box 310
              Shippensburg, PA 17257-0310

Call: 1-800-722-6774

Email: orders@destinyimage.com

For a complete list of our titles or to place an order
online, visit www.destinyimage.com.